MERDEKA RISING

Part Two of
BLACK SUN
RED MOON
A NOVEL OF JAVA

Rory Marron

SEVENTH CITADEL

Published by Seventh Citadel (www.seventhcitadel.com).
Seventh Citadel, 10 WA4 2XA, Cheshire.

ISBN: 978-0-9576305-4-3 (paperback)
ISBN: 978-0-9576305-3-6 (eBook-Mobi/Kindle)

Cover design from an idea by Rory Marron, developed by John
Amy (info@ebookdesigner.co.uk).

Quotation from the English translation of *This Earth of Mankind*
(Bumi Manusia) by Pramoedya Ananta Toer reproduced with the
permission of Max Lane.

Keris dagger and Samba *wayang kulit* (shadow puppet) RM
Collection. Photographs: Copyright © 2013 Rory Marron.

Back cover photograph of Borobudur temple by J. Olbertz (c.
1915) with retouching/restoration by Rory Marron.

Maps of Java drawn by L. Maddocks in 1951 for Gale & Polden Ltd.
(Attempts have been made to identify the rights-holder, who is
invited to contact the publisher.)

For a boy soldier, unknown to me…

Mehndi Khan
22575
Sepoy, 2ⁿᵈ Bn. 1ˢᵗ Punjab Regiment.
Died 19th November 1945.
Age 16.
Son of Shafdar Khan,
of Mandi Chani, Poonch, Kashmir.

Headstone inscription,
Jakarta War Cemetery
(Menteng Poeloe)

Names of Characters

Historical fiction often requires reference to actual people and events to give context. Thus the suggestion of someone other than Lord Louis Mountbatten as the head of South-East Asia Command (SEAC) would be odd, so in my story Mountbatten is given (brief) dialogue with a mixture of both historical and fictional characters. In the same way, Sukarno and Dr Mohammed Hatta, key figures in Indonesian history, are not disguised and are given dialogue. My guideline for changing or disguising characters in 'supporting roles' was if there were a danger of taking an historical character beyond a 'reasonable assumption' of dialogue. For example, the characters of Dutch colonial and military officers invented here are creative combinations of dozens of officials whose comments and actions are on record. Other changes were made reluctantly. Official files are full of the names of many men whose service and deeds deserve to be better known. Yet attempts to honour (or vilify) them by using their real names in a work of fiction risk their actions being inaccurately depicted. Most of the names used in this story are therefore disguised.

I also confess to the creation and 'importation' of names that are easier for a native speaker of English to read. In the case of Japanese names, many were chosen randomly from friends and acquaintances. Indonesian names were more problematic, since many Javanese and Sumatrans have only one name, often rather long. Consequently, I invented names. In so doing, unintended syllabic combinations might have occurred. Similarly, relatively few Indian and Dutch names are familiar to, or can be read easily by, the non-native speaker. There were many instances of surname duplication among the 80,000 Dutch and Eurasians interned in camps in Java. For this reason I also used names of Dutch acquaintances, names I read in the KLM Airlines in-flight magazine, and also the Amsterdam and Maastricht telephone directories. I also created combinations of given and family names in memoirs of wartime Java. Fairly late on in the writing I stumbled upon a photograph album of a family by the name of van Damme (a not uncommon Dutch surname) living in Surabaya in the 1930s. I decided, however, not to change the names of my characters because of this coincidence.

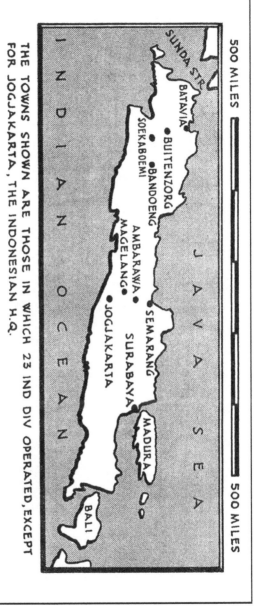

500 MILES

500 MILES

SUNDA STR.

BATAVIA

● BUITENZORG

SOEKABOEMI ●

● BANDOENG

AMBARAWA ●

MAGELANG ●

● SEMARANG

● JOGJAKARTA

SURABAYA

MADURA

BALI

INDIAN OCEAN

JAVA SEA

THE TOWNS SHOWN ARE THOSE IN WHICH 23 IND DIV OPERATED, EXCEPT FOR JOGJAKARTA, THE INDONESIAN H.Q.

12000'

12000'

° JAVA °

● APPROXIMATE CROSS SECTION THROUGH JAVA & BALI ●

7

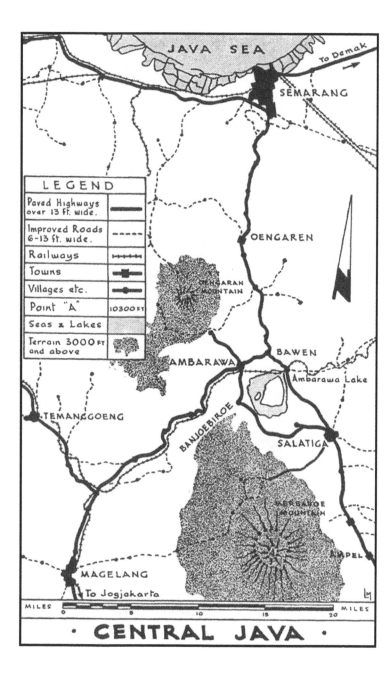

JAVA SEA

To Demak →

SEMARANG

LEGEND

Paved Highways over 13 ft. wide.	——
Improved Roads 6-13 ft. wide.	- - - -
Railways	+-+-+-+
Towns	■
Villages etc.	●
Point "A"	10300 FT
Seas & Lakes	
Terrain 3000 FT and above	

OENGAREN

OENGARAN MOUNTAIN

BAWEN

AMBARAWA

Ambarawa Lake

TEMANGGOENG

BANJOEBIROE

SALATIGA

KERBAROE MOUNTAIN

MAGELANG

To Jogjakarta

KAPEL

MILES   0   5   10   15   20   MILES

· CENTRAL JAVA ·

'...when my island was blanketed in the darkness of night, her country was lit with sunshine. When her country was embraced by the blackness of night, my island shone brightly under the equatorial sun.'

Pramoedya Ananta Toer
This Earth of Mankind (Bumi Manusia)
Translated by Max Lane

A Synopsis of

BLACK SUN
RED MOON
A NOVEL OF JAVA

Prologue

Burma, September 1943: Private Alun MacDonald ('Mac') is on duty by the Chindwin River when he is informed by Captain Miller that a patrol is due back from a reconnaissance mission. is nervous about possible Japanese infiltration. Unaware that the soldiers are Gurkhas, he narrowly avoids shooting one of them, Rai. Mac's platoon crosses the river with the Gurkhas. Mac sees action but cannot bring himself to finish off a dying Japanese and, as a consequence, one of his comrades is killed.

Java, 1944: The Van Dam family are sent to internment camps by the Japanese. As they scramble to pack a few possessions, Kate Van Dam watches her father's Javanese assistant in the municipal engineering department take over their family home (and her father's job).

Nijmegen, The Netherlands, late 1944: American war correspondent Meg Graham shelters with a squad from the 81st Airborne Division... They promise to meet at the end of the war....

Book One

Kate van Dam is living in near starvation in the overcrowded and filthy Tjandi Camp III, a requisitioned school, in Semarang. Kate and her mother share a converted classroom with 30 women and children. Their is no privacy. Kate's mother is suffering from malaria and malnutrition. Relations between the inmates are fractious with squabbles over food, work duties and pre-war social status. Disease runs rampant, with many deaths daily from dysentery, malaria and beriberi. Kate has been assigned to the kitchen detail with her friend, Juliette, a French woman in her mid-twenties.

Like other internees, Kate tends a small vegetable plot. One morning she is doing her washing when, with her friends in tow, she pegs out red, white and blue bunting—the colours of the now illegal Dutch flag—on a line. Kate then realises that she is being watched by a young man from a window beyond the camp. At first Kate is attracted to him but then realises that he is a Japanese officer. When two guards enter the garden, she is afraid of a reprimand over the 'flag' that will mean a beating. But there is no shout from the officer and the guards walk on, oblivious to the 'flag'. One guard then steals the only ripe tomatoes on Kate's plot.

Some days later Kate finds a sack containing tinned fish at one corner of her plot. Her first thoughts are that a smuggler has dropped it or that it is a trap set by the guards. She takes a chance and keeps the contents. Nothing happens and three days later she finds another sack containing soap and medicines. For weeks the mysterious gifts keep appearing. Kate begins to think that one of the camp guards is preparing to make her his sex slave. Now dependent on the food and medicines for her mother she knows she will have no choice but to accept....

Lt Kenichi Ota writes his will in anticipation of his certain death when the Allies invade Java. He goes drinking with his friend, Lt Nagumo, who has heard rumours of white women working at the Sakura Club, a brothel for officers, run by the madame, Kiriko. Ota and Nagumo take a short-cut through the camp. Ota is hoping to catch a glimpse of the girl when they come across some peddle carts. While examining the carts they find some boys peering through a fence. Without thinking Ota does the same. It is an open-air shower area and to his surprise he sees the girl, who he hears called by her name, Kate, by Juliette, a Frenchwoman.

For Lamban, a youth who has just graduated from his Islamic school, the Japanese invasion is the first step towards freedom ('*Merdeka*') for his country. Lamban hopes to travel with his friend, Kerek, to Djakarta, the capital, to work for the Independence movement. Yet Kerek is reluctant to leave the village. At a festival, a *wayang kulit* (shadow puppet) performance about a revolutionary hero enthuses Lamban even more. Lamban is also a student of the *silat* martial art and takes his final test under, Taruna, a famous sword smith. Later, Taruna leads Lamban through a mystical ceremony before forging him a traditional *keris* dagger. Soon afterwards Lamban leaves for Djakarta.

As Kate's health improves she is increasingly keen to know the identity of her benefactor. One night she decides to hide in the vegetable garden. She is dismayed to Anna, one of the cooks, stealing from the plots. As dawn breaks, Kate is about to leave the garden when the young Japanese man appears on the balcony of his room. She is amazed to see him throw a sack onto her plot. Greatly relieved but nervous she bows below his window. Ota is left surprised and confused.

Kate shares some of her extra food with Juliette who, like her, helps in the camp infirmary. The two become much closer and Kate almost confesses to Juliette that the extra supplies come from a Japanese.

Ota is one of the favourites to win the 16th Army's annual *kendo* (fencing) tournament. The reigning champion is Captain Shirai, of the *kenpeitai* (military police corps). Shirai is feared throughout all the camps for his brutality. He also takes a personal interest in young Dutch girls in his cells.

Ota's platoon capture an Australian airman after a bombing raid on Semarang harbour, saving the injured man from drowning in a rice paddy. The next day the inmates of Tjandi camp are assembled and the man is beheaded by Shirai.

The guest of honour at the kendo tournament is General Yamagami, who served with Ota's commanding officer, Major Kudo, in China. Yamagami warns Kudo not to trust the Javanese militia. Ota defeats Shirai in a very close bout. While taking a short cut through the camp Ota meets Kate alone for the first time. They are interrupted by the sudden appearance of Shirai. Ota is forced to slap Kate in order to deflect Shirai's suspicions. That night, angry with himself for hurting Kate, Ota gets drunk. The next morning he is assigned to duty over 30 miles away. He leaves Semarang that day.

In Djakarta the nationalist leaders Sukarno and Dr Hatta meet with an influential and politically astute Japanese naval officer, Admiral Ishida, in the hope that he can persuade the Japanese army to declare Indonesia independent. Ishida disappoints them, though he has his own plans.

While journeying to the capital, Lamban intervenes to save Sarel's life, killing two robbers. Sarel explains they were communist agents. Once they reach safety at his village he reveals that he is the leader of a revolutionary cell. Lamban joins the group.

Ota's sudden disappearance leaves Kate in despair. Her mother's health deteriorates quickly, too, so when advertisements appear for 'hostesses and dance partners' in Japanese officers' clubs in return for pay and regular meals, she faces a dilemma. Kate is a reluctant volunteer. Juliette also accepts. As they leave the camp, Kate sees Ota returning from his distant posting. Kate and Juliette enjoy a pampered few days until they are bought by Kiriko. Ota asks Nagumo for help in finding Kate. When Nagumo discovers that she will start work at the Sakura, Ota is determined to be Kate's first 'client'. He convinces her to return to the camp. Juliette chooses to remain at the Sakura.

Lamban begins his political education under Sarel, gradually becoming a trusted member of the 'Black Buffalo' cell. Finally, in mid August 1945, he is chosen to accompany Sarel on an important mission to Djakarta. At the same time, the Japanese garrisons on Java assemble to hear what they expect to be an exhortation from their Emperor to fight valiantly in the battle ahead. Instead they are left stunned as he announces Japan's surrender. In Djakarta, Sarel and Lamban also hear the momentous news. At Tjandi camp the internees awake to find that their guards have disappeared. When there is confirmation on a hidden radio that the war is over they are ecstatic.

In Djakarta, Admiral Ishida is destroying incriminating documents when Sukarno and Hatta visit, accusing the Japanese of betrayal. They nationalist leaders leave disappointed but determined to act. Elsewhere in the city, students hold pro-independence rallies and Sarel attempts to turn them into anti-Japanese riots. In the chaos, students kidnap Sukarno and Hatta. Ishida works to secure their release and then encourages them to declare independence from the Netherlands.

Book Two

In Ceylon, Lord Mountbatten, head of South-East Asian Command, is reluctant to take on responsibility for the Netherlands Indies but assumes that co-operation with the Dutch will be smooth. For three years, Charles van Zanten, Governor-General of the Indies, has worked for the return of the Indies to Dutch rule. The sudden end of the war finds the Dutch unprepared. Van Zanten seeks assurances that the British presence in the Indies will be short. Mountbatten confesses that he has few troops available. Van Zanten begins to scheme.

Meg Graham, in Berlin reporting on the Allied Occupation, gets an assignment to cover the 'fighting' in Java. In Singapore she boards a ferry and meets Dr Jarisha. He tells Meg of the problems facing his country, something of its culture and of his dreams for the future. The ferry narrowly evades the attentions of a British warship. Meg discovers that Jarisha is one of the nationalist leaders.

In Malaya Mac enjoys watching a surrender ceremony of downcast and dejected Japanese before a hostile Malay crowd. The British soldiers are all looking forward to going home when news comes that they are to be sent as quickly as possible to the Dutch Indies.

On Java, the Japanese are increasingly short of rations, so Ota and Nagumo join a crocodile hunt. Three Dutchmen leave their internment camp and drive into the eastern port town of Surabaya. They find the displays of the new Indonesian flag and hostile demeanour of the nationalists insulting. Their protests provoke an attack by a mob. All three are murdered.

The Kudo Battalion is preparing to move out of Semarang to await repatriation when the local nationalists make demands for weapons. Kudo refuses. Tension rises and the Japanese prepare for trouble.

At Tjandi camp, frustration builds over the non-appearance of the 'Americans'. An air-drop of food and medicines leads to arguments and then a fight between the internees and Javanese women. Next day a group of internees tries to leave the camp. A gunman kills three. The women are horrified to realise they are still prisoners. Sounds of gunfire reach the barracks, so Kudo sends a patrol, led by Ota, to investigate. The frightened internees, who are expecting an attack from the nationalists, are greatly relieved to see their former gaolers. Ota is thrilled to find Kate is safe.

In the Semarang business district some Japanese civilian clerks are packing documents when a gang of Indonesians seizes them. They and nearly three hundred others are taken to a gaol. That night a mob marches on Tjandi camp demanding food. Ota defuses the situation and as the mob disperses, Juliette, disguised as a native, dashes in through the gate. She tells Ota of her escape from the Sakura Club and that Japanese civilians have been rounded up.

Meanwhile, Mac's battalion of Seaforth Highlanders arrives at Djakarta by sea. They are given a cold and suspicious reception. The Seaforths do not yet know that their commander carries secret orders to use surrendered Japanese troops to maintain order if necessary. On the quayside, Mac meets reporter Meg Graham as Van Zanten and other Dutch officials try to land. A hostile, rock-throwing crowd forces the Dutch to retreat. Mac finds it hard to accept that armed Japanese move around the city at will.

In Semarang the Kudo Battalion races to the gaol but discovers the Indonesians have murdered their prisoners and fled. The Japanese pursue them. Ferocious fighting for control of the town lasts for three days. No prisoners are taken. On the third day, Gurkhas, including Miller and Rai, arrive but are mistaken for Indonesian militia. In the confusion, the Japanese open fire...

...five Gurkhas went down in the first hail of bullets. Rai was saved by the corner of the office building and the inexperience of the gunner, who aimed slightly too high. Instinctively Rai dived through the nearest window. A split-second later Major John Miller landed half on top of him.

Bullets were churning up the street, drilling into the brickwork and window frames. Chunks of masonry and wood showered down on them.

Miller's head went back against a desk. His breathing was quick. 'Damn it', he said listening helplessly to the dying and wounded men outside. Their move up from Semarang harbour had met no opposition. Occasional gunfire towards the town centre had alerted them to danger. Professionally executed ambush had not been expected.

Rai crawled among the desks to the end window. He took off his slouch hat and raised it gingerly on the end of his rifle at one side of the window. Glass shattered and the hat flew ten feet across the room to land on a desk. A neat, round hole had been punched through the crown. Rai retrieved the hat and tried the other side of the window. There was no shot. Carefully he lifted his head to peer across the canal. He looked knowingly at Miller. 'They are well-trained. Maybe some Japs have decided not to surrender, Major-sahib', he said quietly.

Miller sighed. 'Jesus, that's all we need! I better inform the CO....

Chapter One

Colonel Harold Edmunds, commander of Third Battalion, 10th Gurkha Rifles, was using the foyer of a looted bank as his temporary HQ. Edmunds was seething over the lack of information that had seen him walk into a trap. His orders had said that he was to secure Semarang, its airfield, guard internees and send patrols to the camps inland.

Miller's report had not helped his mood. He did not relish the thought of fighting renegade Japanese for the town. 'You're sure they're Japs, John?' Edmunds asked. 'Not locals in Jap uniforms like in Burma?'

'No doubt about it, Sir,' Miller replied regretfully. 'Naik Rai got close enough to identify them. It looks like we've run into a few hold-outs from their 48th Division. We've hit two or three but they've got us pretty well pinned down until dark.'

There was a brief exchange of distant fire and both men paused to listen. 'We're trying to plot their positions. Unfortunately, it's a full moon's tonight,' Miller said quietly.

Edmunds nodded. 'When it rains it pours… Right.' He turned to the other officer, Major Timothy Duncan. 'Tim, take your Company and try and get round their flank. We'll bring up some mortars from the docks to give you cover as soon as we can.'

Duncan nodded. 'Right, Sir.'

A Gurkha knocked on the office door, which hung off its hinges. 'Excuse me, Colonel-sahib. There's a Mr Wonabo outside under a white flag. He claims he's the Governor of Semarang Residency.'

Edmunds shrugged. 'Governor? Very well, let's see what he has to say.'

A plump, middle-aged man in a rumpled shirt and jacket rushed in. He was breathless and clutching a small white cloth nailed to a walking stick.

'General—' Wonabo blurted.

'It's Colonel,' Edmunds corrected him.

Wonabo nodded vigorously. 'Colonel? Oh, yes, my apologies. I am the new Governor of Semarang, appointed by President Sukarno. Please, you must stop the Japanese. They are taking no prisoners! It was the Japanese who shot at you—they think you are our militia!'

Edmunds looked quickly at his officers. 'John break out the flag. It's time for a chat.'

Two hours later a small group of officers and Gurkha riflemen watched the Marmon Herrington Mk III armoured car, now in Japanese livery, approach them. A white flag flew from the command turret. Two machine guns and twenty rifles were trained on it as it came to a stop in front of the bank.

Edmunds was waiting in the shade under a shop awning. He stepped forward. Miller stood with him.

The turret hatch on the armoured car opened with a clang and a helmeted figure surveyed his surroundings before quickly climbing out and jumping down nimbly. The man came to attention and saluted. Edmunds returned the salute and waited, noting the thin scar down one side of the Japanese officer's face.

'I am Major Kudo, 48th Division.'

'Colonel Edmunds, 10th Gurkha Rifles,' Edmunds replied sternly. The Gurkhas made no attempt to hide their hostility.

Kudo bowed deeply. 'Colonel, I humbly apologise for the attack on your men. We had no information that British troops would be coming to Semarang. It was a terrible mistake.'

Gravely, Edmunds nodded. 'I accept your apology, Major. We were not expecting to arrive in the middle of a battle. Tell me, what's the situation now?'

'It has taken four days but the town is under my control....'

'Hmm,' grunted Edmunds. 'Well, Major, as of now, consider yourself and your men under my command. Major Duncan and Major Miller here will liaise between our two HQs. How many men do you have?'

'Three hundred and fifty-six are still fit for duty.'

'How many hostiles?'

'Our estimate is six hundred militia and perhaps three thousand *pemuda*.'

The British officers exchanged glances.

Edmunds frowned. *'Pemuda?'*

'Students and youths,' replied Kudo. 'Most are armed with machetes, spears or knives.'

'I see,' said Edmunds. 'What about your casualties and wounded?'

'Thirty-eight dead. Fifty-six wounded.'

'Our medics will let you have supplies if you need them.'

Kudo bowed again. 'Thank you, Colonel.'

Edmunds hesitated, then held out his hand. 'It's not been a good start, Major. Let's hope we can do better.'

Allied Air Corridor, Singapore to Batavia (Djakarta)

The pilot of the RAF Mitchell bomber glanced back and indicated to look below. One of his two passengers was asleep, but the other, Lieutenant General Sir Philip Chrishaw, was waiting expectantly. He pulled himself up eagerly, putting aside a dog-eared copy of Birds of the East Indies and readying a pair of binoculars. Chrishaw was wearing plain green field dress but around his neck he sported a silk beige cravat embroidered with the triple golden V insignia of Fifteenth Army. He carried his broad, six-foot frame economically in the cramped fuselage of the Mitchell.

'We're coming in over the wetland now, Sir,' the pilot informed him.

Chrishaw nodded and pushed his face to the window.

With a concerned raise of his eyebrows to his co-pilot and navigator the pilot pushed the stick forward, taking them as low as he dared. The last thing he wanted to do was risk a bird strike but the General had been adamant about the detour over the lagoons. As they swooped over a large flock of colourful waders he glanced back and was relieved to see Chrishaw smiling. Whatever keeps the brass-hats happy, he thought.

A few minutes later they had left the wetland behind and were circling over the blue- and red-tiled roofs of Batavia. Chrishaw looked down on the spacious city, noticing the impressive twin towers of the cathedral, the wide avenues of the commercial district, and the imposing government buildings flying the red and white flags of the republic. Out in the bay to the north HMS Cumberland looked sleek and dangerous. Chrishaw was very glad she was there.

He leant down and patted Major Taylor-Smith, his aide-de-camp, on the shoulder. 'We're here, George,' Chrishaw shouted. 'In the footsteps of Raffles, no less! Did I tell you he was Governor here during the Napoleonic Wars? Or that the Seaforths fought the French here in 1811? It's remarkable how history repeats itself.'

Taylor-Smith stifled a yawn. 'Fascinating, General. You have told me about Raffles. But I hadn't realised we were at war with France again.'

Chrishaw shot him a weary look. 'I hope the Dutch and the Javanese appreciate your sense of humour. If not, I'll need another two divisions!'

Taylor-Smith arched an eyebrow. 'That will give us a grand total of two then....'

Chrishaw had seen no reason to announce his arrival, so he was surprised to see the waiting journalists.

'Sorry, Sir,' said Taylor-Smith. 'NICA were informed as a matter of course. We didn't expect—'

'They obviously did,' replied Chrishaw moving forward to greet his reception committee. He shook hands with Admiral William Patterson and Brigadier King. 'Hello, Bill, Andrew. Good to see you again.'

Patterson grinned. 'And you, Phil.' The Admiral moved closer and spoke under his breath. 'You pulled the short straw with this one. I can't wait to get back to Cumberland and off! The Dutch are a royal pain in the backside.'

Chrishaw turned and flashbulbs started popping. He noticed the woman among them immediately. 'Who's she?'

'Megan Graham, Robert Jordan's latest ex-wife,' Patterson answered sarcastically. 'Very interesting lady. Experienced, full accreditation. She got here well before us. Spirited and opinionated, to say the least.'

Chrishaw smiled. 'She'd have to be to put up with Jordan. I enjoy his novels, not so sure I'd enjoy his company very much. He sounds like a wild one. I must invite her to lunch....'

Patterson cocked his head, laughing. 'Be warned. If you light the blue touch-paper make sure you retire pretty damn quick.'

Chrishaw smiled. 'Is that so?'

Van Zanten strode over, face beaming, his hand extended. 'General, welcome to the Netherlands East Indies.' He led Chrishaw to a microphone. 'Naturally the press are keen to hear your plans.'

Chrishaw noticed most of the journalists still wore the uniforms and badges of war correspondents even though, strictly speaking, the war was over and, with it, all military censorship of press reports. His own statement had been cleared days before by London.

'Good morning, Ladies and Gentlemen. I am here for what I hope will be a short and uneventful tour of duty. British forces have three objectives. First, to repatriate Allied prisoners of war and internees. Second, to disarm and remove Japanese forces. Third, to maintain law and order. I stress that the British have no intention of meddling in internal political affairs. But we will strive to ensure law and order. In general, our troops will not move beyond certain key areas except to introduce food or for humanitarian purposes.'

'Finally,' Chrishaw continued, 'let me add that I hope soon there will be an understanding and settlement of some sort between the Dutch and Indonesians. Until then, I intend to ask present party leaders to treat my troops and myself as guests and to assist this temporary British administration.'

There was silence as some of the Dutch reporters looked questioningly at each other. Only then did Chrishaw notice Van Zanten staring at him in open amazement. Other journalists raised their hands. One of the Indonesians did not wait.

'Eric Subidi for *Asia Raya*, General. You said "key areas". What do you mean by that?'

Chrishaw answered immediately. 'Provisionally, these are Batavia, Bandung and Surabaya.'

A rotund, red-faced Dutchman spoke as he raised his hand. 'Derk Boer, *Trouw*. Are you including Sukarno as a "party leader"?'

'Indeed, I am,' nodded Chrishaw. 'And the rest of the Indonesian cabinet. This should be no surprise after—'

Boer was aghast. 'But he's a collaborator!'

In the sudden silence Meg caught Chrishaw's eye. 'Meg Graham, *Collins Weekly*. General, does this mean British forces will not be taking action against the Republican Government?'

As he hesitated the reporters surged forward. 'Are you recognising the Indonesian regime?'—'Does the Dutch administration have any authority?'—'Will collaborators be arrested?'

Chrishaw raised his hands and waited for quiet. 'My statement is over. This is off the record. The situation in the Indies is complicated. We have just come through a terrible world war. We fought for political and religious tolerance, and for the right of people to live their lives as they wish with the proviso that they do so without threatening or dominating their neighbours. Let us not forget that, or those who gave their lives for that cause. Thank you.'

Chrishaw turned away, directing a quizzical look at Van Zanten, and re-joined the other British officers.

Meg was both relieved and impressed by Chrishaw's announcement. Around her the few Indonesian correspondents were jubilant but among the Dutch there was consternation. 'Sounds reasonable enough,' she said casually to an Australian reporter who had been on Java for just two days. The man shrugged.

Boer stared at her. 'Reasonable! You heard him. He's anti-Dutch!'

That evening, Chrishaw was sitting in the lounge of his requisitioned suite in the Hotel des Indes, now the temporary headquarters of Allied Forces Netherlands East Indies. He had a bemused look on his face. Nearby an Indian clerk sat with a pad waiting to take dictation.

Chrishaw sighed, wondering how he'd managed it. One day in Batavia and already he had nearly caused the severing of Britain's diplomatic relations with Holland. Soon after his speech, Radio Djakarta had broadcast a bulletin announcing that the British had recognised the Sukarno government and were encouraging the Dutch and Indonesians to negotiate in the new spirit of post-war tolerance and co-operation. Transcripts had been relayed to the Dutch Government. Reaction had been furious. London had already issued one denial, claiming Chrishaw had been misquoted. Mountbatten had warned him before he arrived in Java that he'd have to carry the can if he messed up....

Chrishaw sat up and nodded to the clerk. 'Right,' he said, composing himself, "Chrishaw to Mountbatten. Point one. Off the record comments were taken completely out of context and exaggerated by partisan Dutch press. Point two. I have not recognised the nationalist regime. End." Get that off right away, will you?'

'Sir.' The clerk saluted and left.

Chrishaw closed his eyes and put his head back on his chair. So much for the spirit of moderation and co-operation, he thought acidly.

Taylor-Smith handed Chrishaw a large glass of Talisker whisky. 'It was just bad luck, Sir. Pity we can't control the press anymore.'

'Bad luck!' Chrishaw scoffed. 'I've been here only nine hours and already the Foreign Office are fuming and Mountbatten's laid a brick. Hardly the best of starts.'

'Admiral Patterson will back you up. He's told them what a hornet's nest we're in.'

Chrishaw rested the heavy crystal glass on his abdomen and closed his eyes briefly. 'These things are sent to try us, George. Rather this though than face the Japs in the Arakan again, eh?'

'No question.'

'Talking of the Japs, any word from Yamagami?'

'Not yet. Should I telephone his HQ?'

'No need for that.' Chrishaw savoured his whisky. 'It's a matter of face, that's all. He'll reply soon enough.'

'Has Mountbatten said anything about the extra troops?'

'Yes. Unfortunately he says we have to make do with what we've got.'

Taylor-Smith sighed. 'But that's just a fraction of 23rd Indian Division!'

'Yes', Chrishaw pursed his lips, 'but there's an army here already...'

'Uh...?'

'The Japanese will come under my command.'

'But Sir...' Taylor-Smith stared, 'British and Japanese troops together? Bloody Hell, the war's only been over for eight weeks!'

Chrishaw nodded. 'Actually, Mountbatten gave Brigadier King the option to order Japanese help before he left Malaya. We weren't going to ask a handful of Seaforths to put down a revolution.'

Taylor-Smith shook his head. 'Think of the reaction back home, never mind here!'

'You think Mountbatten hasn't?' Chrishaw shrugged. 'Political and diplomatic niceties are all very well. But "law and order" in Britain means catching burglars and ration-coupon forgers. Here, it means saving innocents from being murdered in their beds. We've no choice.'

'But the Geneva Convention—'

'George!' Chrishaw interrupted irritably. 'The GC is not my bed-time reading but I am fairly familiar with it by now!'

Taylor-Smith reddened. 'Yes, your right. I'm sorry.'

'No need to apologise. It's your job to point out potential pitfalls. Mine's to tip-toe around them. Pour yourself a whisky.'

HMS Cumberland off Batavia (Djakarta)

Admiral Patterson surveyed the room with quiet satisfaction. His formal dinner was going well, or as well as could be expected. So far he and Van Zanten, who sat opposite him, had carefully steered the conversation of their younger officers away from contentious issues. This meant that General Wavell's sudden departure from Java in 1942, the defeat of the combined Allied fleet in the Java Sea not long afterwards, and the ill-fated assault on Arnhem in the Netherlands the previous year had been skirted with good grace.

Patterson's main problem, however, was that they could not avoid talking about Java. To his dismay, Admiral Hurwitz's voice boomed yet again.

'Sukarno's a proven collaborator, a Quisling. He'll be found guilty and hanged. No doubt about it. Things will go smoothly then, mark my words!'

Patterson could not catch the reply from David Fisher, Cumberland's captain, but he could tell from Hurwitz's expression that he was not impressed. Sorry, David, he thought to himself, I put you in a hot seat there. Still, he had wanted to keep the two senior Dutchmen away from Chrishaw, who had enough to think about and certainly deserved a decent meal. Even so, he saw Chrishaw was fielding questions from two unexpected guests. General Overbeck, the head of the Dutch army in Java; and Dr Ruud

Visser, Van Zanten's deputy, had arrived in Batavia only the day before. From what Admiral Patterson could gather, Chrishaw was regaling his end of the table with stories of the Burma campaign. Overbeck had drunk too much wine and sat red-faced, enthralled in Chrishaw's tales. In contrast, the tee-total Visser was watching the rest of the table like a hawk through his rimless spectacles.

Van Zanten, following three discussions at once, drank little. He considered the highly strung Visser unsuited for the task at hand but a useful foil nonetheless. Visser was a passionate believer in the Dutch right to rule the Indies and wore his heart on his sleeve. His radio broadcasts from Australia had threatened Sukarno, Hatta and other nationalist leaders with death.

As the evening went on, Van Zanten's impatience mounted but nothing in his expression gave any suggestion that his British hosts' relaxed geniality was fuelling any frustration. Surreptitiously he scratched his ear. His deputy took his cue.

'Admiral Patterson,' Visser began, his voice a little too loud. 'I was outraged and dismayed to see the rebel flag flaunted all over Batavia. It is a symbol of collaboration with the Japanese and an insult to our armed forces and to Her Royal Highness Queen Wilhelmina. I formally request that it be banned immediately and burned wherever it is found!'

Other conversations quickly died. Patterson glanced at Chrishaw as he answered. 'Doctor Visser, I am aware of sensitivity over this issue but as far as I am concerned people can fly any flag they like. What I dislike is one group forcing another to fly a flag they do not want.'

Visser pushed himself back in his seat, affecting surprise and affront. 'So when innocent Dutchmen are murdered by thugs for defending their country's honour you will take no action?'

Patterson's tone did not change. 'Don't misunderstand me. The deaths here in Batavia and in Surabaya disgust me. Alas my resources do not allow me to play policeman.'

'Merely Solomon!' Visser interjected.

Patterson ignored him. 'Of course, from tomorrow General Chrishaw will be in command of all land-based operations.'

All eyes turned to Chrishaw. 'Flag-flying can be a very dangerous sport, Doctor,' he said calmly. 'The Indonesians appear to have absorbed your countrymen's enthusiasm for it. Frankly, I don't see the point in seeking to aggravate an already difficult situation.'

'So you prefer to avoid confrontation?' Visser quipped acidly.

'While we have so few men, continuing Admiral Patterson's policy seems sensible to me. We must concentrate on real problems not symbolic ones. Until all the internees have been liberated from those dreadful camps I think anything that will make life more hazardous for them should be avoided, don't you agree?'

Visser sat forward raising a finger. 'It depends on the final—'

'A point well made, General,' Van Zanten interjected amenably. Visser would have said more but a sharp look from Van Zanten stilled him. 'Now, this is a rather fine wine, Admiral,' he continued. 'I find it remarkable that I am drinking a 1936 Côtes du Rhône. Where on earth did you get it? A bit of piracy in the Mediterranean?'

Instantly the mood eased and the relief among the junior British officers was palpable. For several minutes Patterson explained some of the more resourceful ways of maintaining a well-stocked cellar on a warship in hostile waters.

At just past nine-thirty, Patterson waited for a lull in the conversation. 'Gentlemen, may I suggest we take brandy and cigars on the foredeck.'

Murmurs of approval ran around the table. Patterson led his guests up to the cooler air where two stewards waited with trays of drinks and a box of cigars. He had given strict instructions for two petty officers and one of his first lieutenants to escort Van Zanten, Hurwitz, Overbeck and Visser throughout the evening in the hope that the presence of junior officers would prevent the Dutch from posing difficult questions. Once on deck, he was disconcerted to see Chrishaw hemmed in by Van Zanten and Hurwitz, with his officers effectively blocked off by one of the ship's gun turrets. Patterson took a sip of brandy and squeezed through to Chrishaw.

'A most excellent meal, Admiral,' effused Hurwitz. 'You must let the Royal Netherlands Navy return the invitation when Tromp or one of her sister ships gets here from Singapore.'

Patterson nodded politely. Upon his request, Mountbatten was refusing to release any Dutch vessels from the joint Allied Naval Command. The last thing he wanted was a Dutch warship operating independently off Java. 'I shall look forward to it,' he replied casually.

'Yes, so shall I,' Chrishaw added. 'I hear a Dutch Christmas dinner is a sight to behold.'

Patterson tried not to smile at Chrishaw's veiled inference of a ten-week delay.

'This really is an impressive vessel,' Van Zanten commented easily. He turned, raising his arm as if to survey the ship, effectively pushing the loitering British officers further out of earshot. Patterson and Chrishaw did not notice the sudden change in Hurwitz's manner as he acted on his signal from Van Zanten.

'Admiral, General, we—that is, NICA—are of the opinion that quick action by the British could end this nationalist nonsense almost overnight.'

The two Britons maintained an uncomfortable silence. Hurwitz waited expectantly.

'Really...?' Chrishaw replied reluctantly.

'Yes, we suggest the British invite the two sides—Dutch and Nationalist—to a meeting on board Cumberland.'

Patterson and Chrishaw exchanged looks of genuine, pleasant surprise.

Hurwitz continued apace. 'Yes. Then once Sukarno, Hatta, Sjahrir and Jarisha are on board they can be arrested and shipped off to face trial for treason!' He smiled and took a gulp of his drink before going on. 'With their leadership behind bars the—' He paused because he had caught Patterson's shocked expression. Chrishaw chose to stare into his brandy balloon.

Hurwitz and Van Zanten waited uneasily.

Patterson's measured reply did not disguise his indignation. 'Admiral Hurwitz, I will do my best to forget what you have just proposed. I am astounded that you could even think that I would permit one of His Majesty's Ships to be used for such a treacherous purpose! Britain's position here is delicate enough. I trust that in the future you will not try to make our situation more complicated than it need be.'

'Hear, hear,' Chrishaw added quietly.

Hurwitz's face flushed in embarrassment and he attempted to laugh it off. 'Only joking, Admiral! I doubt Cumberland's brig is big enough. Hah! But you can't deny it would make our work so much easier.'

For several long minutes they struggled with strained, artificial pleasantries before the Dutch party made their excuses. As their launch sped away from Cumberland Patterson let out a long exasperated sigh. 'Good God!'

'Can you credit it?' Chrishaw snorted. 'We're doing business with a couple of gangsters!'

Patterson shook his head. 'I've got a bad feeling about this place, Phil. It could be bedlam. And the Dutch are our allies!'

Chrishaw raised his eyebrows and nodded. 'Of a kind...' he replied quietly.

Hurwitz managed to contain himself until he and Van Zanten were in the car and heading back to the city. Visser was in a car behind them.

'The British will do nothing for us!' Hurwitz raged. 'They might as well cut out the blue from the Union Jack and fly just red and white! The bastards actually accused me of treachery!'

Van Zanten turned his gaze to the window. 'Yes, I realise now it was a mistake to suggest it. You know the British. Traps are "not cricket" as they say.'

'But you said we needed to know whether the British will support us or not. 'They—' Hurwitz suddenly pointed forwards. 'Oh, look at that Jap shit!

General Yamagami had returned the Governor-General's American limousine late that day. A red, silk Shinto travel amulet still dangled from the rear-view mirror. Hurwitz would have reprimanded the driver but for the closed partition.

'Yes, I did and tonight we got our answer. We must make the British come round to our point of view.'

'But how? You heard them!' Hurwitz was still fuming.

'We agree with the British on one thing at least', Van Zanten put his fingertips together and paused. 'Java is a dangerous place. Eventually British soldiers will be killed. When that happens they will be less keen on "fair play". We must anticipate this happening sooner rather than later.'

Hurwitz's eyes widened.

Van Zanten ignored his unease. 'We are playing for very high stakes, Jurgen. An empire no less! Never forget that.' He put his head back on the seat and closed his eyes. 'Arrange for Visser and Brommer to see me tomorrow morning at ten.'

Ketapang, Djakarta

'Why do you do this?' Fear weakened the thin, elderly man's voice. He knelt to try and rescue the pocket watch and smashed photograph frame from under the heavy, deliberately clumsy boots of the soldiers. He gaped as one soldier swept clear a shelf of crockery with the barrel of his rifle. Sounds of casual, wanton destruction echoed around the small bungalow.

'My name is Kesawana,' wailed the man. 'I work for the railway. Before God I swear I have done nothing wrong! Leave my home!'

A solider trudged in from another room holding a foot-square Indonesian flag. 'Captain Mollet, we found this.' He gave it to the Dutch captain who smiled in contemptuous triumph at Kesawana.

'Look at this, Voss!' Mollet said in exaggerated surprise to a burly Dutch military police sergeant.

Voss grinned.

'Why lie?' Mollet snarled at the kneeling man. 'You ran trains for the Japanese. That makes you a filthy collaborator.'

Voss slid his boot under a carved reading stand.

'No! Please—' Kesawana pleaded, reaching out helplessly.

Casually, Voss flicked the stand sending the green-bound copy of the Koran to land face down on the littered floor.

Kesawana began to sob.

At the doorway, Amit Rahman turned away and walked back to the narrow street. The Indian havildar was deeply troubled. Corporal Nambiar and the rest of his section were facing away from the house in a rough semi-circle in case of any protest from neighbours. Rahman knew his men were listening to the commotion. Their joint British-Dutch patrol had already spent three fruitless hours in the kampong. At each house the routine of damage and brutality had been the same. They had been relieved when they heard that Kesawana, a ticket inspector on the State Railways, was the last on Mollet's list of suspects.

The ransacking continued but Rahman said nothing. He did not want to show his disquiet. While the desecration of the holy book had disgusted him, it would enrage the Muslims among his men.

Force of military habit made him check the street again. It was eerily silent, empty apart from two dogs, one of which was urinating on the wheel of their lorry. Immediately after the patrol had been spotted, villagers had rushed inside bolting doors and shutters. As far as the rest of the kampong were concerned, the unfortunate Kesawana and his family were on their own.

Two women, one a daughter holding a young child, ran out of the house in tears. Rahman stepped aside to let them go past him. His men did likewise.

Voss, his shirt soaked with perspiration, emerged a few seconds later. Behind him a sickly-looking youth, hands tied, was prodded forward by a Dutch private with a rifle. Three more soldiers followed.

'Take him over there,' Voss said gruffly.

Rahman smelt burning. Thin wisps of smoke were drifting through the doorway. The older of the two women moved back closer to the line of soldiers. She was staring at her home, her hands over her mouth in horror.

Mollet appeared next, the small flag crumpled in his hand. He held it up to Rahman in satisfaction. 'No doubt where his loyalty lies.'

Rahman looked at the house. Thick smoke was billowing out of the doorway. There was no sign of Kesawana. Mollet seemed unconcerned.

Two Indians had to restrain the women to prevent them going inside. They were both screaming for the old man to come out. Rahman took three steps towards the door.

'Havildar, stop!'

Rahman turned. Mollet shook his head very slowly from side to side. Rahman frowned, glanced at Corporal Nambiar, then took another step.

'I am in command!' Mollet shouted furiously. His hand moved to the handle of his Colt automatic pistol.

A side glance told Rahman his men had anticipated his action. Nambiar had slowly moved to one side of the Dutchmen. His Sten gun was at forty-five degrees.

Heads turned as Kesawana staggered out of the doorway, coughing. He was groggy and bleeding around the head and face. In each of his hands was an unfastened suitcase stuffed with clothing. Wedged under his arms were the photograph and his Koran.

A burst from Voss's Thompson sub-machine gun almost lifted Kesawana off his feet. He crashed to the ground, dead. The women shrieked.

'That was murder...' Rahman muttered, thinking aloud.

Voss's eyes flared and he started forward with a menacing yell. *'Stront!'*—Shit! 'Who asked you, you little brown bastard!'

Rahman said nothing. Instead, he stared at the barrel of the machine gun which was just inches from his stomach.

Voss snarled, baring his teeth. 'Who's side are you on, boy?'

Rahman looked questioningly at Mollet but the Dutch officer wore an amused half smile.

In the quiet, the metallic clicks from the readying of weapons was jarring. Taken aback, Mollet and Voss looked behind them to see the eight Indians well spaced, their guns trained on them and their men.

Mollet, now uneasy, snapped at Voss in Dutch. 'That's enough! Back off!'

For a moment it looked as if Voss would lose the battle with his rage, then slowly he let the gun barrel drop. Still glaring at Rahman, he stepped back to stand with the dumbfounded Dutchmen.

Rahman looked at Nambiar and nodded. Very slowly his men lowered their weapons. All except Nambiar.

Mollet swallowed, weighing up his options. 'Havildar, you will apologise to Sergeant Voss and retract what you just said. If not, I will put you on a charge.'

'I cannot do that, Captain.'

'You saw a collaborator resist arrest.'

'I saw an old man shot dead and innocent women and children—'

'Innocent!' Mollet scoffed. 'Ha! None of these kampong rats is innocent. I'm surprised at you, Havildar. And you call you yourself a good soldier!'

Rahman held Mollet's gaze. 'I would never say that but General Chrishaw did call me so in Burma when he presented me with the Military Medal.'

Mollet stiffened as if he had been slapped. He had been commissioned in May 1945 and had never seen combat. 'Well, we shall see about that. Come on, Voss!' He turned sharply and led his men off without their young prisoner.

Several times Voss looked back, still glowering.

Rahman let out his breath, untied the youth then slowly went over to the dead man. He picked up the Koran, brushed off the dirt from the cover and placed it on his chest.

As soon as he stepped away the women rushed up to kneel and begin their mourning wails. Rahman led his men back to their transport. Along the street shutters began to open and faces to peep out.

'Bloody hell,' cried Nambiar. 'We nearly shot those buggers!'

'They nearly shot me first!' Rahman replied.

'My God, Hav,' said another soldier. 'What will happen now?'

'Nothing,' Rahman replied calmly. 'But after I make my report I don't think we'll be going on any more patrols with the Dutch.

Chapter Two

General Yamagami opened the hand-written note and read it aloud to Major Miyoshi, his aide-de-camp. 'My dear Yamagami, The war is over. A "traditional farewell" will serve no purpose, so please join me for tea at three on Wednesday. Chrishaw.'

'Out of all the British generals, they send him!' Yamagami laughed.

'What does he mean,' Miyoshi frowned, 'by "traditional farewell"?'

Yamagami was still staring at the note. 'He is asking me not to slit my belly.'

'Oh, I see,' said Miyoshi. 'You'll go?'

'Certainly. As I recall, General Chrishaw makes a very pleasant cup of tea.'

Yamagami saw Miyoshi's confusion. 'In 1929 I spent a liaison year in England, attached to the then Colonel Chrishaw's staff. I enjoyed my time there. He and I exchanged Christmas and New Year cards', Yamagami sighed, 'until 1941... He's a an honourable man, a sincere Christian and a superb commander.'

Miyoshi nodded in understanding. 'Shall I telephone to accept the invitation and arrange for an interpreter?'

'Yes, but not until this afternoon. Don't bother about the interpreter. Chrishaw knows I speak English.'

A clerk knocked and entered. 'Excuse me, Sir. There's an urgent signal from Semarang. Major Kudo reports a serious disturbance.' He handed over the message and left.

Yamagami sat up. 'That's odd. When are the British going to Semarang?'

'They are not informing us of troop movements or numbers', Miyoshi replied. 'We're listening in, of course... They've only a battalion here, so I doubt they would split their forces.'

Yamagami nodded. 'Perhaps we'll find out tomorrow. In the meantime, remind Kudo to tread softly. Let's hope it's just a bit of looting.'

British HQ, Hotel des Indes, Djakarta

Chrishaw stood up from behind his desk as Taylor-Smith showed Yamagami into his office. An elegant, gilded long-case clock was sounding its third and final chime. Taylor-Smith closed the door behind him, so the two men were alone.

'Good afternoon, General Chrishaw,' said Yamagami. He saluted stiffly, bowed and waited. Chrishaw returned the salute then stepped forward, smiling and proffered his hand. 'Good afternoon, General Yamagami.'

Yamagami's shake was formal, his voice hesitant. 'It has been some years, Sir. There are many officers named Yamagami. I had hoped you would not recognise my name.'

Chrishaw shook his head. 'Oh, the British Army always keeps its eye on former guests. In fact, I've followed your career with considerable interest, particularly since 1941.'

Yamagami bowed again. 'I am dishonoured before you now, Sir.'

'And so you should be,' Chrishaw replied sharply. 'For the moment, however, we need to discuss the present, not the past. Have a seat.' Chrishaw pointed to two curve-backed colonial-style chairs separated by a low table. 'Milk and sugar?'

'No sugar, General.'

Chrishaw busied himself with cups and saucers and spoke without looking at Yamagami. 'If Admiral Mountbatten could see us now he would be most displeased,' he said casually. 'He's ordered no social niceties between British and surrendered Japanese. Anyway, that's his view. The Americans see things rather differently. So do I. Did you know that General MacArthur has already had the Emperor round for tea? I thought I'd do the same for you.'

Yamagami was askance. 'The Emperor visited General MacArthur?'

'It was in all the newspapers,' Chrishaw handed him a copy of Pacific Stars and Stripes. 'Take a look.'

Yamagami stared at the photograph. His diminutive Emperor in dated coat and tails stood next to the rangy American commander wearing an open-necked military shirt bereft of any insignia. Yamagami felt a surge of shame. More than Tokyo reduced to rubble, or the USS Missouri in Tokyo Bay, the image spoke volumes. The 'Son of Heaven' had never 'paid his respects' to anyone in his life. Now, humbled, he was at the beck and call of a foreign conqueror who could not even be bothered to dress smartly. Yamagami said nothing but placed the newspaper face down, hiding the photograph.

Chrishaw did not appear to notice. 'Just wait,' he chuckled, 'before long MacArthur will be encouraging marriage between his GIs and Japanese girls!' He paused, his eyes bright as he carried the tea cups to the small table. 'You see my point Yamagami? Already Allied policy is diverging! And as for Anglo-Dutch relations, well I'm sure you know how things are going.' Chrishaw sighed and sat down, crossed his long legs and looked firmly at his guest.

'I read the reports of your speech about British policy in Java. It is hardly my concern.'

'Ah,' Chrishaw raised a finger. 'That's where you are mistaken.'

Yamagami frowned. 'What if Lord Mountbatten finds out about your invitation to me?'

'My HQ, my rules,' shrugged Chrishaw. 'Also, technically the Sixteenth has not yet surrendered.'

Yamagami looked at him questioningly. 'I don't follow....'

Chrishaw intertwined his fingers on his lap. 'Law and order is virtually non-existent here. The truth, as you most certainly know, is that I am very short of troops—or I was. As of midnight tonight, I am declaring all Japanese forces in Java operational under British command.'

Yamagami's jaw quivered. 'I must remind you that the Geneva Convention forbids the use of prisoners of war by the victor in military operations.'

'Perhaps,' nodded Chrishaw. 'But Japan did not ratify the Convention.'

'Great Britain did!'

Unfazed, Chrishaw stroked his chin slowly. 'I believe the key words are "prisoners of war" and "military". As I said, the Sixteenth Army has not yet formally surrendered nor are its men prisoners but the war is over. Japanese forces are officially "surrendered personnel" as requested by General Numata himself at Rangoon. I am assigning you law and order duties, in other words policing.'

'Another war is about to start,' Yamagami said quietly.

'With your help it might be prevented.'

'I disagree, General,' Yamagami said sternly. 'That is playing with words. You are intending to use defeated enemy forces.'

Chrishaw sighed. 'Are we still enemies, Yamagami? Does someone give an enemy his weapons back and ask for help?' He held up his hands. 'No matter. Your assumption is incorrect for another reason. British forces are administering the Netherlands East Indies on behalf of the United Nations. Our authority stems from the UN, not from the British Government.'

'General,' Yamagami shook head, 'I believe you are stretching a point. Japan is not in the United Nations. Many countries are demanding that it never becomes a member...'

'Yes, Japan's rehabilitation may take years but sooner or later your country will want to join, or others will want Japan to join,' Chrishaw countered. 'Either way, helping out here might well help speed up that process. Your co-operation may also ease things for your Emperor, too.' Calmly Chrishaw took another sip of his tea.

Yamagami paused, wondering if the Emperor was truly at risk if he refused to co-operate. 'If Japanese troops were to serve with the British, the order would have to come from our commander in chief, I mean the Emperor himself, as long as His Imperial Majesty approves, I—'

'No!' Chrishaw interrupted. 'The order comes from powers vested in me as Commander of Allied Forces Netherlands East Indies. Your superior, General Nagano, refused to co-operate and he is on his way to a POW compound in Singapore. You are now the senior Japanese Army officer on Java. As far as I am concerned, there is no-one senior to you, except me. I urge you to think carefully. Japan is under Allied occupation. It is suffering. There are reports of starvation, looting and disorder. Your Government is not interested in you. In one sense, the men of the Sixteenth Army are already forgotten. I urge you to take this opportunity to do good in the eyes of the world.'

Yamagami appeared to waver. 'And in the eyes of the Dutch, too? Are they willing to be policed by Japanese? There is much bad feeling.'

Chrishaw shrugged. 'That is understandable but they will obey my orders. Will you?'

'One question, General.' Yamagami hesitated. 'Do you intend to use force to reinstate the Dutch?'

'Certainly not,' said Chrishaw. 'Our intentions are to look after POWs and internees and to keep the peace. I have no other orders.'

Yamagami frowned. 'What if there is war between the Republic of Indonesia and the Netherlands?'

Chrishaw nodded slowly. 'Naturally we hope the Dutch and the nationalists will reach a settlement. We have no agenda other than to evacuate former POWs and the internees, and then all Japanese forces. Do you think that after six years of war the British people would permit their soldiers to become involved in a revolutionary war in Java of all places?'

'Will anyone tell them?' Yamagami asked cynically. 'Perhaps if I could at least consult with my Government...'

Chrishaw smiled thinly, shaking his head. 'The Japanese Government has no authority over Japanese in Java. I do.'

'This will be very dangerous for my men,' replied Yamagami.

Chrishaw sat forward in his seat. 'I don't accept for one moment that you are serious. Six weeks ago, every man in your command was preparing for a fight to the death!'

Yamagami bridled. 'That sacrifice was to have been in the Emperor's name. It was...*taigimeibun*.' He struggled to find the English equivalent. 'It was...expected, sanctioned. This...well, I am not sure that dying for the British or the United Nations is the same thing.'

Chrishaw sighed. 'Look at what's happening. Japanese soldiers and civilians are in increasing danger. By rearming your men, I am giving you the capability to defend yourselves as well as your civilians. You will be safer. It is a simple choice. Now tell me, General, do I have your support or not?'

Yamagami was under no illusions. He knew that if he refused he would be on the next plane to Singapore. Why co-operate, he thought. As Chrishaw had said, the war was over. Sooner or later he would be arrested anyway. Indonesia's fate was not his responsibility, whatever Japan's false promises to the Indonesians! And what of the Imperial Japanese General Staff, he asked himself. What will their decision be? Idiot, he thought, it no longer exists! It was his decision alone. He could not pass it up the chain of command. Chrishaw was right about one thing. Java was not safe for Japanese. They were victims of unprovoked, often deadly, attacks daily. But there was something else. They had lost....

Yamagami stood and bowed formally. 'You have my full co-operation, General but not because of the United Nations. I accept your absolute right as victor to do as you please. Forgive me, I was only testing your sincerity. In Japan's feudal wars, the captured generals of the losing side were either executed or killed themselves but their soldiers were allowed to pledge their loyalty to the victor. This is what I offer you in 1945, a tradition from 1345! For me your word is enough. I will prepare the orders.'

Chrishaw was sombre but grateful. 'Thank you, General. Please believe me when I say the British do not even want to be here. We all want to go home. The sooner this mess is sorted out, the sooner we can all leave. Now, how about another cup of tea?'

Mantraman, Djakarta

'But, gracious American *nyonya*, my lady...look, bright eyes.' The wrinkled trader gave Meg an almost toothless grin and held up the bamboo bird cage for her inspection Inside, the little bulbul fluttered nervously but silently on its twig perch. 'Best singing voice in Java and cheap! Only five Jap guilder!'

She laughed in delight. The Pasar Burung, the bird market, was the busiest place in Djakarta. It was unlike any market she had seen. It was a noisy warren of narrow dirt paths that wound through a collection of lashed bamboo huts. Hundreds of caged finches, turtledoves, parrots, orioles and bulbuls hung from eaves, on high wires and poles, or were piled in haphazard, teetering columns.

Meg had adored a lively red and green parakeet that had been chained to a section of rusting steel bedstead. When she gave it a few nuts it had revealed its recent change of ownership by talking in both Dutch and Japanese.

At times the birdsong was so loud it was painful. At each hut or stall Javanese stood transfixed, often with their eyes closed, as they listened. Haggling was vocal and intense and she realised that even in a time of shortages, money could be found for songbirds, particularly the ever-cooing turtledoves.

Aware that his potential customer seemed unimpressed the Trader tried again. 'Ah! *nyonya*, the *kutilan* no sing free. Every Friday you pay him…only gold! Like this!' He reached for a thin cord around his neck and pulled it from under his shirt. A small gold ring dangled at the end. Slowly he opened the cage, then gently coaxed the little grey-black bird to open its beak by offering it a fat meal worm.

Meg watched, astonished, as the bulbul then let the trader rub the ring over its thin, pointed pink tongue.

'Now he sing,' he assured her. Deftly he reached for a long pole and raised the cage, hooking it on an overhead wire. Hanging a few feet from it was another caged bulbul. Within seconds the two suddenly agitated males began to sing in furious competition.

Drawn by the new contest, Javanese clustered round and Meg copied them, closing her eyes and letting the bright melodies envelop her. After a while several of the Javanese began arguing over which had the more attractive song.

Meg had been unable to distinguish between them. As the debate intensified and the trader sighted more likely customers she took her chance to slip away to the stalls set up by basket- and silk-weavers, bone-carvers and batik dyers. Before long, the delicious smell of roasting meat drew her to the food stalls.

'That looks all right,' said Nesbit, pointing to a row of freshly prepared meats and vegetables on skewers.

Mac wasn't convinced. 'Are you sure?'

'Och, come on, Mac!' Nesbit said impatiently. 'I'm ravenous.'

The smiling vendor welcomed them but adamantly refused to take Nesbit's new Dutch half-guilder coin. Nesbit was prepared and offered him a packet of cigarettes and a bar of chocolate in exchange. Two minutes later they were both chewing on tender, spicy barbecued kid.

'Umm. Tasty,' mumbled Mac.

'Anything's better than tinned ham and beans, mate,' Nesbit said, his mouth also full. 'Watch out for the green chillies though. They'll take your head off.'

'Aye,' added Mac. 'And if you do, remember what the Doc said about not drinking the water!' They laughed and wandered around the stalls, with a string of curious children in tow.

Mac was limping a little. 'How's your leg?' Nesbit asked, his mouth full of food.

'A lot better since the pills from the Doc,' Mac replied. He had suffered an insect bite on his calf that had become infected and swollen to the size of a golf ball. For the time being he was on light duties. He hoped it would last.

Excited shouts from a group of men and youths drew them to the far side of the square. Here the crowd was tightly packed but loud crowing and clucking hinted at what they would find.

Curious, they pushed to the front, the Javanese giving way to the bigger, uniformed men. The pit was circular, about a foot deep and six-feet in diameter. In it stood two men wearing only loincloths and loosely wrapped headscarves. They were baiting two large bantam cockerels, one a bright, almost ginger, brown, the other a speckled white-and brown. Their handlers were keeping them just out of pecking range. Already the birds were in a furious, squawking rage.

Shouts from the spectators grew louder. They were anticipating a good fight. Three bookmakers sitting around the pit were calling out odds and their runners, boys of nine or ten, darted about collecting stakes.

Nesbit grinned at Mac. 'Come on, laddie, let's have a flutter! We're the old Fighting Cock after all!' He pointed to their Divisional shoulder patch, a silhouette of a strutting red cockerel on a yellow background. 'It's a sign!'

'Aye, of madness!' Mac rolled his eyes and reluctantly pulled out a crumpled five-rupiah note. 'This is all the Jap stuff I've got. On "Ginger", all of it!'

'Aye, he's the one for me too!' Nesbit grinned. 'I'll be back in a sec.'

Mac finished his kebab as Nesbit, pointing repeatedly to his shoulder patch, managed to place the bet.

With shrill, angry squawks the two birds launched themselves at each other. Feathers swirled as they kept jumping, pecking and kicking. The spectators roared.

Mac was surprised by the ferocity. 'I'll remember this next time I eat cock-a-leekie, Nessy,' he joked.

Handlers stepped in, dropping bell-shaped wicker baskets over the birds to separate them. Mac and Nesbit watched them tie long, needle-like steel spurs to the backs of the birds' feet. Then, once again, the birds were baited and set loose in the pit, this time for the final round. They crashed together, then jumped and spun as if glued together at the chest, their wings beating madly.

Suddenly the speckled bantam staggered backwards. Spots of dark blood were splattered across its chest plumage. A mixture of cheers and groans erupted from the crowd.

'He's not so "cock-sure" now, eh, Mac!' Nesbit laughed.

Yet again the birds charged. Beaks, chests, feet and wings blurred together. Blood started to drip over the red bantam's feet into the dust.

'Oh, no!' Nesbit nudged Mac. 'Ginger's hurt!' He leant forward, cupping his hands to his mouth. 'Come on you useless chicken!'

'Get him, Ginger!' Mac shouted, his words lost amidst the noise.

Suddenly the speckled cock sat down. A large, glistening patch of blood was spreading across its chest.

'Yes!' Nesbit punched the air. 'Come on the Fighting Twenty-third!'

Ginger let out an angry squawk and charged. Valiantly its weakened opponent stood up but there was an audible snap and it scurried away sideways trailing a broken wing, its head lolling forward weakly.

Before the victorious Ginger could strike again, its handler trapped it under a basket. The winning punters cheered.

'We're in the money!' Nesbit clapped Mac on the arm. 'I'll go and see Java Joe over there for our winnings!' He left and started to push his way through the crowd to the now rather glum-looking bookmaker.

Mac watched the owner of the injured bantam scoop up the limp mass of feathers and snap the bird's neck with a flick of his wrist. Ignored by the crowd, he dropped the bird into a sack and walked dejectedly away. At least he's taking home food for the pot, thought Mac.

Nesbit was soon back, grinning as he held up a wad of crumpled, dirty rupiah notes. 'We won't have to barter our chocolate for a while, anyway! Fancy another "flutter" old boy?'

'Why not, me old cock-fightin' sparrow!' Mac joked in return.

'Hello there!'

They both turned. Mac smiled broadly. 'Oh, hello, Miss.'

Meg raised a finger in recognition. 'Didn't I see you at the harbour last week?'

Mac nodded. 'Yes, that's right. Small world!'

'It sure is. I'm Meg Graham. Good to meet you.' She held out her hand.

'Alun MacDonald. Mac to my friends.'

Nesbit cleared his throat. 'Oh, sorry! This is Stan Nesbit, Nessy for short.'

'As in Loch Ness?' Meg asked.

'That's right, Miss,' Nesbit replied. 'Pleased to meet you.'

'Likewise', Meg said cheerfully.

'Are you sightseeing?' Nesbit asked.

Meg nodded. 'Kind of.'

'Miss Graham's a reporter,' Mac added quickly.

'I see you backed a winner,' said Meg looking at the money.

'Yes,' smiled Mac. 'We had a bit of luck with—'

Heavy revving of a large engine and repeated honking of a horn drowned his words as a big Isuzu troop lorry lurched into the market square. People scattered, clutching at their children as stalls were knocked over and the vegetables and fruits laid out on the ground were crushed.

Meg stared. 'What the hell?'

'Christ knows!' Mac replied.

They backed away as the lorry passed them, continuing its slow, destructive circuit around the square In the back, gaunt wild-eyed, white soldiers were training rifles and machine guns randomly on individuals including Meg, Mac and Nesbit. Defiantly the Javanese stared back. The Isuzu came to a sudden stop.

A tall, stooping man in a newly issued Dutch uniform climbed down from the cab and approached them. A pistol hung loosely in his hand by his thigh.

'Jesus!' Meg gasped.

'Watch yourselves,' Nesbit warned.

'No sudden movements,' Mac cautioned quietly. He was acutely conscious of being unarmed. As a sign of good faith to the Javanese, General Chrishaw had ordered off-duty British troops to go without weapons.

The Dutchman wore Captain's insignia but the clothes hung off his thin frame. He was unshaven and his sunken eyes bore the yellow tinge of jaundice. 'So my British friends,' he sneered in a heavy accent, 'you trade with rebels?' He was staring contemptuously at the cash in Nesbit's hand.

Meg remembered that Van Zanten, desperate for any Dutch authority in the city, had armed former Dutch prisoners of war. 'I'm an American. I just see people shopping,' she replied calmly.

He smiled mirthlessly and shook his head. 'No, traitors and Quislings at a rebel market. Be careful, you could get a knife in your back!' He turned dismissively and walked back to the Isuzu.

As it moved off, it veered deliberately to demolish a stall laden with spices. Resignedly the traders started to clean up.

Hotel des Indes, Djakarta (Batavia)

Major Taylor-Smith opened the office door and beckoned to the visitor. 'Sorry about the wait, Major, you may go in.'

Chrishaw had his head down over a pile of paperwork. As he looked up, Miller saluted.

'Afternoon, John,' Chrishaw said affably. 'I apologise for the rush. Take a pew.'

'Not at all, Sir,' Miller replied sitting. 'Things are pretty quiet just now.' He had been whisked from Semarang on a transport plane at short notice.

Chrishaw smiled, partly to himself. 'Well, it's good to know that at least somewhere on Java is quiet!' He looked at the clock. 'Ask someone to put the kettle on.'

Taylor-Smith signalled to an orderly.

'John', began Chrishaw, 'this must remain absolutely confidential. We have a growing problem that can no longer be ignored. Batavia is in the grip of a killing frenzy. There's no end to it! Random shootings are happening daily. Every night someone is taken in a tit-for-tat murder-kidnapping. They say if you sit on the bank of the Kali Besar a body drifts past every hour!'

Chrishaw paused to sip from a glass of water then methodically brought the spread tips of his fingers together on the leather-topped writing surface. 'Last week alone, thirty-seven people were murdered. We know it because we have the bodies. Governor Van Zanten is shouting about law and order, about innocent Europeans being butchered in their beds. Scandalously, the Dutch correspondents are saying there's a serious risk of massacre.' He uttered a short, dismissive laugh. 'The trouble with those thirty-seven bodies is that thirty-two of them were Javans…. This inconvenient fact is being ignored by the Dutch reporters but not by those from other nations who are asking legitimate questions about bias and apparent complicity. We have identified twelve of those killed in the last week as individuals previously accused by NEFIS—that's Dutch Intelligence—of collaboration during the Japanese occupation. Others are probably linked in various ways with the nationalist movement, though many may have simply waved a flag at the wrong time. You are here to reduce this murder madness.'

Miller gave a short nod. 'How can I help, Sir?'

Chrishaw's expression darkened as he reached for a file on his desk. 'Nineteen of the thirty-two corpses bore similar chafing marks on their wrists and ankles; and other bruises probably caused, I am told, by an expertly used cosh. Most had been shot in the back of the head at close range with a forty-five.'

'A forty-five?' Miller's eyes were thoughtful. 'Dutch vigilantes?'

'Alas nothing so simple,' Chrishaw said shaking his head. 'More like well-organised death squads. This is absolutely confidential. We believe there is a secret prison in an old fort just beyond our security zone.' He sat back and stroked his chin. 'A prison-cum-torture chamber by the sound of it, run unofficially by the Dutch 10th Battalion. The trails of many missing Javanese lead there. All the information we have is in that file, which you are to read next door and return to me personally.'

Chrishaw saw Miller's confusion. 'I want you to watch the fort for a few days, note comings and goings, numbers of guards and so on. When we pay a visit, your men will be inside to let us in.'

Miller's surprise showed. 'I see. But why not use the Seaforths, they're here?'

Chrishaw held his gaze. 'Two reasons. First, disguised as local farmers and labourers your Gurkhas can move about unsuspected by the Dutch. Second, when we go in it could get messy. I don't want any mistakes. The fort has narrow passages and underground cells. In poor light Dutch uniforms will look very similar to ours and, of course, the NEFIS and 10th Battalion men are white. It has to be your Gurkhas.'

'I understand, General,' Miller said quietly.

'Good.'

Miller was at the door when Chrishaw stopped him. 'John, one more thing.'

He turned. 'Yes, Sir?'

'Our conversation did not take place.'

Fort Michiels, near Batavia

Rai heard the slow movement in the bushes behind him and whispered the challenge in Gurkhali. 'Home of the Eight Tribes?'

'*Athrai!*' Limbau replied immediately.

Rai turned back to watch the only entrance to the old fort. There was little activity. The last vehicle had entered two hours previously.

Limbau settled down next to Rai who pushed over the glasses in silence. The bright moonlight made them redundant so close to the wall. For a few moments both men lay still to ensure that the single sentry pacing the crumbling rampart of the fort had not noticed anything amiss. Nothing stirred, then the sentry's face and hands were illuminated as he lit a cigarette.

Rai took advantage of the sentry's loss of night vision and backed away from the fringe of sago palms. As he left, the two Gurkhas exchanged a look that combined boredom, confidence and even wry amusement that had begun when they had donned the sarongs and headscarves.

Rai headed back to a secluded copse some two hundred yards back where Miller was waiting with six more Gurkhas, all of whom were dressed as Javanese farmers. Each man carried a Japanese Arisaka rifle. In place of their trademark *kukri*, Miller had acquired hefty *bodik* daggers from a market stall.

For over seventy-two hours the Gurkhas had kept a round-the-clock watch on the fort. In that time the Dutch had sent out no perimeter patrols or even flashed a searchlight except to illuminate their own approaching vehicles. Rai and the others had driven ox-carts and led water buffalo and goats back and forth past the fort but they had been ignored. Every aspect of the occupants' routine had been noted down. Miller had taken the information back to Chrishaw personally. Now, though, the waiting was over.

Rai made his report to Miller. 'The last of the lorries returned two hours ago, Major. Its covers were down, so we don't know how many prisoners. As usual the sentries are sloppy.'

Miller nodded and updated his list. 'That makes seventeen or eighteen enemy—er, I mean Dutch or Ambonese—inside. General Chrishaw is going to come calling at five thirty.' He looked at the luminous dial on his watch. 'That's forty-five minutes from now. Time to go. Tell the men.'

Rai nodded and went to pass the word.

Once again Miller ran through the plan in his head. Chrishaw had named it Operation Jumble Sale. In addition to case histories and letters from worried relatives of the missing, the secret file contained a pamphlet and floor-plan published by the Batavia Tourist Office. He now knew that Fort Michiels was an eighteenth-century star-fort built by the East India Company. The city's suburbs were just a mile away. Abandoned for years, the fort had been a minor tourist attraction until the arrival of the Japanese, whose military police had appreciated its relatively isolated location and its thick, sound-deadening stone walls.

Miller was assuming the Japanese had altered little inside the fort. Each of his men had committed the floor-plan to memory. Infiltration was easy enough, but avoiding injury to the Dutch once inside was a different matter. If his men were seen they would be shot at yet they were under orders not to return fire. Rai and Limbau were to go in first. Miller did not like it. Worse, he was to be the last man in. He liked that least of all.

As the Dutch sentry passed a small tower that hid the narrow parapet walk behind him the Rai and Limbau began a silent count and moved off. Miller watched the two slight figures dart across the open ground, then scale the twenty-foot wall, their rifles strapped across their backs. He held his breath as they rolled over the top of the wall and disappeared. So far so good, he thought.

Up on the parapet, Rai and Limbau pressed themselves against the tower. Twenty seconds later, as expected, the sentry returned. He was wearing a soft cap and was mumbling to himself. Rai padded after him, his bare feet noiseless on the stone. He clubbed the sentry just behind his right ear and the man crumpled quietly into his arms. Limbau caught the man's rifle soundlessly.

Miller heard the birdcall and signalled his other men. Six shadowy figures darted from the fringe of palms to the wall and began to climb. His main worry was the second sentry. If the alarm was raised the mission was to be aborted. He flicked the safety catch off his Thompson sub-machine gun. In front of him were four spare magazines. Chrishaw had said nothing about covering fire....

A second, and then, finally, a third birdcall sounded in the still, dawn air, signalling that the other two rampart sentries had been taken care of. Miller let out a long breath. They were almost there. He looked at his watch and then at the sky. There was a definite brightening to the east. His eyes went back to the dark, eerie outline of the fort. Now all they had to do was hope the gatehouse sentry was the only one who stirred when the General arrived.

Rai and the others perched on the parapet walk, watching for any activity in the tent-dotted courtyard below. There were no lights but they could hear heavy snoring. They had allowed seven minutes to deal with the sentries. In the end they had needed under five.

The sun rose, the walls casting long shadows and keeping much of the courtyard in darkness. Limbau checked his watch and nodded to Rai. They moved down to the door of the gatehouse. Soon they heard the rumble of engines. They waited as the noise grew but the column of armoured cars and troop lorries was less than three hundred yards away before the snoozing sentry inside awoke. When he unlocked and threw the door wide to raise the alarm Rai's rifle butt caught him squarely in the midriff. He fell gasping to the floor. His groans were quickly silenced by a blow from Limbau. In seconds the man was bound and gagged.

Rai, Limbau and the others raced to the large double doors no longer concerned about stealth since the noise from the vehicles was now a constant drone. They lifted out the two thick crossbeams and dragged back the gates. Moments later, an armoured car swept into the courtyard, followed by a troop lorry. Seaforths jumped out, rifles ready, taking to the ramparts and lining the fort's wall. A second lorry was disgorging more soldiers as Chrishaw's jeep raced through the gates.

The General sat impassively, watching half-dressed Dutch soldiers being roused out of the huts and tents. They were herded unceremoniously into a group.

Gradually they overcame their shock and began to protest. 'What's going on!'— '*Stront*!'—'Who do you think you are?'

Chrishaw let them mutter for a few more seconds then stood up. 'Be quiet. I am General Chrishaw. You are all under arrest!'

Instantly the talking stopped. A major stepped forward. 'This is a Dutch-controlled area, General. I protest. You cannot enter here without permission from our commanding officer—'

Chrishaw's voice rumbled with controlled fury. 'I am Senior Allied Commander in the Indies! I have every right to enter and inspect all military bases as and when I see fit.'

Uneasy now, the major swallowed. 'I demand to speak with General Overbeck!'

'And so you shall, Major,' Chrishaw said with a half a smile. 'General Overbeck was expecting to meet me this morning at six o'clock for details of a surprise security operation. When he arrives at my headquarters he will be escorted here.'

Crestfallen, the major retreated to stand with the rest of the Dutch and Ambonese.

Chrishaw turned to the Seaforths officer. 'Captain, you may commence your search.'

Sounds of chains scraping over stone woke Lamban. He could see nothing in the darkness. His head ached. Three more men had been put into the cramped cell during the night. The stench of faeces and urine coming from the overflowing bucket in the corner filled his nose, mouth and throat.

Beside him Sarel shifted. 'I think it's morning,' Lamban whispered.

'Perhaps our last?' Sarel replied.

'If God so wills,' sighed Lamban, easing the manacles that were chafing his wrists. He was still cursing their carelessness. They had been returning in darkness from a meeting to co-ordinate business and food boycotts against non-Javanese when they had come upon the Dutch army checkpoint. Boxes of their leaflets had been discovered and both he had Lamban had been brought in handcuffs to the old fort. For two days they had been questioned and beaten. They were under no illusions as to their fate. Among the prisoners it was rumoured that no-one returned from questioning after three days in the cells. Today was their third day.

An electric light flickered casting a dull light around the cell. Soon afterwards heavy, booted footsteps echoed along the corridor. Lamban eased himself up against the wall and grimaced as pain surged through his dislocated shoulder. 'When they take these irons off us I pray I have a chance to kill one of them.'

'There is someone else I would rather kill,' Sarel muttered. 'Only one other person knew our route and he left the day before us.'

Lamban looked at him sharply. 'Yarek?'

Sarel nodded. 'If you live, settle the score.'

Along the corridor doors clanged open, followed by brisk, spoken orders.

'Try to get an officer!' Sarel said quickly.

Sudden, excited shouts from other cells told them something unexpected was happening. *'Inggris!'*—British!

The two Javanese looked at each other in bewilderment as two soldiers stepped cautiously in to the cell wrinkling their noses. 'Och, God, Sarge,' said one of them, 'This is even worse!'

Lamban did not understand the words but he knew that the uniforms and words were not Dutch.

Forty-one bedraggled prisoners were led blinking into the sunlight. There they saw their gaolers, ringed by British soldiers. After they were photographed in their chains they were ushered to the shaded side of the crowded courtyard where they were given bread, water and fruit. While they ate, British soldiers removed their manacles.

They cheered as an officer announced that they would be free to go in one hour. Not long afterwards several of the

Javanese, sensing they were safe at last, found their voices. Abuse flew at the Dutchmen.

When General Overbeck and Lt-Col Brommer arrived at the fort their Dutch escort was stopped at the gate. The Dutch officers looked distinctly ill at ease as they were shown across the courtyard and into the main offices by two British military policemen. Inside they found Chrishaw and a translator behind a desk, flicking through a NEFIS file stamped 'Top Secret'. Every desk and filing cabinet drawer was open. Soldiers were loading the entire contents of the cabinets into boxes under Brigadier Taylor-Smith's direction.

'General,' Overbeck said firmly, 'What is going on here?'

Chrishaw did not look up. 'I am listing names, General,' he said quietly. 'Names of Javanese who have recently died.'

Brommer thrust out his chest. 'Just what you are inferring? This unit is not part of our official Dutch forces, its just a camp for ex-POWs. And those documents are confidential files reported stolen from NEFIS some time ago. While we congratulate you on recovering them, we demand their immediate return!'

'I'm afraid you can demand nothing here, Colonel Brommer,' Chrishaw said sharply. 'This is a crime scene. Several murder and kidnapping investigations are about to start. These files are to be held as evidence. I am confident that they will be returned when the investigations are complete.'

Brommer's face was puce. 'I protest. My Government shall hear of this within the hour!'

Chrishaw held his gaze. His voice was measured. 'I doubt that because my Provost Marshal will be interviewing the two of you later this morning. I am ordering you not to leave the fort until he has done so. You may wait in your vehicle or one of the tents.'

Dumbfounded and furious Dutchmen were led outside.

Taylor-Smith could hardly contain himself. 'Sir, how on earth did you know they would say the files were stolen?'

Chrishaw smiled. 'Well, they had to have a cover story ready in case the unit was exposed, so it had to be something like that. That way they can deny anything. At least I managed to get their files for a few days.'

'Are we to let the Javanese go?'

'Yes. Arrange transport for them to the nearest station and buy them a ticket home. Use the cash found here.'

Taylor-Smith paused. 'You know that some of them could be rebels, even murderers?'

'I don't doubt it, George,' Chrishaw sighed. 'Not for a second. But no jury would convict on this evidence. They must go free.'

Book Three

Chapter Three

Quay number three was a hive of activity. Landing craft and wherries were plying back and forth to the two supply ships that had arrived from Singapore the previous evening. Next to them was the troopship that had brought two companies of Mahratta infantry and Rajpurtana Rifles, and a few dozen Dutch marines. Shouts in Urdu rang out along the quay as equipment and provisions were unloaded and stacked.

Quartermaster Bandur Patel was a stocky forty-five-year-old with seventeen years' experience of moving men and machines. The work was going well, and the lines of pencilled ticks on his battered clipboard showed everything in order. Except, that was, for one thing. Brand new and gleaming in dark green, it stood in its own space on the quay. Patel scratched his head again as he tried to work out how a brand new jeep, complete with stencilled, white American star and four jerrycans of precious petrol in the back, was listed in his inventory.

The unusual always made him uncomfortable, mainly because it meant a lot of paperwork. It was not, he thought sadly, as if this was an extra case of medicinal rum or saccharine tablets whose loss could be attributed to the 'fog of war.' No, someone, somewhere was missing his transportation and would want it back. That would mean extra work for Bandur Patel.

Another possibility suddenly struck him. Someone might have sabotaged his inventory... Patel's eyes narrowed. He looked for Gupta, his deputy. 'I bet it's that bloody bugger, Sinda! He probably won it at cards from a Yank and decided to cause me administrative aggravation!'

Gupta nodded sagely but did not look up from daubing the bottom of a bucket with bright red paint. The jeep had been virtually the sole topic of conversation all morning. 'Maybe it's his revenge for that cheap Siamese "scotch" you sold him.'

'The "Loch Taye"?' Patel looked pained. 'It was a perfectly good scotch... For the price.'

Gupta sighed. 'Yes but it would have been sound business practice to have first checked the labels.'

Chagrin flashed momentarily on Patel's face. The bottles had been emblazoned 'Lok Thai'. He grunted as he watched Gupta press the bucket down on a piece of square white cloth then lift it off leaving a print of a solid red circle. Gupta smiled and gave him the thumbs up. A dozen more 'Japanese battle flags' were drying on lines hidden amongst the stacked crates, ready for sale to newly arrived, gullible conscripts.

Patel turned as two British officers walked over to the jeep. All morning it had drawn admiring, envious glances. Most of the British vehicles were patched-up survivors of the Burma campaign. The jeep was easily the most desirable piece of kit anyone had seen in months.

Patel laughed under his breath. 'Guppy, look there! More Captain-sahibs wishing they were Major-sahibs, so they could have that jeep and be photographed just like Mountbatten-sahib!'

As the British left, they passed three Dutch officers coming on to the wharf. They also gave the jeep a studied once-over. Patel could not follow their conversation but he saw their condescending smirks as they observed the Indians unloading their own equipment. He watched them move to the area set aside for the Dutch supplies. Patel was more than a little envious of their brand new, lend-lease American equipment. Most of the crates had come from the stocks earmarked for the invasion of Japan.

In contrast to the Indians, the Dutch were using Javanese coolies. Patel shook his head in silent disbelief. He would rarely let anyone near his supplies and certainly not on the first day of a landing in unfamiliar and insecure surroundings.

Dutifully he went back to his checklist. Suddenly there was a loud bang and shouting from over by the Dutch section. Two coolies had dropped a large crate and it had broken open. Boxes of ammunition and spilled loose rounds were strewn across the wharf. A furious Dutch NCO was berating the hapless Javanese.

Patel could see that the coolies showed no sign of being intimidated. Instead, they were shouting back and pointing angrily at the ammunition. More of them gathered. The Dutchman's hand flashed up as he struck one of the Javanese across the face.

Patel began to walk towards the fracas. Gupta and several other Indians followed him.

The protestations by the Javanese were too much for another of the Dutchmen and he waded in, pushing them back to the crates. Some went back to work and Patel stopped, thinking the browbeating had worked. A sudden shout of 'Indonesia Raya!' told him he was wrong.

Two more coolies lifted another crate to the edge of the wharf and then hurled it into the harbour. A murky brown plume spouted as the box vanished. Others cheered and rushed to do the same. In seconds another half-dozen boxes had joined the first on the harbour bottom. Chanting 'Strike!', the coolies walked away.

Enraged, the Dutchmen watched their workers leave. One had his hand on his pistol holster. Some of the younger

Indians soldiers were laughing. When the Dutchmen saw them, their mood worsened. The biggest Dutchman, well over six feet tall, turned and took a step towards one of the smaller Indians. His voice was a snarl. 'You think that's funny, boy?'

'You cannot go about beating coolies,' Patel called out jauntily as he closed the distance.

'No indeed,' added Gupta in a monotone. 'It creates a terrible relationship between management and labour.'

'Is that so?' snarled the Dutchman. 'Well you don't tell me what to do, you brown bastard!' He stepped forward menacingly.

Patel smiled and glanced at Gupta who raised his eyebrows. Some fifteen Indians closed in, forming a tight semi-circle around the three Dutchmen trapping them against the stacked crates.

'You don't appear to get on well with brown bastards, do you, gentlemen?' Patel grinned. 'I wonder why? But never mind, we'll help you recover your ammunition.' He looked around at his men then spoke in Urdhu. 'In the harbour with them!'

His men rushed the helpless Dutch, grabbing them, then casting them into the water one after the other.

The Dutch swam to some steps. They clambered out glaring and stinking of waste and diesel. Humiliated, they began the long walk back to the harbour entrance past dozens of jeering Javanese.

Hotel des Indes

'All right, MacDonald,' Taylor-Smith beckoned, 'in you come.' Chrishaw had his head down over a pile of paperwork.

Mac saluted. He knew only that the General wanted to see him.

'Afternoon, MacDonald. Take a pew,' Chrishaw said affably.

Taylor-Smith ushered Mac to a seat directly in front of the desk which was positioned to give the General a view of the luxurious hotel gardens.

'How's the leg?'

'Much better, thank you, Sir. But still painful...' Mac replied warily. In truth he was surprised that Chrishaw knew or cared. He glanced at the cluttered desk and saw two books among the papers. One was a thick, leather-bound copy of History of Java by Stamford Raffles, the other was Birds of the Netherlands East Indies.

'Painful? Hmm... I've got driving duties for you,' Chrishaw said suddenly. 'Is your leg up to it?'

Mac sat up keenly. 'Oh, yes, Sir!'

'It gets better,' Chrishaw laughed. 'You are to be a chauffeur for a lady.'

Mac's eyes widened. 'A lady?'

'Yes. An American war correspondent to be precise. Her name is Megan Graham, Miss Graham to you. You might have seen her wandering about the town in all the wrong places?'

'Yes General. I have as a matter of fact. I saw her at the harbour when the Dutchies—I mean the Dutch Governor— tried to come ashore.'

'Right,' Chrishaw mumbled in a non-committal manner. 'Of course from the journalistic point of view, Miss Graham's usually in the right place. She's experienced and very independent. Even so, I'd be happier if she had a British driver for a few days just in case. Murder, rape and robbery are rife, in addition there's always the risk of the odd sniper!'

Mac nodded gravely. 'Yes, Sir.' Only the night before a patrol had been ambushed and two soldiers killed.

'Listen,' Chrishaw continued. 'You're to be her driver. She's the boss but use your judgement about where she wants to go. I don't want you both kidnapped, or worse. Is that—'

Chrishaw was sitting stock still, his mouth open. Mac saw he was peering over his shoulder and out into the garden. He started to turn.

'Don't move!' Chrishaw's commanded hoarsely. Mac and Taylor-Smith tensed.

They both watched as Chrishaw's right hand began to inch slowly across the top of the desk. 'He's in the nearest tamarind tree!' he whispered. 'MacDonald, I want you to stay absolutely still. George, you can back away. He can't see you.'

Relieved, Taylor-Smith took several, quick steps until he was pressed against the wall.

Mac sat rigid, staring at Chrishaw's hand as it moved at what seemed a snail's pace towards the desk drawer. He felt a moist chill between his shoulder blades and his heart began to race. His mouth went dry. 'Just say the word, Sir,' he managed to croak.

'Hmm?' Chrishaw muttered, not seeming to hear. His hand was now hovering over the drawer. 'He's well camouflaged,' he said under his breath. 'I don't know how I saw him!'

Mac, amazed by the General's composure, braced himself for the shot. He wondered if he would hear it, then remembered the adage that you never hear the one that gets you. His pulse was surging, his throat felt parched. Beads of perspiration dotted his forehead. He glanced pleadingly at Taylor-Smith who leant calmly, even indifferently, against the wall. Chrishaw's hand dropped below the desk top.

Mac heard the drawer slide open. He's too slow! His chest tightened as Chrishaw's hand reaching. 'I'm ready to move, Sir,' he gasped.

'What was that?' Chrishaw muttered distractedly. His eyes were bright but he seemed completely oblivious to Mac. His hand was out of the drawer and was moving furtively back to his lap.

Mac could not see the pistol. His mind was jumping. What was Chrishaw doing? A handgun against a sniper!

He was about to fling himself to one side when, at last, Chrishaw's hand rose above the desk to his face. Mac's jaw dropped.

The General was holding a pair of field glasses and was grinning widely. 'Green hornbill, male, a real beauty! It's native to Java. I was hoping to see one while I was here. What a bonus! Apparently, someone freed the birds in the zoo aviary last week, so anything is possible at the moment!'

Mac's shoulders sagged as he relaxed. He let out a loud sigh. Taylor-Smith was laughing at Mac's expense.

Chrishaw lowered the glasses to reveal amused, twinkling eyes. 'Are you all right, MacDonald? You look a bit peaky suddenly. What was that you said?'

'Nothing, Sir,' Mac managed a wry grin. 'Pity you haven't got a camera handy.'

'That's not a bad idea! Remind me to get one, Major.' Now, back to business. We—'

Mac jumped as shot sounded from near the front of the building.

'Bloody hell!' Chrishaw stood.

Taylor-Smith was rushing to the door. 'Very close!'

'Probably the Dutch offices,' Chrishaw agreed. 'Come on!'

Outside they saw a noisy crowd forming in front of the tall, iron gates of the municipal building that housed NICA staff. Dutch marines and native troops were trying to force the Javanese away from a sentry box. Chrishaw pushed his way through. Sprawled on the pavement was a dead Javanese youth. A bullet wound in the middle of his chest showed clearly on his white shirt. Beside the body was a small

Indonesian flag. Chrishaw fixed his gaze on a Dutch captain. 'What happened here?'

'I'm not sure, General. The guard felt it necessary to open fire.'

'I'll bet he did!' Chrishaw whirled to face the guard. 'Why?'

The guard, an Ambonese, not much older than twenty, shrugged then spoke in Dutch.

'He says he was abusive and threatening,' the Captain explained casually.

Chrishaw was staring at the nonchalant guard. 'Was he armed?'

Again the Captain interpreted. The guard's answer was short.

'No, Sir, he was not armed but he could have been. Protesters gather here regularly throughout the day.'

'What about witnesses?' Chrishaw looked at the accusing faces in the crowd. 'This is a busy street. Somebody must have seen it!'

Much less enthusiastically the Captain turned and addressed the crowd. A middle-aged, neatly dressed Javanese man raised a hesitant finger to point at the guard and spoke in English. 'I saw the boy carrying the flag as he went past. He was shot for no reason!'

'You can't believe these rebel sympathisers,' snarled the Captain. 'They'll say anything!' He glared balefully at the Javanese who shrank back.

Chrishaw's frustration was obvious. 'Captain, perhaps the guard can explain the threat to his life from an unarmed youth?' His tone was steel-like.

Shaking his head and shrugging, the guard mumbled a reply. Chrishaw did not wait for the translation. 'Then in God's name why did he shoot him?'

People in the crowd began to shout. The guard was non-committal but unrepentant. Finally the Captain turned to Chrishaw. 'I think he was provoked and—'

'Put that man under arrest,' Chrishaw said tersely.

The Captain stared in askance at Chrishaw. 'Arrest? But he was a rebel sympathiser—'

Two British military policemen arrived. 'Sergeant,' Chrishaw snapped, 'arrest that soldier.' He pointed to the Javanese witness. 'Take a confidential statement from this man and bring it to me, no-one else.'

The Dutch officer moved as if to accompany them. Chrishaw raised his hand. 'Captain, you and your men will remain here and assist Major Taylor-Smith and the MPs. MacDonald, come with me. You start your new job this afternoon.'

Meg sipped her tea. It was deliciously fresh. Chrishaw put down his cup and cleared his throat. 'Miss Graham, as someone who's being driven around in a clapped-out Citroen, I have some enviable news. You're to have use of a brand new jeep.'

His amusement showed in his eyes and Meg relaxed. The invitation to tea had arrived shortly after rumours of the altercation at the docks had reached her. She had been wondering if the two were connected.

'To be frank,' Chrishaw went on, 'I do have concerns about your movements. Most of Batavia is outside our control. I think it best if you travel in a very noticeable vehicle.'

Meg's face clouded but Chrishaw carried on quickly. 'You're movements will not be vetted but I do insist that you have a driver. I've already asked Brigadier King to spare one of his men for a few days. His name is MacDonald. He's downstairs.'

Chrishaw missed her slight smile. 'MacDonald's excused patrol duties because he's had a bad leg. Still, he can be useful while he's recovering.' The General waited for the outburst on restricting the freedom of the press but it did not come.

In fact, Meg gave him a beaming smile and mimicked a put-upon southern belle. 'Lordy, Gen'rul, ah thought y'all were going to confine me to ma' quarters.'

Chrishaw's shoulders shook. 'My dear lady,' he laughed, 'the British don't go about doing things like that. More tea?'

'Oh, yes please. It's the best I've ever had! We gave a really good tea party once.'

'Let me guess. In Boston in 1776?'

They both smiled, liking each other. He refilled her cup. 'There you are. It's first-flush Darjeeling. One of the perks of commanding an Indian Army division.'

'But not for much longer, I guess?' She regretted the question even as she spoke. 'Sorry, General, force of habit. I didn't intend to raise the subject of Indian independence.

Chrishaw was unfazed. 'This isn't an interview, we're having a conversation. There have been Indian levies in the British army since before the battle of Plessy in 1767.' He smiled. 'You see, even as we were about to lose one colony we were gaining another!' His expression became thoughtful. 'Forgive me if I sound boastful but today the British Indian Army is probably one of the finest organisations—military or civilian—the world has ever seen. Nearly a million Hindus, Muslims, Sikhs, Buddhists, Zoroastrians and Christians operating together, often in mixed regiments. It's multi-faith, meritocratic, non-partisan as well as efficient and capable. It has worked spectacularly well, Miss Graham. Not a bad epitaph!'

Meg nodded. 'There will be an Indian Army, though, without the British. You're sure it will change?'

He sighed, raising his open palms. 'Oh, vestiges of tradition will remain I suppose. But a political division of British India that leads to a separate Muslim state would mean arguments over borders, and a splitting of regiments, resources and recruitment. That will destroy the whole ethos of the army. To adapt a phrase, it ain't broke, but the politicians will want to fix it!'

There was a knock on the door. 'Sorry to interrupt, Sir, said Taylor-Smith. 'Wing-Commander Ball has just arrived from Singapore.'

Chrishaw nodded. 'Oh, good. Show him in. Miss Graham might be interested in his work. Women's angle and all that.'

Meg frowned accusingly at Chrishaw who smiled. 'Please don't take it the wrong way. Ball is assigned to Recovery of Allied Prisoners of War and Internees.'

'Wow!' Meg laughed. 'That's a mouthful.'

'Isn't it just. It's "RAPWI" for short.'

A short, stocky man with sleek black hair and hard features entered the room.

'Ah, Wing-Commander, good to meet you at last,' Chrishaw said warmly. 'Your reports are first class…if rather disturbing.'

'Very pleased to meet you, too, General,' Ball replied confidently. The two men shook hands.

Chrishaw turned to Meg. 'Wing-Commander, let me introduce Miss Megan Graham. She is with the US Press Corps.'

Ball stepped forward, smiled and offered his hand. 'Tom Ball, delighted.'

'Same here, I'm sure,' Meg replied with a smile. She noticed a burn scar running down one side of Ball's neck.

Chrishaw continued in good mood. 'Wing-Commander Ball has been here for some weeks now, zipping about the internee camps near Batavia, Buitenzorg and Bandung. He even has his own plane—one of your marvellous Dakotas! He'll be going to Semarang and Surabaya. Why don't you go along? I'm sure it would make an interesting article for your readers. I'll assign you a vehicle so you can get about. Your driver can go with you on a temporary secondment to RAPWI. How about that, Wing-Commander?'

Ball nodded quickly. 'Fine with me, Sir. We can always use more help...and publicity!'

Meg eyes narrowed. 'General, is this a reward for not writing about the incident in the market and the squabble at the docks, or do you just want me out of the way?'

Chrishaw feigned outrage. 'My dear, how could you think that of one of His Majesty's Generals? I simply wish to be of service to the Press.'

Meg grinned. 'In that case, General, you've got a deal.' She stood and Chrishaw rose as well. They shook hands.

'I enjoyed our chat immensely,' he said warmly. 'Most Americans, naturally enough, have hostile preconceptions about colonies but I understand that you write very perceptively and even-handedly. I'll be interested to read what you have to say.'

'I'll try not to disappoint,' said Meg. 'Good-bye and thank you.'

'I'll see you at the reception on Tuesday night?' Chrishaw called after her. 'Could be newsworthy!'

She nodded. 'Oh, yes. The Major gave me the invitation before I came in.

'Good,' he beamed, 'you can put me down for a waltz!'

Mac was sitting in a cane-back planter's chair in the hotel lobby. He saw Meg come down the stairs and look around. Nearly every man was in a uniform of some kind. He stood, waved and walked over to her.

'Hello, Mac,' she said smiling. 'Small world...again!'

Mac nodded. 'Aye, so it is, Miss.'

'Won any bets lately?'

'Given it up for Lent, Miss.' He was still thanking his lucky stars for his cushy assignment. Driving for an attractive reporter was a lot better than standing all day in the sun at a checkpoint.

'Please call me Meg', she said, offering her hand. 'It's good to see you again, Mac.' She held his hand longer than he expected, and looked at him curiously, almost challengingly. 'By the way,' she added, 'the jeep's left-hand drive. Can you drive on the right?'

'As long as everyone else does.'

Meg laughed. 'You're hired, soldier!' She looked at her watch. 'Right, Mr Sulosu, the maître d' at my hotel has invited me to a festival at his village. There'll be music and shadow puppets, which I really want to see. It should be great fun!'

'A festival? Any food?' Mac was always ready for a change from bully beef and beans.

'Oh, the usual festival snacks I suppose, roast meats, fish, lots of fruits.'

He grinned enthusiastically. 'That sounds great. Where are we going?'

'Near Krawang. It's about thirty miles east of here on the coast.'

His face fell. 'You realise that's about twenty-eight miles beyond our security zone?'

'Don't worry, I'm an American! And I'm invited!'

Krawang, North Java Coast

Mac was attacking his third kebab of the evening with gusto. 'What did you say this sauce was called?'

'*Satay,*' Meg replied, smiling, pleased that he was enjoying himself. They had taken a break from the puppets and dancing to try some of the food. Sulosu was treating them as guests of honour. Meg had been given flowers when they arrived and the children had clustered round them, shyly at first, despite Sulosu's half-hearted protestations that his guests be shown more respect. After one little boy had dared to touch Meg's face giggling children had started to crawl all over them. They had followed them noisily on their tour of the village and sat around and on them during the first of the *wayang* shows. Meg had been entranced by the puppets even though she had been balancing two toddlers on her knees at the time. She had also noticed that Mac had been very attentive to the children.

'I'm sorry, Miss Graham,' Sulosu said in frustration. 'These little ones are too small to remember the Dutch. They have never seen white people before.'

'I see,' Meg smiled. 'So that's why they thought we were devils?'

Sulosu gave an embarrassed nod then surrendered with a smile as another youngster came to stare at Meg.

Mac pointed to half a dozen youths forming a line in the centre of the village square. 'More dancing? It's the laddies' turn now I suppose? The girls were beauties, Mr Sulosu. My friends will be so envious when I tell them!'

Sulosu smiled. 'Thank you. I will pass on your compliments...after you have left!'

Their laughter was cut short by a fast, staccato drumming on a single gong. Almost as one, the youths dropped into very wide, open-hipped stances, their thighs parallel to the ground.

Sulosu drew closer to Meg and Mac to explain. 'These are students of *silat*, a traditional fighting art. Many of the movements are based on animals. This first one is *harimau* or tiger. You'll see it's quite different from western boxing!'

After a hand salute the youths began swaying, dropping low over their stepping feet mimicking a prowling cat. Periodically their hands slapped their thighs in unison. Suddenly they flung themselves to the ground and jumped up to kick out, then dropped again into a crouch.

As a drum started to accompany the gong the youths stood tall and stretched, balancing on one leg, arms high and outstretched.

'This is the crane,' said Sulosu, watching them whirl, balance and spin, whipping their arms about them.

For their finale, the youths paired off in slow, dance-like combat sequences. Gradually they speeded up until the movements were an acrobatic blur.

Their display finished to tremendous applause.

'That was amazing, Mr Sulosu,' Meg said appreciatively. 'They are so supple. I don't think I've ever seen anyone move so fast!'

Sulosu was very pleased and turned to Mac. 'What did you make of that?'

Mac shrugged. 'Dancing around isn't like proper fisticuffs though, is it? And they use their feet. I don't know how they'd stand up to an old-fashioned straight left or a good right hook.'

'A right hook to what, Mac?' Meg laughed. 'A head that isn't there! I know who my money would be on in a fight between a *silat* player and a boxer!'

Mac shook his head. 'Using feet and knees like that's hardly sporting, is it?'

Sulosu frowned. '*Silat* is not a sport. It's combat. The object is to walk away unharmed. To survive.' Then he smiled politely. 'More *satay*?'

At nine Meg and Mac left the village with full stomachs and much regret. Happy, smiling villagers waved them off.

Meg was pensive on the drive back, so Mac made a stab at conversation. 'That was the best meal I've had in a long time. He's a nice bloke, too, Sulosu.'

She did not reply so he drove in silence until they passed a sign for Krawang Point. 'We're going the wrong way,' he announced. 'I'll have to turn round.'

They came upon a clearing and he swung quickly off the narrow road. Just then the headlights picked out a fallen tree. He was too late with the brakes and the front wheels bounced up and over the trunk. Meg let out a yelp. They jerked to a halt and the engine stalled.

'Sorry,' Mac said quietly, switching off the ignition. The headlights went out. They sat in darkness, catching their breath. Gradually cicadas resumed their chirping and, just beyond a line of palm trees, they could hear the sound of waves breaking on a beach.

Embarrassed, Mac reached for a cigarette. 'Could have been worse,' he said awkwardly.

'Umm… it was my fault, Mac,' she replied softly. 'I was supposed to be navigating. I wasn't concentrating.'

Mac shrugged. 'We're only a couple of miles out of our—'

He stopped as they heard engines. Moments later powerful lights swept the bushes ahead and then flicked past them. An unmarked, canvas-topped lorry raced by. Two smaller Red Cross-marked ambulances followed close behind. They rounded a bend and disappeared.

'Christ!' Mac gasped. 'If I hadn't turned off we'd have hit that! I hope it's urgent, that's all!'

Meg was still troubled. 'My father told me never to joke about being hit by an ambulance.'

'Aye, I see his point!' Mac said getting out of the jeep. 'Er, excuse me, call of nature. I'll be back in a minute.'

Meg nodded. 'OK, I'll be over there.'

There was a gentle, sloping beach and apart from glimmers of light from a few fishermen's huts at one end of the cove it was deserted. Her feet slipped in the soft sand and she took off her shoes and socks. She pulled out a cigarette then went forward to let the water swirl over her feet.

Mac's footsteps sounded heavy in the sand. She turned wondering how he would react if she suggested a swim. 'Isn't it beautiful?'

He looked around slowly and then nodded thoughtfully. 'Aye, it is. I used to hate Asia. I thought it was just sweltering, stinking jungle and leeches. Java's different.'

'How's that?'

'Oh, there are cities, hotels, trains, roads, shops, cafes... I just wish we were more popular. Also I'm not here to kill anybody for one thing. That makes a big difference.'

'It must do,' she smiled, trying to gauge his mood. She felt a strong urge to reach out and take his hand.

He looked at his watch. 'Let's go. We can still beat the curfew.'

'Oh,' she sighed disappointedly. 'I'd like to come back here to swim and watch the sunset.'

'With me?' he replied quickly. Suddenly he seemed embarrassed.

Meg raised her eyebrows. 'Well, you're my driver, aren't you?'

'Oh,' he said awkwardly. 'I see what you mean...' He looked away.

Meg shook her head. 'No you don't, soldier boy.'

With two quick steps Mac was in front of her. 'I'm not a boy, Meg,' he said firmly.

Her voice was husky. 'Then show me.'

Hesitantly his hand touched hers. She smiled at him, letting her fingers intertwine with his. Their gaze held and he leant forward to kiss her. She closed her eyes and raised her face. His lips brushed her cheek then slid to her slightly parted mouth. She pushed against him, letting her hands slide up behind his neck. 'God!' Meg gasped. 'I've been worrying that you think I'm an old hag.'

He frowned. 'You're joking? You're lovely, Meg. Really lovely.' His arms closed firmly around her waist. His breath was quick and hot on her neck.

'Oh, Mac! Don't stop now,' she murmured into his ear. 'I couldn't bear it.' Then she felt his hands on her shoulders, pushing her down on to the sand.

Her hands went to his face and she kissed him, taking his lips between hers. She moaned breathlessly into his kiss, hugging him to her. Their tongues met and she shuddered as his hands squeezed her breasts. He began pulling at the buttons on her blouse.

'Let me do it,' she panted, slipping from his embrace. Quickly she sat up and undid her blouse, then reached back to undo her brassiere which she flung away in the sand. His hand caressed her back and she lay back, her arms open and inviting.

Later they swam to wash off the sand and Mac dried her with his shirt. They dressed slowly, kissing frequently, reluctant to leave their paradise. It was nearly an hour before they were heading back up the beach arm in arm. Meg paused at the palms for one last glance at the cove and the ocean. Thick clouds were rolling in from the north and the last of the moonlight was flashing silver on the wave tops. She was turning back when suddenly she stopped and stared. If she had not seen the image before—a white silhouette of a shark on grey steel—she might have missed it. A chill shot through her.

Mac followed her gaze. 'You look like you saw a ghost!'

She gripped his arm. 'A submarine!'

'A sub!' Mac scoffed, glancing out to sea. 'Don't be daft!'

Meg glanced at him quickly then forced a laugh. 'Well, maybe I am seeing things....'

Mac scratched his head. 'Come on, lass, we're late!'

Meg ambled after him, wrestling with the implications of what she had just seen. *Tigershark* was hunting off Java....

Mac had decided to play safe and re-enter Batavia from the southeast on the main Buitenzorg road. He was concerned about the risk of ambush on the narrow winding lanes that linked the paddies and isolated kampongs to the east of the city. Even so, he drove at speed until they saw the signs for Meester Cornelis, a small township on the outskirts of the city. As the familiar landmark of a church came into view at the Salemba junction, he slowed and let out a quiet sigh of relief.

Meg turned to him with a smile. 'Hey! We've made first base!'

'Uh? Oh, yes, nearly there.'

He turned right on to the wide road without stopping. They sped past poorly lit bungalows and houses. Before the war, Meester Cornelis had become a continuation of suburban Weltvreden. Now it lay well beyond the British-Japanese security zone. Native squatters had already laid claim to many of the houses.

As the lights of the first roadblock appeared Mac slowed to a crawl. He did not want to raise the slightest suspicion because the Japanese were known to shoot first and ask questions later.

At least four rifles were trained on them from behind two cars staggered across the road. Once again, Mac felt his stomach tense at the sight of the Japanese. The weight of the Sten machine-gun resting against his thigh was comforting. He kept his hand on the gear-lever, just inches from the weapon. Even as he did so, he knew it was a useless and even dangerous idea.

Meg was rooting in her bag for her papers but they were not needed. To Mac's relief Meg was already known to the Japanese who seemed relaxed. The lieutenant in command waved them through as soon as they saw the jeep and its passengers.

Mac drove slowly around the cars and pulled over a few yards past the roadblock. 'We need some more petrol—I mean gas.'

Meg nodded and he jumped out of the jeep to reach for the jerrycan. Behind them more lights were approaching the roadblock.

Meg stretched in her seat. 'Do you always drive so fast?'

He grinned. 'Only between roadblocks!'

A squeal of brakes distracted them. An ambulance was drawing up at the roadblock. 'The Red Cross are busy tonight,' Meg said watching the Japanese inspect the driver's papers.

Suddenly the Japanese lieutenant began shouting at the driver. Two more soldiers moved towards the rear of the vehicle.

Mac swore. 'They've no bloody right to stop an ambulance like that. I'll report it when I get back.'

There was more shouting as the guards started banging on the back of the ambulance with their rifle butts. A door flung open and two shots rang out. One of Japanese fell back clutching at his chest.

Mac grabbed for Meg. 'Shite! Keep low!'

He saw the driver try to flee. The Japanese lieutenant fired and the man went sprawling. Mac was reaching for his gun when Meg grabbed his arm. 'No! They'll shoot you!'

He saw she was right and let go of the Sten. Another figure leapt from the back of the ambulance. He went down in a hail of bullets.

Mac let Meg up and saw some of the Japanese were now eyeing them suspiciously. Unarmed, Mac began to walk slowly back to the roadblock. Meg caught him up.

'Go back!' he hissed. 'Anything might happen here.'

'I'm a journalist, Mac. Let me do my job.'

The Japanese lieutenant did not seem particularly concerned about them but he checked their papers this time, then beckoned them to follow him. *'Kochi ni kite kudasai.'*

Mac hesitated but Meg stepped past him. The dead Japanese lay unattended on the road. Next to him lay an Indonesian, also dead. Several Japanese were standing around the driver, who had only a minor wound in his leg. As she drew nearer Meg saw he was white, very thin and wearing Red Cross badges on his otherwise plain shirt. Glumly he avoided her gaze.

Pointing, the lieutenant led them confidently to the back of the ambulance and produced a torch. Illuminated by the beam were long wooden crates and some smaller boxes. One had been prized open. The lieutenant invited them to look. *'Mite kudasai.'*

Meg already knew what was inside.

Mac was incredulous. 'Bloody hell! Guns and ammo!'

Beside him, the lieutenant nodded in satisfaction. *'Oranda!'*

Mac frowned. 'What did he say?'

'I think he said "Holland". Gun-runners,' said Meg softly. 'The dead man is probably Ambonese and the driver an ex-POW.'

Mac shook his head. 'Now the Dutch are running guns?'

'So desu, Daatchi!' The lieutenant squatted to pick up a beret. It carried Dutch insignia.

Meg and Mac went back to the jeep to wait. Within a few minutes a British patrol arrived to take the prisoner away. Mac and Meg were questioned briefly, then allowed to leave.

Meg sat half-twisted, resting her chin on her folded arms on the top of the seat back. 'Why do I have a feeling that tonight's fun and games will not feature in tomorrow's bulletin from the Army Press Office?'

'Eh?' Mac half laughed. 'Surely they can't hush this one up. Two dead, and another one arrested running guns in a Red Cross ambulance!'

'If you ever do come across it I think you'll find it described as a regrettable incident involving former POWs having a go at the Japs. Very convenient really.'

'Christ!'

'Hey, it happens all the time. Don't worry about it.'

He looked at her sharply. 'Will you write about this "regrettable incident" then?'

She smiled. 'I have a hunch it's much more. You'll see what I mean tomorrow at Van Zanten's press conference.'

Governor-General's Palace, Batavia

'Doctor Van Zanten, when can we expect new Dutch troops to arrive in Java?' The journalist stood expectantly, pen ready. It was the third question that morning on the same theme but Van Zanten was quite pleased to have another excuse to complain about British delays. Standing to one side near the back of the hall he could see Admiral Hurwitz, General Overbeck and Lt Colonel Brommer were quietly satisfied, in contrast with the far from happy British liaison captain who was taking notes.

Van Zanten raised his hands. 'I only wish I knew. Dutch ships are still under British command. Despite our repeated requests, these have not been released to us.'

There was another planted question. 'Doctor, what about the delay in arresting and trying the rebels? When will courts be set up?'

He paused for effect. 'Naturally our Administration is very concerned that we have not yet been permitted to re-establish a judicial process. NICA judges, counsel and clerks are ready to begin work immediately should the British agree with us that the time is now right for Dutch law to apply throughout the Indies. Sadly, heinous crimes are going unpunished.'

Several Indonesian journalists raised their hands. Van Zanten ignored them and chose another Dutch correspondent.

'Doctor, why has there been no move against the main rebel base at Yogya? Surely the more time they have the better prepared they will be to resist the attack when it is made.'

'It seems that the British are reluctant to honour agreements about returning our territory. They are, of course, busy in Burma and Malaya looking after their own interests. Naturally we feel they are in breach of their obligations to an ally.'

Meg stood up uninvited. 'Doctor, could the British reluctance to risk the reprisals against tens of thousands of Dutch women and children still trapped in camps be another reason for this delay?'

He nodded once. 'The hostages concern us greatly, Miss Graham.'

'Really? Dutch policy would seem to suggest otherwise. Especially with Dutch forces acting independently of the British.'

Perplexed, Van Zanten looked at her. 'Independently? I don't know what you mean. Our forces are very limited in number. We rely totally on the British armed forces for support and logistics.'

One of the Indonesian reporters stood up. 'Doctor, at least five Indonesian fishing boats have gone missing recently.

Wreckage washed up along the coast suggests fire or even explosion. There are rumours of a Dutch warship operating off Java. Is this true?'

Mac was propping up the opposite wall to the Dutch officers. Meg's instruction to him had been to watch Hurwitz and Visser very closely whenever Meg asked a question or someone mentioned ships or boats.

Van Zanten shook his head and laughed. 'That is a fantastic assumption! The nearest Dutch ships are at Singapore.'

Clearly unimpressed by the answer, the Indonesian sat down. Van Zanten ignored him and addressed the Dutch correspondents. 'As for fire and explosions, I agree those are not normal hazards for fishing boats but they are for cargoes such as grenades and ammunition. The hungry people of Java should ask whether their fishermen should be trying to put food on the table rather than aid rebels.'

Meg saw the opening she was looking for and stood up again. 'And what about Dutch gun-running, Doctor? Who is that serving?'

Many of the Dutch journalists shook their heads derisively. Meg ignored them.

Van Zanten rolled his eyes. 'Miss Graham I think you are fishing without a hook!'

Again the Dutch laughed.

Meg shrugged. 'I did go fishing the other night. And guess what? I caught a huge tiger-shark. It was such a shock that I had to be taken home in a Red Cross Ambulance!' She sat down quickly, keeping her gaze on him.

For an instant Van Zanten's eyes flashed cold, then he was smiling again. 'Shark fishing can be very dangerous...' He nodded to a Dutch journalist. 'Jaap, your question?'

'Thank you, Doctor', said the journalist respectfully. 'How long will Japanese currency remain legal tender?'

Outside in the car park, Mac could hardly contain himself. 'How did you know? You should have seen the Dutch admiral's face!'

Meg smiled and began touching up her lipstick. 'I was tempted to look. And the other two?'

'Oh yes! They gave you very dirty looks and went out.'

Meg grinned broadly. 'Then the gun-running goes all the way to the top!'

Mac looked at her accusingly. 'You really did see a submarine didn't you?'

'Yes....' She pursed her lips. 'Sorry I couldn't tell you. I—'

'You don't trust me?' He looked pained.

'Listen, I'm an American journalist. You're a British soldier. The war's over but you still have to follow orders or you could be in big trouble. I don't. I had one chance to link the sub to the ambulance. I couldn't risk you blowing it by telling someone at the barracks.'

Mac stared at his lap quietly. 'You're right. I would have told someone.' He smiled. 'I'll tell you what, I'll drive, you report.'

She laughed. 'Deal!'

Mac started the engine. 'So, Miss Foreign Correspondent, where to now?'

'Where do you think? My hotel room!'

Brommer, the head of the Intelligence Service, turned away from the second-floor window as the jeep moved off. 'That nosey bitch has left,' he snarled.

Van Zanten shook his head reprovingly. 'Colonel, Miss Graham is exceptionally good at her job.'

'Well,' interjected Visser, Van Zanten's deputy, 'she could have got something from the British military police about the guns and the ambulance but how the hell does she know about *Tijgerhaai*!'

'It's worrying,' nodded Brommer.

Van Zanten gave him a sharp look. 'What if she has a source inside NEFIS?'

Brommer's head shot up. 'I don't believe it. My people are—'

'What about the local staff,' Hurwitz shouted. 'I mean some Dutch girls work as secretaries for the British. You get information from them. The British could have bribed one of yours.'

Brommer looked affronted. 'Non-military staff are forbidden inside my HQ. Any leaks must have come from here...or the naval office.'

Hurwitz bridled, 'That's—'

'Enough! Van Zanten slammed the table. 'At the moment it does not matter how she knows. I want a solution. Brommer, that is your department. Any suggestions?'

'Interviewing revolutionary leaders,' Brommer said archly, 'can be very dangerous, especially if there happened to be an assassination attempt on the politician...'

Visser clapped. 'Two birds with one stone?'

Van Zanten slowly stroked his chin. 'Just solve the problem.'

Chapter Four

Yarek entered the office with a part smile and an overly loud greeting. 'We were worried Bung Sarel, Bung Lamban. It's good to see you safe.'

Lamban, Sarel and four of the Black Buffalos from Sadakan village regarded him coldly. He looked around uneasily.

Sarel was leaning against a desk. 'Only you knew our precise travel plans Yarek. You left the meeting early. Lamban and I were arrested at a temporary roadblock on a minor road. Why did that happen?'

Yarek shrugged but paled. 'I have no idea.'

'Don't lie! Sarel snapped. 'We have people watching the Dutch bases. NEFIS arrested you at Krawang with our leaflets. You were taken to their compound. Five hours later you were released and went directly to the *Asrama*.'

Yarek dropped to his knees in supplication. 'I was arrested. It's true! But I didn't betray you. I swear!'

Sarel frowned. 'And yet they let you go unharmed after just five hours. Why?'

Yarek looked from face to face in desperation. 'I was beaten but they got nothing!'

'Really? Sarel half smiled. 'Strip him!'

In seconds Yarek stood before them naked and without bruises. He began to sob.

'Please Sarel, NEFIS know your full name and the houses you have used. They were going to catch you anyway...They threatened to arrest my parents and shoot my brother. I—I had no choice!'

Sarel's expression was pitying. 'Oh, but you did, Yarek. You had a choice to die a martyr for the revolution at the hands of the Dutch, or to die a traitor now.'

'Mercy, Sarel, I'll—' Yarek suddenly gasped, half-turned then pitched forwards.

Behind him Lamban stared at his victim, the Death Shroud *keris* in his hand. Blood began to pool around Yarek's corpse.

British HQ, Hotel des Indes

Ball yawned as he re-read his report. He was pleased. The spelling was perfect, and the paragraphing and indents made his suggestions seem far more measured than they had done in longhand. Emmy Eberfeld sat in front of her typewriter filing her nails while she waited for his corrections. She was one of several Dutch hired by a desperate British HQ for secretarial and typing duties. All the others had left for lunch.

'Emmy, you're a marvel!' Ball grinned. 'I'll bet you've got the fastest fingers in Java!'

Behind her a signals clerk smirked, and Ball struggled to keep his face straight. Emmy sat expectantly, oblivious to the double entendre.

'It's perfect,' he said warmly. 'The cover page should be titled "RAPWI Report No. 2. West Java Evacuation Schedules". Date it and add my surname and initials as well please.'

'Of course, Wing-Commander.'

For a few seconds the typewriter rattled, then Emmy pulled out the sheet and carbon. She clipped the pages together and offered it smiling. 'Here you are, all done!'

'Splendid!' Ball beamed. 'Why don't I take you to lunch as a little thank you?'

'Sorry, Wing-Commander I've got an appointment at one o'clock.'

'Surely not with a man!' Ball put his hands on his heart in pretended agony.

Emmy giggled. 'I'm not telling,'

'Lucky man,' smiled Ball. He reached across the desk for a stamp and pressed it firmly on the two cover pages. Emmy glanced down at the red-inked 'Top Secret'.

Taylor-Smith entered the office. He looked anxious and was relieved to see Emmy.

'Excuse me, Tom. Emmy, this is very urgent. It's only a short invitation. Do you mind?'

Ball grinned at her. 'You mustn't make her late for her date, Major.'

'Just put it there, Major,' Emmy replied. 'I'm taking a late lunch, so I'll do it now.'

Taylor-Smith heaved a sigh of relief. 'Bless you!'

Ball stood up and gave Taylor-Smith a copy of his report. 'Would you pass this to General Chrishaw? I'm flying to Semarang today and then on to Surabaya to check out the camps before our transports arrive. You won't see me for several days. God knows what I'll find. Each camp I visit seems worse than the last.'

Taylor-Smith nodded sympathetically. 'I'd hate your job. The General's enormously grateful.'

'Well, I'm off,' declared Ball. 'Have a nice lunch, Emmy. Cheerio!'

'Bye, Wing-Commander. Take care,' she replied.

As soon as the two officers had gone Emmy pulled out a small mirror from a desk drawer and applied some lipstick. When she finished she stared mournfully at the clock on the wall, then set about layering the sheets and carbons for her next job.

Five minutes later three copies of the invitation were ready on the desk. She reached down into a large straw shopping bag and took out a folded buff-coloured envelope marked 'Batavia Women's Institute'. Quickly she slipped copies of the report and invitation inside. By twelve fifty-five Emmy had walked to the end of Noordwijk and was on the Waterlooplein West. In the square to her left the twin, open ironwork towers of the cathedral shimmered in the midday heat. Moving briskly, she turned south, making the best of the shade offered by the tall buildings. She was a little out of breath when she arrived at the Concordia Club and, once past the guard, paused to dab her perspiration-dotted forehead. After straightening her hair she made her way to the garden terrace restaurant. Several tables were occupied, most of them by Dutchmen in NICA uniforms.

A young officer stood and waved, giving her a dazzling smile. He took her bag and touched her arm affectionately. 'You had me worried, Emmy. I thought you weren't coming!'

'I'm sorry, Hans,' she sighed apologetically. 'I had to do an urgent report.'

'Well, I suppose that's all right then,' he said cheerfully. 'Emmy, you look lovely today.' He poured her some chilled water. 'So what was so important that it was allowed to keep us apart?'

Her eyes sparkled and her voice lowered. 'Oh, this and that. You know…' she said teasing him, enjoying his attention. She reached for the menu. 'Hans I'm so hungry. Have you ordered? I wonder if they have any fish today.'

'I'm sure they have', he grinned. 'By the way, are you free on Saturday? We're having a picnic. If you like you could bring some of the girls from the office. There'll be lots of single men there.'

'Oh, thank you, Hans,' she gushed. 'They'll all want to go!'

His face suddenly clouded. 'I hope I don't have to work...'

Emmy's face was full of concern. 'Oh, Hans, are you still in trouble with your Colonel?'

He shrugged. 'These days I can't tell,' he sighed.

She reached across the table and patted his hand. 'Don't worry. I brought you something that will put your Colonel in a good mood!'

'Really?'

Emmy giggled. 'Now what time on Saturday?'

By two-fifteen, a still-smiling Hans Kern had reached his tiny office at the rear of the Governor's palace. He was delighted with his lunchtime's work. With RAPWI officers heading for Semarang and Surabaya it meant that the British would occupy them soon, which was good news—the rebels had been given free rein there for long enough, he thought. The real gem, though, had been the other document.

There was only one cluttered desk in Kern's office. He sat down quickly and took out Emmy's envelope from his attaché case. As he re-read Chrishaw's invitation to Dr Jarisha he smiled. Now he even had the date, time and location of their meeting! Elated, he let his thoughts run on. His superiors would be more than impressed.

He reached for a phone and dialled. While he waited for the connection he drew a large, embellished 'J' on a desk diary page. 'Got him!' Kern mouthed quietly.

After three rings a voice answered. 'NEFIS HQ.'

'This is Captain Kern, I must speak with Lieutenant Colonel Brommer!'

British HQ, Hotel des Indes

Major Taylor-Smith was irate. 'Seven guilders to the pound!'
'That's the pre-war rate for God's sake. It's ten-and-a-half in
the Netherlands, fifteen on the black market here. What damn
cheek!'

'Take it easy, George,' Chrishaw said patiently, closing a
file on his desk. 'We'll have to expect things like this.'

A week before, London had agreed that 23rd Indian
Division would make all local purchases through Van Zanten's
Administration in Dutch guilders. That morning the first of
the bills had come in.

'A formal complaint at least...' Taylor-Smith sighed. 'It's
so...ungrateful.'

Chrishaw shook his head amiably. 'There's nothing we can
do about it. Inform London and let them see the error of their
accounting ways.'

'But Sir, our costs have just risen by a third!'

'Only on paper, George. The Indonesians won't accept the
new guilders anyway. I think Doctor Van Zanten is simply
showing his displeasure after I refused to declare Jap currency
illegal tender.'

Taylor-Smith was calming down. 'But you'll have to at some
point. We did it immediately in Hong Kong.'

Chrishaw nodded. 'Yes but what do you think the likely
outcome would be if I, backed by all of fifteen-hundred men,
suddenly decreed that the wage packets and savings of forty-
odd million hungry and aggrieved Javanese were worthless?'

'Well, yes, you're right,' Taylor-Smith conceded with a
shrug. 'But what will London—and The Hague—make of it?
Van Zanten is bound to make another protest.'

Chrishaw pursed his lips. 'To misquote Rhett Butler,
"Frankly, my dear Major, I don't give a damn". The economy

must keep going. People must be able to buy food, everyone—our men, ex-POWs, internees, natives—even NICA staff.'

Taylor-Smith nodded in agreement. 'Talking of food, Sir, there's rumour of a boycott of Dutch customers by native traders.'

'Our troops as well?'

'No, not so far. But as you say, they can't make purchases if they receive their allowance in Dutch guilders.'

Chrishaw began to straighten his silk cravat. 'Hmm. I'll have to do something about that. Every time Governor Van Zanten holds a press conference he manages to upset another group of locals. On Monday he revoked all promotions given to rail, water and power workers during the Jap occupation.'

Taylor-Smith frowned. 'What's he trying to do?'

Chrishaw laughed. 'Oh, stir things up for the nationalist government by trying to undermine its authority. As a result, we now face the threat of an island-wide rail, water and electricity strike.'

'Any advice from London?'

'Heaps of it,' Chrishaw said, swallowing a laugh. He cast an eye at the mound of papers in his in-tray and pulled out a sheet. 'This gem came from the Foreign Office only this morning. I quote, "We suggest joint route marches by British and Dutch troops throughout Java to publicise and reinforce Allied authority." How very useful.'

Taylor-Smith rolled his eyes.

Chrishaw leant back in his chair with both hands behind his head. 'I rest my case!'

Meg felt a little self-conscious as she entered the brightly lit hotel lobby. For the first time in weeks she was wearing a dress, nylon stockings and high heels instead of tunic, long shorts and boots. She handed in her invitation and was escorted into the reception by a smiling young sepoy, his red tunic freshly ironed and starched. He left her at the end of a short line of guests being met by General Chrishaw and his senior staff.

She waited patiently, glancing surreptitiously into the hall at the other women guests and congratulating herself on her foresight in shopping in Alexandria en-route to Java. Her light blue silk dress, copied from a two-month-old issue of Vogue, had taken the Singaporean dressmaker only one afternoon to run up. It had cost Meg just a few dollars. In Java the silk was worth a small fortune. She was only sorry that she had no escort, but she was used to it and, she reminded herself, she was working. At first she was quietly pleased by the envious looks but then she found herself feeling guilty about her unfair advantage over the recently released internees.

'Miss Graham, delighted you could join us!' Chrishaw greeted her jovially. He was resplendent in dress uniform, his chest encrusted with medals and braid. She looked him over appreciatively from head to toe.

'No-one can dress up like the British, General. If only General MacArthur would take a few tips from you!'

Several of the officers laughed. Chrishaw's eyes flashed in amusement. 'I'm glad you said that! Perhaps I should send him one of my cravats?'

Meg shook her head smiling at him warmly. 'Oh, I don't think so. Try him with a tie first!'

Chrishaw chuckled but was already looking past her and extending his arm to shake hands with a short, dapper Indian man in a high, round-necked Nehru jacket and plain, round-rimmed metal-framed glasses.

'Good evening, Mr Panjabi,' said Chrishaw. 'What excellent timing! Do you know Meg Graham, the war correspondent?'

Meg turned, sensing something in Chrishaw's tone.

'Miss Graham…,' continued Chrishaw, 'Mr Panjabi, a businessman of these parts, who also happens to be Mr Nehru's eyes and ears in Java.'

Meg was suddenly very alert. Pandit Jawaharlal Nehru was president of the Indian National Congress and was expected to be the first prime minister of independent India. The British had recently released him from prison for the ninth time.

Panjabi shook Meg's hand. 'Delighted! You must ignore the General, Miss Graham. I have no idea why he should think I am involved in Indian politics in any way. I am merely an overworked entrepreneur.'

There was genuine humour in Panjabi's eyes. Meg warmed to him immediately. Chrishaw started to introduce his officers to Panjabi, so Meg moved away, collecting a gin and tonic from a busy waiter and chose a vantage point by a large marble fireplace. Above it, a rectangular patch of lighter wallpaper served to remind the guests that the Dutch royal portrait, taken down and destroyed by the Japanese, had not been replaced. There were several other bare patches. British, Dutch and Indonesian flags had been placed in three corners of the hall by the hotel's temporary new management.

Meg watched the guests closely. Despite the frequent clinking of glasses, there was a distinctly frosty atmosphere. The British had decided to invite Dutch and Indonesian officials, with the result that the evening was ruined for both sides. They stood in two groups at each end of the hall in splendid diplomatic isolation. British and British-Indian officers were buzzing between them trying to break the ice but without any success.

She leaned back against the pleasantly cool marble and listened to a chirpy waltz being played by a group of rather tired-looking Dutch musicians tucked away on a corner podium. Only four couples, all of them Dutch, were dancing.

She noticed an extremely handsome Sikh officer approach a group of Dutch girls and invite one of them to dance. Blushing deeply under the stern gaze of her friends the girl refused and turned her back. Meg felt a surge of annoyance and was thinking about asking the Sikh for a dance when she saw Panjabi standing alone between the Dutch and Indonesian groups, looking rather ill at ease. She caught his eye and smiled. He came over to her gratefully. 'Thank you for the safe haven, Miss Graham. "No man's land" is such a lonely place!'

'Or maybe it's any port in a storm?'

'Good gracious me no! Not in your case, I assure you! We are, after all, both neutrals in this dispute.'

Meg feigned surprise. 'I can't believe India, about to become independent, is not championing a free Indonesia.' She pointed to the patch on the wall. 'When the Imperial portraits do come down in Delhi you'll have the same interior decoration problem.'

Panjabi laughed then smiled thoughtfully. 'Ah, but we will still have our rajahs, just as the Indonesians have their sultans.'

'Hmm. Same frame, different portrait?'

He was eyeing her studiously. 'Do you really wish to debate the relevance of monarchy in our modern, post-war world, Miss Graham?'

Meg shook her head smiling. 'No I don't.' She wanted to talk politics. 'So future Prime Minister Nehru doesn't trust the British to look after his soldiers in Java? Is that it?'

Panjabi's was suddenly serious. 'On the contrary, I'm sure Mr Nehru has immense faith in the British Army... It's the British politicians who worry him...so I have heard.'

Meg pressed further, wondering just how close Panjabi was to Nehru. 'Some American papers argue the British are using Indian soldiers to do their own and Dutch dirty work. Is that the view in India, one colonial power helping out another in suppressing a native population?'

Panjabi smiled. 'It is true that some influential individuals are calling for the return of our soldiers on religious and political grounds. I—'

A sepoy waiter came by them carrying a tray of drinks. They both took a refill. Panjabi nodded after the sepoy. 'One of the oppressed, perhaps?'

'That's how it looks to Uncle Sam. Don't you object?'

He shook his head, tut-tutting. 'Let me tell you why the sepoys are waiting on. None of the Javanese hotel staff would agree to serve the Dutch. And none of the Dutch would acknowledge Indonesian management of the hotel. General Chrishaw was about to cancel the party when the Mahrattas volunteered their services because they did not want their General to lose face! Of course they might also get a "souvenir"—in officially worthless but still useable Japanese rupiahs—for their pains.'

'I see,' Meg nodded. 'Still, I don't know. White officers, coloured troops. It screams "discrimination" to me.'

'And what of the American coloured regiments, Miss Graham? The prohibition on coloured men becoming officers?'

She closed her eyes. 'Touché! It's not something we should be proud about, nor the British...'

Panjabi shook his head. 'Miss Graham, forgive me but I don't think you know much about the Indian Army.' He took another sip of his drink. 'In India the British do not discriminate by colour or creed. Look at it this way. To them my country is rather like a gentlemen's club. Some of the members are coloured. Some non-members are white... Both whites and coloureds seek membership. Both can get "black-balled"—no pun intended. Does that help?' He laughed. 'It's rather complicated!'

Meg shrugged. 'It goes against our constitution, ideas of equality and rights.'

'Hmm,' Panjabi was unimpressed. 'I have two stories for you. In 1943, the top commanders of the Indian Army were invited to Washington for a policy conference.' He raised a finger. 'Remember, this is during the midst of the Japanese advance when Indian military assistance was crucial to the Allied war effort and when Indian troops were needed for the liberation of Europe. What happened when the Indian generals arrived in Washington, some eighty years after the abolition of slavery in your country?'

Meg frowned, anticipating more embarrassment.

Panjabi merely smiled. 'The hotel which had taken the reservations from the Pentagon refused to admit them! Eventually they found rooms at a military club.'

Meg sighed. 'Oh, dear. I—'

'Unfortunately there is more,' Panjabi added quickly. 'When they went out for dinner with American officers five restaurants refused to serve them! That does not happen in London at the Ritz or the Savoy!'

She grimaced. 'That doesn't make us look too good, does it.'

'No, but you really shouldn't worry about it. Most Indians certainly don't. You should know that no-one is more discriminatory against Indians than other Indians! It's perfectly true. Have you not heard of our caste system? If you are born Dalit— Untouchable—in India, may Lord Shiva help you.'

'I'll remember that. Thank you,' Meg nodded thoughtfully. 'You said you had two stories?'

'Oh, yes. A British officer told me this just the other day. At the battle of Keren in Abyssinia there was a tremendous fight by some Mahratta infantry and a Scottish regiment to take an Italian position on a ridge. As you will know, Abyssinia is terribly dry and hot, and the Mahrattas assumed that they would be more or less babysitting the Scotsmen. Well, the battle was won and the Mahrattas reached the ridge but among the dead Italians they found several dead Scotsmen.

Clearly the Mahrattas were not the first there! Afterwards the British and Indians patrolled together with their little fingers linked in a "chain" of friendship and respect. Rather "touching", don't you think? It's a pity the story isn't more widely known... When the British leave India I like to hope we will still be linking our little fingers!'

Meg felt chastened. 'My apologies. Sometimes we journalists think we know it all.'

Panjabi shrugged and surveyed the hall. 'Look carefully at what is happening here in Java, Miss Graham. Like will find like everywhere. Tonight, outside, British privates and Indian sepoys are sharing pots of tea and those awful compo rations. Already those same fellows are trading and playing games of cricket, soccer or hockey among themselves or with the natives, as well as chasing the Javanese girls! In here, we see their officers hobnobbing with diehard Dutch colonialists who speak as if the white empires had never been humbled by the little yellow men. Listen to them! They talk of polo, weekend shoots on estates, summer retreats in the hills and, most of all, how coloured people—Indians and Indonesians alike—are not ready for self rule. You could certainly be forgiven for thinking they have learned nothing.'

'So you think the ranks are sympathetic to the Indonesian cause but their officers are pro-Dutch? That's a recipe for disaster.'

Panjabi scratched his chin in thought. 'Or mutiny...I think that the British need to play their hand very carefully. General Chrishaw was a good choice but alas the Dutch already have their knives out for him.'

Meg nodded. 'So I've heard.'

A shout interrupted them. 'Panjabi-*tuan*, please join us!'

They turned to see a small group of Indonesians waving cheerfully. Panjabi raised a hand then turned to Meg. 'You must excuse me, business calls. I am in the market for rice.

Hundreds of tons of the stuff! I hope we can talk again. Perhaps a dance later or even lunch?'

'I'd love too!'

Panjabi excused himself and with regret Meg watched him join the Indonesians. As she was waiting for a waiter to replenish her glass she saw Chrishaw greeting Jarisha. She waited for a reaction and saw a junior NICA officer was already informing Van Zanten of Jarisha's arrival. He barely nodded and continued his conversation whereas others turned to look. Admiral Hurwitz, true to form, managed a scowl.

Meg tried to mingle but no-one was as interesting as Panjabi. Secretly bored, she listened to snatches of conversations and decided he was right. The Dutch were behaving as if nothing had changed since 1942.

On a whim she went in search of the rejected Sikh officer and danced with him and his delighted friends for almost thirty minutes. The Sikhs were good company and excellent dancers. Meg thoroughly enjoyed herself, especially the disapproving looks from some of the reforming Batavia establishment.

Even so, she kept one eye on the main figures, waiting for the inevitable meeting. When she saw Chrishaw deftly bring Jarisha and Van Zanten's group together in a small group in the middle of the hall, she gave them a couple of minutes to exchange pleasantries then excused herself from the disappointed Sikhs. As she neared the group she read a hint of caution in Chrishaw's glance.

'Hello, Dr Jarisha,' she said warmly.

'Miss Graham! You look wonderful,' Jarisha said bowing. 'I hope you'll save me a dance?'

'But of course,' she replied beaming.

For once Chrishaw seemed surprised. 'The Senior Allied Commander has priority, Dr Jarisha,' he said jovially. 'I didn't realise you and Miss Graham were acquainted.'

'Oh yes, indeed. I have given her a number of exclusive interviews.' He and Meg smiled at each other, enjoying the private joke.

The Dutch group exchanged glances. Only Van Zanten remained at ease. 'I was wondering why your writing is so blatantly anti-Dutch, Miss Graham. You must visit the palace soon. I'm sure your readers would appreciate hearing the other side of the story.'

Meg returned the smile. 'To tell the truth Dr Van Zanten there is not much interest in Indonesia in the States.'

'The Netherlands Indies,' Hurwitz muttered caustically. He was slightly the worse for drink.

Van Zanten ignored him. 'That may be so but your articles are also read in Europe and even Australia. You should not underestimate your wider influence.'

'Thank you, Doctor. My motto is "I write what I see". That's all,' Meg said deliberately. 'Whether it's people dying from neglect or a people demanding their freedom.'

Hurwitz sneered again. 'Rabble swept along by traitors!'

Van Zanten shot him an irritated look and asked quickly. 'Tell me, what have you seen recently that you intend to share with your readers?'

Meg took a sip of her gin and tonic knowing she had drunk too much to be taking on Van Zanten. 'Oh, maybe I'll write something about a would-be colonial administration in denial.'

He frowned. 'Denial?'

Hurwitz and the others were regarding Meg with barely disguised hostility. She ignored them. 'Yes, after all, you abandoned the Indonesian baby in '42. Now, for better or worse, it's standing on its own two feet. You can't put the clock back.'

'Nonsense!' Hurwitz said gruffly. 'It's nothing more than the leftovers of a collaborationist regime—'

Van Zanten's voice was suddenly severe. 'And you know what can happen if a baby tries to run before it can walk, unless the parents are there to catch it?'

Jarisha cleared his throat softly. 'Perhaps I may speak for this infant? Why is it, Dr Van Zanten, that the Dutch would deny this child the very thing that they themselves celebrated so joyously only in May? I refer, of course, to freedom! As President Sukarno has asked many times: If it was wrong for the Germans to rule the Netherlands why is it acceptable for the Netherlands to rule Indonesia?'

Hurwitz's face was puce. His voice boomed. 'You dare compare us to the Nazis!'

Chrishaw rolled his eyes in despair.

Jarisha looked pained. 'It is such a simple question yet you have no answer!'

'I'll answer it with troops and tanks—'

Van Zanten stilled Hurwitz by placing a hand on his forearm. 'The Admiral needs some fresh air.' He nodded to a Dutch captain who led the listing Hurwitz away. When he spoke he looked solely at Meg.

'Mister Sukarno's premise is false. The Indies are sovereign territory of the Netherlands. Dutch rule is established in international law.'

'Oh dear,' Jarisha said holding up his palms, 'There is one set of rules for white nations and another one for Asians.'

'I am sorry you see it that way, Dr Jarisha,' Van Zanten said casually. He turned back to Meg. 'You also mentioned "neglect", Miss Graham. The Netherlands has hardly neglected her colonies. Industrial investment, transport infrastructure, healthcare provision—'

Meg shook her head. 'No, I mean the thousands of half-starved, sick women and children still stuck in camps weeks after the end of the war. Women and children, neglected—no, abandoned—by their safe and well-fed countrymen—and I stress the men—who are more interested in flagpoles and military parades.'

Van Zanten looked almost amused. 'Those former internees are being held hostage, Miss Graham. You should ask Dr Jarisha why his followers will not free them. It is immoral, is it not, to keep women and children in camps just like the Nazis and Japanese?' He paused looking pleased with himself.

Meg held his gaze. 'Oh, yes Doctor, I agree it's immoral. I've seen the Dachau death factory and the awful state of the internment camps here on Java. But I also saw another camp opened by the good, free citizens of Nijmegen. It was full of scared young Dutch women and their babies.' She looked from one confused Dutch face to another. 'Surprised, gentlemen? Their crime was to have given birth to babies fathered by Germans.'

Van Zanten stood rigid, his expression studiedly disdainful. His staff stared at her balefully. Meg continued with a shrug. 'What I am trying to say is that after six years of war there is no moral high ground left. It's all mud and we're sinking fast.'

'An interesting observation,' Van Zanten said coldly. 'Your readers are indeed fortunate. For tonight at least, let us agree to differ.' He turned to Chrishaw. 'General, my thanks for a most… instructive…evening.'

If Chrishaw was disappointed he did not show it. 'My pleasure, Doctor. I hope this will be the first of many face-to-face meetings between Dutch and Indonesian representatives.'

Van Zanten inclined his head dubiously and moved away, ignoring Jarisha but stopping here and there to greet other guests on his way out.

Chrishaw turned and smiled at Meg sarcastically. 'Well, that was a resounding success wouldn't you say? Now, Miss Graham, I don't believe I've ever danced with an American journalist before. May I?'

Laughing, Meg took his arm. The mock southern belle accent returned. 'Why, Gen'rul, I'd be delighted!'

Near Bekassi, Central Java

Several darkly clad figures eased through gaps in the bamboo fence an hour before dawn. Their rubber-soled boots made no sound on the packed earth as they approached the cluster of half-a-dozen living huts and storehouses. Penned livestock—three scrawny water buffalo, and a few goats and chickens—were the only witnesses to their silent progress towards the centre of the hamlet. Nearer their goal, the men fanned out, walking openly, purposefully.

They began their sweep; pausing briefly beside each hut and communicating with quick, precise hand signals. In their wake they left small showers of sparks and bright orange light as the flares spluttered into life. Then the figures turned and formed a line across the path to the well and water trough, and the exit.

The palm-leafed roofs and matting walls of the huts were tinder dry. Shouts of alarm, then screams of panic punctured the night quiet. Men and women, many clutching babies or toddlers, began rushing from doorways, blinking in stunned disbelief at the bright circle of flames that almost surrounded them. Instinctively they moved, the women towards the safety of the path, the men shouting for buckets.

Machine guns blazed until magazines were emptied. Then the second sweep began and the soldiers walked methodically among the moaning mass of twisted, twitching bodies looking for those still living. When they found them, they were finished with point-blank bursts.

A single blast of a whistle brought the men back to regroup at the well. They had not spoken. Carefully they retraced their way through smouldering huts back towards the fence. As the last man crossed the open area he turned and tossed something near the entrance to one of the huts. A tiny flicker of movement back at the killing zone caught his eye. A survivor was crawling towards the water trough. The gunman watched with disinterest. Someone, after all, would need to find the British army hat and feed the fires for revenge....

Chapter Five

Hotel des Indes

Mac took the keys to Meg's jeep from the hotel valet and re-parked it in the shade of the covered entrance. It was only eight o'clock in the morning but the metal around the seats was already hot. There was hardly a breath of wind. He got out and flexed his shoulders to try to lift the clammy shirt off his back.

Meg appeared in a calf-length, blue batik skirt and a loose, white long-sleeved blouse. She noticed his discomfort immediately. 'Hey, it's sticky today!'

Mac looked her up and down. 'You aren't exactly dressed for the weather.'

She laughed. 'You should see the white women in the American south on days like this. Bonnets and long gloves all day. Anything to prevent a tan.'

He smiled. 'The only hats at home are wool! I can imagine my grandfather in this heat though. He'd be in his vest and long-johns but he'd never take his cap off!'

Meg laughed. 'Well, it's not all day. We'll have finished with the Doctor around eleven.'

She was to interview Jarisha later that morning, but before that he had offered to show Meg something of the old city. Since it was also an Islamic festival day, Meg did not want to embarrass Jarisha in public by wearing shorts. Mac thought she was worrying too much when most of the Javanese women were walking around half-naked.

Meg held up a small canvas rucksack. 'What about the swim at Krawang?'

Mac grinned. 'My things are in the back. And I've some sweets for the village kiddies.'

They smiled at each other and this time it was Meg who looked away first. 'I'm too old for you, soldier boy,' she said only half-joking. 'Let's go!

'This is the Penang Gate,' Jarisha told them as they walked three abreast through a high but unimposing stone arch. 'It's all that's left of the old city wall.'

Meg walked between the two men. Jarisha's two bodyguards followed a discreet but watchful ten yards away.

'And this is the *"Si Jagoer"* gun,' Jarisha continued. He was pointing to a bronze cannon about ten-feet long supported on a low cradle. The patina of the aged bronze was a deep, rich blue-black.

Meg remembered the cannon from her guidebook and went for a closer look. Its rounded base was etched with a delicate floral motif and the cascable was fashioned into a large, clenched right hand with the thumb-tip protruding between the index and middle fingers. The metal hand glistened from constant touching by human fingers. A large patch on the top of the barrel just behind the swell of the muzzle was also burnished.

Jarisha watched as both Meg and Mac were drawn to touch the fist. 'No-one knows its history,' he continued. 'It is said to be Portuguese and to have come here in the 1640s as a war trophy. Other than that, it is a mystery.'

Meg nodded. 'But isn't there an inscription somewhere?' She bent over to look. 'Yes, here it is! *Ex me ipsa renata sum.*'

She frowned. 'Damn! I read it the other day but I've forgotten what it means…'

'Out of myself I was reborn,' Jarisha intoned. 'Presumably it means it was recast out of another cannon.'

'Like a phoenix,' suggested Meg.

'Or even a country from a colony!' Jarisha joked. 'There's a superstition that this cannon is one of a pair, and that on the day it is joined by its mate, Dutch rule in Java will end.'

'Where's the other gun, Doctor?' Mac asked interestedly.

'There's supposed to be one like it in Banten.'

'But that's not far away,' said Meg. 'You could go and get it!'

Jarisha laughed. 'I heard the Dutch are guarding it day and night!'

High, happy voices sounded from under the arch. Three Javanese girls in their best festival sarongs and *kemban* tops were approaching with flowers and sticks of incense.

'Ah-ha,' Jarisha pointed. 'I was not going to mention it but in Java a fist shaped like the one on the gun is considered an obscene gesture. Add the obvious symbolism of the barrel and you have a very powerful totem of fertility…for the less devout at least. Women make offerings here in the hope of becoming pregnant. *"Si Jagoer"* means—how can I put this delicately?— "Mr Sturdy", I think is close.' His eyes sparkled.

They laughed.

Jarisha greeted the three girls and they bowed back demurely. He moved aside and waved them towards the cannon to perform their ritual.

Now a little self-conscious, the girls placed their flowers next to the barrel and threw a few precious grains of rice down the muzzle. Then they lit the incense and stood in quiet prayer. Suddenly inhibition left them as one after the other they lifted up their sarongs and sat astride the barrel, giggling hysterically.

'Well, this wasn't in my guidebook, Doctor,' Meg said dryly. She saw Mac staring at the girls and she jabbed him with her elbow. 'Glad you came now, Mr Sturdy? I suppose the girls in Glasgow wear underwear?'

Mac blushed a furious red. 'Well—I, er… Oh, God!'

Jarisha and Meg chortled but Mac could only manage a sheepish grin as the girls waved goodbye.

Horns and shouts admonished Mac as he weaved through the cars, *becak* trikes, bullock carts and military vehicles crowding the road. Jarisha's red Chevrolet was leaving them behind. He swore in frustration. 'Christ! I wish his bloody driver would slow down!'

They were about to turn off the main Rijswijk shopping street towards the wide Koningsplein square and the State Railways Hotel where Jarisha was due to meet General Chrishaw.

Meg was holding on to her seat and the dashboard handle. 'If you were Jarisha, would you want to stop with all these trigger-happy Dutch on patrol?'

Mac shot her a cautious look. 'Aye, I suppose you're right.' 'What do you make of him?'

Ahead the road suddenly cleared and Mac made a quick gear change to get moving. The Chevrolet was fifty yards away, slowing to let a cart cross the road.

He shrugged. 'Seems like a decent bloke.' He glanced at her quickly. 'You like him don't you?'

She smiled. 'Are you jealous?'

He shook his head a little too quickly. 'Me, why of course not!'

'Good. Don't be,' she said gently, reaching across to place her fingers on top of his on the steering wheel.

Mac grinned at her.

A sudden, searing pain in her hand made her yelp. 'Oowwh!'

The jeep's windscreen shattered. 'Shit!' Mac yelled in pain. Blood oozed from both their hands. Another burst of shots left a neat line of holes across the wing and bonnet. Meg ducked instinctively.

'Hold on!' Mac tried to swerve but they went into a spin and veered across the road into a cartload of mangos.

'Keep down!' Mac shouted, reaching for his Sten gun. Ahead there was a tremendous crash as a lorry rammed Jarisha's car, sending it broadside across the road. Three gunmen in the back of the lorry began to fire into the stricken Chevrolet. Bystanders fled in panic.

Mac opened fire at the lorry cab. Seconds later it sped away.

He turned and saw Meg's wound. 'You're hit!'

'I'm OK,' she yelled. 'Help Jarisha!'

As Mac started towards the battered, bullet-ridden Chevrolet, he was amazed to see the back door open and Jarisha, bloodied about the head, step out on to the road. There was no other movement in the car.

Suddenly two Javanese hopped off a *becak* and ran towards the dazed Jarisha. One held a pistol. Mac was thirty-five yards away and the accurate range of the Sten was nearer twenty. He charged, shouting and firing short bursts into the air.

The assassins threw Jarisha against the side of the car and thrust the pistol hard against his head. Miraculously nothing happened. Mac saw consternation on the face of the gunman as he repeatedly pulled the trigger. A blaring horn sent the two men running. A jeep screeched to a halt and a British officer jumped out, revolver in hand.

Mac reached Jarisha just as his legs were giving way. He slid slowly down against the car until he was sitting on the road, gasping for breath.

Meg ran up, a bloody handkerchief around her hand, and clutching the jeep's first aid kit. 'God, that was close!'

Jarisha looked up at her and smiled weakly. His face was very pale. 'Close indeed, even for my God!'

Dutch Administration HQ, Governor's Palace, Batavia

Captain Peter Henssen saluted smartly, keeping his face expressionless even though he suspected he was to hear something to his advantage.

Hurwitz wasted no time. 'Sit down, Captain. Tell me, how does "Commander Henssen" sound to you?'

'Sir?' Henssen, an office in the Naval Reserve, allowed his surprise to show. A promotion and full commission were worth both money and status.

Hurwitz nodded. 'Yes, indeed! Follow my instructions and the rank will be yours within six weeks.' He saw he had Henssen's full attention. 'This is confidential, of course. You must mention it to no-one.'

'I understand, Admiral,' he nodded eagerly.

Hurwitz pushed himself up from behind the desk and crossed the room to a large wall map of Southeast Asia. A large, orange-red swathe denoting pre-war Dutch possessions ran from the northern tip of Sumatra to half of New Guinea. His back was to Henssen as he spoke. 'Did you know that so far not one Japanese sailor, soldier or airman in the Indies has surrendered to a Dutch officer?

'No, Admiral. I didn't.'

Hurwitz turned round to face him. 'Well, Potsdam Agreement or not, after what they did to us I think it's a disgrace!'

'I agree, Sir.'

'Surabaya!'

'Sir?' Henssen interest quickened. Before the war he had lived in Surabaya. He was keen to get his house and possessions back.

Hurwitz nodded. 'Our contacts there report that the Japs are itching to be repatriated.'

'That's good news, Sir. We can bring in our own troops and—'

'Ha!' Hurwitz shook his head slowly. 'The Jap commander in Surabaya, Admiral Shimizu, has informed Mountbatten directly that sending Dutch troops would be "inadvisable". Can you believe the arrogance of the man!' He began to pace up and down the room. 'In a few days the British are going to deploy a brigade of Indian infantry in Surabaya!' he added bitterly.

Henssen could not tell whether Hurwitz objected more to Indians or to infantry.

Scathing, Hurwitz went on. 'Chrishaw says they are going in to evacuate internees!' His voice rose. 'Think of it, a bunch of chupatty-eaters taking the Jap surrender at our most important naval base! What are the natives going to make of that!'

Since Henssen was not sure where his Admiral was leading he did not reply. The silence dragged. Finally, Hurwitz stopped pacing and turned to face him. His eyes were shining. 'Well, if I have anything to do with it,' he muttered, 'Surabaya will be an exception to the Potsdam rules. We must be first in!'

It occurred to Henssen that his promotion was not such a sure thing after all. 'It's strange to be trying to put one over on the British…' he said guardedly.

Hurwitz heard the doubt and stared at him hard. 'Captain, Japan is beaten. At stake now is the trading wealth of the Indies. Once the British have even so much as a toe-hold in Surabaya they'll be difficult to shake off. Have you forgotten our sacrifice at the Battle of the Java Sea?'

Henssen was suddenly indignant. 'Never, Sir! My brother was lost on the *De Ruyter*.'

'I'm sorry, I didn't know,' Hurwitz lied smoothly. His tone became softer as if he had been humbled by the name of the sunken Dutch flagship. 'If we are not careful, more humiliation awaits us. Never forget that it was Wavell and the British who deserted us on Java! And now they have the gall to deny us our own ships and men while they rush troops to reclaim their own colonies!'

Henssen nodded his agreement, deciding that Hurwitz must have made detailed preparations. 'You have a plan then, Admiral?'

A prim, satisfied smile appeared on Hurwitz's face. 'Fortunately I have convinced the British to send a naval officer to inspect the yards in advance and make preparations for the arrival of the Allied troops. You know the city well, so you are the perfect choice. Your instructions and travel orders, signed by Admiral Patterson, are here. You are to be Chief Allied Representative in Surabaya. You'll leave this afternoon by flying boat. Two junior officers will accompany you. Perhaps you could also take one or two of our reporters along? Just in case anything newsworthy should happen!'

Henssen relaxed, his confidence now fully restored. He could scarcely believe his good fortune.

Kemajoran Airport, Djakarta

Despite the ache from his injured hand, Mac was in a good mood. His job as Meg's driver was the envy of the Seaforths. It had not taken long for the wags in the Battalion to notice that his right hand was bandaged in much the same way as Meg's left. He was relieved he was escaping Batavia and the ribbing about the danger of holding hands. A tour of the internee camps would be a breeze after the events of the last few days. Apart from the flying.... It would be his first flight. He was both nervous and excited.

Meg had caught him smiling. 'Let me guess. You're thinking of all those young damsels who haven't seen a white man in years.' She fluttered her eyes at him.

'Is it that obvious?' Mac smirked.

'Well, let's just say you've got a "sturdy" smile on your face.'

They laughed, then Meg became serious. 'This isn't going to be as pleasant as you think, Mac. Here the internees have had help from the Navy, and extra food and supplies for weeks. Wing Commander Ball says that at Semarang and Magelang they've had almost nothing. I think you are going to be in for a shock.'

'I understand,' he said softly.

The Douglas C-47 Dakota dwarfed every other aircraft at the airfield, including the Mitsubishi Ki-213 Japanese bomber parked a few yards from it down the strip. Ball was supervising the loading of the last of the stores. He heard the jeep and turned with a wave.

'Glad you could make it, Miss Graham.'

'Thank you, Wing-Commander.'

MacDonald saluted Ball and Meg introduced him. 'This is my driver, Mac—I mean Private—MacDonald.'

'Welcome to RAPWI,' Ball said affably. 'Once you get your stuff loaded, Frenton here will show you where to leave the jeep.'

A wiry, ginger-haired RAF Flight Sergeant nodded a greeting.

'Please don't delay,' Ball added. 'I'd like us to be off soon to make the most of the daylight when we get there.'

Mac and Frenton sat together at the back of the Dakota. Mac chose a window seat. Frenton sat in the aisle, one eye on the kettle in the galley, the other on an issue of SEAC News.

'It must be exciting, flying around all over the place,' Mac said trying to hide his anxiety.

'The more they fly 'em,' replied Frenton, 'the more I 'av to service 'em.' He grinned. 'I prefer short flights and long stays. These last few weeks have been absolutely barmy.'

'You're not nervous about flying then?' Mac asked uneasily.

Frenton's brow wrinkled. 'Scares me to death! Nearly came a cropper over the Java Sea. Lost an engine, so we had to dump the cargo. It was touch and go. We were skimming the treetops at the end. When we landed six monkeys were sitting on the wheels!'

Mac managed a weak smile. Meg turned, saw the alarm on Mac's face and smiled gleefully.

Frenton carried on blithely. 'From what I've heard, Semarang's a bit dodgy. This morning that Jap bomber flew in loaded with body bags and wounded Gurkhas. Word is that Jap renegades are putting up a fight!'

'Jesus....' Mac said quietly to himself. Suddenly patrols in Batavia seemed much more attractive.

Semarang

The two-hour flight over central Java's lush and contrasting mountainous landscape proved uneventful. Apart from handing out cups of tea and coffee Frenton dozed most of the journey, so Mac was left to his own thoughts. By the time they began the descent he had more or less convinced himself that he was flying into a war zone. The landing was bumpy but he kept looking out of the window. A glimpse of a line of twin-engine Japanese bombers complete with Japanese ground crew made his stomach twist.

Frenton was up on his feet as the plane began to taxi. He looked out and also noticed the Japanese. 'Blimey! I hope that lot know the war's over!'

Ball opened the door and Mac heard a familiar voice.

'Wing-Commander Ball? Good afternoon and welcome to Semarang. I'm Major John Miller, Tenth Gurkha Rifles.'

Mac sat in silence with unpleasant memories of Burma. Somehow he wasn't surprised Miller was now a major.

Ball greeted Miller. The other passengers followed. Ball was introducing Meg to Miller when Mac came down the steps.

'MacDonald!' Miller exclaimed. 'I wondered if you'd made it to Java with the Seaforths.'

'Hello, Sir,' Mac said quietly. He looked at Miller, who seemed older than he remembered.

'You two know each other?' Meg asked.

'Yes, from Burma,' Miller replied cheerfully. 'We can have a chat later, eh, Mac?' He turned back to Ball. 'Your team will need to be on its guard, Wing-Commander. There's been heavy fighting between the Indos and the Japs over the last few days. Some of the internee camps were attacked and women and children have been killed.'

'How awful!' Meg grimaced.

Miller nodded. 'It's very sad, Miss Graham. Anyway, the Japs saved the day! The Jap unit here is armed, too, so the airfield's reasonably secure.'

Frenton cast a quick, sceptical glance at Mac. 'I've heard that one before,' he murmured under his breath.

Miller carried on. 'The ground crews will help you unload. We also managed to get you two Jap six-wheelers. They're a bit shaky but at least they're right-hand drive!'

Two lorries drew up carrying Japanese. Mac noticed that they all had rifles. In contrast with the Japanese at the surrender ceremony in Malaya there was no sullenness or obvious resentment. They set to the task quickly, talking among themselves as they worked. Mac realised they knew they were needed and with that came a confidence and dignity so lacking in Malaya. He was astonished at the difference. With a nod he joined the chain unloading the sacks.

Meg and Ball went in Miller's jeep to Tjandi. Mac followed them, driving one of the big Isuzus. Frenton and a guide took the other to a camp in the west of the town.

They found the gate to Tjandi III wide open. Inside some boys were playing soccer with several Gurkhas. A small group of ragged, under-nourished women was cheering them on. 'Look at them!' Meg gasped as the jeep pulled to a halt. 'Have we got any clothes with us?'

Ball shook his head. 'Afraid not. Just medical supplies and vitamins. It might not look it but actually this camp is fairly well provided for. They've had a few weeks of increased rations and Red Cross parcels.'

'How many internees are there in Java?' Meg asked, notebook and pen in hand.

Ball shrugged. 'We don't even know how many camps there are. Dutch estimates were fifteen thousand internees. But the Red Cross have counted that many in just five camps near Batavia. People are turning up everyday from places we've never heard of and telling us they've come from a camp of several hundred. There might be tens of thousands.'

'Well let's hope not,' Miller said shaking his head.

Ball changed the subject. 'If Major Miller approves, the day after tomorrow we'll take a quick look at Borobudur temple. All work and no play makes Jack a dull boy, eh Major?'

Meg found the prospect of a cultural diversion very welcome. 'Oh, can we? I've read about it, an Asian wonder of the world!'

'It's a slight detour,' said Miller, 'but I don't see why not for an hour or so. We'll have to leave here before dawn.'

'Right,' said Ball. 'Since we've got an escort I'm going to ask for a few volunteers to come along as nurses.' He left them and headed for the infirmary.

'Ma-ku-don!' The shout came from the soccer players.

Curious, Mac turned to see someone holding a ball and waving. The wide grin was unmistakable. Suddenly much of Mac's anxiety about Semarang vanished.

'Rai!' He waved back. 'Bloody hell!'

Meg spent three hours talking with the women of Tjandi. She found many of them surprisingly cheerful. They pressed her for news of the outside world. Meg did her best to answer questions which ranging from the amount of damage to Amsterdam, Nijmegen and Paris, to gossip about Hollywood film stars and what was available in Batavia's shops. But one question came up more often than any other: 'When can we leave?' She told them that she did not know. In the end, she managed to escape the questions by saying she wanted to interview the camp doctor.

As Meg entered the infirmary the smell of carbolic was almost overpowering and she pulled a face. She would have left, except for a smile from a cheerful and fairly healthy looking girl who was kneeling and busy with a scrubbing brush and a pail of soapy water. 'Hello! Dr Santen will be so pleased to see you.'

Meg frowned. 'She will?'

'Aren't you a nurse?' Kate asked.

'Oh no, I'm a journalist.'

'Sorry,' she apologised with a laugh. 'I saw the uniform and thought—'

Meg smiled. 'Sometimes I wish I were... By the way, I'm Meg Graham'

'Kate van Dam. Pleased to meet you.'

Meg saw the door to the balcony and went out for some fresh air and a cigarette. Kate followed her. 'It must be so exciting to be a journalist! Travelling, meeting people, seeing everything that goes on.'

Meg inclined her head. 'It has its moments. The last few years have been mainly bad ones.'

'Same here, Kate sighed.'

Meg offered her a cigarette. 'Smoke?'

'Oh, er, no, thank you.'

They stood side by side looking over the parapet and watching people milling around the RAPWI lorry. Mac was unloading supplies. Two Japanese soldiers came into view from behind one of the huts as they patrolled the perimeter fence. Kate glanced at them as did Meg. 'You must hate the sight of them.'

Kate was caught off guard. 'I—I don't know. They helped us...'

'I heard about the mobs,' Meg said sympathetically. 'It must have been frightening. Were you surprised the Japs helped you?'

'No, I wasn't...' Kate said quickly but softly, almost to herself.

Meg noticed her distant look.

Behind them the balcony door opened. 'There you are, Kate,' said Juliette. 'Some men want to talk to us. Let's not keep them waiting!'

Meg laughed and Kate introduced her to Juliette. They went down together.

Two uniformed officers were chatting with Jenny Hagen. Meg thought they looked a little hesitant but then decided that the state of the women would make anyone who was clean and properly dressed feel awkward. Kate and Juliette said goodbye. Meg went with Jenny back to the lorry.

'Miss Geroux and Miss van Dam? Good afternoon,' said the older of the two officers. He peered at them through thick glasses. He was around fifty with silver-grey hair. 'I am Major Liddleton. I work in the Army Legal Office. This is Group Captain Bowman of the Australian Air Force. We have the rather unpleasant but necessary task of investigating war-guilt charges. If we may, we would like to ask you some questions.'

'Of course,' said Juliette. Kate nodded.

Bowman cleared his throat. He was in his mid-thirties, thin-faced with a slim build and wore a trim moustache. 'We are seeking statements from witnesses to the public execution of an Australian airman at this camp. Did you see this incident, ladies?'

'Yes,' said Kate, suppressing a shudder. 'I was just a few yards away.'

'Hundreds saw it,' Juliette added, smiling softly at Bowman.

'How terribly distressing for you. We have detailed statements from seven other witnesses so far. For the time being, we simply wish to ask whether you can identify the Japanese officer involved.'

Juliette spoke quickly. 'It was Shirai, the *kenpei* captain! Him and his...how do you say, in English, *partisans*?'

Liddleton nodded. 'I think "henchmen" is the word you are looking for,' he said casually.

'Yes, it was Shirai,' Kate's voice was cold and detached. 'The monster chopped off the poor man's head.'

Bowman proffered a sheet of paper. 'Are you both prepared to sign a statement, to that effect?'

They both nodded but the men paused, exchanging sideways glances. Liddleton rubbed his chin awkwardly. 'As it happens, there is something else,' he said softly. 'There are reports of a number of women from internee camps being pressed into, er, work at certain clubs run by the Japanese.'

Kate felt a quick tap from Juliette's elbow. She wondered whether the questions about the airman had been just a front. Someone had been talking! She felt herself start to blush and looked at Juliette who was still smiling, though much less warmly, at Bowman.

'We intend to bring charges against the Japanese and other nationals involved,' continued Liddleton. 'Naturally, we need preliminary statements. Would you care to tell us what happened?'

'Why us?' Juliette replied frowning.

Bowman and Liddleton regarded each other again. 'Well, your names were mentioned,' said Bowman.

Kate and Juliette exchanged another quick look. Liddleton pressed them further. 'We realise it must be rather embarrassing for you but—'

'Major!' Juliette said demurely but firmly. 'I think you have been listening to gossip!'

The two officers were looking at them intently.

Kate nodded. 'Yes, idle gossip.' She felt her face burning

'I see,' Bowman sighed. 'In fact, your names are listed in an accounts book for a club called the Sakura. This was found there....'

In near disbelief Kate watched as he produced a fire-blackened ledger from his leather document case. He opened it at a flaking, bookmarked page. On it was a list of handwritten names and camps. Most of the page was singed but, still legible in the centre column, were several names, including hers and Juliette's.

Kate stared at the ground in embarrassment. Juliette took her hand in hers. She felt a gentle squeeze.

Liddleton was trying to be tactful. 'I can assure you that all we want to do is punish the guilty. We also have what might be a bar slate of regular "patrons", probably Japanese officers. It has not been translated yet but if you could name any—'

'Sorry, gentlemen,' Juliette said sternly, 'but you have made a mistake. It must be other women with the same names. We were not at the Sakura.' She dropped a shoulder coquettishly. 'And even if we had been, how could we help you? You know how the Japanese all look alike to us...especially naked. Au revoir!'

Kate and Juliette strode off arm in arm. The two men stared after them, open-mouthed.

'Oh, Juliette, did you see their faces!' Kate gushed, still blushing. 'I don't know how you could be so calm!'

'Those spiteful, fucking cows!' Juliette snapped.

Kate gripped Juliette's arm in sudden panic. 'But they have a list!'

'They have a burnt piece of paper, that's all.'

Kate was not reassured. 'They said there would be investigations. I don't want people to know. Before, it didn't matter, but now—'

'You were there for one night!' Juliette said dismissively. 'I was there a month. It was my choice. I wanted to live. To live I had to eat, and to eat I had to sell myself. But I am alive and well. So are you. Others are dead! If we say nothing, they can do nothing. Soon you can leave here and start a new life. You'll never see these people again. Forget about it!'

Mac stacked the last of the cartons destined for Magelang in the back of the lorry and jumped down. It was six-thirty in the morning and he had a palm-wine hangover. Shout in Japanese and revving engines near the gate distracted him. 'I'm still not relaxed about them,' he said uneasily.

'Um?' Meg looked up from her map and followed his gaze to the Japanese soldiers climbing aboard an open-topped six-wheeler. 'I know what you mean,' she said. 'No-one will believe this back home, not even my editor!'

'It doesn't seem right,' replied Mac.

Meg smiled at him. 'So how's your Gurkha buddy?'

'I hope he's got a hangover.'

'Some party…' She had expected Mac to join her later but she had been disappointed.

Mac missed her sarcasm. 'Yeah. He doesn't speak much English and I don't speak Urdu or Gurkhali but after the third tin of whatever it was it really didn't matter.'

She laughed. 'Is he coming inland with us?'

'Aye, thank God!'

'Will you introduce me?'

'With pleasure.'

Ball appeared with four women in tow. Meg recognised Kate and Juliette. She waved cheerfully.

Kate made to wave back but then stopped and turned. Juliette had come face to face with a Japanese lieutenant. To Meg's surprise, the smiling Japanese bowed, then Kate and Juliette bowed back. When they reached Meg their faces were slightly flushed.

Ball saw Meg and waved. 'Here we go again! We've heard there are two more camps at Ambarawa. Let me introduce Juliette, Kate, Marja and Anna, our latest volunteers.'

Mac helped them up and fastened the tailboard. 'There we go, ladies. First class all the way!'

Miller pulled up alongside in a jeep. 'Wing Commander, we'll change the column order at Srondol. For now, your vehicle should keep behind the Jap half-track. Their commander is Lieutenant Nagumo. He doesn't speak English but seems capable. We'll be leaving in ten minutes.'

Srondol, south of Semarang

A steady stream of travellers was passing through the checkpoint. Some had made the hazardous journey from the interior but most were local farmers or traders with bullock carts piled high with rice, maize or barter goods. Their mood was cheerful and good humoured. Srondol was the first of the checkpoints into Semarang. From here on the possibility of robbery was unlikely. They and their goods were safe until they ran the gauntlet of bandits once again on their return.

Ota watched them casually through the office window of a disused Shell petrol station. Its paintwork was flaking and its single pump sat rusting on the pot-holed forecourt. Later that day they were due to be relieved by Nagumo's platoon. They had been on duty for seven consecutive days.

Corporal Suzuki entered the office without knocking—the door was missing—and stifled a yawn. 'Well, Lieutenant, the men won't be sorry to leave here and neither will I!'

Ota nodded. 'I know what you mean but it's better than a gaol!'

Suzuki was pouring himself a cup of cold Java tea when he stopped to listen. 'Something heavy coming out of town,' he said, gulping down his drink. Ota followed him outside. Motor traffic through the checkpoint was sparse. Only military or Indonesian Red Cross vehicles risked venturing into nationalist territory.

'Brits moving in some force,' said Suzuki looking through field glasses. 'I count nine vehicles, mainly lorries. Not our relief.' His disappointment was clear.

'Hmm, I thought it was a bit early in the day for Lieutenant Nagumo,' Ota said lightly.

Before long all of his platoon had gathered to watch the approaching vehicles. 'Right,' shouted Ota. 'Get ready to move the half-track off the road. And shift the locals out of the way!'

Minutes later, the jeep leading the column stopped in front of him. In it were two British officers and two Gurkhas. Ota saluted.

'I'm Major Miller. Do you speak English?'

'A little, Sir,' replied Ota.

'That's good,' said Miller. 'We're going to Magelang via Ambarawa. The platoon that was going to relieve you today is coming with us instead. Major Kudo gave me this for you.' He handed over an envelope.

Ota read quickly. His platoon was to remain at Srondol for another two days. 'I understand, Sir.'

'We're changing our column order here,' Miller said turning in his seat and waving the column off the road by the petrol station. The jeep pulled away.

As the column parked, Ota saw a Japanese half-track flying a small, rising-sun pennant from its whip antenna. He went in search of Nagumo.

'Hello, Kenichi.'

He spun round, knowing her voice. Kate was beaming at him beside a lorry. His mouth opened in half-smile, half-shock. 'Kate!' He frowned, 'But you should not be here—'

Kate's face reddened and her smile vanished. She had not expected him to be disappointed. 'Well, there are no ships yet, so I've volunteered to help at Ambarawa,' she replied firmly.

'Ambarawa? But it's dangerous there...' Ota rushed, not catching her tone. He could not believe she was taking such a risk when she had promised to stay safe.

Three more women came around the back of the vehicle. He recognised Juliette. They were regarding him with interest.

Kate forced a laugh and turned away. 'Oh, the rebels won't dare attack all these soldiers! We'll be perfectly safe.'

He wanted to shout at her. You fool, they will attack! We trained them how to ambush convoys and plant mines! How can two hundred defend you from thousands? Conscious of the curious looks from women, he said nothing.

Gurkhas toting Bren guns and ammunition boxes walked between them. Any chance to talk further was lost. Kate and the others climbed back into the lorry. Ota glanced at her helplessly then walked away to hide his anger.

A hand clapped him on the back.

'Oi!'

He spun around to see Nagumo. 'Hey, What the hell's going on?'

His friend shrugged. 'All I know is we're going up to Ambarawa to supply a camp. Anyway, I can't stop. I heard you will be relieved soon. Any trouble?'

He shook his head quickly. 'No. Listen to me. She's here, Kate!'

'I know,' grinned Nagumo. 'And do you know who else is here? The Frenchwoman! She even said "Bonjour".' He scratched his chin thoughtfully. 'I don't suppose I'll get another chance with her now though...'

Ota gripped Nagumo's arm. 'Don't even think it! You'll be hanged for rape!'

'Balls!' Nagumo scoffed. 'Not even the British would give me the drop for having a screw!' He looked quickly at Ota, 'Would they?'

'They've won, they can do whatever they like,' Ota replied sharply. 'And the Dutch will also want revenge. Keep your head down and don't give them any excuses!' He paused, his voice calmer now, 'And something else, please, watch out for Kate.'

Nagumo nodded slowly. 'If I'm there...'

As Nagumo's platoon passed, several of Ota's men called out, joking and waving at their comrades. Nagumo went by, saluting from in the half-track. His mind only on Kate, Ota stepped further into the road, watching the column head off. He did not see the dark blue Plymouth PJ convertible until it was almost upon him. Ota sprang back and the car screeched to a halt a few feet away. Four Japanese officers were inside. He saluted automatically. Three of the four returned it. One did not. Ota tensed.

Shirai was watching him with a half-amused, half-challenging look. 'So Ota, you've chosen dishonour after all.'

Slowly Ota glanced around him but saw his men were out of earshot and none was aware of anything unusual. 'I obeyed the Emperor, Captain,' he replied calmly. He saw Shirai and the others were wearing the uniforms of engineers. He understood why. The British were allowing Japanese technicians to move between pump and power stations without restriction in order to keep the electricity and water utilities functioning. Shirai's car had simply tagged on to the column to pass through the checkpoints unhindered.

Ota considered his options. Shirai was now a wanted man. But the man was not his enemy... His indecision showed. Shirai slowly looked down at his lap. Ota followed the gaze. Under a map a pistol was pointing at his chest. He suspected that the others were similarly prepared. If he tried to stop them he and several of his men would die pointlessly. He would not risk it, not over a fugitive *kenpei*.

Shirai gave him a pitying look. 'You're risking your life for the British. Just what are you expecting in return? A few comfortable weeks on Rempang and then a ship back to a barbarian-ruled Japan?' Rempang island, south of Singapore, was the main confinement area for tens of thousands of Japanese.

Ota met Shirai's stare but said nothing.

'Well take it from me,' Shirai said almost gloatingly. 'There's no food on Rempang. Men are dying every week. Some are escaping and coming to Java and Sumatra to join the Indonesian cause. They prefer to die in battle with honour than from hunger. Think about it, Ota. You still have time to redeem yourself and your family's honour. If you change your mind, you'll find me near Magelang.'

'I have made my choice, Shirai-san.'

'Yes, I see you have…' Shirai's eyes were cold. 'Next time I shall not hesitate to kill you.'

Shirai nodded to the driver and the car sped away to catch up with the column, which was labouring up a hill. Ota watched helplessly as the car nestled audaciously behind the last vehicle in the column then turned off unchallenged as the road forked.

In the back of the lorry the ride was hot and jarring. Kate sat with her eyes closed and her head on Juliette's bony shoulder. They were hemmed in by sacks and boxes.

'Are you all right, ma cocotte?' Juliette whispered.

Kate pretended to be asleep. For the first time since the end of the war, Kate was feeling miserable. Meeting Ota at the roadblock had proved disconcerting. She had been longing for the chance to talk with him before she left Java and above all to part as friends. Countless times she had pictured the scene in her mind: a whispered word of best wishes, a gentle embrace followed by a warm smile of farewell. She craved a happy memory of them both safe and sound. In itself it was so simple… Yet when she saw Ota she had been thrilled, with a strength of feeling for him that had disturbed her. She would have talked with him much more but she had noticed the questioning looks from Marja and Anna. Embarrassed, Kate had forced her smile into a pinched, bloodless line and spoken sharply. Ota's hurt expression had turned a knife in her stomach but she had not been able to stop herself. Her sudden fear of gossip and scandal had been too great. Now she was full of regret.

Juliette gave her shoulder a squeeze and she opened her tearful eyes. 'How much longer?'

'Just a few kilometres now,' smiled Juliette.

Kate stared blankly, hardly seeing the valley scenery below. She was facing an uncomfortable truth. Peace had brought with it the return of convention and propriety. So far she had ignored it, though already in Tjandi the old snobbery was raising its head. Kate had scoffed at first but now she realised she too was being dragged back, if unwillingly, to her place in the old order. Once again she was the daughter of Pym and Marianne van Dam of Magelang. Marja's critical looks had said it all. Surely Kate van Dam would not show friendliness toward a Jap?

All her assumptions about life after the war had swiftly crumbled. Three months before, all that had mattered was survival for herself and her mother, survival by any means. In the camp she had dared to dream of how she would live if she were free. Now, after just days of that freedom, she felt others controlling her, caging her dreams. Worst of all, she was helping to close the cage door.

West Semarang

The night air was heavy and clinging, so the two men drove with the jeep's windscreen down. It had been a long day and they were chatting about their families. Neither the driver nor his passenger noticed the tiny glints of reflected moonlight across the road ahead.

They hit the taut, thin steel wire at nearly forty miles an hour, slewing off the road and slamming a palm tree. Steam hissed from the smashed radiator. Petrol began to spill from a broken linkage.

The driver's body hung out of the jeep, blood spurting from the stump of his cleanly severed neck. Back on the road, his severed head rolled many feet before catching in a rut, eyes fixed in a blank, uncomprehending stare.

His passenger lay sprawled and unconscious over the bonnet. One side of his face had been sliced off from below the chin to the ear. Blood sprayed from a severed carotid artery. In a few seconds he, too, was dead.

Cautiously the ambushers emerged from the thick vegetation along the side of the road. Some went to the jeep while others took down the wire. One retrieved the head and tossed it into the back of the jeep. The corpses were stripped. Pistols, uniforms, underwear, socks and belts were taken, as well as cash and cigarettes. A briefcase was upended and the contents scattered.

One man opened a document wallet stamped RAAF. He cursed when he found no cash, only scraps of half-burnt pages and handwritten notes. Disappointed he dropped the wallet and its contents back into the jeep. He stepped back as the vehicle and bodies were doused in petrol. A match was struck and thrown. Instantly the jeep was engulfed in roaring flames. Long before the petrol tank exploded the ambushers had vanished into the night.

Chapter Six

The Ambarawa Road

From Srondol the relief convoy travelled only ten miles before one of the commandeered Japanese lorries started to overheat. Wing-Commander Ball called a halt outside a small, hillside village. Its Gurkha passengers dismounted then sat in small groups while the mechanics went to work.

Ball, Mac and Meg got out of the car for a cigarette. Afterwards the two men went to check the progress with the problem engine.

Meg was enjoying the view back towards Semarang and the sea. They had climbed steadily and they were now on the lower slopes of Mt. Oengaran, which rose to a steep, green six-thousand foot pinnacle at her back. White-painted buildings shone in the heat and the *sawah* rice terraces shimmered blue-green. She noticed that few others showed any interest in the panorama. A few feet away, Miller was talking with Rai and another Gurkha. She took her opportunity for an impromptu interview.

'Major Miller, will you introduce me to Corporal Rai? I've heard a lot about him.'

'Certainly,' said Miller. He explained who she was to Rai.

Rai seemed shy. 'Pleased to meet you, Madame.' His English was slow and a struggle.

'Oh, is it so obvious?' Meg grinned. 'War really is hell. I started it a Miss!'

Rai frowned in confusion but Miller interpreted. Meg patted his arm to put him at ease. 'Sorry, I was being unfair. May I ask him some questions…with your help, of course?'

'Of course,' said Miller. 'Freedom of the press and all that. By the way, we don't have corporals in the Indian Army. His rank is naik. It's the equivalent though.'

'I see!' Meg said. She turned to Rai. 'First, Naik Rai, why did you join the British Army?'

Rai listened to Miller's translation and replied hesitantly. 'My father was soldier. Father's father soldier.'

'I see, a family tradition,' said Meg. 'So why do you want to serve in the army of a foreign country?'

Miller cleared his throat and gave Meg a slightly affronted look before translating. Rai seemed confused by the question but did not hesitate. 'Army very good!' He grinned again.

Meg tried a different tack. 'Where are you from?'

Rai reverted to Urdu. 'The valley of the Dhud Kosi,' Miller interpreted. Rai looked at her as though he expected her to know it well.

'It's in eastern Nepal,' explained Miller.

'That doesn't help me too much, Major! Oh well, hmm, how do you get to be a Gurkha?'

Miller and the other Gurkha laughed at Rai's reply. 'He said he walked a long way! You see Gurkha recruiting posts are in India not Nepal. We are not allowed in. Nepal isn't part of the British Empire. Recruits have to come to us. They walk for days to sign up.'

'Days? How many days, Naik Rai?' Meg asked.

'Twenty-four,' Miller said enjoying her look of surprise. 'Remember Miss Graham. In the Himalayas there are few roads or bridges. It really is quite a feat!'

Meg turned to the other Gurkha. 'Where are you from?'

Smiling, the man spoke quickly and excitedly. Miller hesitated. 'He says he walked for thirty days from the east of the Tambar river. Technically that means he's from Tibet.' He shrugged. 'Our recruiting officers don't ask too many questions in wartime. In fact, we've got men from Sikkim, Bhutan and Burma as well.'

Meg was amazed. 'Really! I've only heard of the French having a Foreign Legion!'

'Well, we don't see it quite that way,' Miller said uncomfortably. He nodded to the two Gurkhas who moved away politely. 'Let me try to explain. Our treaty with the Kingdom of Nepal is long-established. Gurkhas have fought as part of the British army for over a century. I suppose in this day and age it might seem unusual but it works well and both countries gain immensely.'

Meg cocked her head. 'Do they get the same pay rates as British soldiers? The same invalidity allowances?'

'Not exactly,' Miller said flustered. 'But for people in Nepal the pay or pension is very high.'

Meg became conciliatory. 'Look, Major, I'm not trying to give you a hard time. I'm after an angle for my story, that's all. I know there's blatant racial discrimination in the US military. Some of the ideals we professed to be fighting for are missing from our own backyard. Take the coloured regiments for example. Did you know that in 1941 the US Navy would only permit coloured men to serve as cooks?'

Miller shook his head. 'I had no idea.'

'Well, now it's possible—in theory—for them to become officers. But you know what, I don't know if I can write about the Gurkhas. Most Americans just wouldn't understand the relationship. They'd probably see them as underpaid imperial mercenaries doing the dirty work for peanuts and a few shiny glass beads.'

An engine turned over then sprang into life to sarcastic cheers the waiting soldiers. Miller ordered the remount and walked Meg back to the car. He closed the door after her.

'Miss Graham,' he said earnestly. 'These are the bravest, most loyal soldiers in the world.'

Meg nodded. 'I believe you, Major.'

Beyond Oengaran the road was poor. Potholes and debris from landslides made it a jerky, slow descent into Ambarawa. Miller, ever wary of ambush, called frequent stops while Nagumo's platoon scouted the jungle and ridges ahead.

Ball was concentrating on the road and was unusually quiet, so Meg lost herself in the landscape, enjoying the cooler, drier air in the mountains but not the fumes from the lorries in front. Her guidebook described Ambarawa as having 'nothing of interest for the tourist'. The town sat at the southern foot of Mt Oengaran, facing a small, lush valley hemmed in by majestic volcanic peaks. Below them lay a small lake fed by a meandering river that shone blue-white. Across the valley, farming hamlets nestled in the foothills. It looked peaceful. Meg thought of the guidebook and smiled. Only in Java could something so beautiful merit no comment. 'May be nothing of interest for the journalist either,' she said under her breath.

'Hmm?' Ball grunted and looked at her.

'Oh, I was just thinking aloud,' said Meg.

Ball pointed across the valley. 'See those two villages? To the south is Banjobiroe, to the southeast is Salatiga. The Japs say there's a camp at each. In any case, we'll need more supplies.'

They rounded a sweeping bend.

'About time!' Ball said.

Meg glimpsed a few colonial-style houses and the white steeple of a church before the road bent again and the buildings were hidden. Soon the more modest structures and huts of a kampong appeared on either side of the road. Apart from a few farmers in fields, she had seen few Javanese on the journey. Now they passed them in their dozens, standing outside their houses and staring blankly at the troops. Most were dressed in rags or fraying sack cloth. Babies and toddlers went naked, their thin limbs and bellies distended from malnutrition. Bare-breasted teenage girls watched, disinterestedly, as the Gurkhas gestured and waved.

Soon the kampong buildings petered out and the convoy headed down a leafy, residential road lined with once fine but now dilapidated bungalows. Beyond it was a wide expanse of open ground.

'This reminds me of some of the hill stations in India,' said Ball. 'I suppose wives and children would come up here to escape the worst of the heat. Husbands would join them for the weekend then go back to Semarang or Surabaya. Mustn't have been a bad life....'

Meg was about to add 'for some' when they passed through the high wooden gate of the Ambarawa camp. 'Jeez!' Meg stammered as she saw the pallid, fearful-looking women.

As soon as the vehicles pulled up the internees surged forward. Many were laughing and crying at the same time.

'They're so thin....' Meg sighed. She found herself forcing a smile at two scruffy boys who had jumped on the running board of the car and were pressing their faces against the window.

Ball nodded. He had seen it all before. 'Yes, but it's amazing what a week or two of increased rations will do for them.'

Meg looked around her. 'It looks a bit like Tjandi,' said Meg. 'I mean the main building. Was this a school as well?'

Ball nodded. 'Yes. The Japs used a lot of schools as camps.' He looked at her and grinned. 'Well, here goes. It's the same every time. First they love me, then when I haven't got enough food they hate me!' He opened the door and soon disappeared as the women smothered him with kisses and hugs.

Caught up in the joyous mood, Meg got out after him and saw the same happening to Miller, Mac and the delighted Gurkhas. She saw that the Japanese did not dismount but were watching the jubilant scenes in studied silence.

A small hand slipped into Meg's and she looked down at a naked, fair-haired boy of about three who was as thin as the children in the kampong. She picked the toddler up and he said something to her in Dutch that she did not understand. All she could do was smile as tearful women embraced her one after another. 'Thank God you've come,' said one hoarsely. Meg patted her back and felt the protruding bones of her rib cage and spine.

'What took you so long?' asked another, trembling with emotion.

The boy's mother boy reached for him with a beaming smile. 'This last two weeks has been the worst of all,' she said. 'We only had a bit of rice each day. Bandits stole the rest. We couldn't stop them. Look, the bastards are still there!' She pointed at the low hills and Meg saw figures on a ridge overlooking the camp. Beside her a woman began to sob.

Meg embraced her. 'It's over now,' she said gently. 'The soldiers are here. You're safe.'

In hectic shifts the Gurkha field kitchens fed fifteen-hundred excited internees with small portions of cabbage soup, rice and tinned beef. While the cooking was under way, Miller assigned sentries and sent patrols into the mountains to see off the bandits. To the amusement of the internees, he assigned building repairs and latrine-digging duties to the Japanese.

Meg wandered aimlessly around the camp. Though it was much smaller than Tjandi she found a host of similarities: the rice sacks cut up for clothing; the duty rosters; the stench of the latrines; double lines of barbed wire; feral-looking children roaming in packs; and, beyond one low perimeter wall, row upon row of unmarked graves. Inwardly she shuddered.

Some two miles beyond the graves, on a hill overlooking fields of knee-high ripening maize was a convent. Its high, grey-white walls and bell tower were tranquil symbols of another time. Ball, Mac and the volunteers from Tjandi had gone there with medical supplies for the clinic run by the nuns. Suddenly Meg craved quiet. She left the camp and ambled up the gentle slope in the late afternoon sun, pulling at a head of maize between her fingers.

The pathway took her half-way around the hill. A single-storey hotel came into view. A faded sign advertised twelve private rooms and hot-spring baths. Excited by the possibility of a bath, she started down the drive hoping it was open.

She halted in disappointment when she saw the Japanese lieutenant from the convoy on the veranda, directing some repairs. High above his head, painted on the white stucco gable was a bright red circle. The effect was to make the front of the building resemble a giant Japanese flag. Her anger rose at the thought of the soldiers enjoying comforts when a stone's throw away women and children had been living in utter filth and squalor. She sighed, surprised that she had let her emotion run unchecked. 'Snap out of it, Meg,' she said to herself. 'It's only a dab of paint!'

With an effort she put the Japanese out of her mind and carried on walking up the hill. Ten minutes later she stood before a weathered, iron-studded door.

The Convent of St Agatha

Meg followed a white-robed nun along narrow, stone corridors. A strong scent of disinfectant hung in the air. She was relieved when they finally entered a courtyard whose shaded cloisters were crammed with patients on thin mattresses. As in the camp below, the atmosphere was joyous.

Inside the hospital wing it was quiet, orderly and spotlessly clean. Nuns moved quickly and efficiently along rows of beds and mattresses, changing dressings and bed pans. Here and there the carbolic was not quite strong enough to mask the cloying smell of sickness. Meg's nostrils wrinkled in distaste.

She saw two of the Tjandi girls carting medical supplies and flirting with Mac at the same time. She caught his eye and she winked, indicating the girls. He shrugged and grinned.

Wing-Commander Ball was talking with an elderly nun and a young woman. He waved. 'Ah, Meg! Glad you're here. We were just talking about you. This is the Reverend Mother Beatrice and Dr Richie.'

The three women shook hands. 'Actually,' said the younger woman, it's student doctor but please call me Gwen.'

Meg detected an Australian accent. 'How did you end up here?'

'Oh, just lucky I suppose!' Gwen joked. 'I was on a training placement at a Surabaya hospital when the war caught me by surprise. The Japs sent me here soon after.'

'Bad for you. Lucky for the others,' said Meg.

Gwen shook her head. 'I had a lot of help. I ran the clinic at the camp but fortunately I could ask the Reverend Mother for help with the really serious cases. She's the real doctor!'

'What nonsense!' Sister Beatrice smiled. 'Gwen is already a marvellous physician. What are a few examination papers after such a gruelling apprenticeship?'

Gwen blushed shyly. 'Thank you.'

A few minutes later Meg, Gwen, Mac, Kate, Ball, Marja and Anna were taking a break in the walled convent garden enjoying glasses of the nuns' home-made mango wine. They were surrounded by the sweet scent of red and orange bougainvillaea.

'I could get used to this,' said Ball holding up his glass. Meg nodded. Suddenly the war seemed very long ago. The only reminder of conflict was an ugly, eight-foot breach in the wall caused by a Japanese artillery shell. Yet the gap also provided a stunning view over the plain and lake below.

It did not take long for the conversation to turn to thoughts of home. Gwen Ritchie turned to Ball. 'Wing Commander, when can we go to Semarang? To be evacuated I mean?'

He shifted uncomfortably. 'Oh, in a few days I expect. We have to arrange for transport. There are thousands more internees than we were led to expect.'

'Really?' Gwen asked. 'Surely the Dutch government knew about us. Where did they think we'd all gone?'

Ball snorted. 'I'd like to ask them that very question.'

By dusk the sing-alongs were well under way. Bonfires lit Ambarawa camp. Improvised Dutch flags and bunting hung from the huts and windows. Gramophones or internee musicians and choirs provided the music as the Gurkhas danced with two or three women at a time. The festive mood was infectious and Kate and Juliette were also enjoying themselves, their own memories of the joy of liberation very fresh. They were breathless and almost dizzy as they took a rest from the dancing, enjoying the cooler night air of the hill country. Giggling, Kate reached for an enamel plate and began to fan Juliette who did the same to Kate.

'It's a pity there aren't enough men to dance with,' laughed Kate.

'But the Gurkhas aren't worried', Juliette said pointing. 'Look at them! We were lucky so many came to Tjandi.' She paused and Kate saw her glancing at the gate where Nagumo was talking with two Japanese guards. He was glancing frequently and enviously at the festivities. Then he saw them, nodded politely to Juliette and walked away.

'There's a spare man!' Juliette whispered challengingly.

Kate stared open-mouthed. 'Juliette, you wouldn't dare! I don't know how you can stand the sight of him after what happened.'

'*Oui, chérie* but he helped save us from those murderers. You can't choose your knight in shining armour. You of all people should know that….'

Kate blushed but Juliette merely smiled at her. 'Monsieur Nagumo is just a man; and not a bad man. And he made me laugh, can you imagine that? When we did not understand a word each other said! I know it sounds terrible but each time he visited me he brought a little present.'

Kate did not reply. She had no memento of Ota.

'Oh, it doesn't matter now', Juliette laughed. 'It's over! Come on, let's get dancing!'

Meg was looking for Mac. Eventually she saw him dancing with a giggling, clinging girl with orange ribbons in her hair. Meg started to wave then noticed half a dozen other girls standing excitedly nearby waiting for a turn. She hesitated, then let her hand drop. Let them have some fun, she thought. God knows, they deserve it. Mac too. She half-turned and was edging away when he was at her side. He was short of breath but smiling. 'May I have the pleasure?'

She took his hand quickly. 'Oh, how the other women will hate me!'

At first he held her away from him but the crush from the dozens of couples jostled them closer. A slow number started, bringing cheers. Meg moved quickly against him, resting her head on his shoulder. His arms closed around her and she closed her eyes. 'I think I'm getting tired of war, Mac,' she whispered.

'Join the club,' he replied softly.

His hand touched her hair and she hugged him. 'You'll be home soon.' Mac did not reply and she held him, enjoying his warm breath on her neck.

Around them the party continued raucously but now she watched without real interest. The ever-cheerful Gurkhas were in great demand as dance partners…and more. One after another couples were breaking away from the tumult and heading for the dark anonymity of the huts. She smiled when she saw Rai and a Dutch girl hurry away hand in hand.

Mac's fingers stroked her neck. Slowly she lifted her head to see him staring after Rai. He glanced down and they shared a nervous, excited smile. Mac stopped dancing and led her through the throng towards the maize field.

Borobudur

Massive and dark, the bell-shaped mount rose out of the pale greens of the *sawah* and palms, wrapped in broken spirals of early morning mist. Meg, Mac, Ball and Miller approached in silence, awed by the looming, balanced outlines of the ten, concentric stone terraces.

Meg felt her chest tighten. White, cobweb-like strands hung in the moist air. She tried to breathe slowly so as not to disturb them. On the temple walls, half-hidden in shadow were intricate, life-size bas-relief carvings of animals and men.

Ball had taken the lead and he stopped at the base of a narrow staircase. 'I was told it's best to watch the sunrise from the top then climb again to see the reliefs in the light,' he whispered, almost apologetically.

Equally reluctant to break the silence, they nodded and began the steep, dark ascent to the tenth and smallest terrace. They emerged to find themselves almost hemmed in by a ring of bulbous, grey-stone forms. To the east, beyond the ridge tops bordering the Kedu Plain, the sky glimmered in a soft gold and warm orange-red as the first rays of sunlight reflected off wispy clouds. Around the temple base patches of palm tops and a patch-work of glinting *sawah* were emerging through the fast-dissipating mist.

On the terrace the stone forms were gradually revealed as bell-shaped, ten-feet-high stupas, replicating the shape of the temple. As the tops of the stupas caught the first of the sunbeams the weathered stone appeared to glow, shaking off shadow as though welcoming the still gentle heat.

Meg could not remember a more exhilarating dawn. She took a photograph but knew her camera could not possibly do justice to the beauty before her. Surreptitiously she slipped her hand into Mac's and gazed as the sunlight flashed around them. All too soon the fleeting tapestry melded into the bright disc of the rising sun in a blue sky.

She squeezed Mac's hand. 'Wonderful!'

'I had no idea', he shook his head. 'Thanks for dragging me along.'

Now that the temple top was revealed, they began to explore. Beams of light were piercing the diamond-latticed openings of the stupas, illuminating the faces of meditating Buddha figures inside. Meg went from one to another.

'Mac, it's good luck to touch the hands and feet!' Meg chuckled.

Tentatively he reached inside one of the stupas. 'I hope I don't shake hands with a scorpion!'

One Buddha was uncovered and sat open to the elements. Meg looked at the serene, eroding face with its heavily lidded eyes and the hint of an indulgent smile. She felt warmed inside and smiled. 'I get the feeling this guy would forgive me anything!'

Mac patted the clasped, weathered hands. 'He's a thousand years old. I'm sure he's a good listener.'

After a while Meg again felt the need for solitude and was relieved when Mac said he would stay at the top for a bit longer. 'See you later then,' she said quickly and left him. Looking back at him she saw a calmer man. She was glad, too, that they had shared such a memorable dawn.

Miller was by the staircase, sweeping the plain below with his binoculars, half-sightseer, half-soldier.

'Thank you, Major,' she said softly, not wanting to break the peaceful, contemplative mood that still held them.

'Oh, I didn't need prompting to come here,' Miller said in slightly hushed tones. 'I read about this place at school. Marvellous isn't it!'

'For sure,' replied Meg.

Miller jiggled his binoculars. 'It's good to be able to reconnoitre an area and catch up on a bit of history at the same time!'

Meg nodded. 'Actually, I'm embarrassed to admit that I hadn't known about the temple until I read about it in my guidebook. I'm going down now to have a look at the reliefs.'

'Fine, we'll all meet at the bottom terrace staircase in half-an hour or so. My men are guarding the perimeter but please don't wander off.'

Meg nodded and started down, looking forward to being alone. Borobudur fascinated her and she wanted to make the most of it. She started at the east gate in order to walk the narrow corridors clockwise like a pilgrim and observe the ten levels of the Mahayana-Buddhist universe. Depictions of mythical beasts, heroes, elephants and sailing ships were interspersed with scenes from daily life. Some were remarkably contemporary: farmers ploughing with buffalos, bountiful rice fields and smoking volcanoes. Most of all, she liked the scenes of earthly pleasures: feasts with musicians, provocatively posed dancing girls, libidinous princes and graphically entwined lovers. After the pleasures came the punishments: scenes of hellfire, demons and torments for the guilty, watched over by sombre monks.

Finally she was back, alone, on the tenth terrace among the stupas. According to her guidebook, this was the level of enlightenment, with no earthly distractions for the closeted Buddha figures. Once again she was drawn to the single, unprotected statue. In the full morning light the Buddha looked serene. She took a photograph, hoping to capture his smile. On an impulse she reached for his now warmed hands and briefly closed her eyes.

On her way back down to rejoin Miller and the others she tried to imagine how the terraces must have looked when Stamford Raffles stumbled upon the jungle-covered ruins in 1815. Borobudur had been lost for several centuries. Idly she wondered how much longer it would stand. Signs of subsidence, erosion and damp were all around her. In truth, the temple was crumbling. The thought that the Buddha's smile would be erased by the tropical winds and rains and that someday the statue would topple upset her. Another paradise to lose....

Meg quickened her pace. The Gurkhas were already back at the vehicles. She was glad they had respected the temple. It was not a place for guns.

As they drove away off she craned her neck for a last glimpse of the temple mound but all she could see was the half-track and Rai training his Tommy gun at the tree-line. Under his bush hat his eyes were never still. The gun had a drum magazine. In silhouette he reminded her of a 1920s Chicago gangster. Quickly she turned away.

It was hot and sticky in the car and she reached for her canteen only to remember it was almost empty. Ball, next to her, offered her his. 'The sunsets up there must be quite something,' he said enthusiastically.

Meg did not answer. The image of Rai and the gun had spoilt her mood.

'Next time, Wing Commander,' Miller said, 'we daren't risk the roads at night.'

Meg was curious. 'But I thought the bandits had gone?'

Miller shrugged. 'So did I, but we found signs of movements of large numbers of men.'

'Where are they heading for?' Ball asked quietly.

'Probably for Yogya or Surabaya,' replied Miller.

Meg sat forward. 'Yogya? That's where one of the sultans has his palace! I'd like to meet a sultan...'

Miller shook his head. 'Somehow I don't think we'd be welcome there. You might be safe, Miss Graham, being an American and a reporter but not us.'

Ball was pensive. 'Well, I hope it is Yogya. I'm flying to Surabaya the day after tomorrow. I don't need the bother of bandits!'

'The day after tomorrow is another day,' Miller joked, head-down, studying a map. 'A few miles on there's a temple ruin with a natural spring. We'll stop there refill with fresh water.'

At the second stop they walked about a quarter-of-a-mile along a narrow but well-trodden jungle path with the Gurkhas front and rear. As a precaution, Miller had sent Rai ahead.

They came upon two stone pillars of an ancient arch entwined in thick creepers. Beyond, Meg glimpsed a rectangular-shaped pool. It was the first of five, linked by a stone rill fed from a larger pool at the base of a broad expanse of rock. Hewn from the rock face was a life-size alto-relief of a half-naked, full-breasted woman. The figure leant forward, palms together as if in greeting. Two narrow jets of spring water arced from holes in her nipples over the pool. Rai was squatting below holding the mouth of his canteen under one of the arcs.

'Good Lord!' Miller said with a grin.

'Heavens!' Ball stammered.

Rai turned and grinned, saying something to Miller in Urdu. The other Gurkhas started giggling. Miller chose not to interpret.

Meg stared appreciatively. 'We don't have fountains like that in New York!'

'It would cause a bit of a stir on Oxford Street, too,' Ball added dryly.

'She must be a goddess...,' Miller said smiling.

'Of water perhaps,' Ball ventured with a raised eyebrow.

'Or motherhood...' Mac said trying to keep his face straight.

'Well, her cups runneth over...' quipped Meg, sending the two men into convulsions.

Miller's shoulders shook. 'Whichever you prefer, Wing-Commander. Either way, it's a nice spot for a picnic isn't it Miss Graham?'

'It certainly is, Major. But first I'm going to soak my aching feet.'

While they ate, Meg sat next to Rai. Like everyone else his eyes were frequently drawn to the figure of the goddess.

Meg laughed with him. 'Does she remind you of the women in Nepal, Naik Rai?'

Miller moved closer to interpret. Rai looked wistful as he answered. The other Gurkhas and Miller roared. 'Not those in his village,' he explained. 'They have a saying, "Breasts are bigger further down the mountain".... It makes sense, there's a better diet in the lower valleys.'

'Are you married, Rai?' she asked quickly. Then she remembered she had seen him with a girl the night before. She hoped he was not embarrassed.

'No, Memsahib,' Rai said with a smile. 'When go home, marry.'

'Oh, you're engaged? What's her name?'

Rai's answer was convoluted.

'He likes a girl in the village next to his,' began Miller. 'Her name is Sarita. He plans to win her in the traditional way. One day he will wait for her when she takes her washing to the river, then he'll challenge her to a singing competition. If he wins the girl has to marry him. Of course she has to agree to the challenge first, and she can choose the song. He's learnt her favourite ballad by heart. Every night he recites the words so he doesn't forget them.'

'You must be good singer then, Rai!' suggested Mac.

Rai shook his head and grinned. 'Terrible bad!'

Around her the others giggled. Meg was intrigued. 'What about Sarita's voice?'

Rai replied a little sheepishly.

'Like a warbler in spring,' said Miller.

The Gurkhas started joking among themselves, clearly at Rai's expense.

'Then how will you win?' Mac asked.

Rai spoke animatedly to Miller, who smiled. 'The same way his father won his mother. He'll bribe the judge! It's always the best friend of the girl. The day before the challenge he will slip her some rupees. He says Sarita is very beautiful, so her friend can demand a lot of money!'

Meg clapped her hands together. 'Wow! I see a girl's got to know who her friends are in Nepal! I can think of a few of mine who'd see me married for the price of a whiskey and soda!'

Miller interpreted. The Gurkhas thought it hilarious and could not stop laughing.

Meg looked about her, beginning to understand why Miller was so proud of these tough, respectful men. She had rarely seen anyone laugh or argue as easily as a group of Gurkhas. Somehow she found it hard to picture them as the ferocious fighters she knew they were. But the sturdy, curved *kukri* knives were always within reach. Meg hoped she would never see one drawn in anger.

In the afternoon, Miller and most of the Gurkhas left for Magelang, a town about twenty-five miles from Ambarawa. Mac and Ball went with them with the intention of returning the next day to fly to Surabaya. Magelang boasted a large military hospital and Ball was keen to see it restocked with medicines.

Meg stayed in Ambarawa to interview more of the women. In truth, she did not want to face a third 'liberation' party or the same, tired questions about Holland and Hollywood stars. Meg strolled about the camp. All everyone wanted to do was leave. They kept asking her when they could go. Few would talk of the struggle for survival, and most were already trying to forget.

For Meg the brief excursion to Borobudur had been a refreshing change. She had realised she was bored with the 'women's angle' on Java, however distressing life still was for the internees. She was being selfish, she knew, but also she wanted some time away from Mac. That morning she had decided that after her trip to Surabaya she would head for the sultan's palace in Yogya then return to Singapore. She wanted time to prepare her goodbye.

Around the corner of one hut she bumped into Kate, Juliette and Gwen Richie. 'Hello, Meg,' Kate said warmly. 'We're going to have a bath,' she whispered. 'Why don't you come with us?'

Meg had seen the grime-encrusted bathrooms. 'Oh, I'm fine. I can get a wash later.'

Gwen read her mind and laughed. 'Not the camp baths! Ones at the hotel up the hill. Juliette says they're hot springs!'

The thought of a hot bath was instantly appealing. 'Give me a minute to get my things!'

'All right,' said Gwen, 'but keep it a secret or we'll be sharing with five hundred!'

Together they walked up the valley, carrying sacks which hid their Red Cross soap and shampoo.

'I saw Japanese there yesterday,' Meg said. 'It must have been a billet of some kind. How did you find out about the hot springs?'

'From someone at the camp,' Juliette murmured.

Meg saw Kate shoot a quick glance at Juliette.

A single Japanese sentry stood at the hotel entrance. Juliette took the lead and they walked on, ignored by the sentry.

Inside the hotel it was clean and tidy. The *nyatoh* wood panelling in the reception was polished and even the stuffed hunting trophies on the walls appeared dusted. Armchairs were arranged in fours around small tables. Apart from a Japanese calendar behind the reception desk the war did not seem to have touched the hotel.

Kate, Juliette and Gwen stared. Meg noticed a narrow roll of carpet across the hall on which were lined up several pairs of open Japanese slippers.

Juliette was already slipping off her shoes. She saw the others hesitate. 'The Japs don't wear shoes inside,' she explained.

'Juliette, I don't like the idea of bathing with half the Jap army,' Gwen said apprehensively.

'You won't,' Juliette smiled. 'If they turn up they'll use the men's baths. Come on, I'll show you!'

They followed her almost at a run down some stairs to a basement corridor that was also panelled with rich dark wood.

Scenic photographs of Ambarawa were mounted on the walls but the women paid them no attention. Juliette stopped in front of a door marked Dames. The kanji for 'women' had also been chalked on the door.

Meg laughed. 'That's me, a real dame at last!'

'Follow me, ladies!' Juliette said grandiosely as she opened the door. Inside it was dark. Juliette let them savour the smooth, cool tiles on their bare feet then flicked on the light. The entire room was tiled in a simple blue and white square pattern. Two walls were taken with teak lockers complete with brass hooks and hangers. Along another wall was a row of gleaming porcelain sinks and mirrors.

Gwen let out a small shriek and ran to a sink to turn on a tap. 'It's hot! It really is! So clean!' Then she caught her reflection in the mirror. 'Oh, Christ, I forgot I look dreadful!'

'Et voilà!' Juliette said opening a sliding door. They peered through excitedly. Swirling vapour and a slight smell of sulphur filled the air. Set in the middle of the room was a large, tiled and overflowing *mandi* tub fed by constantly flowing water from open pipes set in the wall. Beyond the *mandi* was a row of frosted glass cubicles, each with a typical western bath.

'Beauty!' Gwen said breathlessly, already unbuttoning her blouse.

They washed themselves and then washed each other's hair before they got in the large bath. Meg had been a little modest at first, partly because the others were so thin. Unlike them, she was not used to group bathing but the hot water soon had her as relaxed as the others.

'Oh this feels so good! Can you believe it, Meg, two and a half years without a hot bath!' Gwen sighed as she stretched out in the water. 'How long for you two?'

'Too long,' Juliette said casually. She shot a quick smile at Kate who blushed a little under her already flushed cheeks.

Meg noticed and wondered why. Kate was nervous about something. Then she remembered Juliette's comment about the Japanese on the way to the baths. Was the person 'at the camp' the same Japanese who had talked with her at Tjandi? And how did she know him? Meg had heard the Tjandi gossip about the brothels. A thought struck her. Slowly she began putting two and two together, then stopped. She knew she could never judge any of these women. It was one story she would never write.

'This has got to be the hottest hot tub ever!' Meg sighed holding up her arm. Her skin was bright pink. 'I'm cooking,' she said tiredly and pushed herself out of the water. She sat on the side of the bath, watching the vapour rise off her .

One by one the others got out to cool off by lying or sitting on the tiled floor. They were in and out of the bath for an hour.

Conversation was unrestrained. They compared the camp routines. Meg listened in horror. Then they talked of what they would do as soon as they reached home or a big city. Gwen made them laugh, 'My dad will give me a big hug but then he'll want to give me a back-hander for letting myself get caught by the Japs!'

Kate seemed a little melancholic, so Meg tried to cheer her up. 'And you, Kate, where will you go?'

She shrugged. 'I think I'd like to live in Canada.'

'Why?' Meg pressed her.

'There's lots of space. I want a new start.'

'That's interesting,' Meg said sympathetically.

Kate looked at her blankly. 'It is?'

'Yes. You were born here but you want to leave. I've heard a lot of Dutch say they intend to stay, even if it means fighting another war.'

'Java isn't worth it, Meg,' she said with a soft shake of her head. 'It's broken my heart.'

The Makassar Strait

Dawn was breaking when the five B-25 Mitchell bombers took off from Balikpapan airfield. At ten-thousand feet they levelled out over the Makassar Strait and then turned due south in a loose V-formation, heading for the Java Sea.

Angry crackling sounded above the drone of the twin, 1,700 horse-power Wright Cyclone engines as the leading B-25 tested its .50 calibre machine guns. Bright, burning tracers streaked into the blue sky ahead, above and behind them as the other B-25s copied their flight leader. Below them palm-tops and sandy, surf-ringed bays along the east coast of Borneo glinted in golden sunlight.

The same rays also hit the nose of each bomber illuminating 'Mrs Sweeper', the squadron's emblem of a smiling washerwoman in a headscarf with brush and dust pan.

At the B-25's optimum cruising speed of three hundred miles per hour, the flight to the Java coast was a short, easy hop of just over an hour. It was a familiar route for the crews because they had already made a dozen similar trips to drop food and supplies over internment camps. Today, however, for the first time since the Japanese surrender, the bomb bays were full.

They made steady progress over a tranquil ocean. When they reached their first marker at the Kangean archipelago they corrected their heading slightly southwest to take them over the small Bali Sea. Ahead of them, the lush forested peaks of the islands of Java, Bali, Lombok, Soembawa and Flores lined the horizon like a giant bracelet of green jade. Soon the planes changed to a single-line formation then, upon their leader's signal, dropped steadily to five hundred feet

From sixty miles out the soaring, barren crest of the Merapi-Raung crater shone like a beacon in the morning sunshine. Nestled at its foot lay the small port of Banjoewangi.

Few of its thirty-five thousand inhabitants had stirred. The first of the day's ferries to Bali from the Ketapang terminal was not for another two hours. Only a few fishermen tending their nets on the slender strip of black-sand beach paid brief attention to the noisy black dots in the sky.

Banjoewangi's nine massive storage sheds were built in a neat row and ringed by a narrow gauge railway that ran to the harbour. They had whitewashed walls and rounded, corrugated iron roofs painted alternately red or blue. Their large, sliding steel doors bore a white, stencilled number.

Each of the B-25s made its run thirty seconds apart at mast-skimming height as they had often done against Japanese ships at Timor, Tanimbar and Koepang. Today was no different except that there was no anti-aircraft fire to distract the aim of the bombardiers.

Dark, stick-like bombs punched holes through the brick walls and brittle roofs of sheds six, seven, eight and nine. As the last B-25 cleared the sheds, the first of the delayed-action fuses ignited the high explosive. Banjoewangi shook as the sheds' roofs were blown open and their walls collapsed.

Three planes made a second run. Sticky, blazing napalm gel smothered the exposed, closely packed sacks. The pungent smell of burning petroleum engulfed the town. Their bomb bays empty, the B-25s made a leisurely turn through the billowing black clouds to return to Balikpapan. By the time the first of the fire appliances had reached the storage sheds the fishermen had already lost sight of the aircraft.

British HQ, Hotel des Indes, Batavia/Djakarta

'The raid was a totally unwarranted and highly provocative act!' Chrishaw's eyes blazed as he confronted Van Zanten and Hurwitz. His first notification about the attack on

Banjoewangi had come from news reports on nationalist-controlled Radio Surabaya. Chrishaw had summoned the two senior Dutchmen expecting to hear a denial.

Instead, Van Zanten was prepared to raise the stakes. 'General,' he replied firmly. 'Please remember this is the Netherlands East Indies. You must expect us to undertake some independent operations as our resources increase.'

'Absolutely!' Hurwitz gushed in agreement.

Chrishaw was struggling to remain calm. 'I do not expect deceit from an ally, Gentlemen. The RAF commander at Balikpapan was informed that your squadron was on a training flight!'

'Standard operating procedure, General,' Van Zanten said casually. 'One does not publicise bombing missions.'

'Quite right,' Hurwitz added gruffly. 'Standard procedure.'

Chrishaw ignored him and stared at Van Zanten. He was glad now that he had decided to meet the Dutchmen alone. 'Rice, Doctor! There is a food shortage across Asia and you incinerated or contaminated thousands of tons of rice!'

Van Zanten shrugged. 'Regrettable, I agree, but necessary. The rebels negotiated directly with the Indian Government over the heads of local Dutch officials. We cannot allow the rebels to make international agreements. To do so would confer legitimacy on their illegal regime. It is a matter of principle.'

'I wonder if the people of the Netherlands would agree? Last winter they were experiencing severe famine. I cannot believe they would wish the same on anyone. You two must have suffered gravely in Australia.' Chrishaw let his gaze drop deliberately to the prominent paunches of the two men whose faces reddened at his accusation.

Van Zanten smiled thinly. 'I think, General, that you are trying to provoke me. I doubt that the incident will be of much concern to the people of the Netherlands.'

'Quite,' replied Chrishaw quickly. 'They won't know about it because your newspapers will neither report it nor comment on the hardship that will follow in India!'

'The Indians are hardly sympathetic to our interests anyway,' Hurwitz interjected dismissively.

Chrishaw looked at him sharply. 'Please tell me, Admiral, whether you think the seven Indian soldiers murdered across Java over the last six days were "unsympathetic" to Dutch colonial interests?'

Hurwitz looked down, his expression was now sheepish. Van Zanten nodded earnestly. 'We are very grateful for the Indian Army's efforts to maintain law and order, General,' he said diplomatically.

Chrishaw sighed. 'Yes, let's talk about law and order shall we?' He shook his head. 'Doctor, your re-armed ex-POW "policemen" are no more than trigger-happy vigilantes. I have reports from British officers who witness random, cold-blooded killings daily. They themselves have been ordered off pavements by Tommy-gun toting Dutch and native troops. There is an air of terror in Batavia and it is by no means all the fault of the nationalists. The recent discovery of the captives at Fort Michiels is evidence of that. Your officials have not shown the slightest bit of remorse or even attempted to rein in the worst offenders. You must know that the British and foreign reporters are very critical. My Government is becoming seriously embarrassed but you choose to see it purely as some vast, anti-Dutch conspiracy!'

Van Zanten was suddenly irate. 'Those soldiers have suffered. It is natural that they will be hostile to Jap collaborators.'

'They are not fit to peel potatoes, Doctor, never mind provide security. I want them disbanded and disarmed.'

Hurwitz was outraged. 'Out of the question! We need more troops here, not fewer!'

'Really?' Chrishaw sat back. 'How will that help the sixty thousand of your women and children held hostage inland?'

'It will help us expand areas under our military control.'

Chrishaw snorted. 'My view is that it would effectively sign the death warrant for those people.'

Van Zanten opened his hands in a gesture of helplessness. 'General, I will be quite frank with you, confidentially, of course. My Government now considers the internees...expendable.'

Chrishaw was open-mouthed.

'You must understand', Van Zanten continued, 'that our empire is at risk here. The Netherlands needs the oil, rubber, coal, lumber, sugar, quinine, everything. We are talking about the life and wealth of a nation. What are a few thousand lives in comparison?'

Chrishaw eyes narrowed. 'I confess I am astounded by such callousness. But I am a soldier not a politician. Yesterday I attended Admiral Hurwitz's press conference. He said—correct me if I'm wrong—that Dutch forces had surrendered here in 1942 in order to save massive civilian casualties. Today, Sir, you are Pontius Pilate, ready to wash your hands of them! What would the Press make of the change in policy? No doubt it will also be of interest to the relatives in Holland of these unfortunate hostages.'

Van Zanten rose suddenly and Hurwitz jumped up in his wake. 'This meeting is really serving no purpose, General,' Van Zanten said icily. We will return to the palace.'

'Very well', said Chrishaw politely. He was leaving his own bombshell until the last. 'I called this meeting to inform you that in the interests of public safety, I have ordered that no more Dutch troops arrive in Java without my express authorisation. Ships now en-route carrying Dutch troops have been instructed to disembark them in Malaya, where they will stay until further notice.'

'I protest!' Van Zanten blustered. 'Mountbatten will hear from my Government this afternoon!'

Chrishaw gave him a polite smile. 'Actually, Admiral Mountbatten approved my order an hour ago.'

Chapter Seven

Bekassi

Arman Sharma's knuckles showed white as he clung to the mesh of webbing stretched behind the narrow bench seat of the Douglas C-47 Dakota. Again the aircraft see-sawed in the gale force winds. Steel hats, back packs and kit bags came sliding past him on slicks of vomit. He closed his eyes and prayed. Then he was sick again.

The ferocious monsoon storm had blown up ten minutes from Semarang. After two hair-raising attempts at landing, the flight of two Dakotas had decided to return to Batavia. All the way back the wind had followed them and, although the buffeting was lessening, the vibration and misfires from the Dakota's starboard engine was shaking everything inside.

A lull came suddenly and the roar of the weather and straining engines was replaced by soft moaning and retching from the platoon. Sharma felt terrible but as havildar he took his responsibilities seriously. There was, he knew, only one thing that might take the men's minds off their predicament. His throat burned and he had to shout over the worrying, irregular engine warbling. 'Sourav, whose going to bat fifth? Jah or Samonath?'

Several bloodless and utterly miserable faces looked up at him and then at Nehra.

Lance-naik Sourav Nehra, the fastest bowler in the 19th Kumaon and captain of the Third Battalion's cricket First XI, was sitting a few places down from Sharma on the narrow bench seat. He looked up pensively. 'I haven't decided yet, Hav. The Mahratta spinners are pretty good. Actually I'd prefer it if we bat second. Mehboob, pass me a fruit drop will you? A strawberry one.'

One or two of the men nodded in agreement then began to chat among themselves about the upcoming match. Sharma relaxed a little. At home these men would think nothing of walking alone through miles of forest inhabited by tigers, wild boar and cobras, yet the 30-minute roller-coaster-nightmare in the air had turned them, and him, into nervous wrecks.

As the lightning and squalls gave way to drizzle, the men began to recover. Conversation, if any, was about cricket. Most of them were exhausted. Some even managed to doze, including Sharma.

There was a cannon-like backfire from the port engine. Sharma was immediately awake. All talking stopped as they listened in silence to the weak spluttering as the pilot tried to feather the engine back to life. The Dakota dipped. At the same time the starboard engine was given full power to try to compensate. Amidst the engine roar Sharma felt the plane losing height rapidly. Suddenly then the nose pitched forwards forward and the speed surged.

'Oh God!'—'We're going to crash!'—'Lord Vishnu, save us!'

All of them heard the pilot's frantic radio call as he hauled back on the stick. 'Mayday! Mayday! Oscar Niner Bravo engine failure. Attempting emergency landing near Bekassi. Mayday! Mayday! Oscar Niner Bravo...'

Although the Dakota was falling fast it was also starting to respond to the pilot's efforts. The starboard engine had not cut out. Slowly they were pulling out of the dive. Sharma watched view through the cockpit windscreen change from a hypnotic mass of swirling green to treetops and a grey-white horizon.

He grabbed hold of a strut and yelled. 'Brace yourselves! Hold on to something!'

Loud scraping and drumming reverberated in the plane as it brushed branches. 'Hold on!'

A slight rise of the stricken Dakota's nose took it over the southwest corner of a large village. Miraculously it cleared a railway embankment and bounced twice on light scrubland before slewing sideways into a dried-up river bed. It came to a juddering stop.

Sharma untied himself from the webbing and started to help his dazed but apparently uninjured men. Billowing black smoke filled the fuselage. He smelt aviation fuel. 'Quick,' the pilot yelled, 'everybody out before the tanks go up!'

As they scrambled clear they saw the flames were already spreading from behind the engine cowling along one wing. They ran, chests bursting until they were out of danger.

Standing with the RAF crew, Sharma counted his platoon twice then flopped down on his back in relief. 'Lord Vishnu, that was a close one!

'My best bat is in there, Hav,' said one of them sadly.

'Bugger!' Sharma sat up in dismay. 'The scorebook's in my bag.'

'Forget your bloody belongings!' The pilot berated him. 'Be thankful that we're in one piece. Any broken bones?'

Eighteen bruised and bleeding Kumaons shook their heads.

Heat forced them back from the plane. As the flames took hold they stood in a loose semi-circle in quiet contemplation of what might have been.

An engine drone high above started them waving. Heads craned to look for the second Dakota. The pilot, aged about thirty with a thin moustache, was almost cheerful. 'Well, they can't miss this signal fire!'

Smoke was rising, too. The other plane came in low, circled twice then rocked its wings in confirmation. Sharma and the others waved at the faces in the cockpit as it turned west for Batavia.

'Right, then,' said the pilot pointing. 'Batavia's about ten miles that way. Let's start walking. With any luck we'll meet the crash party coming for us. We'll be home for din—' He stared as a hundred or more young Javanese brandishing swords, spears and a few rifles appeared on the earth banks above them.

With wild whoops of triumph the Javanese rushed down the slope towards them. Hemmed in against the burning plane and unarmed apart from a couple of salvaged rifles, the Kumaons were trapped. They looked around in dismay.

Two Indians and one crewman tried to bolt through the lines but they were beaten down mercilessly with staffs and clubs. Sharma spun round, looking for his way to escape. A club struck him on the side of the head. He fell to the ground, unconscious.

A burst of pain in his thigh roused him. He blinked to try and focus but he felt only a pounding ache in his head. Another kick brought him fully awake. Someone was shouting in Malay.

'Get up, pig!'

He tried to curl up to protect himself but found his arms were tied behind his back. Around him the other Kumaons and the RAF crew, all of them now naked, were being pulled to their feet. He saw he, too, had been stripped. Rough hands jerked him up, then a fierce-looking youth came close and spat in his face. Sharma saw the youth was wearing his tunic.

Helpless, the Kumaons and airmen stood in a tight group surrounded by their near-hysterical captors. Anyone who reacted to the ferocious taunts or slaps was beaten.

Finally the Javanese forced them to form a ragged line. Jabs from spears and bayonets prodded them into a shambling walk in the direction of kampong Bekassi.

Sharma estimated they walked for about three miles. He was relieved when he saw the outlying buildings. It meant a rest, perhaps an opportunity to escape. His feet were raw and bleeding but he had decided to take any chance that came.

Bekassi was ready for them. Abusive men, women and children lined the road pelting the prisoners with rubbish, dung and stones. Hundreds of armed youths strutted about self-importantly, leading the chanting.

'*Merdeka!*'—'Indonesia'—'Sukarno!'

Eventually the humiliated captives were led into the walled enclosure of the single-storey Bekassi gaol. To one side of the gate under a carpet of flies lay the bloodied, broken bodies of four men and two women. They passed the corpses in grim silence. Once inside they collapsed in exhausted heaps.

Sharma lay on the packed earth. He was streaked with human and dog excrement. Gashes and bruises dotted his body. All he wanted to do was sleep.

Drumming woke Sharma. It was very early morning and armed youths were among them, shouting and kicking their prisoners to stand. He tried to move but he had lost all feeling in his hands. His throat was parched. Nehra was lying on his front next to him with his eyes closed. With alarm Sharma looked at the discoloured, bloodless hands and knew his own would be just as bad. He risked a whisper. 'Sourav, can you get up?'

Nehra managed to open his right eye. His left was badly swollen from a stone cut. He nodded weakly.

'We'll have to make a run for it,' said Sharma. 'If we stay here we're dead.'

Nehra tried to move and grimaced in pain. 'I can't feel my hands.'

A guard bellowed above them. Sharma gasped for breath as a foot slammed into his stomach. Nehra shrieked in agony as he was pulled to his feet by the ropes around his wrists.

'Water, please,' Sharma pleaded. The youths looked at him with bland indifference then laughed. Sharma looked around him in desperation. Across the courtyard he saw a young Chinese woman in another cell. Their eyes met and she looked at him with such deep compassion that a chill of foreboding ran through him.

A sharp jab in his thigh from a bamboo spear urged him on. Once again they were forced to march. Nehra walked with Sharma at the back of the line. 'Hav, there are no villagers around.' he croaked through his parched lips.

Sharma saw it was true. They were the only people on the streets. After several minutes they came to a large clearing by a steep section of the river bank. Several hundred youths stood waiting and jeering. Among them were clusters of frightened Chinese who were being forced to watch the proceedings.

In the centre of the clearing stood three powerfully built men wearing only loincloths. They held straight-bladed swords about two feet long. Four blood-covered corpses lay nearby. Sharma's last, already faint hope that it was all an attempt to intimidate them vanished. Bile rose to the back of his throat. He swallowed forcibly.

A man in his early twenties with long, coiled hair and wearing the uniform trousers and leather boots of a Japanese officer walked into the centre of the clearing. He carried a Japanese pistol. Chanting began.

'Merdeka!'—'Sarel!'—*'Merdeka!'*

Sarel called for quiet then spoke rapidly to the crowd. His occasional looks at the prisoners were disparaging. More than once the audience laughed as he made sarcastic comments. Few of the Chinese laughed. Then, at last, Sarel turned to face the Kumaons and the airmen. He paused before speaking in slow, accented English.

'We are the Black Buffalos and *pemuda* battalions, defenders of Free Indonesia. You are enemies of the Republic.'

He pointed at the men in loincloths. 'Your punishment is death at the hands of the loyal slaughtermen of Bekassi!'

'But that's not true!' Sharma heard the anguish in the voice of the pilot. 'We're not here to—' There was a sudden silence as he was knocked cold by a vicious blow to the head from a rifle butt. Cheers ran through the watching mob.

Sarel smiled coldly at the four naked white men. 'RAF bombs burn our rice. You move troops and weapons to help the Dutch, our enemies. It is very simple. Your guilt is beyond doubt.' He turned then to address the Kumaons. 'But I am sorry to see our misguided Asian brothers helping the heretic white imperialists… We offer you a chance to live. Water and food await any Muslim who will join us, and denounce the British and Dutch!' He scanned the Kumaons slowly. Not a man moved or spoke.

Sarel shrugged as if expecting the outcome. 'As God wills….' he said quietly. At his signal the first three Kumaons were prodded forward. Sharma tensed when he saw Nehra among them. Nehra struggled defiantly but two of the youths quickly clubbed him into a dazed submission, forcing him to kneel facing the other Indians. Two guards each placed a foot behind one of his knees as they cut his bonds, then pulled his arms out to his sides. Nehra grimaced in pain as the circulation returned to his hands.

His fellow Kumaons shouted indignation and disbelief. Irate, Sharma took a step forward. A rifle muzzle was thrust in his face by an eager, gloating guard. Sharma could see that the youth would have no hesitation in pulling the trigger. Reluctantly he backed off, still glaring.

A drum began to beat as the three stern-faced butchers took their positions behind their victims. The man behind Nehra was stocky and bald. Sharma watched him grasp the hilt of the two-foot long straight blade with both hands and hold it point down an inch above Nehra's left shoulder.

Nehra, too, sensed the moment had come. He appeared to tense, then spat heavily and contemptuously towards Sarel. Eyes closed, Nehra bellowed the traditional Kumaon battle cry. *'Nizam Asaf Jah ki jai!'*—Victory to Nizam Asaf! It echoed over the river as the blade plunged into the triangle of soft flesh behind his collar bone and down into his heart.

'Merdeka!' Great roars from the Buffalos and *pemuda* drowned the gasps of horror from the prisoners who watched the executioner withdraw the blade and raise it high above his head in triumph. Thick blood bubbled up from the wound. Nehra's head sank limply on to his chest.

Two youths ran forward with cleavers and hacked off Nehra's arms. His body pitched forward, legs jerking sporadically. Another *pemuda* came forward and hacked off Nehra's head, tossing it contemptuously down the river bank.

One by one the Indians died until the earth in the centre of the clearing was churned red under the feet of the blood-splattered slaughtermen.

Standing in a slowly diminishing huddle, the Kumaons honoured their doomed comrades, shouting their names. Yet each chorus was weaker than the one before it.

Tears of rage and pride filled Sharma's eyes. Fifteen times he watched the blade fall and the mutilation that followed. Not one of the Kumaons had faltered or pleaded for mercy. And each time Sharma made a point of scowling at the Buffalo guard nearest him.

Finally it was his turn. His mouth was parched and he felt embarrassed because he knew he would not be able to spit like Nehra. What courage his friend had shown! Beside him the last two of his men wore blank, numbed expressions. They said their farewells.

Sharma glanced at the RAF crew who stood or knelt with pale, hollow expressions. Most of them were mouthing their own prayers. Clearly the Buffalos were saving them for last.

He straightened and nodded to the airmen. 'May your God go with you,' he called softly but did not notice if they heard him. He was turning away when he saw a young girl on the other side of the river. She was in her mid-teens and holding a water jar. Sharma thought of his own daughter whom he had not seen for three years. They would be about the same age. She stood staring at the pile of butchered corpses, transfixed.

Some of the youths saw the girl and began rushing across the sturdy, multi-piled bridge over the river. Sharma willed her to run. Too late she dropped the jar and bolted. When they seized her Sharma's rage returned. With it came the taste of saliva.

As the Buffalo guard prodded him forward Sharma whirled. His grin was manic. Surprised, the guard took an uncertain step backwards. 'I am Arman Sharma of Hyderabad,' he raged, 'havildar in the 19th Kumaon! Who are you, you worthless, cowardly little shit? You're not fit to wipe the arses of those warriors!'

His guard did not understand the torrent of foreign words but the contempt and fury in the voice was clear. His rifle came up ready.

Sharma laughed shrilly, baiting the youth one last time. 'Fuck Sukarno!' Then he charged. '*Nizam Asaf Jah—*'

The shot boomed over the river, echoing off the opposite bank, silencing the mob.

Surabaya

Two large Plexiglas, gun blisters on the Catalina-PBY flying-boat gave Henssen a wonderful view over a familiar, bustling central Surabaya. To his amazement there were cars, carts and bicycles in the bustling streets. Unlike Batavia, wartime camouflage had already been removed from the roofs of buildings and people were seated at tables on café terraces or sitting in parks. Small crowds stood outside cinemas and work crews were out repairing roads. It seemed the city was fast returning to its pre-war normality.

Encouraged, Henssen directed the pilot to circle over the harbour and naval base at Tandjong Perak. There was little obvious damage to the infrastructure of the shipyards, quays, submarine docks and warehouses. He smiled, glad now that Java had been spared Allied bombing. It meant his mission would be so much easier.

His eyes raked over the Japanese vessels in the harbour as he jotted down types and numbers. Here he was disappointed. A fire-gutted destroyer sat in dry dock. There were also two submarines but even from the air these showed crippling damage from depth-charge attacks. Other craft were mainly small torpedo boats and river patrol launches. Only a Hasutaka class minelayer, anchored out in the roadstead, appeared serviceable. Henssen had an idea. If the minelayer were seaworthy she might be used to ferry Dutch reinforcements over from New Guinea.... He made a note to suggest it in his first report to Admiral Hurwitz.

The Catalina's engines changed pitch as it banked to begin its final approach. As they descended, Henssen noticed at least ten Japanese Navy reconnaissance planes as well as three large transports lined up at Morokrembangan airfield. He scribbled more notes.

A rising-sun flag fluttered atop the airfield flagpole. Henssen frowned. 'We'll see about that...' he said under his breath. Several Dutch flags were packed in his luggage.

The flying boat came in low over a few brightly coloured fishing boats. Red and white nationalist flags flew from their sterns. Henssen did not see the fishermen making obscene gestures in response to the Dutch markings. On the calm water the Catalina skipped just twice, then settled in the gentle swell of the landing dock.

'There's a reception committee,' the pilot called out with evident relief. He had been far from keen to fly over the city.

Through one of the portholes Henssen saw a line of Japanese marines drawn up near the jetty. 'Yes, they were advised I was coming,' he said casually, enjoying the emphasis he put on the 'I.'

A neat, young Japanese captain greeted him with a crisp salute as he stepped off the jetty. 'Captain Henssen?'

Henssen nodded, paused, then saluted in return. The Japanese continued in slow but precise English. 'My name is Saito. Welcome to Surabaya.'

'Thank you, Captain,' he said casually. 'Actually, I know the city well. I have a house here.'

Saito nodded. 'Yes, 15 Weltgarten.'

Henssen tried to hide his surprise. Then he realised that the Japanese had had over three years to examine the files abandoned in 1942. They would know everything about the Surabaya base and its officers, including the fact that he was actually a Naval Reserve officer with a wartime promotion. He wondered if that would lose him status in dealing with Admiral Shimizu. No, he decided quickly. He was still SEAC's representative…

'I'm sure the house is in very good repair, and my car too,' he replied easily. He introduced his companions. 'These are my aides, lieutenants Vlek and Croeuf.'

Saito's face remained expressionless but he saluted again and led the three men towards a gleaming, white Mercedes 290 Mannheim cabriolet. 'Admiral Shimizu is expecting you.'

Henssen stopped. 'First, I'd like to take a tour of the naval base.'

Saito checked momentarily and looked at his watch and frowned. 'I think you should first see Admiral Shimizu. Today he is—'

'I think you forget, Captain,' Henssen said firmly. 'I am the chief Allied officer in Surabaya. I will decide when I see your Admiral.'

Saito swallowed his objection and issued new instructions to the driver.

Henssen switched on the light in his hotel suite, closed the door, threw his attaché case on the bed then kicked at a rattan chair, sending it sliding across the floorboards. 'Bloody hell!'

When he had eventually arrived at Second Expeditionary Fleet HQ, he was informed by a polite but less than sympathetic aide that Admiral Shimizu had just left Surabaya to visit naval personnel in Bali and would be back the next day. The Admiral had been expecting his visitor to arrive much earlier and had delayed as long as possible. Henssen had seethed in silent humiliation through a very uncomfortable dinner, convinced that everyone—including Vlek and Croeuf—was laughing at him.

A few minutes later there was a knock on his door. He opened it to find an anxious-looking Vlek.

'Captain,' said Vlek uneasily, 'there's a demonstration gathering. Word about us has got round!'

'Demonstration?' Henssen opened the windows to his balcony and heard shouts. 'Freedom or Death!'—'Indonesia Raya!'

On the street below him about fifty young Indonesians faced a line of Japanese marines guarding the hotel. The scene did nothing for Henssen's foul mood.

That night the Dutchmen's sleep was disturbed several times by bursts of gunfire. Henssen decided he would complain to Admiral Shimizu most strongly about his lax interpretation of Allied instructions.

Henssen filled his time before Shimizu's return by demanding detailed inventories of arms and equipment from the Japanese army and navy representatives assigned to assist him. He ordered the canals swept for mines and inspected the barracks that would house Allied troops. He also visited his own house to check for damage. Three Japanese officers were living there, one of whom was Saito. He took great pleasure in giving them twenty-four hours to find alternative accommodation.

Yet Surabaya made him feel uneasy. He travelled in a Japanese staff car with an escort of marines because Saito told him bluntly that if he were unescorted he would be killed. From the car he saw the bands of armed youths on street corners often jeering at Dutch civilians trying to buy food. Despite Saito's objections he insisted on stopping to intervene when an elderly woman was being jostled at a stall. It had been a mistake, for the sight of his uniform turned a few abusive youths into a potentially riotous mob. Saito had only managed to diffuse the situation by whisking the angry but chastened Henssen away from the market.

Later the Japanese took him to the Return of Allied Prisoner of War and Internees office that had been set up a week earlier. To his astonishment there was just one Javanese policeman on duty outside and the door was wide open. British and Indonesian flags stood side by side at the entrance. Henssen fumed silently. Inside he found two junior British RAPWI officers discussing civilian evacuation plans with the town's new republican mayor. There followed an awkward few minutes. Henssen's resentment was plain and the mayor soon left. The British were polite but visibly uncomfortable over his presence. Henssen's resentment soared.

For a second night there was gunfire and a much larger demonstration outside the hotel. The Dutchmen's shutters were pelted with stones. None of them slept.

Japanese Naval HQ, Surabaya

'I hear you have been busy, Captain Henssen,' Admiral Shimizu said genially. He was a short, stocky man in his late fifties with cropped, grey hair, a rather bulbous nose and thin lips. His dark dress uniform had a Prussian collar that seemed too tight and which emphasised his round features.

Henssen had read the man's file. Shimizu was a much-travelled, well-read and popular officer. He was also fluent in English after years of international liaison duties. As the Commander of the Second Southern Expeditionary Fleet and the senior Japanese naval officer in the Indies, he was the big fish for the Dutch navy. Two weeks earlier he had been flown to Singapore to witness the surrender of the Tenth Area Fleet and the Japanese Fifth Area Army to Lord Mountbatten. Hurwitz had wanted him in custody. Mountbatten had allowed him to return to Surabaya.

Shimizu introduced another officer. 'This is Rear-Admiral Ishida, my representative in Djakarta.'

Henssen gave Ishida a firm look. 'I think you mean Batavia'. Dutch Naval Intelligence were eager to question Ishida. If he could deliver him it would be another feather in his cap.

Maeda bowed but said nothing.

Shimizu gestured for Henssen to sit but he had prepared his speech and wasted no time. 'Admiral, your absence was unexpected. I would appreciate it if you would keep me informed of your movements.'

'Yes indeed, Captain Saito told me of the unfortunate miscommunication over my schedule.'

Henssen bristled slightly and went on. 'There is considerable disorder in the town. Groups of armed Javans are roaming around at will, Dutch civilians are insulted and assaulted daily, rebel flags fly on municipal buildings, and rebel news-sheets are sold openly. This is not acceptable. SEAC instructions state—'

'Two things, Captain...', Shimizu sighed, sitting down heavily. 'First, until two weeks ago there was no disorder because there were no Dutch here. Now there are over five thousand. I don't know why they are coming here. They have put enormous pressure on limited food supplies and accommodation. Second, the day before yesterday, sixty of my men were murdered by nationalists in Denpasar.'

Henssen's disturbed night suddenly took on a different perspective. He could scarcely believe his ears. 'In Bali?'

'Yes, in peaceful, gentle Bali...' Shimizu said dryly. 'The situation is extremely tense. Surabaya, in contrast, is fairly calm. Even so, last night I lost four men who tried to prevent a mob from taking their weapons. You will understand me when I say that minor assaults, flags and news-sheets are not my biggest problems.'

Henssen tried to recover his poise but knew that he was already at a disadvantage. Shimizu turned the screw.

'Where I can assist you, Captain, I will, even with my limited resources. But I must remind you that as long as I am not a prisoner of war, I will continue to uphold the responsibilities of an admiral in the Imperial Japanese Navy and the associated responsibilities to my officers and men. No doubt, you see the situation in these islands differently to me. Surely, though, we can agree that it is not as it was in early 1942?'

Henssen nodded warily. 'I agree there is some tension.'

'Tension created by SEAC's orders that we Japanese use force to prevent Indonesians obtaining weapons. Now that you have arrived and the arrival of Allied troops is imminent, I hope to reduce tension by removing most of my men some kilometres inland. This will also free some accommodation for Allied troops.'

'That seems logical,' Henssen replied carefully, aware that Shimizu was getting ahead of him. He took out a sheet of paper from his briefcase and handed it over the desk to Shimizu. 'These are to be given priority.'

Shimizu read through the list quickly. Henssen was asking for a transport plane and crew to be put at his disposal twenty-four hours a day, daily minesweeping of the channels into Surabaya, that barracks be prepared for Allied troops, that Japanese troops serve as porters in the docks, and that weapons be confiscated from all Indonesian civilians.

Shimizu passed the list to Ishida then looked at Henssen. 'A plane will be made ready immediately. Minesweeping will be difficult—'

'I fail to see why,' Henssen interrupted. 'You have ships,'

'But no captains. They have been kidnapped.'

Henssen did not mask his surprise. Shimizu continued with a hint of irritation in his voice. 'The Indonesian commanders have not been idle, Captain. If sweeping begins the hostages will be killed.'

'That is not my concern, Sir. The ships must go to work whatever the consequences. The risk to your men is unfortunate but unavoidable under the circumstances. You must draw a line.'

'I understand.' Shimizu said resignedly. Neither his nor Ishida's face registered any emotion.

'Please keep me informed of progress.' Henssen saluted casually and left.

Shimizu shook his head. 'Why didn't the British send a Royal Navy officer after I reported the anti-Dutch feeling?'

Ishida shrugged. 'That one's only interested in appearances.'

'Yes, the sooner we are out of here the better.'

'Your plan is working,' Ishida added. 'Our losses are unfortunate.'

Shimizu frowned. 'Where was last night's attack?'

'Near the Marine School. The platoon requested permission to return fire three times. It was denied. The four men were dead by the time our reinforcements arrived.'

'And the others?'

'They were beaten and their rifles, ammunition and bayonets were taken. Later the Base Force's armoury was besieged for a short time. There were no injuries there.'

Shimizu took a cigarette from a red and black lacquered box then pushed the box over to Ishida. The two men smoked in pensive silence until Shimizu stood and began pacing.

'This cannot go on,' he said wearily. 'Henssen will have us mixed up in a civil war. If we use force the Indonesians they will hate us for centuries! I will not be responsible for that, even though it means disobeying a direct order. Now I am merely a defeated commander. If I must lose what little honour I have left to preserve peace, then so be it. Our men ceased hostilities for the sake of the Emperor. I will not send them to fight on the whim of a Dutch naval reserve captain!'

'It will mean imprisonment,' Ishida said quietly.

Shimizu raised his eyebrows and half smiled. 'I suspect the Dutch have more permanent plans for us both.'

'Yes, indeed,' laughed Ishida. 'I sometimes forget we are already judged.'

'Even so, you must return to Djakarta. There's no need for you to be associated with what happens here. You have done more than enough.'

'I expect to be arrested as soon as I return.'

Shimizu nodded and paused, thinking. 'Turn yourself in to Admiral Patterson himself. If he sends you to Singapore then that might keep you out of Dutch hands...for a while at least.'

'And you, Admiral?'

'I must work on Henssen,' Shimizu frowned. 'He may yet solve our problem for us. If our men are no longer armed then the Indonesians will have no reason to attack them.'

'But that would mean a formal surrender?'

'Yes. Somehow I must force Henssen to act.'

'But surrender has to be to the British.'

'That's what's chafing at him. Perhaps with a little encouragement....'

'The British will be furious.'

Shimizu's lips formed a thin smile. 'Yes, they will. But that will not be our problem.'

Ishida stepped forward and bowed. 'Admiral it has been an honour to serve on your staff.'

Shimizu stood and bowed back with equal formality. 'Thank you. I could not have asked for a more loyal officer. Good luck!'

As the door closed, Shimizu reached for another cigarette. After a while he rang for his aide.

Saito entered. 'Admiral?'

'Ask the Chief of Police, the Mayor and the militia commander if they can join me for dinner this evening,' Shimizu's voice was business-like once more.

Bekassi

Major Clive Roberts took a long drink from his canteen and looked around in frustration at the blackened shell of the Dakota. Clearly whoever had been here was long gone. The only trace of the missing crew and passengers were a few pages torn from army pay books. He wiped the perspiration off his forehead and summoned his havildar. 'Raina, that's enough. We'll rejoin the rest of the column and swing over to the kampong.'

'Yes, Major,' said Raina resignedly and went off to call in the still searching soldiers.

Two days earlier a small search party had found the wreckage of the C-47 but they had been forced to withdraw by a large, hostile crowd. This time Roberts had brought with him a Stuart tank, two armoured cars and nearly two hundred troops. Their search took time and it was midday before the column reached the outskirts of the deserted kampong. Packs of aggressive, hungry dogs roamed the streets.

Roberts set up his HQ in the main square and was about to order a house-to-house search when news came that a patrol had found prisoners in the gaol.

'There are six Chinese and four others, Major,' said Singh, a captain in the Patalia Regiment. 'One of the Javans speaks some Malay. She says she saw our men.'

'Right,' Roberts nodded. 'Fetch Gupta to interpret. His Malay's good after all that trading in Penang.'

In the gaol's office, the girl sat fidgeting across a plain wooden table from Roberts and Gupta. Captain Singh stood to one side.

'She's Ambonese, Sir,' explained Gupta. 'Her father was a teacher here.'

'Where is he?'

The girl's head lowered as she replied.

'She doesn't know. The Japs sent him to Malaya as *romusha*, a labourer.'

'What about our men?'

Gupta smiled at the girl to try and put her at ease. Eventually she began to speak, hesitantly at first and then at speed. Tears ran down her cheeks.

Roberts could see Gupta was shocked. 'Well?'

'They were all killed…Black Buffalos—revolutionaries— chopped off their heads, arms and legs, then buried them along the river bank. She says the soldiers were very brave…'

'Did she witness it or just hear?' Roberts's face was grave. 'I must know!'

Gupta questioned the girl again. 'She went to get water. The Buffalos saw her but she was too frightened to run. They made her watch and afterwards brought her here. They were going to kill her and the others today but fled when they heard we were approaching.'

Roberts looked carefully at the girl. 'Ask her how many Black Buffalos and youths?'

She replied very quickly.

Gupta eyebrows rose. 'About two thousand!'

Roberts exchanged a concerned look with Captain Singh.

'Can she show us where it happened?' Roberts asked quietly.

This time Gupta had difficulty in keeping up. 'She says she will take us to the spot if we will take her to Batavia with us.'

'Ask her if she'll come out here with us tomorrow.'

The girl nodded and Roberts turned to Singh. 'We're sitting ducks for snipers here, so we'll go back to Batavia. Free the other prisoners. They can come back with us if they wish. And Gupta, don't take your eyes off this girl for a second.'

Ten minutes into the dig the Mahratta volunteers unearthed the first evidence of the slaughter. A severed arm was soon followed by a head and a maggot-ridden torso. As the stench of rotting flesh rose up from the river bank Roberts indicated to the Ambonese girl that she could leave the scene. She walked back to the tanks, armoured cars and lorries that ringed the clearing.

The Mahrattas retched as they dug but they did not stop work. Other volunteers—Patalias, RAF, cavalry, engineers and ambulance crews—waited with petrol-soaked cloths over their noses and mouths to take a turn. No-one lasted very long.

'Croc shot!' At the alert men stopped digging and turned. Every few minutes RAF Regiment sentries fired at one of the large, lurking crocodiles attracted by the odour of decay. Their death rolls churned the river water red and sent other crocodiles into a frenzy.

After four and a half hours a gruesome display of exhumed heads, torsos and limbs was laid out along the top of the river bank. Two army doctors and five medical orderlies struggled to piece together the puzzles of blackened flesh and bone.

A wan-faced Captain Singh climbed up the bank and went to report to Roberts who was standing amidst the bodies with Captain Patel, a doctor. 'Excuse me, Major,' Singh said quietly, 'We're down quite deep and wide now but we've found nothing for the last twenty minutes. I think this is all we're going to get.'

Roberts nodded wearily, his own face pale and drawn. 'Doc, what's the tally now?'

Patel referred to his clip board. 'Twenty-two heads and nineteen torsos... The girl said that three or four Chinese had also been killed, so in fact we don't know how many there were to start with, or even if they were buried here. At the moment we are missing roughly four heads, six torsos, eight arms and nine legs.'

'The crocs and lizards will have had some of them,' suggested Singh.

Roberts spat to try to clear the cloying smell of decay from his mouth. 'I don't suppose there's any chance of making an identification?'

Patel shook his head. 'They've been dead for days. With the mutilation, the heat and the humidity, putrefaction is extremely quick. We can't even tell the Indians from the Europeans. I'm sorry.'

'Don't apologise, Doc,' Roberts replied heavily. 'This is above and beyond the call…. I'd intended to bury the British and cremate the Indians but now I think they should all be cremated together and the ashes collected.'

'Fire it!' Roberts shouted, his voice barely concealing his rage. Petrol torches burst into flame. Quickly and purposefully the teams dispersed outwards from the central square. They moved methodically, street by street, house by house. There was to be no looting. Only the Chinese Quarter was to be spared.

Darkness was falling before the column started on the short but hazardous return journey to Batavia. Behind them the night sky reflected an angry red. Bekassi was burning.

Surabaya

Henssen's hotel-room phone rang just after six o'clock in the morning. He reached for it groggily but came sharply awake when he detected the tension in Saito's voice.

'Captain Henssen, Admiral Shimizu would like you to come to the base at once. There is a problem. The Mayor is also here and the chief of police. We have sent a car for you.'

'What sort of problem?' Henssen could hear drums and shouting in the background. He swung his legs over the edge of the bed and stood up.

Saito hesitated. 'Protestors have surrounded the armoury. They are demanding the weapons. We are trying to reason with them but there are too many!'

'How many?'

'Thousands….'

Henssen was alarmed. The armoury contained thousands of rifles, hundreds of machine guns, and well over a million rounds of ammunition. If it fell into nationalist it would be disastrous. Worse, he would fail in his mission… Shimizu was going to ruin everything! 'The Admiral has his orders from SEAC', Henssen barked. 'Civilians must not be allowed to obtain weapons. If necessary, Japanese troops are to open fire,' he barked.

There was silence at the other end of the line. Henssen's patience snapped. 'Saito, do you hear me? Where is Admiral Shimizu?' Again there was no answer. Henssen swore under his breath. 'Shit!'

'This is Shimizu.' The voice was calm.

'Admiral, SEAC orders require you to—'

'I know my orders, Captain. I am trying to follow them. The situation is extremely volatile. I have sent a car.'

'You are authorised to open fire.'

Shimizu did not reply and seconds passed. 'Admiral, I said you are authorised to open fire.'

'Your authorisation is noted, Captain.'

Henssen's knuckles showed white around the receiver. He was convinced Shimizu was toying with him. 'Admiral, will you give the order to open fire or not?'

The line clicked once, then went dead.

Henssen rushed out of the hotel lobby with Vlek and Croeuf trailing in his wake. He saw the waiting car and driver and got straight in the back. Only when two uniformed Javanese sat on either side of him did he realise it was a police car. Before he could protest a third policeman jumped in the front passenger seat and the car drove off.

Henssen glanced behind to see Vlek and Croeuf standing dumbfounded on the hotel steps staring after him. There was no sign of the usual marine escort car. When he turned back he saw the red and white pennant at the front of the car. Idiot! he thought. You've let them kidnap you! Suddenly he was feeling very uncomfortable.

Eventually the policeman in the passenger seat shifted round to face him, resting his arm along the back of the seat. He was about thirty-five, with the typical light, wiry frame of the Javanese. No emotion showed on his thin face or in his eyes. His tone was terse. 'Captain Henssen, I understand you speak Javanese fluently?'

Henssen replied that he did.

'I am Superintendent Shafan. The Chief of Police sent me. He did not think the demonstrators would allow a Japanese military vehicle to pass.'

'I see,' said Henssen carefully. 'How did the demonstration start?'

Shafan's hand lifted casually. 'Ha! It doesn't take much to start a riot in Surabaya these days. But the people don't like seeing the Japanese still in charge.'

Henssen bristled slightly. 'The Japanese are not in charge. They are just following orders until Allied troops arrive.'

'I know that, of course,' Shafan nodded diplomatically. 'But the people don't understand what's going on. They just want all foreigners to leave.'

Henssen let the inference pass and they travelled in silence. At the base guard posts were unmanned and the gate was wide open. Two cars blocked the entrance. Around it milled hundreds of young Javanese, many armed with staves or swords.

Forced to slow down, the police driver began pounding his horn. To Henssen's surprise the crowds parted.

'How did they get inside?' Henssen asked sarcastically.

Shafan kept his eyes on the demonstrators. 'I've no idea. Captain, please sit back. It's better that they don't see you.'

Once they were through the gates, the crowds thinned out and the car headed for the administration buildings. There were a few civilians outside but they were keeping their distance from a line of Japanese marines drawn up with fixed bayonets across the steps to the main entrance. A small group of armed police stood to one side. Thunderous chants emanated from near the armoury.

Henssen was ushered quickly into a meeting room. Inside, seated at a round conference table were Shimizu, a Japanese interpreter, and four Indonesians. Henssen had met Tabarano, the Chief of Police and Suwosa, the recently appointed republican mayor. The police were at best ambivalent about Allied authority but generally co-operative. Henssen felt insulted by Suwosa's presence. The other two Indonesians were militiamen, barely in their twenties but wearing the rank badges of a major and a colonel. Flushed with self-righteous revolutionary fervour, the young Colonel was haranguing Shimizu.

'If you refuse, we shall be forced to attack. Why risk your men's lives over a few guns?'

'But the guns are not yours,' replied Shimizu evenly, evidently not for the first time.

The Colonel began to shout. 'They must be given to the Republic. How can you deny us?'

Shimizu looked weary and seemed relieved to see Henssen. 'Thank you for coming, Captain,' he said politely. 'You have met Mayor Suwosa and Chief Tabarano. Let me introduce Colonel Barata and Major Malik.'

Henssen gave the two men a curt nod. They stared back balefully. Shimizu continued. 'As you see, we face a dilemma.'

'Yes, you do, Admiral.' Henssen said quietly, letting the words hang. 'How do you intend to resolve it?'

'Somehow I hope to calm the Indonesians. They hold several dozens of my men hostage around the base. I have some armed men guarding the armoury itself but they are exhausted, surrounded and greatly outnumbered.'

The two militia men, who did not speak English, looked suspiciously at Henssen who ignored them.

'Admiral, will you give the order to open fire?'

Shimizu's expression hardened. He shook his head. 'No. I am concerned that to do so might constitute a breach of the agreement made at Rangoon between General Browning and General Numata on behalf of Field Marshal Terauchi. Until I have confirmation from Tokyo—'

'Tokyo?' Henssen interrupted frostily. 'Admiral, I am the senior Allied representative in Surabaya. As you well know, Lord Mountbatten has ordered your forces to maintain law and order and that the use of force is permitted. If you fail to—'

'Captain, Admiral, please...' Suwosa said standing up with a smile and gesturing to an empty chair at the table. 'Sit with us. No-one wants bloodshed, either Indonesian or Japanese.' He switched to Javanese. 'We are here to search for a peaceful solution. I am confident we can find one.'

Henssen shot a glance at the middle-aged police chief ,wondering if he would dare challenge the mob. He turned and replied in Javanese. 'Chief Tabarano, do you intend to restore order here? Civilians should not be on this base.'

The young militia colonel slammed his fist on the table. 'The Peoples' Defence Force are not civilians!'

Tabarano ran his fingers nervously over his thin moustache. 'The powers of civilian authorities are limited in an unusual situation like this, Captain.'

Suwosa cleared his throat. 'Gentlemen, this is getting us nowhere. It seems to me that the dispute is over the nominal ownership of the weapons in the armoury. Colonel Barata, understandably, objects to the Japanese keeping them. What if the ownership changed and they became the property of the Allies?'

Henssen's eyes narrowed. 'Of the Allies?'

'Yes,' Suwosa smiled. 'The Admiral could sign them over to you.'

Henssen's thoughts began to race. Was this his chance? Could he present the British with a fait accompli? A surrender to Dutch forces—to him! 'That could only happen after Admiral Shimizu's formal surrender of the base,' he said in measured tones. 'That depends on the Admiral. If he were to refuse a direct Allied order then I would be forced to insist on his immediate surrender, and that of his men. They would become prisoners-of-war. At that point the base and armoury would pass to Allied control under my authority.'

Shimizu's interpreter was racing to keep up. The Admiral sat bolt upright in his chair and scoffed. 'What! Me? Surrender to a Reserve Captain? Ridiculous!'

Henssen reddened but ignored him. 'If it is acceptable to Chief Tabarano, I am prepared to agree to he and I having joint custody of the weapons until Allied troops arrive.'

Shimizu glared but the Javanese began to debate. The Colonel and Major seemed reluctant but Suwosa pressed them until they acquiesced. All eyes were on Henssen and Shimizu.

The Dutchman stood. 'For the last time, Admiral, as the senior Allied officer in Surabaya I order you to disperse the demonstrators by force. Will you carry out the order, yes or no?'

Shimizu stared down at the table. 'No.'

'Very well, you leave me no choice,' Henssen said stiffly. 'You and your men must now consider yourselves my prisoners.'

Shimizu stood slowly. 'Very well, Captain, I accept.' He reached down for the blue-black, polished shagreen scabbard of his sword.

Henssen shook his head. 'Not here, Admiral. This must be done publicly.'

Thirty minutes later two hundred armed Japanese marines had formed ranks in the middle of the parade ground. Henssen, Suwosa and Tabarano flanked by about thirty policemen stood beside the table upon which Shimizu would sign the surrender. Vlek and Croeuf who had finally arrived in another police car were smiling in quiet satisfaction.

Suwosa had calmed the demonstrators by summoning the leaders to Shimizu's office. News spread quickly and the crowd around the parade ground was chanting jubilantly.

Henssen was feeling increasingly confident. His most anxious moment had been when a police contingent took over from the marines at the armoury. Yet nothing happened. The atmosphere even became relaxed and good-humoured.

Slowly, Henssen started to enjoy himself. He straightened as a Javanese reporter came forward to take a photograph with Vlek's camera.

'This will look good printed in *Trouw*, eh, Captain,' Croeuf joked.

Henssen allowed himself a smile at the thought of his photograph in the newspaper, and of his reward.

Shimizu appeared at the head of a group of junior officers. The Japanese marines snapped to attention. Shimizu alone had changed into a dark blue, full-dress uniform. Henssen thought he looked suitably tired and weak, his assurance lost in defeat. A quiet settled over the crowd as Shimizu stopped in front of Henssen and saluted.

Henssen read his speech. '...And now I call upon Rear-Admiral Shimizu, Commander-in-chief of the Second

Expeditionary Force, Southern Regions, to come forward and sign the instrument of surrender.'

Shimizu approached and bowed, then signed. Slowly and deliberately he unclipped his sword and laid it down across the table then backed away. One by one, his officers did the same. On command, the Japanese marines marched smartly off the parade ground, stacking their weapons neatly in front of the armoury.

Beside Henssen, Suwosa and Tabarano applauded.

Henssen was giving an impromptu press conference to some Surabaya journalists when the '*Merdeka!*' chanting started again. He ignored it until Vlek's shout.

'Captain! They are taking the guns! The police have gone!'

Henssen whirled on Suwosa and Tabarano. 'The weapons are Allied property,' he gasped. 'You witnessed the surrender. We agreed!'

Tabarano looked uncomfortable but Suwosa gave him a condescending smile. 'Yes, we agreed. But apparently the citizens of Surabaya did not.'

Speechless and suddenly pale, Henssen walked towards the armoury. A long, winding line of young men and youths brandishing rifles and boxes of ammunition passed him, heading out of the base. He watched helplessly with Vlek and Croeuf as the armoury emptied before his eyes.

Rage gripped him. Shimizu! At least he would have the Admiral in custody. He stormed back to the parade ground to find Suwosa talking with Colonel Barata and Shimizu. Henssen could not help noticing Shimizu's suddenly relaxed attitude or that Barata held the Admiral's sword. The three men paused as Henssen approached.

'Admiral Shimizu, you will come with me,' Henssen said firmly.

Shimizu looked at him almost pityingly. 'Captain, surely you realise now that the Allies were never in authority here?'

Barata smiled. 'Admiral Shimizu is my prisoner, Captain. As are you and your men.' He raised a hand and half-a-dozen militia levelled their weapons at the stunned Dutchmen. They were quickly seized.

'Your sword, Admiral,' said Barata casually, handing back the weapon. 'Indonesia does not require such trinkets... For the time being, please confine yourself to your house and garden.'

'Thank you, Colonel.' Shimizu bowed to him then faced Henssen. 'Thank you for resolving my dilemma, Captain. My duty was and still is to my men. The personal consequences for me are of no significance whatsoever.' He turned and walked to his waiting limousine.

The full realisation of how he had been duped finally hit Henssen. 'Colonel Barata', he raged, 'this is disgraceful! Release me immediately! Allied soldiers are due here any day!'

Barata shrugged. *'Insh Allah.'*—As God wills. 'Surabaya is ready!'

NICA HQ, Djakarta

Hurwitz was standing next to the wall map. He was fuming. 'Those British bastards want us to lose the Indies!'

Van Zanten seemed unconcerned. 'Of course they do! So do the Americans, the Australians, the Malays, the Indians, even the Chinese. We are not very popular.'

'How can you be so calm when Mountbatten and that biased swine Chrishaw are denying us our own troops?'

Van Zanten smiled. 'Just a few companies of young, inexperienced troops—conscripts for the most part—who have never seen combat. What use would they be?'

'But the British refuse to take action!'

'Patience, Jurgen, policies can change. They have just lost over twenty men at Bekassi. In retaliation they razed the kampong. Understandable but rash. Now more natives will suspect them, even hate them. There will be reprisals and the British will lose more men. They will retaliate and so it will go on.' Van Zanten leaned back in his seat, satisfaction playing on his face. 'Slowly but surely the British are becoming involved. The longer they stay the deeper they dig. It's only a matter of time before they are forced to launch an offensive. It will get very messy, so why risk our men when we have experienced British, Indian and Japanese troops here to fight for us?'

Understanding dawned slowly on Hurwitz's face. 'Then you aren't worried about the delay?'

'For those few companies, no. They are a diversion, just like the internees. We ask for troops to be brought in and for our internees to be evacuated. Delays with both are to our advantage.' Van Zanten's eyes shone. 'Think about it, Jurgen. Those camps are all over Java. The British must try to reach them and protect them. Of course, when they leave we must be ready immediately with our own troops but with divisions not companies. That's why we must encourage the British to move into and hold Surabaya. We need them caught firmly in the web. Talking of which, what has Henssen reported?'

Hurwitz shifted uncomfortably. 'Erm, it's been some days since he last reported.'

Van Zanten fixed him with a stare. 'How many days?

Chapter Eight

Two landing craft left the troopships *Princess Beatrix* and *Pulaxi* at anchor in the bottleneck of the Surabaya Strait. They moved steadily across the estuary of the Kali Mas, the main river of Surabaya. In their wake the ocean churned brown with sediment and waste.

To the right of the river mouth, the imposing concrete wharfs of Tandjong Perak harbour, once the centre of Java's great sugar and coffee trade, stood bare and disused. A Japanese minesweeper was the only large vessel in sight, its flags and guns lowered in deference to the victors.

It was a hazardous journey in to the wharfs. The helmsmen's faces were tense as they threaded the ungainly, noisy craft through the graveyard of mastheads, rusting wires and funnel tops of the sunken ships that clogged their approach. Surabaya itself was hidden from view, lost behind the high roofs of the dockyard sheds and warehouses.

Crammed in the boats, the soldiers of the 4th and 6th battalions of the 5th Mahratta Light Infantry, part of 49th Infantry Brigade, looked beyond the rooftops to the massive, cloud-topped Mount Ardjeono and, in the far distance, the dark, smoking cone of Mount Smeroe. Only when they drew much nearer to the wharfs did they notice the thousands of silent spectators strung out in a blur of red and white.

The Indians sat uneasily, watching their observer pan left and right with his field glasses. His news was not good. 'Two o'clock! HMG on warehouse roof!'

Fifty heads swivelled to look for the heavy machine gun. At that distance it was not visible to the naked eye, yet every one of them knew they would soon be within killing range.

'Steady now, Mahrattas!' Subedar Dada Jadhav's calming voice carried over the chug of the diesels. The men were still, if not reassured.

'Listen to the Sub, Laxi!' Sepoy Ankul Nakish whispered under his breath to the man next to him, Laximan Salunke. 'The sod's only happy when there's a gun pointed at us.'

Salunke nodded grimly. 'I just hope it's not a "warm" welcome.'

With small Union Jacks fluttering at their sterns, the two landing craft continued towards the mass of colour on the wharfs. At one hundred and fifty yards the observer no longer needed his field glasses and he let them hang against his chest. The distinctive silhouette of the machine-gun and its hunched two-man crew was now in full view. The wide, cylindrical barrel panned slowly, following every turn of the leading craft.

Once the boats entered the inner harbour they were less than a hundred yards from the projecting wharf and the soldiers could make out English slogans daubed on the walls of the warehouses:

> *A Government of the People, for the People, by the People! — Indonesia Free! — President Truman, see the Nation State of Indonesia exists!*

To the majority of the Indians they were meaningless. Their British officers did not translate.

Jadhav began readying the men. 'Third and second platoons to disembark first. Check your gear and don't leave any presents for the Rajrifs. You'll only have to buy them back!'

Nervous laughter answered him. The 5th Battalion of the Sixth Rajpurtana Rifle Regiment—or Rajrifs—was waiting on the troopships. It would be next to disembark, provided the Mahrattas landed without opposition.

Nervous fingers tugged at clips and webbing. They were close enough now to count the staves, bamboo spears, rifles and swords carried by many in the still-quiet crowd. Sullen, suspicious faces stared down at the boats. One nervous, twitchy finger, one shot, and a slaughter would begin…

A dull, metallic clang echoed as the bow of the craft scraped against the wharf. Two sailors leapt ashore with bow- and stern-ropes. The Surabayans maintained their silence watching the Mahrattas form ranks on the quay. Within minutes the two landing craft had cast off and begun to retrace their winding course back to the transports.

49th Indian Infantry Brigade HQ, Hotel Michiels, Surabaya

'My name is Moestopo. As mayor and representative of the people of Free Surabaya, I welcome you to our city.'

Moestopo was in his mid-forties, wearing a casual, open-necked white shirt and trousers that contrasted with the militia uniforms of the four youths who had insisted on accompanying him into the hotel. They stood, glaring defiantly, with pistols thrust in their belts

'Thank you very much. I'm Brigadier Allenby.' The British officer was a head taller than the Javanese with aquiline features and a slim, athletic build. He offered his hand.

'The people of Surabaya are not happy to see your men here, Brigadier,' Moestopo said bluntly. 'You were allowed to land only because you are a British force, not Dutch, and because we understand you intend only to evacuate the internees.'

'That is our priority,' Allenby replied crisply. 'I hope you will be able to offer us assistance with transportation from the Darmo camps to the docks.'

Moestopo broke into a smile. 'Of course. I shall give instructions immediately. Tomorrow I will bring a list of the vehicles available.'

'Thank you. In the meantime our medical and ambulance staff will be deploying south of the Ferwerda drawbridge to the Darmo hospital. I assure you our intentions are purely humanitarian.'

'Naturally we are delighted to hear that,' Moestopo nodded eagerly. 'You will understand that our militia will be observing your movements.'

Allenby frowned. 'Very well. But please keep them at a distance. We don't want any misunderstandings.'

'No, of course not.' Moestopo's eyes narrowed suddenly. 'Also, there are rumours of Dutch forces on the ships...' he let the words hang, gauging the reaction.

'That is not true,' Allenby said quickly. 'There are a few Dutch medics, interpreters and logistics staff but that is all.'

'I see,' Moestopo seemed unconvinced. 'Thank you, Brigadier. Until tomorrow.'

Allenby and Colonel Leonard Hughes, his second in command, were studying a large-scale street plan. Prominent on the map was the canalised Kali Mas river which cut Surabaya in two.

'What's our furthest position south on the river, Len?'

'The Rajrifs are on the west bank here,' Hughes pointed. 'Two companies of Mahrattas crossed over to the east bank via the Ferwerda drawbridge an hour ago. No obstruction reported but still a couple of hundred or so armed spectators.'

Allenby was measuring on the map with a pair of dividers. He shook his head. 'Look, it's nearly seven miles from Darmo to the docks. We're going to be badly stretched. We've got twelve-hundred men at best, including medics, and nearly everyone in the town is armed to the teeth!'

Hughes murmured in agreement, 'But it seems quiet enough tonight. I still can't believe that Dutchman let the Japs scuttle away like that and then lost the bloody weapons!'

It had not taken long for 49th Brigade to hear the news of the Japanese surrender and the subsequent looting of the naval armoury.

'HQ should have known about the surrender fiasco days ago,' Allenby said scathingly, pinning small blue flags on the map. 'The Intelligence boys described this as a low-risk evacuation. We've got lightly equipped platoons dotted all over the town. It could get nasty at any moment.'

'Let's hope Moestopo can deliver what he says...' Hughes said gravely.

'Right,' said Allenby, indicating on the map. 'I want strong positions at Ferwerda and the International Bank overlooking the Red Bridge. Those are the two main crossings. Once the convoys leave the hospital at Darmo, the only defendable spot big enough to house several hundred is the Marine School but it's across the river.'

Hughes did some mental arithmetic. 'What about 3rd Field Regiment? Fixed artillery isn't going to be much good to us here. They could provide escorts for the convoys through the town.'

'Yes, we'll base them at Darmo with 71st Field Co., 5th Rajrif and 47th Field Ambulance. At least it'll give the impression of numbers. If there is trouble, we'll have to protect the internees as best we can. The waterworks and electricity sub-station are near Darmo, so it will be good to have the sappers of the 71st close at hand in case of any supply problems.'

'What about here?' Hughes asked, pointing to Morokrembangan airfield.

Allenby rubbed his chin. 'Yes, there's a RAPWI coordinator flying in from Semarang tomorrow morning at ten with some press people on board. Just what we don't need! Get one company of Mahrattas there by nine and secure the area. Leave those two companies at the drawbridge and bank. They stay put no matter what.'

Ferwerda Drawbridge

The luminous hands on Nakish's watch read 8.35 pm. Three minutes had elapsed since the last time he looked. Beside him Salunke yawned, hawked then spat into the dark water of the Kali Mas.

'Ankul, do you see that?' Salunke hissed under his breath.

'What?'

'Down there! It's a body!' Salunke pointed.

Nakish peered for several seconds and then made out a shape. His flashlight illuminated the limp form of a dead mongrel.

Nakish let out a sigh of exasperation. 'For God's sake, Laxi!'

'Sorry,' said Salunke. 'It's getting to me.'

Subedar Jadhav called out from the other end of the bridge. 'What is it?'

'Nothing, Sub, false alarm,' Nakish replied apologetically.

Since sunset few people had crossed the drawbridge yet the town was far from still. There was the frequent noise of cars stopping and starting on nearby roads. The Indians could see nothing but the backs of the buildings abutting the bank of the Kali Mas.

Seconds later headlights flashed and a large saloon turned quickly onto the approach road increasing speed. The driver saw the soldiers late, braked hard, then reversed into a wall. Its engine stalled and the driver fled down an unlit side street.

Half a dozen Mahrattas fanned out around car, a Packard 120. It was crammed with rifles, stick-grenades and boxes of ammunition.

Salunke spoke for them all. 'There have been cars moving around all night. If they're all loaded like this one...'

Subedar Jadhav, nodded. 'Let's get on the radio to HQ.'

Just after eight o'clock the next morning an unexpected aircraft came in low from the north and circled over the town, leaving leaflets swirling in its wake. The four-engine, RAF C-87 Liberator long-range transport had flown directly from Singapore. The soldiers of 49th Infantry Brigade, on duty in the docks, bridges and crossroads, paid it little attention. They had seen plenty of leaflets before....

'What the bloody hell's going on!' Allenby crumpled a leaflet and threw it to the floor. It demanded the immediate surrender of all unauthorised weapons and ammunition in Surabaya within twenty-four hours. Failure to comply would result in forced confiscation.

Hughes sighed. 'God knows. The Psychological Warfare Section operates out of Ceylon. This proclamation must have been authorised days ago. The same as for Batavia and Semarang.'

Allenby shook his head in anger and frustration. 'Too many surprises here, Len. The Javans are jumpy enough as it is. This has put us right on the spot. Get the extra ammo off the ships asap.'

'It's being done but it was loaded in a rush and its under tons of bloody food.'

'God, what a mess! Clear the harbour of locals before it's landed. No need for Moestopo & Co to know what we're up to.'

'Right.'

There was a knock on the door and an aide entered. 'Brigadier, Mr Moestopo to see you. He's alone this time.'

Allenby nodded. 'Send him in.'

Moestopo almost fell into the room. He was clutching one of the leaflets. 'Brigadier,' he panted, 'what is the meaning of this?'

Allenby sat back and opened his hands calmly. 'All Japanese arms in Java must be surrendered to British forces. These leaflets have been authorised by Lord Mountbatten.'

'But the people will not give up their weapons!'

'I'm afraid they will have to,' Allenby said pleasantly but adamantly.

Moestopo wrung his hands in agitation. 'If—if you give them more time I could explain over the radio....'

Allenby smiled. 'I can be flexible, Mr Moestopo. I'm willing to extend the deadline to midnight the day after tomorrow.'

'Yes? Thank you! I'll telephone President Sukarno in Djakarta immediately.' Moestopo hurried away as quickly as he had come.

Allenby and Hughes grinned at each other and went back to the map.

Hotel Michiels

'The priority is, of course, the safe evacuation of all who wish to leave. Any questions before we have some lunch?' Several of Allenby's audience of journalists raised their hands, including Meg.

'Miss Graham, your question'.

'Brigadier, what sort of co-operation are you getting from the locals?'

'Fair, so far,' he shrugged. 'We aren't popular. For the wrong reasons, I hasten to add. I think the people of Surabaya understand that we are here to do a job and nothing more. Our—'

'You are saying that British troops will not be staying in Surabaya?' Boer, who Meg knew from Djakarta, interrupted loudly.

'Our deployment is seen as short term,' Allenby said diplomatically. Meg sensed the reply was mainly for the benefit of the Indonesians who were writing down his every word.

Boer tried again. 'Do you have any information on the whereabouts of the Dutch naval officer, Captain Henssen, who took the formal surrender of the city some days ago?'

Allenby's eyes narrowed slightly. 'Alas no. We hope to locate Captain Henssen very soon.'

'There are rumours that he is being held by rebels,' Boer continued. 'Do you intend to free him?'

'I cannot comment on rumours. At the moment he is not a priority.'

Hughes came in looking concerned. 'Excuse me, Brigadier, I'm sorry to interrupt but I think you and the correspondents should hear this.' He opened the door wide. In the office beyond, the staff had paused to listen to a passionate, measured voice on the radio. A Dutch liaison officer was interpreting.

'...Citizens of Surabaya, now the time has come to fight for a Free Indonesia! Yesterday the British arrived saying they came to evacuate the Dutch. The infidels lied! You have read their demands. They want to disarm us. As I speak, Dutch troops are landing at Tandjong Perak! We must resist. Allah is with us! Prepare for jihad. Let it be freedom or death!'

The broadcast ended and activity resumed in the outer office. Allenby looked earnestly at three young journalists working for the Surabaya news-sheets. 'Gentlemen, I would be grateful if you would stress to your editors and readers that our presence here is purely humanitarian. I repeat there are no Dutch troops with us.'

The serious young men excused themselves and left.

Allenby turned to Hughes. 'Put everyone on alert. Are the docks secure?'

'I'll check immediately, Sir,' he replied.

'Ladies and gentlemen of the press,' Allenby said regretfully. 'Please limit your movements to the Darmo area. We hope that there won't be any trouble but as you heard the locals are nervous and suspicious.'

'Of course, Brigadier,' Meg nodded, admiring the British preference for understatement.

Radio Surabaya Building

Mayor Moestopo sat glumly as he listened to the broadcast. Around him stood a group of excited *pemuda*, most of whom brandished swords or knives. A few also had Dutch army revolvers. He had gone to the radio station with the intention of keeping his promise to Allenby. Black Buffalos had been waiting. Their leader, a man with cold, piercing eyes had scoffed at his plea for co-operation and accused him of disloyalty to the revolution. Sarel scared Moestopo. It was he who was making the broadcast.

'… Let it be Freedom or Death!'

As the harangue ended, Moestopo rose to leave. A youth shoved him back down in his seat. 'You don't go anywhere until Sarel says so!'

Moments later Sarel came back from the studio. His eyes were bright and his cheeks flushed. The youths congratulated him loudly, punching the air in enthusiasm. Moestopo stood up again, unchallenged this time. Sarel eyed him dismissively.

'Those were words of madness,' Moestopo stammered. 'What good will it do to make the British our enemies as well as the Dutch? Thousands will die needlessly!'

Sarel threw his head back and laughed. 'That was the call to revolution, old man! To build a free nation!'

'But the British soldiers will—'

'The British came here as our enemies,' Sarel spat. 'They will leave or die.'

Again the youths cheered. One of them stepped forward grinning, brandishing a sword. 'When Sarel? When do we kill the infidels?'

'Patience, Kalim, wait—'

The door opened and Lamban entered. Like Sarel he was bare-chested and in military trousers and leather boots. A sword hung at his waist. There was a sudden, respectful quiet. Lamban looked only at Sarel. 'The weapons and ammunition have been distributed. Everything is ready.'

Sarel turned back to the others. 'Yes, wait... until four-thirty. Then sweep them from the city!'

Darmo Barracks

'And what is this?' The dark-haired woman was pointing to a bird in a tattered picture book. Half a dozen tiny hands shot skyward. She smiled. 'Now Heidi, you've answered one before.'

Meg watched the open-air class for a few minutes, impressed yet again by the Dutch women's determination to educate their children despite their difficult circumstances. In the barracks and the neighbouring streets ex-internees were living five or six families to a house in conditions only marginally better than their former camps.

Meg had bumped into the teacher, Daphne James, earlier that day. Over a cup of coffee brewed on a camping stove, Meg had learned that she was English and married to a Dutchman. She had lived in Surabaya for ten years. Daphne had also confessed she had no plans to stay on.

'Why not?' Meg had asked her.

'Oh, well, everything changed. It wasn't easy being British among this lot,' she had said rather hastily.

'What do you mean?'

'Most of them blame us for the Nip invasion!'

Meg had stared. 'What?'

'Oh, yes!' Daphne had continued. 'Believe me, it didn't take long for the bickering to start. "General Wavell deserted us" and all that rubbish…. People became very selfish and bitter in the camps. In the end it was easier to keep to our own…if you see what I mean.'

'What about your husband?'

'The last I heard he was in a camp near Bandung. I'm not sure I'm ready to see him just now.' Daphne had sniffed and smiled wanly. 'I know now it sounds awful of me but I want a little time. I'll see these children off home first—they were in hospital—and got separated from their mothers. Then I'm going to England alone….'

Meg nodded in understanding. 'It will take time for everyone,' she had said sympathetically.

'Next one,' Daphne smiled and pointed to an apple. 'Jopie! Your turn,' Jopie was golden-haired girl aged about four who was holding a ragged teddy bear in a vice-like embrace.

'Appural!' Jopie shouted, then giggled.

'That's right, well done!'

Meg found herself smiling, cheered by the happy children. She left the garden to watch the scene in the street. Hundreds of women and older children were gathered in the front drives and gardens of once-impressive, detached houses waiting to board lorries. Around them, piled on the driveways, were suitcases, boxes and their other belongings. British and Indian officers were having a difficult time convincing them to abandon their possessions, even though it was obvious that there wasn't enough space.

She watched uneasily, knowing that Wing-Commander Ball had expected to find no more than four thousand internees in Surabaya. The count had already passed seven thousand.

'They're taking too long,' Meg said to herself. 'Way too long.'

Central Post Office, Surabaya

Sepoy Padurang Rane was counting the pre-loaded 30-round box-magazines for the Bren light machine gun but he had other things on his mind. 'Eighteen, nineteen, twenty, that's the lot. You know, Maruti, those lucky sods will get the best billets as usual, and they're near the women at Darmo!'

Maruti Chavan laughed. 'You never stop, do you, Padu? You've moaned all the bloody way from India, all through Burma and now to Java!' He leant the Bren against one of the square pillars at the entrance to the Post Office. Other men in the platoon were still bringing in kit bags and equipment. Three companies of Mahrattas had finally disembarked, without much of their kit, at midday.

'My mother always wanted me to work in a post office,' Chavan said cheerfully. 'I should write to her and let her know.'

Rane rolled his eyes. 'My mother always worried I'd end up robbing post offices! Do you suppose there's any cash left in there?'

Chavan was about to reply when someone answered for him.

'Only Jap scrip but plenty of paper and stamps though, so you can write to your dear mother during your tea break.' Rane recognised the sarcastic tone of Jemadar Nimse.

'Why isn't that Bren set up?'

Rane turned with a weak grin and looked up at Nimse's six-foot-three frame. 'Give me a chance, Jem.'

'Right then, set it. And help bring in the rest of the kit. Major Cane's due to inspect at 1800 hours.'

Chavan and Rane groaned in unison.

International Bank of Surabaya

A raised, stone porch provided welcome shade for sepoy Shantaran Nambir as he stood guard. It also put him head and shoulders above those around him. The paving stones of the square were shimmering in the full glare of the sun. Opposite the bank, on the wall of a department store, was a large clock. It gave the time as ten-past four.

Nambir had been at his post for just over an hour. Already he felt something was amiss. Earlier the square had been teeming with people on their way to or from the east side of town via the Red Bridge across the Kali Mas. Now the few who crossed, even women and children, did so hurriedly. Something seemed odd. Nambir was not sure what it was exactly, other than an air of tension.

Behind him, the heavy brass door knob clicked as it turned. Havildar Satish Shinde appeared, his narrow eyes squinting in the bright sunshine. He was lean with angular features.

'Anything unusual, Shant?' Shinde asked as his eyes raked the square.

Nambir shook his head. 'No, Hav, apart from very few locals.'

'How long have they been there?' Shinde's hawk-like eyes had settled on a group of youths standing on the opposite side of the square. Two of them were bare-chested with shoulder-length hair.

'They come and go. Sometimes more, sometimes fewer but always the same two with the lovely tresses.'

'Keep your eyes peeled,' Shinde said scanning the square once more before he went back inside.

A little later, Nambir heard engines. There were few vehicles on the roads, mainly because the British were seizing them for use in evacuating the internees. It was an unpopular policy with the Surabayans who had heard rumours the cars were being taken in order to return them to their former Dutch owners. Nambir had seen several scuffles between irate drivers and soldiers.

Three Nissan 180 one-and-a-half-ton lorries entered the square on their way to Darmo. Their Rajrif drivers waved. One called out that he was glad someone could take it easy in the shade. Nambir laughed, trying to think of a riposte for when they returned. He watched the lorries until they were out of sight then looked back into the square. It was totally deserted. He glanced up at the clock and saw it was almost four-thirty.

Behind the clock face, the sniper was waiting for the minute hand to reach the half-hour. The cross-hairs of his telescopic sight were centred on the chest of the tall Indian soldier in the doorway of the Bank. Above the sniper, the clock mechanism whirred and the minute-hand moved. Just then the soldier stepped out of the shade and raised his face to look directly at the clock. At the last second, the sniper switched to a head shot and squeezed the trigger.

Ferwerda Drawbridge

Sepoys Nakish and Salunke were watching a fishing boat glide sedately through the raised drawbridge when a sleek, red Chrysler Imperial Le Baron cabriolet approached them from the British side of the Kali Mas. They recognised Captain Simon Hunter at the wheel and saluted respectfully. Hunter had been with the Mahrattas through thick and thin since 1942.

Hunter was alone and returned the salute. He saw them staring at the car and grinned. 'Not bad, eh? I chose this one from the motor pool myself.' He became serious. 'With any luck you won't be here too long,' he said easily. 'This isn't what we expected at all but stick with it. I'm going over to talk with the local militia commander to try and get more transport. I should be back in an hour.'

'Yes, Sir,' replied Nakish.

The bridge dropped back into place with a heavy clang and the car crossed to the east side. The Indians watched as it turned into a side street, then Nakish noted Hunter's name and time—1530 hours—in the log.

An hour passed. No-one else, British, Indian or Indonesian crossed the drawbridge. A slow drum beat sounded in an adjacent street then stopped.

'Nakish! In the river!' Salunke called out in alarm.

'What?' Nakish grinned. 'Another dog?' His smile vanished when he saw Salunke's expression. He moved to the rail and saw the khaki-clothed body bobbing in the water. As it drew nearer they saw it was Hunter. His throat had been cut.

'Lord Shiva!' Nakish exclaimed. 'Get him out!' He was halfway across the bridge to the radio operator when he heard a menacing roar.

Shots rang out and Nakish turned to see dozens of armed figures pouring out of the side streets and charge towards the bridge. Bullets zinged off the ironwork around him. As he dived for cover the Mahratta's Bren guns returned fire.

Screaming as if possessed, the Javanese came on, surging across the open approaches to the ramp. Against the prepared positions of the veteran soldiers it was certain death. In seconds the human wave broke and retreated, leaving over forty dead or wounded. Minutes later the *pemuda* charged once more.

Darmo

Meg and Daphne heard the shooting. They were in a small, ornamental park with eight of the children from the English class. The barracks was only a few streets away but the firing was between them and the British positions.

'We've got to go right now,' Meg said urgently.

Daphne's face was pale. In Dutch she called the children from the swings. They came obediently and quietly, the younger ones already a little unnerved by the constant gunfire. She knelt down to look her charges in the eye. 'On the way back, we're going to play explorers,' she said as cheerfully as she could manage. 'Everyone get in a line and pretend to be in the jungle!'

'Like in Sumatra, Miss James?' asked one of the boys excitedly.

'Yes, Hans,' Daphne said smiling. 'Pretend you're in Sumatra. Everyone must keep quiet, so we don't scare the animals!'

Hans turned to the little girl who still clutched her teddy bear. 'Jopie, the tigers are going to eat your stupid bear!'

Frightened, Jopie began to wail. 'I don't want to play!'

Meg held out her hand. 'Come on, Jopie,' she said gently. 'Let's play together.'

Sniffling, Jopie gripped Meg's fingers tightly. Meg led her to the back of the line. Daphne was at the front.

Outside the park the streets were deserted but Meg saw some Javanese women watching them from the upstairs windows of houses. All doors and ground floor shutters were closed. She knew they would get no help.

Daphne, too, had seen the women. Undeterred, she pressed on, leading them through a maze of empty back streets towards the barracks, but nearer the shooting. As they approached one junction, drumming began. Daphne held up her hand. Quickly she led them down the drive of an abandoned house and into its back garden.

Where there once had been a neatly tended lawn, grass and weeds grew waist-high. Daphne turned and whispered at the children. 'See! We really are in the jungle now!'

A thin wooden lattice fence, flaky and brittle from lack of attention, barred their entry into the adjacent garden. Daphne glanced quickly at Meg then kicked out a section to lead them through. Giggling, the children followed, still enjoying their game.

On they went, climbing over walls, breaking fences or pushing through hedges until they reached the garden of a house on a street corner. Daphne signalled a halt. The firing was very close now and they could hear shouting in Javanese.

'Stay here and don't make a sound,' Daphne said firmly but quietly. She crouched and went on alone to some thick bushes behind the wall. Meg saw her blanche, then she beckoned Meg to join her.

'It's awful!' Daphne whispered.

Meg peeped over the wall and her face fell. They were opposite a T-junction and streets lined with small shops and boutiques. Several bodies lay sprawled in the open. At least three were white women.

'Jesus!' Meg mouthed.

'The Indian soldiers are down there,' pointed Daphne.

Meg took another quick look. A hundred yards away she could see a line of cars, upturned carts and piles of sacks protecting the approach to Darmo barracks. Every few seconds a shot rang out from the roof tops. Meg realised that the Javanese snipers were trying to get into positions overlooking the British perimeter by using the large rectangular chimney stacks as cover. There had to be another route, she thought desperately. She glanced at the road to their left and caught her breath. She nudged Daphne. 'Look over there!'

'Oh, my God!'

Hundreds of waiting youths and militia sat or stood, apparently resting between assaults on the British position. In the midst of them, three bare-chested youths with long hair were shouting and gesticulating, leading chants.

'We'll have to make a run for it,' said Meg, her stomach churning. 'They'll see us soon if we stay here.'

Daphne nodded nervously. 'You don't think they'll shoot, do you? Not at children….'

Meg looked firmly at Daphne. 'Tell them to run zigzag'. Her throat was dry.

Piru Singh was on a roof top perch just in front of the Rajrif's street barricade. He had waited five minutes for the shot at the sniper. At last his target peered around the chimney stack one inch too far. Singh squeezed the trigger and watched with quiet satisfaction as the body rolled limply over the edge of the roof and crashed to the pavement below.

He was scanning for his next target when he saw the small figures appear at the junction and start weaving towards them.

'Hav!' Singh shouted. 'Children in the street!'

Havildar Ashok Ram risked a glance over a pile of rice sacks. 'Cease fire! Cease fire!' he shouted. 'Push that cart back, quickly!'

Half a dozen Rajrifs dropped their weapons and strained to push the cart aside. Slowly it began to move, scraping on the tarmac.

Anxiously the Rajrifs watched as the children, legs pumping, darted left then right past the corpses towards them. Behind them came two women.

Meg, Daphne and the children had sixty yards to go when the first shot rang out. More followed as the *pemuda* forced them to run the gauntlet. Bullets ricocheted off the tarmac. At the barricade they watched in horror.

'Covering fire!' Ram roared.

Many of the soldiers stood openly to shout and draw fire. 'Don't Stop!'—'Run!'—'Keep going!'

In fury the Rajrifs sprayed the rooftops and junctions. Two *pemuda*, tempted out of cover by the defenceless targets, quickly paid the price.

Meg's head was pounding. 'Zigzag! Zigzag!' She panted to herself as she dodged, trying not to look at the dead in the street. Her chest felt tight and her legs were like lead. The barricade seemed no closer.

Behind one chimney stack a sniper took his time tracking the brunette in the khaki jacket, trying to anticipate her movements. He knew that at some point she would have to make for the gap in the barricade, so he waited for the easier shot.

At twenty yards, Meg glanced up to see the Indians waving. The first of the children had reached safety. A boy tripped, fell heavily and lay stunned. Meg changed course, knowing that she did not have the strength to lift him. A shot whizzed past her. Then she saw a turbaned Indian sprint out, scoop up the boy and dive back over the sacks.

Meg cut in once more and made a last straight dash, head down. The waiting sniper came up a little higher on his elbows. A little too high. His rifle dropped from suddenly senseless fingers He slumped with a bullet in his head, courtesy of Piru Singh.

A Rajrif grabbed Meg and pulled her down behind the barricade. She knelt head down on her hands and knees, her chest heaving. Nearby a frantic Daphne was gathering the sobbing children to her and counting aloud.

'…six, seven. Seven! Jan, Heidi, Molly, Jaap—Oh, Jopie!— Where's Jopie?'

Havildar Ram caught Meg's eye and shook his head. Cautiously she peeped back down the street. Her stomach twisted. Twenty-five yards from the barricade a ragged teddy bear sat upright on the road. Nearby lay a tiny figure with golden curls and outstretched hands splashed with blood.

'Oh, God, no.' Meg groaned.

'Jopie!' Daphne screamed. She rushed for the gap in the barricade. Ram was ready and caught her.

'No, Memsahib! No, please,' Ram consoled her. 'There is nothing you can do. The little one is dead.'

Daphne struggled vainly for a second then slump against Ram in tears.

Gently Meg prised her away from the slightly uncomfortable Havildar. They huddled together, trying to comfort the weeping children.

Drums pounded at the end of the street followed by angry roars.

'Here they come again, Hav!' Singh called down. Unhurriedly he reached for another five-round clip.

Book Four

Chapter Nine

Captain Deshi Chopra of 123rd Field Transport Company allowed himself to relax a little. His convoy from Gubeng to Darmo was making good time. A few minutes earlier they had checked in with the Rajrifs at the Brugstraat Bridge and were now turning on to the wide, tram-lined Palmenlaan. Chopra estimated they would reach the hospital on Darmo Boulevard in another ten minutes. At least now they were over the river, he thought with relief. He did not enjoy shepherding women and children.

Behind his jeep were sixteen T-16 six-wheelers crammed with over four hundred internees and their meagre belongings. Darmo would be their last stop before a ship to Singapore and beyond. Despite their cramped and uncomfortable conditions, the internees were in good spirits. Occasionally Chopra could hear them singing folk songs and nursery rhymes.

His watch said four thirty-five. This last trip of the day had gone fairly smoothly—under two hours in total—but he had wasted nearly an hour enforcing the one-suitcase rule.

'Captain...' the driver said indicating ahead and already slowing the jeep.

Their road ahead was blocked by a palm-tree trunk placed on top of oil drums and two dilapidated cars at right angles across the street.

'Stop now!' Chopra ordered.

The jeep jerked to a halt twenty-five yards from the barrier. A squealing of brakes followed as the convoy also halted.

Chopra counted half a dozen youths manning the roadblock. Two held rifles, the rest were armed with bamboo spears. He looked around him. Rows of houses with low-walled front gardens lined the street. Automatically his eyes swept along the roof-lines. If it was a trap they were sitting ducks....

A jemadar sitting behind Chopra readied his rifle.

'Easy, Jem,' said Chopra, getting out of the jeep. 'No sudden movements.'

Young, impassive faces stared malevolently. Chopra heard heavy footsteps behind him as Sevkani, the tall, powerfully built Mahratta havildar in charge of the convoy's escort, came up to see what was happening.

'Trouble, Captain?' Sevkani asked quietly, taking in the scene ahead.

'We'll know soon enough, Hav. Ask Subedar Ratra to come up here,' said Chopra. He wanted to confer with his second in command and was wondering whether to show force or to try and talk his way through. With the twenty-two Mahrattas and his thirty-two drivers and co-drivers he had just over fifty men. All were armed but they were strung out almost three hundred yards along the road.

Chopra made his decision. 'Hav, you stay here.'

He walked forward alone. Five yards from the barrier he stopped in surprise. About two dozen more youths armed with rifles had been hidden from his view behind bushes. They were all aiming at him.

He cleared his throat. 'I am an Allied officer on official—'

'*Merdeka!*' The shout triggered a volley.

Chopra was flung back five feet before his torn, already lifeless body hit the ground. Several of the bullets passed through him, shattering the jeep's windscreen. His driver and the jemadar died in their seats.

Other concealed ambushers took their cue. Sevkani dived behind a lorry wheel as rifle and light machine-gun fire raked the vehicles. Canopies shredded as bullets and then bamboo spears punched through the canvas piercing mattresses, suitcases or flesh. Shrill, frantic screams of terrified and wounded women and children blended with gunfire and the dull pops of exploding grenades.

Four bellowing *pemuda* ducked under the tree trunk barrier and raced at Sevkani with swords. *'Indonesia Raya!'*

Sevkani shot the first two but the others closed on him and he was preparing to club them with his rifle when three Mahratta sepoys appeared at his side, firing. The pemuda went down feet from them. Sevkani looked back along the line and saw his men scrambling to return fire as best they could from behind or under the vehicles.

Subedar Javagal Ratra, the second in command, had started for the head of the column when the shooting began. 'Take cover!' he yelled frantically to the internees. 'Hold up mattresses!'

Ratra began to run back, certain that the trap was closing behind them. Some *pemuda* were already pushing a car out of a driveway to try and block any escape. He saw one of his drivers manage to turn by crashing his vehicle through a picket fence and race down the road. The car was not yet across the road and the lorry slammed into the front, overturning it and crushing two of the youths.

'Go! Go!' Ratra bellowed.

Three *pemuda* gave chase. Ratra knelt and shot two of them. The third pulled up and flung a bamboo spear that stuck in the wooden tailboard.

The road was now swarming with armed *pemuda*. Ratra retreated to join two Mahrattas who were readying a Bren gun between the rear wheels of the last lorry. Bullets bounced off the road.

'Keep them back!' Ratra urged, quickly loading another clip.

The gas-operated Bren rattled as the gunner squeezed off the entire magazine. Twenty *pemuda* fell in less than ten seconds.

There was a clatter on the tarmac just feet away.

'Grenade!' Ratra shouted, pushing his head against the ground. The blast rang in his ears but he was unharmed.

Shrapnel had caught the Bren loader in the thigh but the man ignored his wound and calmly slotted home a replacement magazine. Another wave of youths surged forward. Again the Bren swept the road.

At the head of the convoy, Sevkani heard the rear Bren and guessed they were trapped. There was a booming roar as a petrol tank exploded and a twelve-wheeler was engulfed in flames. Screaming women and children leapt from it. He saw two hit by bullets.

'Set up behind that wall!' Ratra ordered. The gunners sprinted from under the vehicle and dived over the brickwork. More *pemuda* rushed from behind the barricade but the men with Sevkani picked them off. Six more attacked, uttering wild, piercing screams. A burst from the Bren scythed them down.

As the ambushers fell back to regroup there was a lull. Snipers continued to take pot shots at will.

Sevkani was counting his dead and wounded when he saw Ratra coming towards him.

'We must get them under cover!' Ratra yelled.

Sevkani looked around in desperation. Standing back from the road were five large detached houses. They appeared abandoned. 'Over there,' he pointed. 'It's the only place!'

Ratra nodded and shouted. 'Everyone out. Now!'

His men set off down the convoy, dropping tailboards and urging the occupants out from under mattresses, cases and corpses. Roars erupted from the *pemuda*. Bunched between the vehicles, the internees were easy targets.

Sevkani saw one young woman stagger, pulling weakly at a spear lodged high in her back. As she did so a bellowing youth surged forward and hacked open her chest with a machete. Before Sevkani could bring up his rifle the attacker sprang cat-like up the side of a lorry and on to its roof, sliced through the canvas top and dropped down. Inside there were shrieks. Sevkani swore and started to run for the lorry but then saw a Mahratta leap up, rip open the side canvas with a bayonet and climb inside. Seconds later the soldier jumped back onto the road, his bayonet bloodied.

Other soldiers were already charging to secure the houses but as Sevkani had hoped they were unoccupied. Women and children began bolting for the protection they offered.

Sevkani turned just in time to see movement above him. A *pemuda* balanced on a wheel arch was poised to spear him He raised his rifle and fired at almost point blank range. His attacker fell at his feet. He saw the face of a boy barely into his teens.

Finally, the last of the able women and children reached the row of houses. He gave the order, 'Pull back to the wall!'

As the soldiers retreated, the baying, triumphant *pemuda* swarmed over the rear vehicles. Mattresses, suitcases, dead and wounded were flung on to the road. For man, woman or child still alive there was no mercy as the youths ran amok.

For an hour the Indians kept up a steady fire taking a huge toll. Scores of dead or dying *pemuda* lay sprawled around the convoy and in the gardens. There was no let up. The mob used the bodies of the fallen and some of the lorries as cover to approach ever nearer. In three years of war, Sevkani had never seen so many dead. He flicked back the bolt-action of his Lee-Enfield to load another round and felt the heat escaping from the overused chamber.

In disgust they watched a *pemuda* hack off the legs and then the arms of a wounded and moaning Mahratta. A shot from one of the defenders ended their comrade's agony. As the butcher fled others fired at him.

'Save your ammo for the next attack!' Sevkani ordered bitterly.

Ratra and two wounded drivers worked up the line, handing out ammunition. The chubby Subedar ducked down beside Sevkani, panting and pointing to a half-empty box. 'This is all we have left. Can we hold them?'

There was another lengthy burst of defensive firing. Sevkani shook his head. 'No. The Brens are the heaviest things we've got and we're spread—' He broke off to shoot a *pemuda* charging with a petrol bomb. As the youth fell the bottle smashed on the road, bathing the body in flames. '— too wide,' Sevkani finished.

'Nice shot, Hav,' one of the Mahrattas quipped, 'cremation included in the price!'

Beyond the abandoned lorries, Sevkani could see squads of militia spreading out through the gardens along the other side of the road. 'They're better-trained. They'll work around us and probe for weaknesses,' he told Ratra. 'Once it gets dark, well....'

Hotel Michiels

Piled sofas, tables and chairs barricaded the hotel entrance. Drivers and cooks stood guard at ground-floor windows, and helped the medics ferrying wounded to the operating theatre set up in the spacious lounge. The stretchers returned loaded, this time with water and scavenged ammunition for the Mahratta unit defending the approach.

Inside the hotel, the mood was busy and determined. Messengers were moving urgently back and forth between communications and operations centres set up in function rooms. Officers were poring over street maps, trying to locate and plan escape routes for isolated or trapped units.

Colonel Hughes's face was grim as he headed for Brigadier Allenby's office with the latest reports. He knocked and entered at once, interrupting a briefing by Ball on the situation of the internees at Darmo. Allenby and four officers were present.

'Excuse me, Wing Commander,' said Hughes apologetically. 'Sir, we've had fresh reports from units at Simpang, Ferwerda, the International Bank and the Marine School. They all say the same thing: they face what looks to be thousands of well-armed civilians and hundreds of militia. At two places they're up against light tanks and armoured cars.'

'Casualties?' Allenby demanded tersely.

'Fifty-eight dead, ninety-seven missing at the last count,' Hughes said gravely. 'But that was several hours ago.'

There was silence. Allenby paled.

Hughes consulted his list. 'We've been unable to re-establish contact with two Rajrif platoons that were on patrol in the kampongs this afternoon. Their last reports sounded pretty desperate. A sixteen-vehicle internee convoy is also overdue at Darmo.'

Allenby moved over to a street map. 'What about Indonesian casualties?'

'Estimated at over eight hundred,' Hughes replied.

Allenby looked at him questioningly. Hughes nodded. 'No exaggeration. All positions report repeated suicidal attacks. Again, these figures are hours old.'

Allenby let out a long breath and looked around him. 'Well, there we were worried about a few companies of militia. The entire city has risen against us!'

Outside a faint whistling grew steadily louder.

'Cover!' Allenby shouted. The men ducked as the mortar blast shook the windows.

'Any more news from Batavia?' Ball asked hopefully.

Allenby nodded. 'General Chrishaw telephoned Sukarno. Apparently he's horrified and is coming to negotiate a cease-fire. The General isn't so sure he holds much sway over the hotheads. They will arrive later this morning.'

Ball nodded and made to leave. 'I'd better try and get through to Darmo,' he said. 'The internees will be in a terrible state.'

'No,' Allenby said immediately. 'You must wait until daylight.'

'But—' Ball protested.

Allenby interrupted him sternly. 'If there is no truce tomorrow we face the prospect of surrender or annihilation. God knows what will become of the internees. I won't risk life unnecessarily. We have twelve hundred men against something like sixty thousand. You know Surabaya better than we do and can best help our planners here.'

Ball nodded. 'Yes, yes of course.'

'And in any case,' Allenby said smiling. 'I'll need your car and driver!'

Mac had spent most of the night helping to carry the wounded to and from the operating theatre. He had been relieved at four and found a bench seat in the hotel lobby. Even though he was exhausted his sleep had been fitful. His mind had been on Meg. He had not seen her for hours and he had heard about an attack at Darmo. His breakfast had been a small plate of tasteless, cold baked beans and soy sausage, followed by a cup of tea. The Indian cooks had boiled water in the kitchen's huge rice cauldrons then added tea, milk and sugar to the mix, ladling out the sweet brew to the grateful soldiers.

Ball found him dozing on the bench and tapped him awake. 'Sorry, Mac! Come on, you're taking the Brigadier to the airfield to meet General Chrishaw.'

'Oh, right,' Mac said groggily, feeling for the keys to the La Salle 52 saloon that Ball had been assigned the day before.

Ball grabbed another cup of tea and gave it him. 'Keep your eyes peeled for snipers!'

Mac was suddenly wide awake.

Krembangan Airfield

Allenby was not taking any chances with Chrishaw's safety. In front of the La Salle was a jeep with a mounted Bren gun. Two Mahratta troop lorries followed behind. His caution proved well-founded. Halfway to the airfield they came upon a partially built roadblock. Oil drums and crates had been abandoned as the convoy approached. There was no sign of the Javanese but the Mahrattas suspected they would find it completed on their return.

As they entered the airfield the Mahrattas turned off along the perimeter. Mac followed the jeep and went on to the control tower where two more cars were parked: one a cream, Buick S40 convertible with white-wall tyres; the other a rather more mundane red Ford station wagon. Both were bedecked in red and white nationalist flags. Four Indonesians stood beside them, watching the sky anxiously.

Nearby, Major Derek Cane was watching his men lay a barrage of three-inch mortar fire against militia encroaching along the airfield's southern perimeter. Six bound militia prisoners sat glumly under guard on the tarmac.

'Morning, Sir,' Cane saluted.

'Morning, Derek,' Allenby replied saluting. 'Get anything from them?'

Cane's expression clouded. 'They think we've got a division of paratroopers coming in. Sukarno's reception committee are having kittens!'

A low, increasingly loud drone came from the west. Necks craned looking for the aircraft. Cane saw the Dakota first and pointed. 'There! Ten o'clock!'

The pilot, warned that the airfield was 'hot', was coming in very steeply.

'They'll be in range for a few seconds, Sir, no more,' Cane added calmly.

Bursts of machine-gun fire greeted the Dakota. Seconds later, the Mahratta mortars zeroed in on the source of the line of tracer bullets and silenced the gun.

'Mr Sukarno's not a very popular president then?' Mac ventured.

Allenby laughed. 'I won't be voting for him, that's for sure!'

Safely down, the Dakota began to taxi. Allenby jumped back in the car. 'Come on, let's get there!'

Chrishaw and Sukarno were already out on the tarmac as Mac and the escort jeep raced up. The two nationalist cars followed. Both Chrishaw and Sukarno were looking at the Dakota's tail fin, which had been holed.

'A little extra ventilation, Mr Sukarno,' Chrishaw said casually. Sukarno, clearly shaken by the bumpy landing and the inadvertent attempt on his life, merely nodded.

There was little time for ceremony and most of the greetings were lost as another mortar barrage exploded to the south. Sukarno and his two aides were driven to the airfield's control tower, for talks with Chrishaw and Allenby. Mac waited outside, watching the militia's largely futile attempts to advance while dodging the Mahratta mortars.

Twenty minutes later the Indonesian president emerged with his aides and drove slowly out of the airfield to the Mahratta front line. He sat calmly, exposed, in the back of the convertible, as one of his aides repeatedly shouted news of his arrival through a megaphone.

Mac watched the two flag-draped cars move slowly down the street. Two hundred yards on they were met by a nationalist armoured car, then turned off under escort and disappeared from view.

'Well, so far so good,' said Chrishaw gruffly, 'Let's see what he can deliver.' He turned to Allenby. 'Bring me up to date on the way in.'

Their convoy left the airfield with the six militia prisoners perched on the bonnets of the jeeps and lorries. As expected, the roadblock had been completed. Cement-filled oil drums were now strung across the road.

'Get our new friends to clear it,' said Allenby.

Mahrattas prodded the nervous prisoners forward at bayonet point. They began shouting and waving, pleading with their comrades concealed in the surrounding buildings not to shoot. Half the barrier had been cleared when a hail of gunfire cut down all six. In reply the Bren gun on the leading jeep peppered the windows and doorways.

'Forward!' Allenby shouted. At his signal, one of the lorries raced ahead, the soldiers in the back firing and hurling grenades at the buildings on both sides of the road. It knocked over the last obstructing drum, clearing the way for the others to follow. The firing ceased. As Mac sped through the gap he caught a glimpse of several fleeing *pemuda*.

Two hours later, Sukarno was introduced reverently on Radio Surabaya. He announced an immediate truce and a meeting to discuss a cease-fire the next morning.

Internee Convoy Seven

Sevkani watched another burning lorry explode. Orange flames illuminated the ghoulish scene. Between the abandoned vehicles and the garden wall the ground was carpeted with bodies. Dead, dying and wounded Javanese moaned and babbled in a tangle of torsos and limbs. Over twenty-four hours had passed since the ambush. Gunfire and artillery still echoed in central Surabaya, so he knew they were on their own for a second night running.

He moved forward to the sepoy manning the Bren gun on the overgrown rockery nearest the roadblock which was now their perimeter. 'Karam,' he whispered, 'how many rounds?'

The gunner turned and held up five fingers. A few feet away one of the drivers signalled four. It was the same all along the sparse line. Earlier some of the defenders had sneaked forward to take rifles and ammunition from the Javanese dead. It was not enough. Now each of the houses was on its own. Unbidden, the handful of surviving soldiers had long before fixed bayonets.

Sevkani went back inside the house with a collection of captured daggers under his arm. Women and children were crammed in every room, huddled together. He saw their desperate looks and simply shook his head. There had been no food and no water for hours. The air was fetid.

Sombrely he placed the weapons in the centre of the room. 'There's not much ammunition left,' he said hoarsely. Blanched, fearful faces stared at him. It was not necessary to spell out the choice they faced.

A woman untwined herself from her two young children and crawled forward on her hands and knees. She chose a small dagger then went back to her children, hugging them to her, keeping the blade out of their sight. Tears began streaming down her face. One by one others came forward. Sevkani left them.

Darkness made the attackers bolder. They howled and jeered, scenting victory and—at last—revenge on those who had killed so many of their number.

Their first target was the house furthest from the roadblock. Sevkani heard no more than eight or nine shots from the defenders before it was overrun. Triumphant roars mingled with desperate, pitiful screams as women were seized.

Sevkani made his decision. The only chance—for his group at least—was to try and break out. He passed the word along the perimeter and back inside. Soon afterwards two petrol bombs ignited on the roof on the next house in the row. Flames spread quickly illuminating the massed, chanting *pemuda* nearing the house.

'Now!' Sevkani bellowed.

Three sepoys sprang over the garden wall in a bayonet charge for the road. Five startled youths standing by the nearest lorry fled without firing a shot, their cries of alarm lost in the tumult.

Close behind the soldiers came the internees. The exhausted Indians hurled them aboard like sacks. Sevkani looked back to see the second house aflame but also Ratra leading more internees towards them from the fourth house.

There was a heavy rattle as a lorry engine turned over then fired. Ratra's men started two more.

'What's your plan?' Ratra shouted.

'Simple,' Sevkani shrugged. 'Break through and drive. You're on your own!'

'Good luck!' Ratra yelled as he raced away.

Sevkani jumped into the cab as a final roar heralded the end of resistance at the third house. 'Go!'

Gears screeched as the driver let out the clutch and the lorry swung out, jolting over the dead lying in the road. Sevkani stared grimly at the last, short-lived stand at the houses. Enraged the *pemuda* descended in a wild blood lust. Men, women and children were dragged into the garden. Long, agonized screams punctuated the booming, triumphant chants as the rapes and butchering began. Swords, spears and machetes lifted and fell in flickered silhouette against the flames.

Sevkani turned away. Ahead the barricade loomed in the headlights. Miraculously it was unmanned.

'Ram it!' Sevkani yelled bracing himself as the wing of the lorry clipped the end of the trunk shattering a headlight but forcing a gap. Three lorries sped away.

Surabaya Town Hall

'How dare you demand the BKR's weapons!' The young, swaggering Javanese wearing general's stars folded his arms and glowered. 'We are the national army of Indonesia!'

Chrishaw's face remained calm as the interpreter next to him struggled to keep up. 'General Sombong,' Chrishaw began patiently, 'the proclamation refers to weapons held by unofficial groups. We recognise the BKR. Naturally the confiscation order does not apply to your men.'

Mollified, Sombong sat down. The meeting had dragged on for two hours. The militia and *pemuda* leaders were respectful but in no mood to listen to their new president's pleas for tolerance. Sukarno, desperate for a cease-fire, found himself siding with Chrishaw.

Sombong, a former militia sergeant who had promoted himself, was the main obstacle. Several even younger 'captains' were with him, urging him to resist. Outside in the street, an excited crowd of *pemuda*, barely restrained by the militia, bellowed for blood.

Earlier, the Javanese had demanded the immediate, unconditional British surrender. Chrishaw had categorically refused, repeating time and again to Sombong that the British were in Indonesia on behalf of the United Nations. There were frequent breaks in the proceedings as the Indonesians argued among themselves.

'We all want the fighting to stop—', Sukarno started to say.

'Why?' Sombong flared. 'We are winning! We can drive them into the sea. The Dutch too!'

'For the last time,' Chrishaw said sternly, 'there are no Dutch units in Surabaya!'

The interpreters struggled on.

Chrishaw tried again. 'I suggest that the British control two small zones, namely the docks and the Darmo camps. BKR forces would have authority in the rest of the town but allow us free movement along specific routes between the two zones.

'No! Absolutely not!' Sombong shouted, jumping to his feet yet again. 'You are trying to hem us in!'

Chrishaw and Allenby looked at each other in awe of Sombong's advanced grasp of tactics. Their only advantage in the negotiations was that the Indonesians did not know how few troops they had. Asking him how fifty thousand could be hemmed in by a thousand was not an option. They were alone, unarmed and in a *pemuda*-controlled area. All that protected them was a white flag of truce and Sukarno.

'Our troops would be here for only a few days,' Chrishaw explained, his tone still relaxed. 'As soon as the internee camps are empty we shall withdraw. No more troops will land. BKR observers could be allowed into the docks to remove any doubts.'

Sombong paused, pursing his lips. 'There must be BKR guards at all the camps!'

'Absolutely not!' Chrishaw said wearily. 'Frightened women and children are no threat to anyone. They just want to leave!'

One of the young captains spoke up. 'There could be Dutch spies and saboteurs among them!'

Sombong nodded. Sukarno put his head in his hands.

Three explosions in the street rattled the office windows. Sombong jumped up and ran outside. Two of the militia captains drew their pistols.

Chrishaw looked at Sukarno. 'Mr President, unless this ridiculous shooting stops there will be huge and needless loss of life that will stain Indonesia for years!'

'You are right, General,' Sukarno replied.

Sombong ran back into the conference room. 'The Royal Navy is shelling the town!'

Chrishaw and Allenby, both still sitting with guns inches from their faces, laughed openly.

'My dear General,' said Chrishaw, 'Those were only mortars. They were fired because some of your men must have opened fire on my men, breaking the truce.'

'Sombong!' Sukarno snapped. 'Sit down and negotiate!'

Reluctantly he sat.

'General,' Chrishaw said quietly. 'You have a very simple choice. Let us evacuate the internees without hindrance and leave Surabaya or face massive reprisals from the combined forces of the entire South-East Asia Command. I assure you the destruction of this town and your army would merely be the start. Do I make myself clear?'

'We are not afraid to die,' Sombong declared theatrically.

Sukarno stood up from the table in frustration. 'Sombong, your selfish, stupid arrogance will cost us support all over the world. We need the United Nations, they will reject us—rightly—as a bunch of thugs who make war on women and children! What are you thinking? As President of the Republic of Indonesia I demand that you agree to the cease-fire. If not I will resign as president and blame you!'

Sombong struggled with his rage, then nodded once. 'Very well....'

Mac watched the patched Dakota head down the airstrip to return Chrishaw and Sukarno to the capital. It climbed into the air unmolested.

As Allenby was returning to the car, a loud explosion sounded in the east of the town. Black smoke swirled upwards against the blue sky.

'Oh, Christ...' Mac muttered.

A radio operator came sprinting from the airfield control tower. 'Brigadier, signal from Captain Willot at the International Bank. He says D Company must return fire.'

Allenby's face was grim. 'Tell him a cease-fire has been agreed. He must not fire unless his position is attacked. I'll be there as soon as I can.' He ran over to explain what was happening to the officials who had escorted Sukarno, then rushed to the car with Knowles and Weston, two Mahratta captains, in tow. 'The Indonesians have agreed to come with us to the Bank,' Allenby explained to Mac. 'Follow them!'

The International Bank of Surabaya

Shantaran Nambir watched in frustration as the man moved quite openly and unhurriedly across the rooftop to the shelter of a chimney stack, carrying a rifle with a telescopic sight. Nambir's head, wrapped in bloody bandages, throbbed painfully. He wondered if the gunman was the bastard in the clock tower who had shot off his ear the day before. 'Sniper on the roof!' His frustrated shout was almost a plea. The man was in his sights, the slack gone from his trigger.

'Hold your fire!' Captain Bruce Willot answered reluctantly, his voice grating. All around the square, he could see Javanese using the truce to take more advantageous positions.

Several cars and carts had been brought forward to provide increased cover just yards from the bank. Now the square was filling with chanting *pemuda* who were edging ever closer. Willot's defensive advantage was disappearing in front of his eyes.

'Steady, Mahrattas!' Willot said firmly, wondering just how long his men's resolve could hold.

Two cars entered the square at speed with horns blaring. The first was bedecked with Indonesian colours, the second a white flag. Two agitated Indonesians got out of the first car and began talking to the crowd. Eventually it parted and the cars drew up outside the bank.

To Willot's surprise Brigadier Allenby got out of the second car. Immediately there were angry shouts and the Javanese surged forward, coming between Allenby and the bank. Aggressive *pemuda* stood four deep, refusing to move out of his way.

Immediately Willot and the Mahrattas swung their weapons to cover Allenby. After a few moments, Allenby gave up trying to enter the bank and held up his hands for quiet. He spoke to Willot from ten yards away. 'Captain Willot, this morning President Sukarno and General Chrishaw agreed a cease-fire. The Indonesian representatives will now explain the agreement.'

Willot lowered his revolver as Sukarno's party workers climbed on to the roof of their car and began to appeal to the turbulent crowd. The phrase 'Bung Sukarno' was used repeatedly. After a fifteen-minute harangue the restless crowd finally quietened, then began to break up.

Willot saw Havildar Shinde at his shoulder. He let out a long breath. 'All in a day's work, Hav.'

Shinde was peering across the square. 'Over there, Sahib,' he said quietly, 'near the bridge.'

At the approach to the Red Bridge, several activists were attempting to stir up the crowd once more with chants. Movement out of the square halted. 'Bloody hell!' muttered Willot under his breath.

Sukarno's associates had also seen the danger and were already in their car moving towards the bridge. Without hesitation Allenby sat on the front of the La Salle holding a white flag and shouted to Mac. 'Follow them!'

Mac moved off slowly, admiring Allenby's nerve but not sure if it was wise to move from the bank. Snarling faces pressed against his window but no-one touched Allenby. 'Och, for fuck sake get back in!' Mac muttered, trying to keep his eyes firmly to the front.

Behind him, Knowles stated the obvious. 'One wrong move and we're gonners.'

Mac and Weston did not reply.

It took ten minutes to inch through the excited crowd. Shouts grew louder and fists banged on the La Salle's windows and roof. A door handle were knocked off and the rear lights smashed. Allenby did not flinch. He sat calmly, and unmolested, feet braced on the bumper, under the truce flag.

Mac's knuckles gripped white on the steering wheel.

When they reached the other car Allenby dismounted. Weston and Knowles got out to stand with their commander. Mac could see very little. He kept the engine running.

Sukarno's aides were being shouted down. Suddenly they looked nervous and unsure of themselves. Mac sensed that this time the 'Bung Sukarno' mantra was falling flat.

A long-haired, bare-chested young man vaulted on to the roof of the station wagon. He unsheathed a Japanese sword and raised it above his head. There were more cheers.

'Sarel!'—'Let Bung Sarel speak!'

Crestfallen, Sukarno's aides gave way.

Sarel, pointing contemptuously at the three British officers, launched into an impassioned, vitriolic speech. Shouts of *'Merdeka!'* erupted every few seconds from the excited crowd. Swiftly the mood became ugly. The mob closed on Allenby and the two captains, gesticulating wildly. Hands grabbed at them.

From the fourth floor of the bank Willot was watching Allenby through field glasses. Large numbers of armed *pemuda* were again gathering outside. Some were jostling with Mahrattas at the bank's broken windows.

'Captain!' Nambir shouted. 'LMG!'

Willot looked down and saw a cart carrying a Nambu machine-gun being brought up against the bank's veranda. *Pemuda* started climbing over the wall. When he saw Allenby being grabbed his patience snapped. 'Open fire!'

At the sound of shooting, the Javanese in the square scattered, many firing their own weapons in panic. The La Salle's windscreen shattered. Mac ducked in his seat shielding his face with his arms. 'Shite!' he gulped.

He heard the back doors open and then slam as Allenby and Weston flung themselves between the seats. Knowles joined Mac in the front. A hail of shots holed the back and side windows, punching through the top of the front seats and into the dashboard just inches over their heads. Other bullets hit the front of the car.

'Quiet!' Allenby hissed. 'Play dead!'

They lay still. Seconds later they heard footsteps outside the car. A shadow fell across Mac's face. He held his breath. The footsteps faded.

Mayhem continued around them. Heavy fire from the bank was forcing the mob out of the square.

'Thank God Willot opened fire when he did,' Allenby said heavily.

'MacDonald,' Knowles asked urgently, 'do you think you can start the car?'

'I don't know, Sir. I can smell oil. Maybe we took one in the sump. I can try...'

'Wait until the next round of firing,' Allenby replied. 'It'll hide the sound of the engine.'

Mac was getting cramp in his calf. He was also desperate for a cigarette. 'Anyone got a fag?'

Knowles found one in a battered packet. They shared it , passing it furtively under the car seats.

'I hope the prefects don't catch us!' Allenby joked nervously.

They laughed weakly.

A burst of machine-gun fire swept the square. Quickly Mac reached up and pressed the ignition. The engine turned over several times but would not start.

'Sorry, Sir,' he whispered.

'That's that then,' said Allenby. 'We'll get cut down crossing the square. It'll have to be the river. Agreed?'

There were mumbles of assent.

'Right,' said Allenby purposefully. 'We'll try for the Ferwerda bridge. It's about three miles downstream. What weapons have we got?'

'One grenade and my pistol, five rounds,' Weston said.

'Same here, Sir, five rounds,' added Knowles.

'MacDonald?' Allenby asked.

'My rifle, Sir. I'm sitting on it.'

'Leave it. George, next bit of fireworks, throw the egg and let's run for it. Jump off the bridge—Shhh!'

'Brigadier Allenby?' The voice was very close.

They tensed. Cautiously, Allenby shifted and raised his head.

Mac glimpsed a bare torso and long coils of black hair. 'Indo—!'

Two shots drowned Mac's warning. Blood splattered the inside of the car.

Weston snapped off three quick shots as Knowles threw the grenade. It exploded with a sharp crack, followed by agonised screams.

'Now!' Weston yelled.

Mac flung open his door glancing at the back seat. Allenby lay dead, a bullet hole in his forehead.

They sprinted for the bridge followed by shouts and shots. Weston leapt feet first over the wall. Mac followed. It was a forty foot drop. Dark, cold, oily water engulfed him. He kicked furiously and came up gasping. Eyes stinging, he glimpsed Weston making for a row of boats moored along the far side of the river. Bullets splashed around them.

Knowles surfaced behind him spitting. 'Keep moving!'

Mac launched into a frantic, flaying front crawl. Seconds later Weston grabbed for him, pulling him behind the stern of a fishing boat. Knowles took cover behind a nearby barge. Shots bounced off the concrete walls above them.

Back in the square, black smoke swirled upwards from the burning La Salle.

Surabaya Post Office

Rane was finding it difficult to breathe in the heat, even by the shattered third-floor window. Above him the roof and top storey of the Post Office were ablaze. He knew that the creaking, smoking ceiling would soon collapse but he did not want to give up his vantage point until it was absolutely necessary.

A familiar but unwelcome rattle of an air-cooled diesel engine drowned the sound of small arms fire. Rane took a quick look to confirm his suspicions then shouted down the stairwell to Jemadar Nimse. 'Jem, T-95!'

With dismay the Mahrattas watched as the tank rolled into view. Thick, black smoke billowed from its exhaust. A red and white nationalist emblem had been daubed on the turret, partly obscuring Japanese regimental markings.

Rane fired two speculative shots at the driver's observation slit. The bullets clanged off the steel. He grunted in frustration knowing that a bazooka or PIAT rocket, still in the hold of the supply ship, would easily penetrate the relatively thin armour.

The T-95 came on, crushing the corpses in its path. Expectant chants began in the buildings across the street.

Nimse considered their options. 'Quick, grenades!'

Two Mahrattas rushed to the entrance, unclipping grenades from their chest webbing. They threw slightly ahead of the tank, hoping to damage a track. Both grenades exploded without effect. The T-95's short, stubby 37mm gun boomed. The building shook and masonry fell.

'Everyone down!' Nimse shouted urgently.

Maruti Chavan darted back from a ground-floor window and joined the others taking cover behind overturned desks and tables. He heard the tank engine increase revs to mount the steps, then drop to an idle. The Mahrattas pressed themselves to the floor.

Twin 7.7mm machine guns swept left then right in a thunderous roar punching deep holes in the brickwork and hammering out chunks of razor-sharp mortar. Around the lobby large, plate-glass counter-windows shattered into spinning, jagged shards.

Chavan saw one comrade's eyes glaze as a ricochet caught him in the back of his head. The man's hands fell limply from the stock of his Bren gun. Seconds later another man wailed as a foot-long glass shard pierced his thigh. Swearing under his breath, Chavan began to crawl from desk to desk towards the Bren.

Bullets flew above him but after a few seconds he realised he was below the guns' lowest trajectory. He scurried to the Bren, slipped a bag of magazines over his shoulder and started for the entrance. A sudden burning in his right leg made him grunt. He looked down and saw a ricochet had ripped away a piece of his calf. Blood oozed from the wound.

With one hand pulling the gun, he dragged himself along to an overturned desk nearest the doorway. Straining, he heaved the barrel of the Bren over the top of the desk. He was no more than twenty feet from the tank.

'Let's see how you like this!' Chavan snarled, sending a constant stream of fire at the driver's observation slit. Green paintwork around the narrow opening began to chip away. From within came a muffled scream. Suddenly the T-95 guns were silent. Seconds later it began a jerky, wild reverse.

When the Bren clicked empty, Chavan slammed in another magazine and kept his finger on the trigger. At the foot of the steps the tank lurched to a halt and the turret hatch flew open. Two militiamen clambered out, rolled off the back and fled across the street.

Nimse dropped down beside Chavan and clapped him on the back. 'Well done, Chav!' He saw Chavan's bloodied calf. 'Let's have a medic here! And finish that pile of scrap!'

Another Mahratta darted to the lobby entrance and lobbed a grenade cleanly into the tank's open hatch. A dull boom echoed inside.

Spontaneously the exhausted defenders cheered. Enraged by the set back, the *pemuda* opened fire once again. There was no answering fire from the bank. The Mahrattas were saving their ammunition.

A deafening drumming shook the building as the roof and third-floor ceiling collapsed. The extra weight was too much for the floors below. In turn they gave way. Jagged rafters punched through the ceiling, showering the Mahrattas in hot embers.

Chavan stared at bowing ceiling. 'Rane!' he shouted hoarsely, breathing in ash. 'Answer me, you selfish bastard!'

'Quiet!' Nimse ordered. 'Listen!'

They waited in silence. The building's partial collapse had momentarily silenced the watching mob. Nimse let his head sag to his chest for a moment and closed his red, stinging eyes. Eight men had been on the second and third floors.

Suddenly the stairwell door burst open and three Mahrattas stumbled into the lobby covered in ash and hawking. Rane was one of them. His beard, hair and uniform were singed.

He saw Chavan's bandaged leg. 'Who are you calling selfish? Look at you getting all the attention!'

Chavan and the other Mahrattas grinned, their teeth bright white amidst the grey-black coating of ash.

Behind Rane, smoke was rolling down the stairs. He pushed the door to and helped pull a desk across it. 'At least this heat will keep the mosquitoes away!'

Chavan sat on the floor, watching the white ceiling paint brown and blacken from the heat on the floor above. Minute by minute the temperature rose. Uniforms began to smoulder and so they stripped to their underpants. Body hair began to singe. 'The bastards want us to fry in here!' Chavan spat. With each breath hot air scorched his lungs.

The nine survivors knew that finally they had run out of time.

'Here, Chav,' Nimse said resignedly, handing him five .303 rounds. He went from man to man giving out the last of the ammunition. When he finished, he addressed them all. 'This is it,' he croaked. 'Who'd have thought we'd finish up in bloody Java! I am very proud to be a Mahratta.'

A lookout raised his hand. 'Hav, looks like they want to talk!'

Nimse went to the doorway and saw a militia officer and a nervous-looking older man approaching under a flag of truce. He nodded to let them approach.

From the doorway the older man spoke in halting English. 'Indian soldiers, the building is on fire. It will collapse on you at any moment. Do you wish to die? You are surrounded. We give you a chance to surrender your weapons now and live.'

'There will be no surrender,' Nimse replied. Behind him he heard his men fixing bayonets.

The two Javanese shrugged and walked away. As soon as they were back at the barricade the shooting restarted.

'Two more tanks coming up the street! Militia closing in behind them!'

One by one they fired their last rounds until only the Bren gun covering the main entrance was left, then it too clicked empty. 'That's it!' Chavan mouthed, shaking his head. They waited for the final onslaught.

Above them the burning joists snapped and half the ceiling gave way showering them with burning ash. Pungent smoke swirled around the lobby.

One Mahratta sprang up gasping, his hair on fire. 'Farewell, my friends!' He rushed blindly out of the entrance, rifle braced at his hip. *'Bolshri chatrapati Shivaji Maharaja ki jai!'*—Shout for Victory to Maharajah Shivaji! A ragged, 50-shot volley silenced him in mid stride.

Two more men charged after him. Those inside heard them gunned down. Chavan looked at Rane who shook his head. 'No, the bastards can come and get us,' he said hoarsely. The two men embraced.

There was a roar as the attackers charged.

'Steady, Mahrattas!' Nimse barked.

Bayonets raised, they braced as baying Javanese came rushing through the entrance and shattered windows.

'Shivaji Maharajah ki jai!'

After a few seconds sheer numbers of attackers swamped the Mahrattas. Dozens of hands grabbed for them and they were lifted and carried out like human trophies.

Chavan was flung down and struck his head on the road. Dazed he saw Nimse held while he was run through with bayonets and spears. He could not see Rane. Hands grabbed at him. He fought them wildly until a rifle butt slammed against his head.

Kali Mas

A large, ocean-going tug chugged past the three tired, sodden men clinging to a log nestled against the sheer concrete wall of the Kali Mas. They had been in the canal for nearly two hours, working slowly downstream, using moored boats, barges and flotsam and jetsam for cover. Dusk was falling.

Mac was caught unawares by the bow wave. It splashed him in the face and open mouth. He gagged and spat. 'Christ! The taste of home. It reminds me of the Clyde.'

Knowles peeped around the front of the log and saw yet another group of pursuers seventy yards away on the far bank. They began shooting wildly at something floating in midstream.

'The bloody canal's full of bodies,' said Knowles. 'They can't tell if it's us.'

'Let's keep moving,' whispered Weston. 'It'll be dark in twenty minutes. We're sitting ducks here.'

Mac and Knowles looked up and saw a large apartment or office building built flush to the concrete bank. They nodded.

'Off we go then!' Weston said without enthusiasm. He ducked under the water and surfaced a few feet away behind a rusting iron barge. The other two followed.

As darkness fell their pursuers lobbed flaming torches over the water, firing at random targets. Eventually they lost interest in the chase.

When they reached a wharf the saturated soldiers took the opportunity to rest and warm up. Mac eased himself out on to the steps gratefully. His uniform was covered in a film of oil, algae and faeces. He shivered as he examined the puffy and wrinkled skin on his arms and hands.

Weston, equally stained, looked at him. 'God, Mac, you stink!'

Mac managed a laugh. 'Thank you, Sir.'

'We should split up,' Knowles whispered. 'The water's tidal from here on. We'll stand a much better chance alone. With any luck C Company will have held the drawbridge and the harbour....'

There was a long silence as they weighed up their chances. Anything could have happened in the last few hours. Mac knew Knowles was right but it did not make him like the idea any better. He suddenly remembered the bird calls of the Gurkhas back at the Chindwin. 'What recognition signal should I use? Sentries at the bridge are likely to shoot at anything that moves.'

'Good point,' replied Weston. 'Try "Maharajah Shivaji" followed by "British". That should do the trick.'

They moved off at ten-minute intervals. Weston first, then Knowles. Mac counted the minutes then, reluctantly slid back into the river. He swam slowly into mid-stream, trying not to splash and praying that the moon would remain hidden.

After a few minutes a wooden crate bobbed alongside him and he clung to it, letting the tide take him. As his eyes grew accustomed to the darkness he made out other objects in the water. Rats were congregating on them, gnawing and squeaking. At first Mac assumed they were grain sacks. Later one of the 'sacks' bumped against his crate. To his horror he saw it was a headless and limbless torso in what was left of a uniform tunic.

Time dragged and the water drained his body heat. He began to feel numb and sleepy. Light flickered over his face and he opened his eyes. Ahead of him torches flashed over the water. Behind them loomed the dark, angular framework of a drawbridge. Instinctively Mac rolled on to his back, closed his eyes and played dead for the second time that day. Muffled voices reached him, then a beam hit his face. He tensed, waiting for the shot.

'It's MacDonald! Damn, he was so close!' It was Knowles's voice.

Mac grinned. 'Call me the Maharajah of Glasgow!'

'Marvellous cuppa, Sir!' Mac shivered as he gulped the hot, sweet tea.

The two officers led him along the bridge to the bullet-riddled gatehouse. Weary but still vigilant Mahrattas sat in small groups, their weapons near to hand. With every footstep Mac trod on spent cartridge cases.

'What's been happening?' Mac asked looking inquiringly from Weston to Knowles.

'It's quiet now but it's been a shambles', Weston sighed. 'Colonel Hughes has taken over the brigade. Somehow he managed to get from the Marine Hospital to Brigade HQ by jeep. He and Major Cane have been negotiating with the Javans for a cease-fire. We've lost a lot of men.'

'And Darmo, Sir?' Mac was thinking about Meg.

'We haven't heard much', replied Knowles. 'But there are reports of an attack on an internee convoy. Many killed and missing.'

Mac's head dropped. 'What now?'

'A formal cease-fire is due to come into force at 0900. General Chrishaw and Sukarno will be here at ten.'

'And guess who'll be driving the General!' Knowles added, clapping Mac on the shoulder.

Mac's face fell. 'Uh? I thought I'd get a day off at least.'

'Not a chance, Mac', Knowles said quickly. 'We're at war here—whatever the politicians might say back home. Allenby's death has already been reported by the BBC. General Chrishaw wants first-hand accounts from the three of us as soon as he arrives. He's been on the radio and threatened Surabaya with a pasting if the Indos don't grant the internees safe passage and hand over the Brigadier's killers. I think Java will now have London's undivided attention.'

'About bloody time!' Weston grumbled. 'The General also wants written reports on the Brigadier's death for Lord

Mountbatten and the Chiefs of Staff in London, so the sooner we get cracking the better. Come on, we can get cleaned up at the HQ.'

Mac gulped down his tea and shivered. 'No rest for the wicked...' he muttered to a red-eyed Mahratta sentry. The English was lost on the sepoy but not the universal tone of the much-put-upon enlisted man. The sentry smiled briefly then his gaze went back to the canal.

Hotel Michiels

Mac's morning had passed in a blur of activity. He had driven Colonel Hughes to meet General Chrishaw's plane at Morokrembangan in a five-vehicle convoy. Sukarno had flown in separately.

Back at the HQ, Chrishaw had listened to his account of Allenby's death without interruption, then congratulated him on his escape. Afterwards Mac had resumed helping out in the busy HQ hospital.

He was taking a break when Wing Commander Ball arrived from Darmo with news that Meg was safe. 'She had a close shave,' Ball told him. 'It was sickening.'

Just then a Mahratta military police sergeant strode into the hotel and went through to Hughes's office. Two more policemen were outside, escorting a white male prisoner in the uniform of an Indian Army sepoy. Conversation and activity stopped. A ripple of anger ran round the servicemen in the foyer.

'Who's that, Wing Commander?' Mac asked casually.

'Well, well,' Ball replied sardonically. 'I suspect it's the infamous Captain Henssen sprung from his Surabaya cell. I heard he was being brought in today. Word has got round.'

'I'd like to punch him,' grunted Mac.

'Many in 49th Brigade would string him up if they got the chance,' said Ball. 'The MPs had to bandage his head, stain his face with coffee and dress him as a sepoy for his own safety. General Chrishaw wants him expelled from the Indies. Of course, the Dutch have protested to London.'

Haggard and shoe-less, Peter Henssen was escorted into the lobby. His hair was unkempt and an almost full beard covered his lower face. He was also sporting a very recent black eye. Muted but audible comments followed his progress. 'Imbecile!'—'Stupid bastard!'—'Arsehole!'

Henssen's eyes flared briefly then his head dropped and he let the MPs lead him up the stairs, followed by the armed Mahratta who was to stand guard outside his door.

Mac turned the ambulance into the drive of the Simpang Hospital. Ahead, half-a-dozen Indonesian militiamen were lounging by the entrance.

'Slow down, Mac', Ball said calmly. 'And look confident!'

'That's not so easy for a mere enlisted man, Sir.'

Ball laughed. 'That's the spirit!' His face darkened as he noticed the Lee-Enfield rifles sported by some of the militia. 'We know where they got those...' he said bitterly.

Mac nodded. Images of the mutilated corpses in the Kali Mas came back to him. He felt a flush of anger.

Surabaya had been a disaster for the British. On the way to the hospital Ball had given him a quick summary. 'It was touch and go for quite a while. If Sukarno hadn't come and broadcast, and if Chrishaw's bluff had failed, then the entire Brigade would have been wiped out. As it is, we lost over four hundred and thirty men in three days! There must be easily five thousand Indonesian dead.'

'I still don't know why we're here, Sir,' Mac's dejection had been undisguised.

'Yes you do!' Ball had said quickly, one eyebrow raised.

'Oh, yes,' Mac had nodded in understanding. 'Because we're here!'

'Exactly!'

'But how can we trust the Indos after this?'

'Allenby gave his life for the truce,' Ball had replied earnestly. 'It's fragile but it must hold...if only for a few days. Colonel Hughes insists we must abide by it to the letter. Allenby had to agree to Indo guards on the convoys from Darmo to the harbour. Understandably enough that won't go down well with the internees. Basically we've got just a few days to get nearly seven thousand women and children out. HMS *Sussex* and HMS *Bulolo* are waiting to ferry them to Singapore. But the Indos keep delaying things. And the General's ultimatum isn't making things any easier, either.'

'Will he really order the town shelled?' Mac had asked.

'No question,' Ball had said emphatically. 'He's a man of his word.'

'Christ!' Mac had blurted. 'What a mess! We'll be stuck here for bloody years!'

Ball had eyed him reproachfully but aware of Mac's recent experiences, said nothing.

Mac stopped the ambulance outside a little way from the main hospital entrance. They were watched suspiciously by the young militiamen but an officer soon appeared to lead the unarmed Mac and Ball inside. Corridors, offices and waiting areas were crammed with wounded Indonesians, nurses and anxious, angry relatives.

Icy stares and jeers followed them as they went through to a small room guarded by two more militiamen. In the room were three bandaged-swathed Indians.

'I don't understand how these blokes are alive and the others aren't', Mac said quietly.

'Luck of the draw', Ball replied, glancing at a list of names on his clipboard. 'The militia took some prisoners but the mobs did not. Twenty-two men have been returned to us so far, mostly from hospitals or prisons.'

Only one of the wounded Indians was conscious. His expression brightened at the sight of the British uniforms.

'Good afternoon!' Ball beamed at him jovially. 'You're coming with us. Name and number?'

'34125 Chavan, M, 6th Battalion, 5th Mahrattas, Sir.'

Ball searched through his list and then made a tick. 'Ah, here you are. Chavan, Maruti. You're a lucky man!' He was turning to the others when Chavan spoke in halting English.

'Excuse, Sahib. 35163 Rane? Padurang Rane. Same battalion.'

'Rane...' Ball flicked back through the pages of his list and quickly found the name. He paused then shook his head in commiseration. 'I'm afraid Sepoy Rane is listed as missing.'

Chavan's eyes dropped. He lay back on the bed, his gaze distant.

Simpang Mosque, Surabaya

Sarel was elated. He had addressed the huge, already ecstatic crowd in the square for ten minutes. They stood before him, a sea of expectant young faces, banners and placards held high, hanging on his every word.

After Sukarno's plea for a truce over the radio the militia units had restrained the *pemuda* and taken control of key buildings. Sarel was not concerned. He had seen the fire of revolution lit in Surabaya. Fanning the flames across Java would now be easier.

'*Arek Surabaya!*'—Surabayans! Sarel's voice boomed. 'God has granted us victory against the imperialist Dutch-British and their Indian lackeys! They have lost their stomach for the fight because our cause is a true and just jihad to free Indonesia!'

The crowd roared its approval. *'Merdeka!'*—*'Merdeka!'*

Suddenly sombre, Sarel held up his hands for quiet. 'Over the last three days, many of our brothers have fallen in the battle for Freedom. We who live have an obligation to those glorious martyrs for In—do—ne—sia.'

Again the crowd cheered.

He waited for silence. 'Our struggle is not over. As I speak, our brothers in arms at Ambarawa and Semarang fight the colonialist oppressors. I ask you. Will the heroes of Surabaya go to their aid?'

Shouts of 'Yes!'—'Yes!' echoed around the square.

Sarel raised his hands, this time beseechingly. 'Who will follow me to final victory?'

A new, bellowing chant began, building rapidly. Sarel led them, punching the air in a brisk three-beat count, his face triumphant. 'Am-bara-wa!'

Chapter Ten

A shout from the lookout brought dozens of *pemuda* to the ridge. 'Bung Lamban, another convoy!'

Lamban glanced at the line of trucks winding along the narrow road several hundred feet below then reached for his field glasses. He watched them for a few seconds then sat back against a large rock. A rustle of frustration ran through the half-dozen youths with him on the ridge.

One could keep silent no longer. 'They are within range of our mortars. Let's attack!'

Lamban smiled and shook his head. 'Save your ammunition, Subo. Wait for the sure kill. You are too—' A slight movement by his foot caught his eye.

From head to tail the scorpion was about five inches long. It was a glossy dark brown moving deliberately from stone to stone, keeping to the shade while searching for prey.

Lamban came up on his haunches and placed his hand, palm-down and with his fingers spread on the powdery earth directly in the path of the scorpion. Instantly the it sensed the vibration and stopped.

Conversation among the now perplexed youths petered out. They drew nearer. Lamban paid them no attention. His hand remained motionless.

After several seconds the scorpion continued forward, resuming the hunt. It was three inches from his hand when

Lamban quickly lifted his index and second fingers, spreading them wide, mimicking a large, predatory spider.

Immediately the scorpion shrank back, its tail arching upwards and over its body. At the tip, the comma-shaped sting quivered, ready for the strike. It scuttled quickly left then right, seeking escape.

Deliberately Lamban inched his hand still closer to the scorpion. Some of the onlookers, disconcerted by the strange duel, exchanged uneasy looks.

Suddenly Lamban's hand darted forward in a circling blur. In a split second his hand returned to its start position. His middle finger had gouged a low ring of raised earth around the scorpion.

His face expressionless, Lamban withdrew his hand and sat back. 'Watch and learn.' His voice was dispassionate. 'It could simply climb over the dirt and escape. Instead, it is too excited, trapped by its own instincts. There can only be one outcome.'

Within the traced circle the agitated scorpion began to spin, probing frantically. The youths watched in utter fascination. Tail twitching in an innate response to a perceived threat, the scorpion continued its frenzied scuttling. Seconds later its overloaded nervous system surged. In the blink of an eye the tail flicked forward, sting plunging, once, twice, thrice, piercing its own thick carapace, pumping venom. Slowly the scorpion arched upwards, then flipped over onto its back. It lay convulsing as the fatal paralysis took hold.

Lamban reached down, took the dying insect between his thumb and forefinger and squeezed. It burst, splattering his fingers in blood and entrails. Wide-eyed, the youths watched him unsheathe his *keris* and anoint the blade with the poisoned remains.

When he spoke his gaze was already on the familiar figure working his way nimbly along the ridge path towards them. 'Whites are dangerous like the scorpion but if we are patient they will destroy themselves.'

Eagerly the youths nodded, the awe and fear was still in their eyes when Sarel reached them.

'That was the seventh convoy,' Lamban informed him casually. 'Ten lorries and a few cars each time. They moved about fifteen-hundred Dutch today.'

Sarel looked at the sun. It sat low in the west. 'That's about half of them. This will be the last one today. They won't want to risk the roads at night.'

Lamban nodded and smiled. 'Can you blame them?'

'Not really,' laughed Sarel leading him away from the group. 'Where are their tanks?'

'Two in the centre, near the hotel. Two by the church.'

'Hmm,' Sarel muttered. 'What do you think?'

Lamban picked up a twig and used it to point. 'The British are rushing. We have received no word of any reinforcements coming from Semarang or leaving Djakarta. I think this is all of them.'

'I agree,' Sarel replied in frustration. 'We could have destroyed them at Surabaya if Sukarno hadn't arrived and started bleating about "world opinion". I wonder whether world opinion will save him from the rope if the Dutch ever catch him.'

'We must never let that happen!' Lamban said firmly.

Sarel smiled cynically. 'Of course not!'

At the sound of footsteps behind them, they turned. A Black Buffalo in militia uniform saluted Sarel. 'Sir.'

'Well?' Sarel asked sharply.

'Our main force has assembled to the northwest, ready to move. One battalion is keeping the British sentries occupied as instructed.'

'Good,' nodded Sarel. 'We move tonight. It's time to give them some easy pickings. Spread the word that there's food—and women—at Ambarawa and only a hundred Dutch soldiers.' He stood up. 'Tomorrow morning we'll let Major Shirai demonstrate his loyalty to the revolution. Who's this?'

'Lamban, at last! I've been looking everywhere for you!'

A figure was scrambling up the bank. Two Black Buffalos escorting him stood watching, waiting for instructions.

'Kerek!' Lamban grinned.

Sarel looked at him inquiringly.

'He's a friend from my village. I can vouch for him.' With his white shirt, long shorts and short hair Kerek looked as though he had come straight from a class at the *pesantren*. Lamban waved the escort away.

'Loyal lieutenants are hard to find,' Sarel said quietly. 'Train him.'

Kerek reached the top of the bank panting. Lamban embraced him. 'You've finally left home!'

'Yes, three days ago. I sneaked away!' Kerek was staring at him in admiration. 'You look so different. Like a real warrior!'

Lamban laughed. 'This is Bung Sarel, one of our senior commanders.'

'I've heard of you!' Kerek beamed.

Sarel nodded politely. 'Welcome, Bung Kerek. You are here just in time for the battle!'

'I'm ready!' Kerek's eyes blazed.

'Not before we get you a gun!' Lamban said quickly. Kerek was armed with only a *keris*. Lamban carried a *klewang* sword, two keris and a Thompson sub-machine gun.

'Your parents and sister are well...' Kerek said unsure if he ought to continue.

'Good,' Lamban answered uncomfortably, with a quick nod. He had barely given them a thought for weeks. 'I will see them soon enough. Now, how did you find me in just three days?'

'First I asked where I could find Lamban of Sadakan. When people did not know you I asked where I could find the most skilful fighter! Someone told me about a Black Buffalo known as "Death Shroud". I knew Taruna forged you a *keris* with that name. It had to be you!'

'Well done,' said Lamban.

Sarel laughed and clapped Kerek on the shoulder. 'Soon,' he said casually, 'that name will spread terror among the Dutch! But for now let's get you something to eat...and then a rifle!'

Fifty cheering, armed youths escorted the Ford station wagon as it crept slowly towards the Hotel van Rheeden. An excited, almost hysterical voice blared alternately in Javanese and Malay from a loudspeaker mounted on the car's roof.

Rai and Miller watched uneasily from the hotel's veranda. Miller looked at his watch. It was close to midnight. Ambarawa was all but controlled by the *pemuda* and relations with them were already at breaking point. Ominously, local women and children had been seen leaving the town all day. Tension was rising by the hour. Earlier that day, the Gurkhas had seized a number of cars at roadblocks and returned them to their Dutch owners. Ferocious arguments had ensued but the local police had sided openly with their fellow countrymen, accusing the Gurkhas of working for the Dutch.

A couple of hours before, Miller had led an emergency patrol to a nearby kampong. A local stall-holder who had ignored a *pemuda* warning and served the Gurkhas had been made to watch as his wife and two young daughters were clubbed and hacked to death. Afterwards the man was shot dead. The Gurkhas had driven the youths from the kampong but on their way back they had come under fire.

The Ford drew nearer and Miller caught some of the words. 'My Malay's poor,' he said quietly to Rai, 'but I don't like the sound of that.'

Rai nodded once. 'Sunwar speaks good Malay, Miller-sahib.' He beckoned to a sentry by the hotel's entrance and the soldier trotted over to them.

'Well, Sunwar, what are they going on about?' Miller asked, not taking his eyes from the street.

The young rifleman listened to the harangue. 'He says the British have been defeated at Surabaya...It's everyone's patriotic duty to rise up and throw out the whites and their Indian servants.'

Miller sighed in exasperation. 'Nice to know we're appreciated! I'd better pass it on.'

Lt-Col Edmunds sat at the hotel manager's desk and listened to Miller's report along with Major Timothy Duncan.

Edmunds shook his head gravely. 'There might be something to the claims. Signals have been picking up some of 49th Brigade's radio messages. They were facing heavy opposition and they requested urgent reinforcements.'

'I'll tell the men to be on their guard,' said Miller. 'Not that they aren't already with these fanatics around.'

Duncan interrupted, 'Sir, we've got platoons scattered all over. Here, the hospital, the schools and so on. Shouldn't we put the internees in larger groups?'

Edmunds shrugged his shoulders in frustration. 'Yes but do it tomorrow. I don't want them out in the open in the dark.'

'You're probably right,' Duncan nodded thoughtfully. 'I keep thinking about the reports of roadblocks and large groups of Indos in the east.'

'Me too, Tim', Edmunds nodded. 'If they're accurate it won't be long before we're surrounded. HQ Batavia has asked me to evaluate our chances of making a dash to Semarang.' He turned to Miller. 'John, you're the only pilot we've got. Can you handle the plane the Japs left at the airfield?'

Miller stood up enthusiastically. 'The trainer? Yes.'

'If that damn thing is safe. I'd like you to see if the road is still open.'

'I had a look at it yesterday, Sir. It's a bit tatty but it seems sound enough. I'm a bit rusty though!'

'Just like riding a bike isn't it?' Edmunds asked, raising his eyebrows. 'I'm sure it'll all come back in a couple of minutes!'

They all laughed nervously, well aware that the mission could easily prove a death sentence.

'Well then,' Miller said heading for the door, 'I'll give the engine the once-over just in case. I'll take her up at dawn.'

Miller coaxed the Tachikawa Ki-17 bi-plane along the dirt strip runway. Its engine spluttered briefly as it rose into the hazy orange dawn sky then settled. Two low circuits of the airfield gave him the feel of the very basic controls.

Ambarawa, nestled beside the large, almost circular lake looked tranquil. The water reflected a deep, iridescent aquamarine. Miller swung northeast to follow the road towards Semarang some twenty-five miles away. Low, pale-green hills, stacked with flooded rice terraces shimmered to the north and south. In the distance, Semarang's church spires stood out in brilliant white against the vast, rich blue of the Java Sea. For the first time in days he relaxed, losing himself in the breath-taking view. Much of the landscape reminded him of the hill country in central Assam where he had spent his childhood summers on his father's tea estate.

Something across the road caught his eye and he took the plane lower. There were five roadblocks in all. From the air they resembled a series of hurdles on a racecourse. Some were substantial, incorporating vehicles and sandbags, others were more simple barriers made with oil drums. He circled them all at 1,000 feet, ignoring pot-shots and making notes on a pad tied to his thigh.

His task completed, Miller resisted the urge to buzz the last roadblock and turned the Ki-17 around. As the airstrip appeared below him he saw several vehicles nearing a railway crossing south of the town and went on to investigate. British flags on the roofs identified an internee convoy. He put the biplane into a climb and continued south-west.

As Magelang came into view he was distracted by the graceful, grey stepped dome of Borobudur looming out of the trees just twenty miles away. He suddenly regretted not having a camera with him. A reflected flash of sunlight on a windscreen below ended his reverie. 'You're not a tourist today, Johnny,' he said testily to himself. He eased the plane lower.

The enemy column had evidently rested overnight and was reforming for the short march to Ambarawa. It stretched back for nearly a mile. At the head was an advance guard of an armoured car, six troop carriers and a dozen cars. The bulk was following on foot or bicycle with dozens of supply carts.

Miller circled over the station as a tram car draped in red and white banners was disgorging yet more fighters. Another tram, with dozens of figures clinging to its roof and sides, was less than a mile behind. To his dismay he estimated there were at least five thousand *pemuda* heading for Ambarawa.

Ambarawa Station

A bell rang shrilly and the heavy gates slowly began to rise. Rai acknowledged the signalman with a wave from the passenger seat of the Isuzu T-94. The three-tonner rocked forward over the level-crossing, the driver trying not to jar the women and children crammed in the back.

Rai's watch said seven forty-six. He was a little behind schedule but that was not what was bothering him. Ambarawa was strangely quiet.

Up in the signal-box, Lamban watched from the shadows as four Isuzus crossed the rails ahead of an assortment of overloaded cars.

As a battered Oldsmobile saloon nosed forward Lamban nodded to the signalman. 'Now!'

Reluctantly the man reached for a lever. Again the bell rang. Seconds later, the gate came down, missing the front of the saloon by inches. The driver, a twelve-year-old boy, sounded the horn.

Rai heard and stopped the convoy. He jumped down and began to walk back towards the crossing. By now the boy was out of the car, shouting and gesticulating at the signal-box. Then, still shouting, he started to climb on the gate. A single shot rang out and the boy pitched backwards. A woman's scream inside the car was immediately drowned in bursts of fire from the station buildings, the freight yard and roadside houses.

Rai spun and sprinted to the front lorry. Behind him there was chaos. In the vehicles women and children were screaming in terror. The Gurkhas were returning fire but they were exposed and hopelessly out-gunned.

'Go! Go!' Rai ordered.

The driver crashed through the gears and the Isuzu lurched forward. Rai leant out through the open door to look back at the crossing. Beyond the gate cars were backing away.

'Ahead!' The driver yelled urgently.

Rai turned and saw two *pemuda* in the middle of the road taking aim. A burst from his sub-machine gun cut them down. The T-94 barely bounced as it ground over their bodies.

In the distance mortar fire rumbled over the town.

'Keep your foot down!' Rai yelled. 'Don't stop till we get to the school!'

Hotel van Rheeden

'And that's about it, Sir,' said Miller finishing his report. It had not been positive. 'If we moved in at least company strength within the next two hours we could probably punch through with heavy casualties but once enemy reinforcements arrive...'

Colonel Edmunds and Major Duncan were looking doubtful. The Colonel cleared his throat. 'Hmm. You're assuming the bridges aren't mined.'

'That's true,' Miller admitted. 'I can't vouch for the bridges.' He glanced through the open window. Little groups women and children were relaxing or eating breakfast in the hotel's overgrown shrubbery.

Edmunds shook his head in exasperation. 'Internee numbers here are swelling all the time. Almost two thousand have come from Magelang in the last three days. Another seven hundred from Banjobiroe. That brings the total to over eight thousand! Protecting them is a full-time job for two regiments, never mind two companies!'

There was a sharp knock on the door. A havildar entered and saluted crisply. 'Excuse me, Colonel-sahib, lookouts report armed Javans are entering the shops and houses opposite. Also, C Company has reported activity near the school and hospital.'

'Thank you, Hav.'

Edmunds looked sombrely at Miller and Duncan. 'The locals must have been encouraged by the news of reinforcements.' The words had barely left his mouth when they heard shooting.

'It's to the south, near the station,' said Duncan.

Miller went quickly to the open window to listen. Several internees were sitting in the garden. 'You're right. Damn! The first convoy from Magelang is due at the crossing anytime now!'

Three high-pitched whistles sounded high overhead. 'Take cover!' Miller yelled into the garden, then dived for shelter behind the desk.

Crump! Crump! The ground shook as two mortar shells exploded along the side of the hotel. Crump! A third blew up a shrubbery. Those in the garden rushed inside screaming.

'Swine!' Miller spat. 'They don't care who they kill!'

Shots blazed from across the street. Windows in the hotel shattered and ricochets zinged along the hallways. Seconds later a Bren gun in the lobby hammered out a reply.

'Get the internees into the basement and interior rooms!' Edmunds shouted urgently. 'And do something about those bloody mortars!'

Kate was in the infirmary, applying a new dressing to a middle-aged woman's leg ulcer, when the distant shooting started. She went to the window. Below her, mothers were shouting anxiously for their children, then gathering them up and rushing for their huts. In stark contrast, a few Gurkhas were calmly preparing firing positions along the walls. Others were issuing weapons to the Japanese work party.

First she heard, then saw the convoy racing out of the town and across the open ground towards the school. Several Japanese rushed to open the gates. As the lorries swept through, she caught glimpses of distraught, shocked faces of the passengers.

Gwen, Juliette and Anna came in running. 'Quick!' Gwen shouted. 'Lots of hot water and bandages!'

Within minutes the injured were being brought up.

Major Miller arrived with five Gurkhas with minor wounds. 'We were lucky that the road to hear was clear,' Miller said sombrely. He was staring out of the window. Seven women, five children and two Gurkhas had been killed in the ambush. Another seventeen internees had a range of gunshot wounds. 'Doctor, I'd like to put a man here. There's a commanding view of the approach.'

'Of course, Major,' Gwen said, forcing a smile.

Miller addressed them all. 'I've been in contact with Colonel Edmunds at Magelang. He's conferring with our HQ in Batavia. Reinforcements will be leaving Semarang soon.'

'But we have trucks here…' Juliette said quickly. 'The sick and wounded could leave.'

Miller shook his head. 'There are too many roadblocks.'

'Major,' Gwen asked calmly, 'just how many revolutionaries are there?'

'Oh…er,' Miller mumbled, caught off guard. They noticed his hesitation and he sighed in confession. 'We estimate about four thousand.' He gave up any pretence. 'Please keep it to yourselves. It's true we're out-numbered but we've got sound defensive positions,' he said with a slightly forced bonhomie. 'The relief column will fight its way through. They should be here by late this afternoon. You won't believe it but some of them are Japanese!'

Kate felt her chest tighten. Suddenly she was sure Ota was coming to Ambarawa.

'Then—' Juliette stammered. 'Then we are trapped?'

'I'm afraid so,' he said firmly. A short, awkward silence followed until one of the wounded groaned and Gwen went to help. Miller left them.

Kate went back out on to the veranda. Over to her right she could see Duncan directing Nagumo and the other Japanese as they placed sandbags around a machine gun behind the gate. Juliette and Gwen came and stood by her. Nagumo said something to his men and they laughed together. Duncan clapped Nagumo on the shoulder and hurried away.

'I don't believe it!' Gwen said bitterly, her cigarette shaking in her hands. 'Now every fucking Jap's a good Jap!'

'Gwen!' Kate shot back sternly. 'We all have to fight! Now's not the time for—'

'Oh, isn't it?' Gwen shrieked. 'When will it be fucking time? Those bastards are already getting chummy! I don't see any of them suffering! Look at them, walking around bold as bloody brass! When will the bastards get what they deserve? Or is it better to forget the torture and starvation!'

'Gwen, stop it! Please,' pleaded Juliette. 'They're helping us!'

Gwen covered her face with her hands and burst into tears. 'I— Oh, I'm sorry,' she sobbed. 'I don't know what came over me.'

Juliette embraced her. 'I do, *chérie*,' Juliette said gently. 'You're exhausted. Come and rest.'

Later, Kate slipped out for some fresh air. She walked aimlessly, head down. Thoughts of Tjandi, the Guttman house, the Sakura and Ota mingled in her mind. Now she felt guilty about leaving Semarang. Because of her Ota was in danger again.

'*Konnichi-wa!*'

Startled, Kate looked up and saw Nagumo inclining his head in a slight bow. Without realising it she had wandered almost to the main gate.

'Konnichi-wa, Nagumo-san,' Kate replied politely.

Nagumo turned back to issue more rapid instructions to his men. Kate wanted to say more but she was too embarrassed. Instead, she walked on, Gwen's comments about 'good Japs' heavy on her mind.

When she returned to the infirmary Gwen, Juliette, Anna and Rukmini were waiting for her.

'Ah, here you are!' Gwen said, now back to her usual self. 'The Reverend Mother has asked for some help at the convent. I thought two of you could go—just for a few hours—in shifts. I'll be going there later. We thought drawing lots would be fair. Is that all right with you?'

'Yes, of course,' said Kate.

Gwen held up three straws pulled from a mattress, levelled their tops but hid their lengths with her fingers. She smiled. 'Long straws stay here with me.'

They made their choices. Kate and Anna drew the shortest straws.

'Gwen, there are no soldiers at the convent,' said Kate softly.

'Oh, you'll be quite safe!' Gwen said lightly. 'It's a holy place and a hospital.'

Kate was at the convent when she heard explosions in the town. In the nearby kampongs drums began a frenzied beat. With Anna and two of the younger nuns she rushed to the top of the bell tower. From their vantage point they watched anxiously as the human tide rushed towards them. Kate held her breath as the revolutionaries reached the path that led to the convent. Miraculously the horde swept on.

'Praise be to God,' one of the nuns whispered.

At the edge of the swathe of grassland the *pemuda* halted and fanned out, surrounding the school buildings. Their defiant jeers echoed over the valley. Then they began shooting.

Hotel Michiels, Surabaya

Mac was helping to carry Chavan's stretcher when he heard the shouts.

'Mac! Mac!'

Meg was waving, pushing through the hotel's crowded reception. She kissed him on the mouth. 'Wing Commander Ball told me you were safe but it's good to see for myself.'

'Same here', Mac grinned.

Chavan and the Indian stretcher bearer were smiling at them.

'Excuse us, fellas,' Meg laughed. 'It's just a demonstration of Anglo-American friendship!'

Mac and Meg left Chavan with some of his fellow wounded and found themselves a quiet corner. They held each other for a long time.

'Hey,' Mac said suddenly, running his fingers through her hair. 'This is a hotel! Do you think we could get a room?'

'One day, maybe,' she laughed. 'But it won't be at wartime rates!'

He looked at her carefully and changed the subject. 'That run down the street must have been scary.'

Meg put her cheek against his chest and hugged him tightly. 'Yeah...shitty. And for you too in that stinky river! I can smell it on you!'

He became pensive. 'I really thought I'd had it.'

Meg sighed. 'I liked Brigadier Allenby. It's always the nice guys who get it. Tell me about it sometime. We were both lucky.' She dabbed at her eyes with the back of her hand. 'Damn! I'm crying again! It's not like me.' She forced a smile. 'Still a few more articles left in this body, soldier!'

Mac kissed her forehead. 'That's the way! What are you going to do?'

She shrugged. 'I'm at a loose end. General Chrishaw's playing hard to get and the Dutch and Aussie correspondents have already skedaddled! They were besieged in the Tourist Office the whole time. They had a nasty surprise!'

'I wish we could leave,' he said tiredly. 'I mean the British leave Java.'

She nodded. 'Well, war is never fair. Java's yours whether you like it or not.'

He sighed. 'Aye, like it or not. Let's hope we can at least go back to Batavia.'

She was suddenly uneasy and shook her head. 'Uh uh, the Wing-Co said that if the evacuation here goes smoothly we'd be flying to Semarang early tomorrow. There's been trouble there, too.'

Mac frowned. 'Semarang again? I suppose it's better than here...'

'Some worrying news, Mac,' she said softly. She pulled back from him and gripped his arms. 'The Wing-Co told me there's heavy fighting at Magelang.'

Mac's smile vanished. 'Rai's lot?'

She nodded. 'They're cut off.'

'They can take care of themselves,' he said gruffly.

'Mac, listen to me,' she said softly. 'There are only three-hundred Gurkhas against ten thousand or more. I'm so sorry,' she said softly. 'I had to tell you.'

Semarang

'Suzuki, that's the one!' Ota hissed, pointing with his pistol to a closed, glass-panelled front door of a house. He was across the street from Suzuki, sheltering in a shallow doorway. Semarang's electricity supply was out again but the moonlight cast long, deceptive shadows down the street.

Ota yawned. It had been a tense and gruelling day. The British had assigned them the task of flushing out hundreds of militants from the northeast section of the town. Night had fallen with three streets still in the hands of the *pemuda*. The battalion had already lost six more men.

Suzuki nodded back to Ota, then bobbed underneath a window and across the doorway to stand flat against the wall beside the door. A quick backward jab with the stock of his sub-machine carbine smashed a glass panel. Shots from within shattered the others. Suzuki ignored them and calmly struck the tip of a grenade against the wall. Sparks spluttered from the lit fuse. He began a silent count then flung the grenade inside and pressed back against the wall. Two seconds later, a loud bang echoed. Suzuki went in low, firing from the hip, followed by two other soldiers. There were two more bursts of gunfire before Suzuki appeared in the doorway and signalled the house was cleared.

Just as Ota moved out of the doorway he glimpsed a brief blue muzzle flash. Instinctively he jerked backwards and the bullet struck a drainpipe a foot from his head. He crouched down and darted across the street.

Suzuki grinned and offered Ota his canteen. 'That was a close one, Lieutenant!'

'I think Harada trained their snipers too damn well!' Ota replied, his breath heavy with relief. He looked at his watch. 'I'll lead the next one.' It was going to be a long night.

'Well, it's...different,' Sgt-Major Tazaki said hesitantly. 'I always thought our rations were tasteless but this is foul. No wonder we took Singapore if they were fed on this shit!'

Kudo, Captain Seguchi and Ota laughed. The sweep through the suburbs had finished just before dawn and they were resting in an abandoned house. Their early, cold breakfast consisted of tinned potato and soya sausages donated by a grateful British HQ.

A runner scurried through the charred doorway with a note for Kudo. He read it, noticed their inquisitive faces and shrugged. 'It looks like the Brits haven't finished with us yet. I'm to report to their Brigadier.'

'More "house clearances", Major?' Tazaki asked casually.

'Probably,' replied Kudo sounding weary.

'Where are all their troops? That's what I want to know,' Seguchi complained.

Kudo shrugged. 'Get some sleep if you can.'

When Kudo entered the Operations Room at the British HQ he recognised only the tall, lean British area commander, Brigadier Bentham. He was studying a wall map of central Java with some British and Indian officers. John Miller was among them.

Kudo saluted. To his surprise Bentham returned it immediately, in contradiction of standing orders. 'Thank you for coming so promptly, Major,' Bentham said. There was a slight tension in his voice.

All eyes in the room turned to Kudo as Bentham continued. 'Splendid job last night and much appreciated.'

Kudo glanced around and saw the looks of genuine gratitude. He also noticed red eyes and stubble and realised that, like him, no-one in the room had slept much the night before.

Miller came forward with a cup of coffee. 'You look like you could use this, Major.'

'Thank you,' Kudo replied gratefully.

Bentham let him take a sip then sighed. 'To be honest, Major, we face another crisis. Reports of the uprising at Surabaya have encouraged every would-be revolutionary to attack us. Thanks to your men, we've managed to contain the trouble here. Elsewhere it's a different story. We need your help again.'

To Kudo the sombre faces spoke volumes. 'What kind of help, Brigadier?' he asked quietly.

'You must know the Ambarawa area well,' Bentham said stepping back over to the map.

'Yes, quite well,' Kudo replied cautiously. 'It was within my command area.'

Some of the officers moved away from the wall map and he saw the single, blue 'friendly' pin-flags at Magelang and Ambarawa, Semarang and Surabaya. He was stunned to see no other blue flags except far to the west at Djakarta and Bandung. In contrast, red 'enemy' flags were clustered beside the British ones. Kudo could not believe his eyes. The British had less than a division in the whole of Java!

Bentham pointed at the map. 'At Ambarawa three hundred Gurkhas and the fifty of your men seconded as a work party are defending over eight thousand women and children. They are massively outnumbered and surrounded by mobs and some militia units. Late last night, a couple of infantry platoons managed to get through from here. Since then, roadblocks have been set up. My men are getting low on ammunition and this morning they radioed requesting reinforcements.' Bentham paused to look keenly at Kudo. 'Major, I have insufficient troops to keep Semarang secure and send aid to Ambarawa. You, on the other hand, command a company…'

Kudo stared at him.

'Of course,' Bentham added quickly, 'I realise this is outside the terms of the agreement on the use of Japanese forces. I have already involved your men in costly operations. I will fully understand if you feel that you cannot—'

'Can they hold out for another few hours?' Kudo asked quickly, stepping closer to the map table.

Relieved smiles appeared around the table and some of the tension left Bentham's face. 'Thank you, Major! Your men could make all the difference.'

'It's only twenty-five miles,' interjected Miller. 'Will it take hours?'

Kudo pointed to the mountain passes. 'The road is narrow and easily defended. Some of the bridges might have been re-mined.'

Bentham nodded. 'Two Gurkha companies are pinned down in Magelang, twenty miles away. Your approach from the east should ease the pressure sufficiently to allow them to march on Ambarawa.'

'Yes,' Miller agreed. 'Is there any way we can swing round to the west and link up?'

Kudo bent over the map. 'We can take the main road through Oengaran as far as the Sikoenin junction, then turn west to Bodjong and Bedono. If there are no roadblocks it will add an hour, perhaps less, to the journey. It's an easier route into Ambarawa, and the Bedono summit overlooks the town.'

'Good,' Bentham said impressed. 'We'll rendezvous with the Gurkhas at Bedono.'

Kudo scratched his chin. 'We have only two armoured cars…'

'The Gurkhas have armour with them: four Stuarts,' said Miller. 'They should be enough.'

'For God's sake let's hope so,' Bentham added sombrely. 'Major Kudo, let me introduce Major Miller who's just flown in from Ambarawa…. He'll be in overall command of the relief column.'

Kudo tensed and looked carefully at Miller, trying to gauge the man who would hold the fate of his men in his hands.

'I understand how you feel, Major,' Bentham interjected. 'But your men are officially under British command. The column must be led by a British officer.'

Kudo nodded. 'Of course, Brigadier.'

'Right,' continued Bentham, 'leave as soon as possible. In the meantime I'll get on to the RAF.'

Miller stepped forward, extending his hand. 'I never expected to say this to a Japanese, Major Kudo,' he said sincerely, 'but thank you. I dare say you never expected to be helping the British army…'

Kudo shook Miller's hand, still watching the younger man keenly. 'No, Major,' he said calmly. 'These are strange times.'

Chapter Eleven

Some small but rapidly growing black dots appeared in Major Duncan's field glasses. 'Right on cue!' he exclaimed. He was pressed against a large rectangular, brick chimney stack. A Gurkha rifleman lay next to him. They had just finished arranging several linen table-cloths into a large X across the flat roof of the hotel.

Five single-engine RAF P-47 Thunderbolt fighter-bombers roared over head. The   leading pilot rocked his wings, acknowledging the roof-top signal.

'Welcome to Ambarawa!' Duncan added with obvious relief. The rifleman grinned then trotted back down the stairwell to rejoin the fight.

The day was not going well for the Gurkhas. They had played a tiring game of cat and mouse with the nationalists, hunting them in the houses and kampongs to the north, while units in the south had shepherded the internees into the more easily defended hotel, hospital and high school. Eventually sheer weight of *pemuda* numbers and lack of ammunition had forced them to give ground.

Two wild, suicidal charges against the hotel had left the main street littered with dead but they had succeeded in splitting the Gurkha forces. At ten that morning, Edmunds had been forced to inform his HQ that they could hold out for two hours no more. Chrishaw had not hesitated to order the air-strike.

Three Thunderbolts came in from the south towards the approaching Indonesian reinforcements on the Magelang Road. Muffled explosions and palls of black smoke rose in their wake. Two more aircraft came in low over the town centre. A hundred yards from the hotel they dropped their two 1,000lb and one 500lb high-explosive bombs. Blasts shook the entire hotel.

Duncan peered over the parapet and saw militia and *pemuda* fleeing. Several barricades and buildings had been destroyed. Before the dust began to settle, the Thunderbolts swooped in again twice with their eight, wing-mounted .50 calibre wing-guns strafing the roads and ruins. As quickly as they had come, the planes climbed away quickly into the east.

Another, deeper engine pitch sounded overhead. Duncan craned his neck looking for the transport and saw a chain of white parachutes dotting the blue sky. He watched anxiously. Two chutes drifted over nationalist-held areas of the town but others were landing around the hotel. Delighted Gurkhas rushed out for the ammunition, food and water. Duncan grunted in satisfaction but as he left the roof he could not help wondering if the air-drop had only prolonged the inevitable.

Back in Edmunds's office, he found his commanding officer looking bemused. 'You aren't going to believe this, Tim,' said Edmunds, 'but John's on his way with a bloody Jap company in tow!'

Semarang

The C-47 carrying Ball, Mac and Meg arrived in Semarang from Surabaya at first light. Ball's intention had been to drive straight to Ambarawa to check on the internees. His plans changed when Captain North, one of Brigadier Bentham's aides, met them at the airfield with a staff car. As they sped through almost deserted streets and crossroads manned by Indian soldiers, North explained what was happening.

'Wing Commander, The only way for you to get to Ambarawa is to accompany the relief column. Every available car and lorry has been requisitioned, as well as every able-bodied man. That applies to you, too, MacDonald, North added apologetically. 'Major Miller asked that you report to him. I could drop you off if you like? It's on the way.'

'Thank you, Sir,' said Mac. Meg, was sitting next to him, now looking worried.

Ball turned round in the front passenger seat. 'Sorry, Mac. Bad timing again.'

Mac shook his head. 'I'm up for this one, Sir.'

'That's the spirit, MacDonald!' North said a little too cheerfully. Mac glanced at Meg but said nothing.

North went on obliviously. 'Major Miller has taken over command of a local Jap battalion. They're helping us out. God knows how it'll go down in Blighty!'

Ball turned again. 'Well, here's a story for you, Meg!'

'Hmm, maybe,' she said without enthusiasm. 'I usually write about what fighting does to people. Captain North, what are my chances of going on to Ambarawa with the column?'

'Between you, me and the 23rd Indian Division, Miss Graham, absolutely none,' North replied. 'General Chrishaw's banned all correspondents from Magelang and Ambarawa until further notice. It's not safe.'

Two six-wheeled Sumida M-93 armoured cars and several Isuzu troop carriers almost blocked the approach to the Djatingaleh barracks. North weaved through them to set Mac down outside the gates in front of two sentries. No British or Indian soldiers were in sight.

Mac patted Meg's thigh and got out of the car. North passed him a note. 'You're to ask for a Lieutenant "Otter". He speaks some English. Off you go, best of British!'

Meg waved at him through the back window and he watched until the car turned a corner.

A horn blared and he jumped aside as a Toyota KC flat-bed missed him by inches. The Japanese sentries were watching him curiously. Behind them, through the open gates Mac glimpsed well-armed Japanese milling around, the rising sun flag atop the parade ground pole. He tensed. 'Jesus!' His throat felt dry. He opened the note. It was hand-written and said simply 'Lt Otta.' Below it was a line in Japanese.

As nonchalantly as possible he hoisted his kit bag over his shoulder and approached the sentries. 'Lt Otter?' he asked hopefully.

Blank stares greeted him. He gave up and handed them the note. Suddenly the Japanese were nodding. One of them pointed to the paper. *'Oo–tah chu-ii desu yo! Oo-tah!'* He beckoned Mac to follow him. Mac took a deep breath and went through the gates. He was crossing the courtyard when he heard a shout.

'Mac! MacDonald!'

Relieved, he turned to see Miller standing in a doorway with a Japanese officer. He went over and saluted.

'This is Major Kudo,' Miller said politely, returning the salute, as did Kudo.

'Sir!' Mac said firmly.

'I thought you might want to come along with us,' said Miller.

'Absolutely, Sir.'

'Good man, we need everyone we can get. The Major's going to hold a short meeting for his officers and then address his men. We'll be leaving in about twenty minutes. Someone will get you fixed up with a weapon.' He grinned. 'Don't worry, we won't be charging you for the one you left in Surabaya! I've heard about your swim. Wait by my jeep.'

Miller and Kudo left. Mac watched the Japanese loading food, water and ammunition. To his surprise they completely ignored him. His thoughts had taken him back to Burma and Archie Ferguson when he realised someone was speaking to him.

'I am Lieutenant Ota.'

Mac straightened quickly and saluted. 'MacDonald, Sir.'

Ota waved for him to stand at ease. Mac looked at the young officer, wondering if anyone in the British army had ever experienced an odder day.

Ota was staring at Mac's uniform, particularly at the Red cockerel patch on his shoulder. 'What is your regiment?'

'Seaforth Highlanders, Sir.'

'You are British?'

'Yes, Sir. We're a Scottish regiment.'

'Ah, "high lander." *Sukotorando ka…* Where are you based?'

Mac hesitated. The phrase 'name, rank and serial number' flashed into his mind. He wondered for a moment if regulations allowed him to answer. 'Batavia, Sir. But I'm seconded to RAPWI.'

'Rap—?' Ota shrugged disinterestedly. 'You were in Burma?'

Mac pictured Archie's broken body again and felt his anger stir. 'Yes, Sir,' he replied firmly. 'Were you?'

'Hmm? Oh, no… only Java.'

Mac sensed that Ota was preoccupied and apparently making conversation. A non-commissioned officer came up to them and Ota spoke to him.

'Do you prefer a rifle or a carbine?', asked Ota.

'Rifle, Sir.'

'Juken?—I mean—bayonet?'

'The full set, please, Sir.'

'Go with Corporal Suzuki,' Ota said. 'I am going to a meeting.'

'Yes, Sir!' Mac saluted again. He was walking away when Ota called him back.

'Private!'

'Yes, Sir?'

'I heard there's fighting at Surabaya.'

Mac nodded. 'There was fighting at Surabaya, Sir. I was there. But we're heading south. Some internees at Ambarawa are in danger.'

Ota left Kudo's briefing with his stomach churning at the thought of Kate in the hands of the mob. He saw the vehicles at the gate and fought a sudden, desperate urge to jump in one and drive to Ambarawa.

'Fall in! At the double!' Sergeant-Major Tazaki's voice boomed across the parade ground. It was unnecessary because the men were ready, yet it suited their mood. Word that their comrades were in danger had already circulated. They had prepared for battle without instruction. Many had tied small rising-sun flags to their rifle barrels.

Kudo emerged and there was a sudden hush of expectation.

'Attention!' Tazaki bellowed.

Hands slapped against rifle stocks and feet stamped in unison. An expectant silence followed.

Kudo saluted then his eyes swept slowly over the assembled men. 'Not long ago, I told you that our fighting days were over. I said there was "peace" and that, in time, we were all going home. Alas, I spoke too soon. Already a number of our comrades have been killed in this so-called peace, some just last night. Years from now we should have been reminiscing, sharing sake under cherry blossoms beside the

Kanda river...but they are lost to us. Today, more of our comrades are in danger. A few against thousands. We cannot desert them. They make their stand alongside British Gurkhas! Together, they protect women and children from massacre. You will all remember the slaughter at Bulu Gaol. That day we were too late. Now I ask you to fight again, not for Japan but for the honour of the Kudo Butai! Let us not be late today!' Kudo paused then saluted.

Cheers erupted among the ranks and officers. 'Banzai!—Banzai!—Banzai!'

They quietened and watched as Kudo saluted Miller, who returned the salute smartly. Kudo turned back to his men and gave the command. 'Mount up!'

Ota was climbing up into a lorry cab when Captain Seguchi slapped him on the shoulder. 'They won't get Nagumo easily,' he said encouragingly. 'All the whores would be furious!'

Those within earshot laughed.

Ota managed a wan smile and pulled the door shut. The feeling of dread returned with a vengeance. What if Kate were already dead? And Nagumo too? It had never crossed his mind that they might be separated at the end. Silently he cursed his stupidity in daring to believe he had cheated death. Japan's surrender had been nothing more than a fleeting respite that had tempted, lulled and softened him. Now, in a final, cruel agony, his promise to protect Kate was proving worthless. Java was going to claim her after all....

For the first five miles of town there were no roadblocks or sightings of militia but Miller, ever-conscious of the risk of ambush, led cautiously, stopping frequently to send out scouts ahead on motorcycles.

The two hours from Djatingaleh to Sikoenin were the longest of Ota's life. His knuckles gripped white on the sword scabbard propped between his knees. Yet again the column stopped. Ota fumed quietly when he saw Seguchi walking back down the convoy.

Seguchi waved to him. 'Ota, the Major wants you to hang back and try to raise Nagumo on the radio. Tell him we're on our way. If you reach him, ask his position. Allow no longer than twenty minutes, then catch us up.'

Fifteen minutes later Nishino, the radio operator, smiled in triumph as he handed over a set of headphones and microphone. 'Lt Nagumo, Sir. The signal's poor. Their batteries are low.'

'Nagumo? It's Ota. Over.'

'Where are you? Over.' Nagumo replied.

'About twenty kilometres, repeat two-zero kilometres, from you. ETA is 1400 hours. What's your situation?'

'Surrounded but we're holding them off. Enemy numbers estimated at more than three thousand! Ammunition is getting low. Eight dead, eleven badly...' The signal faded and Ota frowned. Nishino adjusted the tuning dial, then nodded.

He tried again. 'Tell me your position.'

Nagumo's voice came booming back. 'Front and centre at the high school gate.'

Ota hesitated, he had to ask... 'What about the women?' He phrased it as a joke. In Japanese, *onna*, could mean women or woman. The reply would be in the headphones only.

Nagumo sounded amused. 'All of them or just one?'

'You know what I mean,' Ota smiled, already knowing the answer from Nagumo's teasing.

'Don't worry, "Shower Girl" is fine,' Nagumo reassured him. 'She's with the nuns.'

Relief surged through Ota. He remembered the convent from his postings to Ambarawa. 'We'll be there soon', he replied. 'Watch yourself! Column over and out.'

'Ambarawa out!'

Ota handed back the headphones and microphone to Nishino and realised he would have heard Nagumo's reply. He didn't care. 'Well done, Sparks,' he said. 'Let's catch them up!'

As the lorry moved off, Ota leant back in the cab, comforted by the thought that Kate was safe. It was only twenty kilometres, normally a journey of under an hour....

Ambarawa

Shirai lowered the field glasses and returned them to the man beside him. They were in the belfry of the church, the tallest building in Ambarawa. The school was just six-hundred yards away.

'So, the British have rearmed their coolies,' Shirai said dismissively. 'Add another fifty to the total.'

Captain Iga nodded, his face troubled. 'They're probably from Semarang,' he said head down, adding to his notes on the defences.

'Yes, Kudo's turncoats,' Shirai added scathingly. 'I've seen enough.' He was turning to go back down the tower when he saw Iga's expression. 'What's on your mind, Captain?'

Iga hesitated, choosing his words. 'How do you think our men will react when they know they are going to attack their fellow Japanese?'

Shirai's look was icy. 'Those who serve the enemy are traitors,' he snapped. 'Remember that!'

'Yes, Major,' Iga said quickly.

They heard a door open below. Someone started climbing the steps.

Sarel, bare-chested with his long hair unbound, climbed into the belfry. He was followed by a youth in part-militia uniform.

Shirai bowed. 'Well, Major Sarel, do your Black Buffalos scent victory?'

The youth, a graduate from a Japanese-language educational programme, began interpreting.

Sarel did not respond. Iga handed him the glasses. Slowly and deliberately he scanned the school wall and buildings. He spoke casually, without lowering the glasses. 'How do you propose to capture the school, Major?'

'They must have little ammunition left,' Shirai said confidently. 'It will not be difficult, perhaps two days at the most.'

Sarel whirled to face Shirai before the interpreter had finished. 'I remember you saying the same thing two days ago, when the Gurkhas were trapped at Magelang. They are still fighting us!'

Shirai tensed. 'I did not anticipate an air-strike and a supply drop. I will not make the same mistake again.'

'I hope not,' Sarel replied dismissively. 'Did you know a cousin of General Manyar was killed in the bombing? The General is furious. He's demanding an immediate attack.'

'No!' Shirai exclaimed in exasperation. 'We should wait until dark!' Now they are ready!'

Sarel smiled coldly. 'I wouldn't try to change his mind. Not at the moment, anyway. Do not concern yourself, Major. We have plenty of warriors who are not afraid to die for their country.' He let the barb hang as he went back to the steps, then looked back questioningly. 'Will we see your Japanese volunteers at the front of the charge?'

'They will be right beside your Buffalos,' Shirai countered sharply, knowing that Sarel's men were rarely risked in mass attacks.

'Yes, I'm sure they will,' Sarel laughed. He disappeared down the stairs. His interpreter followed.

Iga looked uncomfortable. 'I don't trust him, Major.'

'There is no need for trust...at least as long as we both want the same thing.'

'And when we no longer want the same thing?'

Shirai shrugged. 'We'll all be dead long before then!'

Shooting began and they turned to watch over two hundred *pemuda* charge the school in a reckless frontal assault. Most were cut down by machine gun fire before they got halfway to the wall. The attack petered out and the survivors retreated.

Iga shook his head. 'Pointless! I'll go and prep the mortars.'

'Yes, do that,' Shirai replied enthusiastically. 'Set the range to keep our old Semarang friends on their toes.'

'They can shout as much as they like!' Nagumo called out sarcastically over the jeering. Beside him his men laughed, though they knew another attack would come soon. For over an hour the attackers had been taking pot shots but had made no further attempts on the walls. Some familiar popping sounds from the nearest kampong instantly wiped the good humour from their faces.

'Take cover!' Nagumo shouted. They ran, scrambling for their foxholes. Seconds later six mortar shells landed in a narrow, precise band behind the main gate. The ground heaved.

Nagumo, dizzy and covered in earth, staggered to his feet. One of his glasses lenses was missing.

Two men had been blown out of their foxholes. One had lost both legs, the other had his chest and stomach ripped open. Blood splattered the ground around them. A third man was dead in his hole, his rib-cage splayed open to the spine.

'Shit!' Nagumo swore as his head and ears cleared. He realised the Javanese had guessed the foxholes would be set back that crucial few yards from the machine gun position... A second mortar volley sounded. It would come down on top of the first.

'Back to the gate,' he shouted urgently. His platoon rushed forward. Behind them the earth churned. There was a deep roar as once again the *pemuda* charged.

Major Duncan watched the screaming youths waving rifles, swords, bamboo spears and machetes. Marksmen among the defenders started picking off their targets. At a hundred and fifty yards, Duncan gave the general command. 'Gun crews open fire!'

Brens and Nambus opened up together. Dozens of Javanese were cut down in the hail of lead. At fifty yards Duncan saw the gaps in the their lines were widening. Still the attack came on. Back at the wall Gurkhas with Sten sub-machine carbines were waiting for any who made it close enough to throw a grenade. None did. Cries of *'Allah akbah!'* and *'Indonesia raya!'* petered out as the human wave faltered, then broke. Though the attack was spent, the *pemuda* withdrew defiantly, turning to fire or taunt.

'Cease fire!' Duncan ordered. He holstered his revolver. His face was pale as he surveyed the scattered, twisted mass of dead and wounded. Along the wall he saw three or four dead or badly wounded being carried away on stretchers by internee volunteers. Those still able to shoot were being tended to where they fought. His men, too, stared at the carnage before them. Respite was brief. A bugle sounded in the kampong and the battle chants started again....

Bedono

Light was fading when Kudo Butai entered the British perimeter at Bedono. Ota rushed to the summit clutching his field glasses, arms shaking as he tried to focus on the thin plumes of smoke over Ambarawa. The convent stood out in grey-white on a verdant hillside.

Miller and Mac came to stand with him. They shared a cigarette while Ota pointed out some features of the town. 'Do you know the road well, Lieutenant?' Miller asked.

'Yes, Major,' Ota replied. I have used it many times.'

'An easy road to block,' Miller said to no-one in particular.

'Too easy,' Ota said bitterly. 'It will take us about—' He glanced at the troops below and saw they were preparing to camp. 'Major,' he asked anxiously, 'the Gurkhas?'

Miller nodded reluctantly. 'We're staying here until first light to allow the rear guard to catch up.'

'But we can't stop now!' Ota said loudly.

Miller saw his alarm but shook his head. 'I know...but we haven't eaten for hours and it'll be dark soon. Get some food.'

Ota noticed Kudo and Sgt-Major Tazaki. He rushed down the slope and hovered nearby as Kudo gave out instructions.

'Post sentries to the east and north. The Gurkhas will guard the south and west.'

'Yes, Sir. Immediately.' Tazaki excused himself and left to organise.

Ota approached and saluted. 'Major, let me take a platoon. I'm sure I can make it to the school before dark.'

Kudo looked at him askance. 'You might,' replied Kudo tersely. 'But the Javans could easily take out such a small force. If any British pilots see you they'd assume you were militia and attack.'

'But Sir, we are so close!' Ota pressed.

Kudo looked at him carefully. 'I'm surprised at you. Rest or you'll be useless tomorrow.' He lowered his voice. 'I am keen to reach Ambarawa. Also I heard a rumour that your enthusiasm has little to do with aiding our comrades and has more to do with a skirt.'

'Major, I—I', Ota stammered helplessly in surprise and embarrassment. He stared at the ground.

Kudo let him stew for a several seconds. 'I'll excuse your emotions this once. You are a good officer, Ota, but if for one instant I think you are endangering my men's lives for personal reasons I will shoot you where you stand.'

Guilt flooded through Ota. 'Excuse me, Major, I'm sorry. It won't happen again.' He came to attention and saluted.

'I trust not,' Kudo said dismissively. He turned his back on Ota and strode away.

Ota was shaken awake just before dawn by two Stuart tanks turning over their engines. Thick, acrid exhaust smoke drifted over him and down the hillside.

'Come on, Ota,' Seguchi called to him. 'The Indos started where they left off. They're shelling the Gurkha rear guard.'

He jumped to his feet, amazed that he had slept at all. He felt calmer. The deep, nagging worry was still with him but it was no longer in control. He went back up to the summit and scanned the road ahead once again. This time he did it methodically, looking for likely ambush.

Two more hours passed before a Stuart rattled into view with half-a-dozen wounded strapped precariously on its back. Behind it followed the exhausted Gurkha rear guard, some on foot because they had lost transports to mortars.

At eleven o'clock, with the sun already fierce, the first Indians and Gurkhas moved off the hill. The RAF had reported four roadblocks between Bedono and Ambarawa. Ota's anxiety began to return.

Finally the order came for the Japanese to mount up. Three miles down the road they halted while the Gurkhas advanced on foot behind a Stuart up to the first roadblock. Nearly an hour passed before the all-clear came. It had been deserted but checks for booby traps and snipers had all taken time. Two more roadblocks were all unmanned but at each one retreating bands of armed youths were visible in the surrounding hills.

At five o'clock Kudo Butai caught up with the Gurkhas again. They were a hundred yards from a steel road bridge over a steep, rocky ravine. The unmistakable rhythm of a Nambu machine gun sounded in the distance. A Stuart stood at the bridge, impervious to the bullets clanging off its armour.

The Stuart's 37mm gun boomed. Again the Nambu clattered in reply.

Another hour passed until eventually a blanket mortar salvo silenced the Nambu permanently, allowing the Gurkhas to take the bridge. Ota looked yet again at his watch and the nearby vista. Light was fading. Above Ambarawa the last rays of sunlight were catching the hill tops. The column pressed on.

Powerful lights half-blinded him as three more Stuarts squeezed past the troop carriers, their tracks at thirty degrees on the banks of the narrow road.

Kudo gathered his officers, shouting over the noise from the tanks. 'We're risking the last two miles. Tanks and Gurkhas leading!'

There were murmurs of surprise. In the dark, the tanks would be vulnerable to mines and ambush.

'There are concerns about the convent,' Kudo added. 'It's unguarded.'

Ota felt the familiar icy claw of dread twisting in his stomach.

The Stuarts rolled towards the town in a staggered column of four, their heavy machine guns blazing randomly left and right into buildings and vegetation. Kampongs emptied as villagers abandoned their homes in panic. Along the roadside, strings of fragile wooden huts crumpled under metal caterpillar treads. Roaring orange jets from flame-throwers briefly turned night into day, leaving the air heavy with the clinging stench of burnt petroleum. Their speed was slow, no more than five miles an hour but it was relentless, a glacier of steel and fire sweeping all before it.

Behind the tanks the troops followed. Tense, weary and hungry, they marched beside their vehicles, expecting ambush or snipers at every turn, shooting at any movement. In their wake, a chain of spreading fires marked their desperate, destructive progress.

St Agatha's Convent

One by one the shadowy figures slipped through the gap in the Convent's garden wall, creeping quickly past the flowerbeds and pergola to gather at the bolted patio door. Two of the intruders linked hands to propel a smaller, lighter third up and over. There was a slight metallic scraping as the bolt slid back, then the door swung open to reveal a dark corridor.

Kate was dozing on a mattress on the infirmary floor when the youths burst in.

'Merdeka!' —'Death to the Dutch!'

In the confusion Kate managed to roll under a bed, pressing herself against the wall. One after another, patients were hauled, screaming, out of their beds A middle-aged nun rushed in, her arms high in protest. 'This is a hospital! How dare—'

A rifle butt thwacked against the side of her face. She crumpled in agony, clutching at her broken her jaw and spitting out teeth and blood.

Kate felt a hand seize her hair and drag her up.

'Kate! Kate!' Anna's shout was tearful.

'Anna!' She reached out and Anna grabbed her hand. They clung to each other.

Kate felt a stinging pain shot across her shoulders as a bare-chested youth with unkempt hair began lashing out indiscriminately with a buffalo whip. 'Get the Dutch scum outside!'

Prods from bamboo spears forced them out into the garden which was now lit by torches and a now burning pergola. Two dozen women and children were lined up against the high stone wall. Teenaged boys armed with rifles and pistols stood laughing and joking.

An older youth strode forward and began to insult them in a mixture of broken Dutch and Javanese. 'Listen to me white bitches! I am Rakasa, demon of the *wayang* come to haunt you. We, the Black Buffalos, are the law. In the name of the revolution, all Dutch are sentenced to death!'

Casually he lifted his revolver and fired randomly, hitting a middle-aged woman in the shoulder. She slumped to the ground.

Rakasa brought the pistol up again. Almost as one the women bolted along the long wall screaming.

Emboldened now, other *pemuda* began taunting. Another shot rang out and a boy of about ten fell, blood streaming from his head. His mother sank to her knees, wailing, clutching his body to her.

Rakasa stared contemptuously, hawked then spat. In silent terror, Kate and the others watched him unclip a stick grenade from his belt and strike the fuse tip on the patio. Grinning mirthlessly, he lobbed the sparking grenade amongst them. In panic they ran back to the other end of the wall.

Kate sprinted, gripping Anna's hand, pulling her along. They were trapped in the mass of bodies, sandwiched between slower runners. She ran blindly until she collided with those already against the far corner of wall. There was a loud bang close behind them. Someone crashed into her. Ignoring the pain, she looked back, her heart racing.

Two white, bloodied shapes lay face down and unmoving in the dirt border. One was an adult, the other a young girl.

Panting nervously, the women watched and waited. Another grinning youth was waving a second grenade.

'No!'—'Please don't!'—'Have mercy, please!'

The grenade sailed high overhead. Again the group ran. All Kate could think of was to get away. Screams and groans followed the blast. When she reached the far wall and looked back two more figures lay still. A third woman was clutching her bloody, shrapnel-ripped legs.

A girl ran to her, shrieking, 'Mother!'

On the patio, the Buffalos and *pemuda* were laughing hysterically. One of them lifted his sarong and shook his penis at the girl. Then he shot at one of the nuns, hitting her leg.

'Make the white bitches run!' Rakasa yelled. He began firing at their feet. His followers did the same. Yet again the captives bolted until they were corralled once more against a corner wall. As they caught their breath, another sparking grenade landed at their feet.

A heavy-set woman in a muddied nightdress, her face set in rage, stepped forward, picked up the grenade and flung it at a group of four startled youths. 'Bastards!' she thundered.

Three scattered but the fourth reached to throw it back. This time the fuse was shorter. It went off in his hand, shredding his face and blowing open his chest.

Several of the women cheered. Rifles and swords rose threateningly but the captives stood their ground. Enraged and wild-eyed, Rakasa fired at the heavy-set woman but missed and killed a nun. Cowed again, the women backed away.

One of the *pemuda* charged the group waving a machete and grabbed at a girl of about fourteen. She tried to pull back but the youth dragged her brutally by her hair to the middle of the garden. A blow with the machete handle stunned her and she collapsed. He knelt over her, tearing off her nightdress and underwear. She began screaming. 'Mummy, help! Please!' A sobbing woman turned away, her hands over her ears. Others shielded their children's eyes.

The girl tried to slither away but her attacker sat on her, punching her repeatedly in the face, chest and belly until she lay pliant, wheezing through a smashed nose and broken teeth. He knelt over her, dropped his shorts and slipped his arms under her knees, forcing back her thighs. She whimpered helplessly. As he penetrated her he began shouting obscenities. Around him, the watching youths began to chant and stamp their feet in unison, urging him on.

Finally the rapist spent himself and he stood up, his hands raised in triumph. Another youth took his place and the chanting began again. The girl lay dazed in shock. When the second youth had finished he reached nonchalantly for his revolver. Quite slowly and deliberately he put the barrel against her forehead and pulled the trigger.

A small, wiry youth in his early teens with long, matted hair came towards the women and the chanting began again. He saw Kate and leered, rubbing his crotch through his sarong.

Suddenly Rakasa threw another grenade. Again the women ran.

Kate saw a flash then all was dark and still. When she came to, she was lying on her back, her head pounding. Above her the moon was blurred. Screams and shouts echoed dully in her ears. She remembered...

Groggily she rolled on to her front. She could barely manage to lift her face out of the dirt. A hot, sticky dampness was spreading over her buttocks and inner thighs. Oh God, she thought, my legs!

She heard a groan nearby. Anna was three feet away, lying face down. Her cheek and arms were grazed. Blood was streaming from her ear. Kate tried to reach out but did not have the strength. 'Anna—'

'Oww!' Kate gasped as she was jerked upwards by the waistband of her shorts and her knees forced roughly under her chest. Rasping, rapid breath on her neck made her shiver. A hand was tugging at the buttons of her shorts.

'No!' she croaked feebly. 'Please!'

Something cold and metallic slid swiftly down inside her shorts and knickers. There was a sharp tug and the clothing fell away from one leg and buttock. She saw a hand stab a long bayonet into the ground beside her. A weight pressed heavily on her back and a fleshy hardness rubbed against the inside of her thigh.

'No!' Kate sobbed, utterly helpless. She moaned in despair. 'Help!'

There was a snort of disgust then a blow hammered down on her back. She was sent sprawling, gasping in pain. Her attacker had left her. Short of breath she clawed weakly for her slashed shorts staunch the bleeding on her legs. Her fingers slid in watery slime but she saw it was not blood. In the daze of the explosion she had soiled herself.

Anna was swaying on her hands and knees, still in a stupor. The youth moved over to her, the bayonet back in his hand, his expression full of loathing. He stabbed the blade into the earth by Anna's leg, then knelt and grabbed the hem of her thin white nightshirt. In one motion he flung it over her head and shoulders. Anna was trying to crawl away but his fingers curled around the top of her knickers and yanked them down to her knees.

Laughing now, the youth reached forward and pinned Anna's arms behind her back, holding both her thumbs in one hand. Her head struck the ground heavily. She stared blankly at Kate.

'Anna, run!' Kate mouthed desperately.

Anna's numbed expression did not change. The youth started to thrust, wrenching up her arms. Anna's eyes bulged.

Blind to her pain, the youth thrust repeatedly. Suddenly one of her one of her shoulders dislocated with a sharp pop. With a final grunt, the youth released Anna's arms. Whimpering now, she tried to rise on one hand. Still within her, the youth snatched for her pigtails, winding them around his left hand. His right hand reached for the bayonet.

Kate screamed. 'Anna!'

Anna's head snapped backwards, bridled by her own braids. The blade slashed deeply across her stretched throat. Anna collapsed, fighting for breath in a pool of her own blood. In seconds she was still.

The killer's gloating face turned to Kate. He stood, his penis still erect. She tried to push herself away but her feet slipped in the dirt and she fell back. In three easy strides he was upon her, bayonet raised. Drops of Anna's blood dripped onto her face.

Kate mouthed a silent, pleading, no. His grin revealed blackened, rotting teeth. She closed her eyes, lifting her arms in a last, desperate defence. Beneath her she felt the earth rumble, followed by a mechanical roar and a jolting crash.

Bright, white light bathed the garden. Shouts and gunfire filled her ears. She opened her eyes. Her attacker had vanished. Wedged in the breach in the convent wall she saw the high, angled front of a tank. Yelling Gurkhas were leaping from it, illuminated by a large, turret-mounted searchlight. Relief surged through her. She tried to wave but the effort drained the last of her strength.

Ota was two minutes behind the Gurkhas. He clambered over the tank and stopped aghast at the scene before him. Blood-stained bodies, old and young, littered the flower beds. Distraught women, many with bloody wounds, stood in groups, hugging each other and crying. Others sat by prostrate bodies.

His search for Kate became frantic. Nearly all the women were dressed in white, Red Cross nightdresses or hospital smocks. He pushed his way through the crowd to every blonde, only to be met with shocked or unknowing stares.

He steeled himself to look at the bodies. Hesitantly he moved from one to another, gripped by cold dread.

When he saw her lying half-naked, bloodied, her arm outstretched towards another lifeless girl, tears ran down his face. Exhausted, he slumped to his knees beside her. Tentatively he reached out to touch her neck. He felt her warmth and gave a start. Quickly he put his ear over her mouth and felt her breath.

'Kate!' He touched her cheek.

Her eyes flickered. 'Oh, Kenichi!'

'Where are you hurt?' His hands moved over her body rapidly and methodically, searching for wounds but finding none. He sat back, catching his breath. 'You scared me,' he said whispered. 'I thought...' He cupped her face in his hands. 'I wasn't here to help you. I'm so sorry.'

Her fingers reached for his. 'I knew you'd come,' she whispered softly.

A Japanese medic ran up to them, asking if Kate needed help. Ota shook his head. 'Just water!'

Kate leant against him while he held the canteen for her. She moved to cover her smeared crotch with her shorts. 'I'm dirty...' she whispered apologetically.

He stroked her hair. 'Your alive!'

Two nuns came to kneel in silent prayer by Anna's body then covered her with a white sheet. When they saw Kate's exposed lower half they tried to push Ota away but Kate stopped them.

'No, I want him to stay,' she snapped.

They left them but one of them hurried back with a large bath towel which she wrapped around Kate's waist.

Ota looked around them. Some of the seriously wounded were being treated where they lay in the light from the tank. Others were being carried or led away to the convent's infirmary.

He gave her a smile. 'Can you stand?'

'I think so.'

He helped her up and she managed a few shaky steps.

'Good! Now rest,' he said scooping her up. Her hands locked around his neck.

Ota carried Kate out of the convent and joined a stream of internees, nuns and soldiers heading down the hill. At the fork he turned into the long drive of the spa hotel. A patrol led by Corporal Suzuki met them. 'We've searched the hotel as Major Kudo ordered, Lieutenant, it's clear,' Suzuki reported, looking at Kate. 'The electricity is back on now, too. Do you have any orders for us?'

'Yes, the hotel will be the battalion's base for the night, so first secure the perimeter and post sentries. Internees will be moving here from the convent soon. Help them. And someone go and find Lt Nagumo.'

'At once!' Suzuki cast another quick glance at Kate then led his patrol off at the trot,

Ota barely heard their laughter. He looked down at Kate. She was asleep.

To his dismay the hotel lobby had been ransacked. Tables lay smashed, padded leather chairs slashed and ornaments shattered. He strode on, kicking open a broken door and flicking on a light switch before going along the corridor and down the stairs to the apparently undamaged changing rooms.

Kate woke as he sat her down on a stool. He kissed her forehead tenderly. 'Where are we?' she asked wearily, still clinging to him.

'I thought you would like a bath,' he said. He rummaged in the cupboards, finding her towels, shampoo, soap and a *nemaki* robe. 'I have to leave you now,' he said. 'Can you manage?'

She smiled, 'Oh, yes. I'll be fine.'

He saw that she meant it and he nodded. 'After your bath I'll take you down to the main camp.'

Kate began to undo her blouse. 'Will there be more fighting?'

'No, not tonight. The Javans have retreated into the town. At daylight we will try to force them out.'

'I see,' she said glumly. 'I thought it was over. I—'

She paused at the sound of women's voices in the corridor. Their private moment was at an end. Wearily she let her head sag. 'Thank—' She sighed when she realised she was alone.

Back outside, in front of the hotel's reception, Ota saw a familiar silhouette sitting with Suzuki by a hibachi grill.

A space opened for Ota next to Nagumo and he sat down. 'Domo,' he said politely.

Nagumo sported a three-day stubble and looked exhausted. *'Ambarawa ni yokoso!'*—Welcome to Ambarawa! Nagumo said heartily, handing him a bowl of rice. 'You took your damn time!'

Kate emerged from the hotel with a group of internees. As he had promised, Ota was waiting for her. She dawdled to let the others move ahead.

He came over to her. Without a word or hesitation they kissed, hidden in the shadows of the tree-lined drive. Later they walked slowly, arm in arm, past a bemused Japanese sentry. They both knew that at the end of the drive they would say farewell. Torches flashed busily at the junction ahead and female voices carried clearly on the night breeze.

'The British are evacuating the convent,' said Ota.

Kate squeezed his hand. 'Please be careful, Kenichi. Java isn't worth dying for.'

He was about to say *but you are* when a burst of distant gunfire echoed over them ominously. Their steps became little more than shuffles. Above them the orange-red moon was almost full and the stars stunningly clear. When at last he spoke there was a slight tremor in his voice. 'Where will you live in Holland?'

She halted. Neither of them had ever mentioned a future after Java.

'I'm not sure,' she replied, moving forward slowly. 'Utrecht, I suppose, for a while at least. My grandmother lived there but she's dead now... I don't remember it very well. I've only been back once. I was ten. I'd never felt cold before... Most of all I remember the tulips.'

He frowned. 'Tu—?'

'Yes, red tulips, my favourite flower.' She smiled at his puzzled look. 'They're shaped like a wine glass. They don't grow on Java, so you might not have seen them.'

'One day I would like to give you tulips.'

'That would be...lovely.' Her voice trailed off and she looked away. She wiped her eyes and tried to laugh. 'Silly me,' she said quickly. 'I hate goodbyes. I still can't believe I'm going to Holland or that you are going to Japan. It's so far away.'

'They say we must go to prison and work first.'

'What!' Kate was incredulous. 'They can't put you in prison after what you've done. You've saved hundreds, thousands of people! You're not a stinking *kenpei*—'

'It doesn't matter,' he said softly, trying to calm her.

'It does to me! I'll speak up for you! I'll tell them you—'

He put his palm against her cheek. 'Kate, my Major says people are tired of war. They don't want to hear about another one in Java.'

She gripped his forearms tightly. 'But they must let you go home. It's so unfair!'

He smiled. 'One day I will be free. Don't worry about me.'

'But I will!'

His eyes bored into hers. 'Really? Is that true, Kate?'

'Oh Kenichi, you know it is!' She hugged him to her and his arms went around her waist. Again they kissed, clinging together for several minutes until he straightened and took a step forward, forcing her to break the embrace.

'What will you do in Japan?' Her voice was a whisper.

'I have no idea. Everything will be different now. It will be hard but now there will be many—what's the word—opportunities. I might become an English teacher or even make sake with Nagumo!' He laughed and for a moment she saw the stress lift from his face.

She laughed with him, pleased to see him relaxed at long last. 'What's your home like? You've never mentioned it.'

'My parents are rice farmers. Nagumo's father buys most of our crop.' He pursed his lips then shook his head. 'It's hard work being a farmer. To be honest, I don't think I'm very good at it.'

She smiled up at him warmly. 'I think you'll do well at whatever you do.'

They were in the final patch of shadow on the driveway before the gate. Their steps faltered again. A few yards from them figures were scurrying down the main path with lanterns, mattresses and boxes.

Gently, Ota slipped his arm from out of hers. She looked at him accusingly.

'It's better for you this way,' he said quietly.

'I don't care what they—'

His fingers went to her lips. 'Please listen to me. I don't want to cause you problems, here or in Holland. For many people Japan is still the enemy. I am still the enemy!'

Tears ran down Kate's cheeks. She sniffed and shook her head. 'Not to me! But I understand… I owe you so much.'

'Perhaps one day it will be different.' He swallowed nervously and reached into a pocket. He pulled out a thin package wrapped in oiled paper and placed it in her hand. 'I might not see you again before you leave Java… These two envelopes are addressed to my home. Will you write to me in one year's time to tell me you are safe?'

'Oh, yes, of course!' Kate replied quickly. Her eyes were bright and moist. 'But a year?'

'I don't know what's happening in Japan. Your letter might be lost. If there is no reply, please try again after two years.'

'Two years? Oh, God, I'll be so worried about you!'

Her head fell and he raised her chin up gently with his fingertips. 'Kate, nothing means more to me than knowing you are safe. Please be very careful until you have left Java.'

'And you, Kenichi. Please don't risk your life….'

He smiled. 'We say our karma—our fate—is foretold. We cannot change it. *Ki-wo tsukete*—be careful, Kate.'

She melted against him and for a moment he thought she had fainted. Then he felt her hands on his back and the back of his neck. She pushed up, meeting his kiss, her mouth open and moist.

Finally he broke from her embrace and walked back to the hotel. He did not look back. Head down to hide her fresh tears, Kate left the shadows.

Chapter Twelve

The Second Day at Ambarawa

Kudo ducked instinctively as the shot whistled harmlessly off the top of the brick wall inches from his head. 'That was a bit too close,' he said.

Ota did not reply. He sat with his back to the wall, staring across the road. Private Kondo, sheltered by a burnt-out car, was dragging the limp body of Yano out of the line of fire. He had been shot dead an hour earlier. The pace was slow and deadly, street by street, house by house in the face of determined resistance. Now they were waiting for their own predator to strike.

'Harada's got his work cut out on this bastard,' Kudo said pessimistically.

Ota's face broke into a tired smile. 'Maybe not, Major,' he said pointing behind them.

An F-47 Thunderbolt was skimming the rooftops. The men ducked as the plane zoomed towards a neat crescent of two-storey shops where the sniper had his lair.

Two 1,000lb bomb-blasts merged into one. Ota felt the wall shake and his ears pop painfully. Brick dust filled his nose and mouth. He sneezed then gingerly peered over the wall. One end of the crescent had been reduced to rubble.

'Right on target!' he said in awe of the RAF pilot's precision.

Kudo wiped his face and spat. 'Now you have an idea what it must have been like in Saipan and Okinawa. Day in day out, only enemy planes in the sky....'

Ota watched with mixed emotions as the Thunderbolt climbed away to return to base and rearm.

'*Aka Fuji!*'

Seconds after the shout Harada rolled over the wall next to Ota, rifle in hand. He was covered in brick dust. Only his piercing eyes were free of grime. Already he had five kills to his tally in Ambarawa.

'Whose side are they on, Major?' Harada moaned. 'They nearly got me as well as the Jav sniper!'

Ota nodded, his ears still ringing from the blast.

'Complain to London!' Kudo said sarcastically.

Harada laughed and began scanning the roofline for his next eyrie. His gaze settled on a blown-out, three-storey town house some fifty yards away. 'I'll be over there, Major. I should be able to cover most of the crescent. The hotel is just beyond it.'

A heavy, clanking sound made them turn. A Stuart tank was rounding a street corner. It trundled forwards spraying the crescent with random bursts from its machine gun. There was no answering fire: the *pemuda* were retreating. A second Stuart followed the first. The Japanese cheered.

From the Hotel van Rheeden's colonnaded main entrance Colonel Edmunds watched the Japanese moving up to positions in the houses around the hotel. Duncan, Miller and Rai were standing nearby.

'Well,' Duncan said under his breath. 'I never thought I'd ever be pleased to see a Jap column!'

Miller laughed. 'We'll never live it down!'

Kampong Ambarawa had been quickly abandoned by its residents. Washing hung on lines and food had been left over cooking fires. Ota's platoon had spent three hours in the maze of narrow, twisting alleys, abrupt junctions and dead-ends. Four of his men had been wounded in hit-and-run ambushes.

Ota was peering around the corner of a hut when two shots tore out chunks of the wooden corner post inches from his face. He jumped back. 'There's a low wall,' he shouted to the men with him. 'At least four of them. It looks as though they are going to make a stand. Beyond the wall it's open ground.'

'*Ara! Aka Fuji!*'

Nagumo emerged, waving, from out of one alley with several men. Ota acknowledged him and pointed round the corner, holding up four fingers. Nagumo nodded and signalled he would attack from the side. Two minutes later there was an exchange of fire.

'Let's go!' Ota ordered. He rushed down the alley to find the wall deserted and Nagumo's men firing at three pemuda sprinting across the field and back towards the town some three hundred yards away. Cautiously the Japanese followed, fanning out into a skirmish line. In the middle of the open ground was a roofless, dilapidated brick building.

There was no firing as they advanced. As they reached the ruin Nagumo suddenly halted, peering at the sky. Then Ota heard it, too.

The Thunderbolt closed on them at incredible speed at just eighty feet off the ground. Its eight .50 calibre machine guns opened up at four hundred yards.

Ota threw himself down as bullets punched into the earth on either side of him. Men screamed as they were cut in half.

'He's going to bomb us!' Nagumo bawled, scrambling towards the ruin.

As the Thunderbolt came around for a second pass, Ota saw the large pod under its wing. He dived into a small depression, clamped his hands over his ears and forced open his mouth to try and save his ear drums. The pressure wave sent him head over heels, sucking the air from his lungs. He landed on his back gasping for breath. Tiny pieces of earth were raining down on him.

He sat up, his chest heaving and spitting out dirt. 'Let's get back to the kampong!' There was no answer.

Ota turned. Only one truncated wall of the ruin was left standing. Beside it was a deep shell crater.

'Nagumo!' Ota yelled. Anxiously he ran forward. Two dead *pemuda* lay at the bottom of the crater. 'Nagumo!

'Oh...shit!' The voice was weak but instantly recognizable. Ota ran to the wall. Nagumo was on his knees. He was dazed and swaying. His right hand was clutching at a mass of shattered bone and flesh that had been his left arm. Dark, arterial blood was cascading onto the ground. Before Ota could reach him he pitched forward and rolled limply to the bottom of the crater, coming to rest next to a decapitated Javanese.

Ota clambered over the rubble. As he knelt he saw Nagumo's back was peppered with small, smoking holes. Nearby he noticed a plate-sized piece of bomb casing glowing a dull red.

Quickly Ota untied the muddied bandanna from around his own neck to fashion a tourniquet above Nagumo's left biceps. Then he hauled him on top of the corpse. Nagumo's smashed arm swung uselessly, held only by tendons, blood still gushing. He groaned in pain and opened his eyes.

Ota took a step back, then dropped on to on his left knee and drew his sword.

Nagumo saw the raised blade. 'Do it,' he croaked. 'Finish me!'

Ota's sword flashed downwards and wedged deep in the abdomen of the corpse beneath.

'Huh?' Nagumo's head lolled to his left. He stared in bewilderment. 'What're you...?'

Where there had been ripped flesh and jagged bone there was now a neat but bloody four-inch stump. 'Don't move!' Ota snapped. Hurriedly he pulled off one of his boots, folding over the calf section. Using it as a makeshift glove, he reached for the hot shrapnel. Instantly the leather began to smoulder.

He sat astride Nagumo, pinning his chest and good arm. 'Hold on!' Flesh, bone and blood sizzled as he pressed the hot metal against the stump, bracing it with a clump of brick.

'Aargh!' Nagumo twisted and bucked, then he passed out.

When Ota finally let go the stump was charred and raw but the bleeding had stopped. Exhausted, he lay back, blowing on his blistered fingers.

The Third Day at Ambarawa

A Stuart tank and the Mahrattas' own anti-tank guns had pounded Fort Prins Willem I for over an hour. Its massive, turreted, 17th-century stone walls seemed impervious to the explosive shells. It was the last stronghold of nationalist resistance at Ambarawa.

Inside, five hundred besieged *pemuda* jeered. Outside, the Gurkhas were biding their time, waiting at the base of the steep, star-shaped earthworks. With the arrival that morning of a second relief column of Mahrattas and Rajrifs the outcome was no longer in doubt.

Two Stuarts rolled forward, machine guns firing, covering the crew of a 25-pounder as they man-handled the gun up to almost point-blank range. Five shells slammed into the gatehouse, blowing the great wooden doors to matchwood. Before the last echo of the guns had faded, the Gurkhas were charging forward, their long, heavy *kukri* daggers drawn.

Sarel, Lamban and Kerek stood on the rear wall watching the soldiers surge through the gate. Lamban held a Thompson sub-machine gun in one hand and a coiled rope in the other.

'Stand and fight! Kill the infidels!' Sarel screamed hoarsely. The defenders were forced back, many turning to flee. Gurkha *kukris* were making short, bloody work of those defenders who tried to hold their ground.

A Stuart began firing just ahead of the advancing Gurkhas. Shells burst in the courtyard, exploding among the more modern brick buildings that had been added by the Dutch.

'Time to go,' Sarel said quietly.

Lamban nodded and tapped Kerek on the shoulder.

'We fight another day. Come on!'

Kerek tried to protest. 'But Lamban—'

Lamban grabbed his arm. 'Now!'

They made their way along the ramparts. Around them *pemuda* and militia alike were scrambling to escape over the walls and lose themselves in the mazes of the kampong. From there they could slip out to the surrounding hills during the night.

Lamban tied the rope to an iron step ladder set into the ancient stonework and let it drop over the wall. He was helping Kerek over when several panicking youths rushed for the rope barging him and Sarel out of the way.

Sarel drew his pistol and was about to shoot them when a tank shell hit the wall only thirty feet away, shaking the parapet. Lamban clung on to the rope but Sarel lost his balance, dropped his gun and fell backwards onto the angled roof of a storehouse twenty feet below. He sprang to his feet. 'Quick, the rope!'

Lamban tried to haul up the rope but two youths were still climbing down. He turned and saw three Gurkhas closing in on Sarel. He pointed urgently. 'The steps!'

Sarel nodded then ducked as a Gurkha came around the side of the storehouse. The Gurkha saw Lamban and fired a burst from a Sten gun. Lamban threw himself down on the parapet as a bullet ricocheted off the wall above.

Sarel, sword drawn, leapt off the roof and landed feet first on the Gurkha's neck and shoulders. The man crumpled. Sarel rolled off him, stabbed him in the back and sprinted for the steps. At the far corner of the storehouse he ran into a second Gurkha.

Lamban saw Sarel slash quickly at the Gurkha's head but the soldier did not check. Instead, he used the Tommy gun as a shield, catching the blade in the right angle between the barrel and stick magazine. At the same time, he darted in, slamming a knee into Sarel's belly and sending him reeling.

Sarel was briefly aware of a silvery blur before the foot-long, quarter-inch-thick *kukri* struck him horizontally across the mouth, slicing through the jaw muscles on both sides of his face and smashing most of his top teeth. His head rocked back as choking blood gushed out of his useless, hanging jaw.

A second blow cleft Sarel from the left collarbone to the base of his sternum. Lamban watched grimly as the Gurkha withdrew his weapon with a sharp, bone-snapping twist. Sarel fell backwards, blood frothing in his severed windpipe.

Rai looked up, saw Lamban and fired from the hip. Three more Gurkhas appeared, making for the steps. Lamban fired a quick burst from his machine gun to dissuade them, then slid quickly over the wall.

Willem I Station

Movement in the night-time shadows made Mac tense. He had already raised one alarm that had proved to be a scavenging dog. Even so, he tapped Miller's arm and pointed.

Miller signalled to Ota and the rest of the patrol—six Japanese—suddenly came alert.

They were in position behind a low wall that ran alongside the railway line a few hundred yards from the Ambarawa level crossing. The tracks marked the southern limit of the British-held zone. Dozens of *pemuda* were still at large in the town. Most were trying to escape to the nearby hills.

Mac peered but saw nothing. He was wondering if he had called another false alarm when Miller held up four fingers. A few feet away from them, Ota nodded. Silently his men readied their rifles.

Miller let his quarry get halfway across the tracks then switched on the jeep's headlights. Four *pemuda* froze momentarily then bolted. A second set of headlights stopped them. They dropped their weapons and stood staring nervously, hands raised.

Miller had not expected surrender. He, Mac, Ota and the Japanese soldiers moved forward to take their prisoners unaware that a fifth, cat-like figure had already crossed the tracks, worked behind the ambush, and chosen his ground.

A burst of bullets sprayed the illuminated targets. Miller and Ota rolled out of the line of fire but three Japanese were cut down. On cue, the other youths grabbed their weapons and began firing. Two more bursts from the shadows shattered one jeeps' headlights.

Mac flung himself behind a stack of thick rail sleepers. Bullets from the Thompson followed him, punching out chunks of wood. He crawled around to the shorter end of the stack trying to orientate himself. Mac lay still, waiting; the lessons of Burma not lost. Hasty footsteps on gravel made him turn and he glimpsed three figures running down the tracks past the abandoned fort.

Two minutes passed and then he heard the Gurkha bird-call some distance to his right. Relieved he wished he knew how to answer Miller. Still, he waited. Another long minute passed before he eased up from his crouch behind the sleepers. Six feet away and half-facing him was a Javanese holding a rifle. Both of them fired simultaneously. Mac felt the draught of the bullet against his cheek. The Javanese fell.

Carefully Mac went forward, his vision patchy after the close muzzle-flash. The youth lay on his back, dead, a dark patch of blood spreading under his white shirt.

Mac sighed, turned then gasped in pain as something slammed against his forehead. Dazed, his rifle slipped from his fingers. He staggered, grabbing for his bayonet.

His attacker, a lithe and bare-chested with long coiling hair was staring at the dead Javanese. A Thompson hung from by its strap from his hand. Mac assumed the gun's magazine was empty. His own rifle was by his feet. He went into a defensive crouch ready to spring for the gun. His attacker seemed unconcerned. Mac saw he wore Japanese army boots and trousers and remembered the similarly dressed youths in Surabaya.

Slowly and quite deliberately the Black Buffalo drew a straight *klewang* sword. Mac dipped for his gun but a foot struck his lower chest and he went sprawling across the rail tracks.

Once again his enemy gave him time to recover. Mac took a quick step towards him and lunged with the bayonet. He stabbed at thin air. The *klewang* flashed and Mac felt a stinging pain across his right shoulder. Blood began trickling down his arm.

Shouts came from nearer the level crossing. Momentarily the youth was distracted and Mac tried to circle around. He took just three paces before his effortlessly quicker enemy took a side-step and landed a thrusting side-kick to his thigh that knocked him down into a drainage gulley. Mac rolled to a stop. His leg was almost numb. Desperately he looked for a way of escape. His only option was the old fort. Mac made his move. Even as he did so he knew it was a mistake to go further away from the patrol. As he ran he heard Miller shouting from what seemed miles away.

'Mac! Where are you?'

'Fort!' Mac yelled, half-swallowing the word.

Up on the crossing, Lamban squatted grim-faced beside Kerek's body and pressed his palm in his blood. Then, grim-faced he set out after the man who had killed his best friend.

Mac footsteps rang heavily on the stone pathway to the fort's inner courtyard. Corpses from the day's fighting lay as they had fallen, stripped of their weapons. He dodged behind a burned-out building and waited, pressing himself against the brickwork, trying to quieten his breathing and straining to listen at the same time. His fist gripped the bayonet point down, ready to strike. What seemed like minutes passed and he began to wonder if the Black Buffalo had given up the pursuit.

He lowered the bayonet and let his head sag back against the stone. His breath caught in his throat. The Javanese was staring at him from the roof of the next building. Mac watched him jump down with barely a sound, sword in hand, his gaze never leaving him.

Mac backed away, looking around. He dashed for a doorway. Lamban was there before him, the *klewang* flicking close to his face. Mac slashed with the bayonet but watched in disbelief as the blade circled around his own and twisted it out of his grip. He was trapped. The Javanese was about to lunge for him when he half-turned and jumped aside.

'Zaaa!' Ota's shout boomed as he thrust with a rifle and fixed bayonet.

Lamban parried the attack neatly, forcing Ota to pull up, then he cut quickly for Ota's leading left hand and arm. Just in time, Ota jerked his arm away and the weapon struck the barrel.

Ota snapped the rifle back to his hip, the bayonet tip tracking Lamban's body not his sword. He had the advantage of the longer weapon to keep his clearly skilled opponent at a distance.

Mac moved behind Ota, realising with dismay that the officer's pistol holster was empty. He pulled a five-round clip for an Arisaka from his belt and wondered if he could throw it to Ota. He dismissed the idea. There would be no time.

Lamban made to close with Mac again. Ota cut him off. His frustration showing, Lamban began a sequence of fast left and right cuts that worked along the bayonet and then onto the rifle barrel as he closed. Ota disengaged with deft pull backs and circular parries, fencing with the bayonet, jabbing repeatedly at Lamban's head and chest to keep him away from Mac.

Warily the two circled, Mac keeping behind Ota. Mac saw his bayonet by the wall, grabbed it, then flung it at Lamban. It was on target but the sword flashed and the bayonet deflected harmlessly.

Lamban darted in and tried to close on Ota by grabbing the rifle barrel. Ota whipped the stock upwards towards Lamban's ribs forcing him to release and jump back. As Ota slashed, Lamban stepped forward, dodging past the bayonet. He dropped low into a spinning kick that hooked behind Ota's front foot. Ota rocked back, taking all his weight on his rear leg. Lamban darted in to strike but Ota hopped back, pulling the bayonet to his body line, forcing Lamban to pause and take a new guard.

'Allah akbah!' A second Buffalo emerged from the darkness, crossing behind Lamban as he raised a revolver.

Ota's right hand curled around the butt of his rifle and he hurled it forward underarm. Lamban side-stepped neatly but there was an audible thud as the bayonet speared the second attacker's chest. The revolver went sliding across the stones into the shadows.

With a growl of fury, Lamban came forward slashing at Ota's torso. Ota just had time to unclip his sword from his belt. He caught the attack vertically on the leather-covered metal scabbard, then thrust the tip at Lamban's stomach. Lamban palmed it aside and jumped back, then unsheathed a straight-bladed *keris* with his left hand.

Ota drew his own blade, keeping the scabbard in his left hand as a second weapon.

They circled, making quick probing attacks, each gauging the skill of the other. Mac watched, heart beat racing, knowing his life was in Ota's hands.

Lamban attacked with a ferocious double-windmill action. Ota cut for his head. To parry, Lamban crossed *keris* and sword high. There was a sharp snap and a length of steel clattered at their feet. The *klewang* had broken against the more flexible Japanese steel.

More cautious now, Lamban threw the broken blade aside then flipped the *keris* in his left hand so that it lay along his forearm. As Ota came forward, Lamban moved to close the distance quickly, catching Ota's blade against his own. He chopped hard with the edge of his palm at Ota's inside right elbow. Ota grunted in pain, his arm numb.

Lamban's left heel flicked up behind his buttock, raising a hidden scabbard fastened to his back. Simultaneously his right arm reached behind his head to grasp the hilt. In a split second the Death Shroud *keris* was in his hand. He lunged for Ota's abdomen.

Ota anticipated second blade and pulled his scabbard in vertically, tight against his body and twisted. The *keris* sliced into the thick leather but slid past his torso. A quick jab with the scabbard caught Lamban in the ribs, forcing him to break away.

Their chests heaving, the two combatants began to circle yet again.

Booted footsteps echoed across the courtyard. *'Ota-chu-ii, Doko? Ota-chu-ii!'*

Lamban looked left and right, gauging the distance of the approaching soldiers. He took two quick, long steps back to disengage, then brought his fists together in front of him in salute. Ota lowered his own sword and bowed. Lamban returned it, cast a quick, bitter glance at Mac, and vanished into the shadows.

The Fourth Day at Ambarawa

'Very good, Lieutenant, this will do fine,' said Miller, 'carry on.'

Ota saluted. 'Yes, Major.' Under Miller's command, the Kudo Butai were setting up checkpoints in the central square and the major road junction north of Ambarawa. There was still an air of tension, so they were taking no chances. Light machine gun crews were building sandbag nests and they were still wearing steel helmets.

'Mac,' Miller called out. 'Let's go and see what needs doing at the camps.'

'Aye, Sir,' Mac replied, glancing at second-storey windows. He felt very exposed in the street.

Ota started to show Mac, Miller, Suzuki and Kondo the marks on his scabbard. It's brown leather cover was sliced to the metal beneath and stained.

'What's that?' Mac frowned. 'Oil?'

Kondo shook his head. *'Doku da!'*

Mac looked up questioningly.

'Poison,' Ota explained.

'Christ!' Mac gulped.

A sentry alerted them. *'Jidosha!'*—Car!

A black, open-topped tourer began to slow for the roadblock. Four uniformed Japanese officers were inside. One waved casually.

Miller raised a relaxed hand. 'It's all right they're Jap—'

Ota glanced at the passengers and saw Shirai. *'Teki da!'*—Enemy!' He shouted, dragging Mac and Miller down behind a wall of sandbags just as the front passenger stood and opened fire with a sub-machine gun. Sand spurted from the ruptured bags. Two men manning the machine gun were cut down. The car sped past them.

Ota was up quickly, drawing his pistol and firing two quick shots. He saw a rear light smash. At the same time Kondo leapt for the LMG, swung it around and sending a long burst. Bullets chewed through the tourer's rear bodywork then shattered the windscreen. Suddenly the driver's head lolled and the car crashed into a boarded-up Chinese hairdresser's.

Shirai and another man sprang from the car towards an alley. Ota fired three more shots but they were well out of range. Shirai reached the alley.

As he ran the other Japanese half-turned and fired wildly. A second burst from Kondo hit him across the chest, throwing him hard against a wall.

Ota rushed across the street, then flattened himself against the corner building. Cautiously he peered down the alley. There was no sign of Shirai. A door creaked open and Ota brought up his pistol. An elderly Chinese popped his head out, saw Ota and darted back inside.

Miller joined Ota. 'Have you seen him?'

Ota shook his head.

Right,' said Miller. 'I'll go round the front in case he comes out of one of the shops.'

Ota nodded and went forward. He tried five back doors that opened on to the alley but each was locked. Further on came to a familiar narrow side-road lined with the tailors, barbers, green-grocers and apothecary shops typical of a Chinese quarter. At one end of the road stood a high, whitewashed wall and pagoda-roofed gate to what he knew to be a Chinese cemetery. Shirai was pushing on the heavy double doors. He glanced back down the street, stared challengingly at Ota, then went inside.

Ota reloaded his pistol then sprinted for the cemetery. The door was still ajar. He crept forward, taking cover behind a banyan tree shading the entrance. Rows of room-sized tombs in black or white marble and granite stretched out in a rectangular grid pattern. Waist high walls and narrow, pebbled paths separated the plots. Apart from the occasional chatter of a monkey in the tree the cemetery was quiet.

He stepped carefully, very conscious of the crunching of his boots on the pebbles. His pulse was fast, his breathing quick. Each tomb and pathway provided the opportunity for ambush.

'Over here, Ota!'

He spun round, raising his gun. Shirai was standing openly, not two yards from him aiming his pistol at Ota's chest. For several seconds the two men faced each other in silence.

'Why don't we settle this the old way?' Shirai said calmly, tapping his sword hilt.

Ota nodded but did not move.

Slowly Shirai moved his pistol off aim then returned it to its holster. He turned his back on Ota and headed without urgency towards the centre of the cemetery.

Shirai's back was an open target in Ota's sights but he lowered his pistol and followed Shirai to see a small lawn bordered by benches. Shirai unclipped his sword from his belt. Ota did the same.

Facing each other, they drew their blades and threw the scabbards.

They approached each other warily. Both knew that the contest would be very short. Shirai held his sword slightly above his head. Ota, in contrast, kept his blade angled at his right side, pointing down and away from Shirai. His feet were spread as he took a low stance.

Shirai looked around him. 'Well, it's a different audience this time,' he quipped dismissively. 'An audience of the dead!' He leapt forward, trying to take Ota by surprise, slashing at his left shoulder.

Ota side-stepped and the sword cut only air. His quick counter flicked upwards from right to left, striking the underside of Shirai's steel helmet and cutting through the leather cheek strap.

Shirai jumped back and his helmet fell to the ground revealing a long diagonal cut across his left ear and temple. His fingers traced the welling wound and he grinned maniacally. 'First blood to the farmer!'

Suddenly Shirai lunged fencing-style with a single-hand grip. Ota side-stepped but not far enough and the tip pierced his thigh. He grimaced.

'Aha!' Shirai laughed and again thrust low then slashed at his torso. Ota blocked hard left and cut back horizontally across Shirai's chest, nicking his left shoulder.

Enraged, Shirai cut quickly for Ota's head. Ota deflected the strike but stumbled and had to step back. Shirai pressed his advantage, lunging again. Ota dodged to the side, simultaneously cutting upwards right to left, slicing deep into Shirai's inner thigh. Shirai gasped but his motion took him on. He crashed against Ota, forcing him off the lawn and back over a wide, rounded headstone.

Shirai's elbow whipped across Ota's mouth and chin. His head rocked back against the stone.

The two sword guards locked together over Ota's chest. Eyes bulging with effort, Shirai heaved trying to force his blade into Ota's neck. Perspiration on Shirai's forehead dripped into Ota's eyes. Ota felt the cold steel cutting his skin but he could sense Shirai weakening. Warm dampness soaked his waist and thighs as blood spurted from Shirai's severed femoral artery draining his strength.

Puzzlement showed in Shirai's eyes as inch by inch Ota began to push him away. Shirai was grunting with effort. Suddenly he shifted, coming up using Ota's strength, then slammed his sword hilt down at Ota's eyes. Ota rolled his head and the brass ring pommel glanced off his helmet and on to the headstone, chipping the marble. He flung Shirai to the side and slipped free, taking a low guard position.

Shirai stood unsteadily, looking down at his blood-soaked legs. He raised his sword and took a step forwards but his legs gave way and he dropped, snarling, onto his knees. His sword slipped from his fingers. He glared at Ota, smiling thinly. 'So, Ota, the field is yours again! Now are you going to watch me bleed to death or end it properly?'

Ota reached slowly for his pistol but Shirai shook his head. 'No! My choice in the manner of my death. Will you do me the honour of being my second?'

Tension played on Ota's face as he considered the enormity of the dying man's last request. Despite his revulsion he could not refuse. 'Very well.'

'Good!' Shirai grunted. With a supreme effort of will, he shifted into a formal kneeling position, forcing his back straight. He looked at Ota and leant forward in a controlled bow, extending his neck. *'Yoroshiku onegai shimasu.'*—I beg your understanding.

Ota bowed and repeated the phrase with equal formality. Out of respect for martial tradition he had practised *kaishaku*—the Second's Cut—many times but always on a tied bundle of soaked reeds. In preparation he moved to stand slightly to the left of the kneeling man, so that the readied weapon would be out of his line of sight.

Slowly he raised his sword above his head, slowing his breathing, relaxing his muscles. Shirai's breath was coming in short, noisy rasps. His expression blank.

Ota's eyes were focussed on Shirai's stretched nape and his first vertebrae. His concentration was total. He was unaware of Shirai's trembling fingers creeping up his holster flap.

Ota took one second too long. Shirai twisted, snatching out his pistol. He glared up, lips drawn in a triumphant rictal grin. Ota started his cut, staring down the barrel but knowing he was a dead man. He did not hear the shot. Neither did Shirai who was flung prone at Ota's feet with a bullet through the heart.

For several seconds Ota stared at the body, then slowly looked around the cemetery. His face pale, his gaze travelled on, beyond the wall to the white, square bell tower of Ambarawa church some three hundred yards away. Slowly he lifted his hand in acknowledgement, quite certain he was in the crosshairs of Harada's scope.

Semarang Docks, late October, 1945

Chrishaw, Edmunds, Bentham, Ball and Miller saluted as the three hundred and seventeen members of the Kudo Butai came on to the dockside past the guard drawn from the Gurkhas and Mahrattas. They paraded six abreast behind their flags, with rifles sloped and bayonets fixed. Officers with their swords drawn. Nestled against the wharf, the rusting freighter that was to carry them to internment on Rempang Island was getting up steam.

Wounded men marched or limped alongside their fit comrades as best they could. Many of the battalion were wearing white cotton slings around their necks that supported plain wooden boxes holding some of the bones of their fallen comrades.

At the end of the dock the Japanese halted to stack their rifles, ammunition belts and bayonets. On Kudo's order, every chrysanthemum crest had been filed off the guns. Virtually disarmed, Kudo Butai reformed ranks and marched back. A small table, draped with a white cloth had been placed in front of the General.

Mac was in the front row of a mixed group of servicemen who had joined the Ambarawa relief column. He looked at the table and found it hard to believe it was only three months since the surrender ceremony in Malaya. Then he had been elated, even angry. Today he felt sympathy for dead men and relief at being alive. He looked over at Meg who stood among a small group of RAPWI staff and curious civilians. She had flown in from Djakarta with Chrishaw. The RAPWI plane was returning that evening. Mac would be on it with her, his secondment to Ball's staff at an end.

Chrishaw began his speech. 'Men of the Kudo Butai. In the past weeks you have performed a number of difficult tasks promptly and professionally. One day, I hope full acknowledgement of your effort and sacrifice to protect the innocent on Java will be known by your countrymen. It is something of which you and they can be proud. From this day, you are no longer under arms. As you lay down your weapons and leave this island, know that you have earned the gratitude of 23rd Indian Division and, indeed, of the internees whose lives you helped save.' He paused for the interpreter, then continued.

'I now call upon Major Kudo to surrender his sword. May it never again be drawn against a foe.'

Kudo approached Chrishaw and Bentham with his sword in his left hand and saluted. The two British officers returned the salute immediately. Kudo stepped up to the table, taking the sword in both hands horizontally. His bow was almost horizontal. He straightened, and offered the weapon to Chrishaw who received it in both hands, then handed it to Bentham. 'I think this is better in your care Brigadier.'

Bentham smiled. 'Thank you, Sir.'

Kudo slowly came out of his bow.

'I'm glad you are not joining General Yamagami in Singapore, Major,' said Chrishaw. 'I am pleased that we are no longer enemies.'

'So am I, General,' replied Kudo.

Bentham stepped forward and shook Kudo's hand. 'My best wishes for the future, Major.'

Kudo nodded once, stepped back three paces back and saluted once again.

One after another, the Japanese came forward until the table was piled high with swords. Mac noticed Ota standing beside a man with one arm. The wounded man walked forward purposefully, limping slightly to offer his sword. Then came Ota.

Mac watched with added interest as he added his sword to the pile, wondering if he had really seen him smiling slightly. He hoped so. At that moment he knew that his war with the Japanese was over.

Thirty minutes later the Japanese had boarded the ship and the gangway had been hoisted. With a single long hoot from the whistle the ship cast off. Relaxed, smiling Japanese lined the passenger rails. Miller waved a final farewell to Kudo who stood on the stern deck. Miller came over to Mac, Meg and Rai. 'Well, what a strange way to end a war, waving goodbye!'

Central Market, Semarang

To the clear delight of a stall holder, Meg was examining an antique blue-green, batik-dyed silk sarong decorated with open clam shells and swirling surf. 'I'll have to be careful what I wear with this or the Goddess of the Southern Seas will send a typhoon to New York!'

Mac looked at her in confusion. 'What?'

'I'll explain later,' Meg laughed, handing over a thick wad of Japanese guilders.

'This'll turn a few heads in Glasgow!' Mac said grinning. He was holding up a bright green silk tie. 'What do you think?'

Meg shook her head. 'No greens, Mac. Not till you're off the boat and home.'

'I didn't know you were superstitious.'

'I am here,' she said squeezing his arm.' When in Java, do as the Javanese do!'

They wandered around the market for a few minutes. It was busy and noisy as traders touted their wares. Women shopped with their children in hand, grateful for the air of normality that had returned to the small part of Semarang within the British-controlled zone.

Mac and Meg returned to their jeep. Miller and Rai were nearby, talking with a patrol led by Limbau. In four days the Gurkhas would withdraw to Batavia. They were laughing among themselves.

A boy of about twelve walked past the jeep carrying a basket of coconuts. He started towards Mac and Meg, then noticed the Gurkhas and headed for them.

'Hey, I'll have one!' Mac called after him, holding up a grubby bank note.

The boy quickened his step towards the soldiers.

Mac looked at Meg and shrugged. 'He can keep his coconuts!'

He glanced back and saw the basket on the ground and the pistol in the boy's hand.'

'Look out!' Mac yelled.

'Merdeka!' The shout was shrill and nervous.

Miller whirled, his arm rising in a protective reflex. Two shots blurred into one as a Gurkha flung himself forward. The boy ran, weaving among the panicked bystanders. Limbau and the others gave chase. A bullet had caught Miller in the left shoulder.

Rai had landed heavily but managed to push himself up into a sitting position. He stared blankly at the blood welling from the centre of his chest. Slowly he fell backwards.

'Oh no!' Miller gasped. He knelt, easing the Gurkha's head off the ground. 'Medic!' he bawled.

Rai was wheezing and coughing up blood, and trying to lift his arms.

Mac raced to him, helping Miller hold his head. He pressed a handkerchief against the wound. 'Rai, laddie, hang on!'

Rai tried to smile.

Meg reached them, her hand over her mouth. 'Oh, God!'

Rai stared at Miller, speaking in Gurkhali.

'What's he saying?' Mac asked, his face white with shock.

Miller shook his head in puzzlement. 'He says he can't remember the words. I don't understand.'

Meg clasped one of Rai's hands in both of hers. 'He means his courting song for Sarita!' She smiled, tears welling. 'Tell him he'll remember the words for Sarita tomorrow! Tomorrow, Rai!'

Miller put his mouth close to Rai's ear and spoke urgently. Rai's chest heaved as he strained for breath. He nodded once weakly then the wheezing stopped and his head lolled back in Miller's and Mac's hands.

Miller looked stunned. 'He—he saved my life. Oh, Jesus! The bravest man I've ever known killed by a bloody child.'

'What a goddamn useless waste!' Meg blurted, burying her face in her hands. She sank down sobbing against Mac.

A crowd began to gather. Mac glared at them, his rage building. A few seconds later Limbau and the other Gurkhas appeared across the square dragging the limp and bloodied young assassin on his knees across the market square. The onlookers parted and Limbau knelt beside Rai's body and began to pray.

'Just now,' Mac snarled, 'I could kill every Indo in this sewer of a town, starting with that little shit!'

Miller looked icily at Rai's' killer, then at Limbau. 'Take him away!'

Gently he reached out and closed Rai's eyes and spoke softly. 'O fall'n at length, that tower of strength, which stood four-square, to all the winds that blew...'

He tried to smile at Meg but failed and bit his lip. He sniffed back his tears. 'Tennyson, "Ode on the Death of the Duke of Wellington", he said softly. It was the first poem I ever learned by heart....'

Kemajoran Airfield, Djakarta

The first of the C-47's two huge engines started up, shattering the morning silence.

'Time to go,' Meg said softly and smiled. 'I was determined that I wouldn't say this... I won't forget you, Mac.'

'I'll never forget you, Meg.'

On their flight back to Batavia, Meg had talked of her work and the United States; Mac of Scotland. It had been their way of untying the last of the knots that bound them. They had spent a few last hours together at the hotel. Throughout the night the distant crackle of small arms fire of patrols chasing looters had accompanied their lovemaking. Somehow it had seemed apt.

She kissed him tenderly on the lips. 'Take care, soldier. Find yourself a good Scottish lass!'

Mac nodded and smiled. 'Wherever you go, keep your head down!'

'I've had it with war, Mac,' she said shaking her head. 'No more bullets!'

'I'll drink to that every St Andrew's Day!'

'Me, too,' she said softly.

She slipped out of his embrace and walked quickly up the steps to the plane. At the door she turned. 'Take care, Mac. You're one of the good guys!' She waved once then was gone.

Mac lit a cigarette and watched the Dakota rise into a cloudless, azure sky.

Near Tosari on Mt Bromo, south of Surabaya, 1ˢᵗ November 1945

At precisely eleven in the morning, just as the leaflets dropped in the preceding days had warned, the creeping shell barrage from the assembled Royal Navy destroyers and frigates stationed just off Surabaya began. General Chrishaw had threatened retribution if the killers of Brigadier Allenby were not given up. Surabaya's citizens had sent no reply. Since Chrishaw was a man of his word, Surabaya began to burn.

Bright orange and reds flashed within the billowing white smoke belching from the ships' guns. RAF Thunderbolts bombed the town with impunity. In the bay, the landing craft carrying the Fifth Indian Division waited for the barrage to lift.

From his vantage point on the mountainside overlooking Madura Bay, Lamban had a good view of the destruction. There was no answering fire from the town. Surabaya's women and children had fled but thousands of *pemuda* were sheltering in basements and cellars. The *Arek Surabaya* would fight, street-by-street, house-by-house, to defend their city.

Lamban turned away, leading his battalion inland to fight another day.

Tandjong Priok Harbour, Batavia/Djakarta, January 1946

Excited Seaforths lined the railings of HMS *Bulolo* watching the slow but methodical loading of their equipment and the last of the fresh food for their voyage to Colombo. From Ceylon they would head for Malta, via the Suez Canal, and, finally, Glasgow. Their embarkation had taken most of the morning.

Mac and Nesbit had been on board for three hours. For them the sights and sounds of the docks had long palled. They lay on the crowded deck, resting on their kit bags. Around them card games had already started. Others just lounged and perspired in the hot sunshine simply enjoying doing nothing.

Beyond the Djakarta skyline Mt Smeroe stood out above a carpet of lush green. Few of the Seaforths took any interest in the view. They were impatient to get underway.

Mac smoked, his expression pensive as he considered all he had gained, and lost, on Java. Nesbit let him be.

At first the jeers from the wharf were ignored. A small group of Dutch marines had taken offence at the British soldiers' good humour and some uncomplimentary comments. But the Seaforths were used to it and merely watched.

As time passed the insults rose in volume. 'Go home, Tommies!'—'We are better off without you!'—'We don't need help from Empire losers!'

Eventually the bored Scotsmen standing at the rails lost their patience. 'Keep your bloody island, Dutchy!'—'And your sodding coffee!'—'You look German to me!'

Card games were paused as more men took notice. It was something to pass the time.

'Arrogant, ungrateful bastards!' Nesbit spat.

On the top deck, Brigadier King and Regimental Sgt-Major Cox saw that the Dutch officers on the wharf were making no move to control their men. At last the gangway went up, ironically bringing cheers from both sides.

'Just in time,' King said to Cox with a wry smile.

Cox nodded and shouted down. 'That's enough of that, you lot! We'll be off soon enough so—'

A loud blast from a steam-whistle drowned the rest of his words. He turned in irritation. A freighter, flying the Dutch flag, was easing into the berth next to *Bulolo*. It was the *Johan de Witt*, of Rotterdam. Lining her decks were hundreds of fresh-faced conscripts getting their first look at Batavia.

On the wharf the Dutch marines and soldiers began cheering. Chants of 'Netherlands!' began. A military band struck up the "Wilhelmina" in welcome. Coolies and other Javanese on the docks stared in open dismay as the smiling, waving Dutch soldiers started to disembark.

A native porter ran forward unfurling an Indonesian flag. He managed one brisk shout of *'Merdeka!'* before he was clubbed and quickly hustled away by a Dutch shore patrol. It was clear nothing was going to be allowed to disturb the welcoming ceremony.

'They don't know what's waiting for them,' Mac said shaking his head.

'They'll find out soon enough,' replied Nesbit, raising two fingers to the crowd on the wharf.

'How can they take on fifty million and win?' Mac asked aloud.

Nesbit uttered a loud, cough-disguised *'Mer-de-ka!'* Gradually it was taken up in unison along the length of the ship.

'Mer-de-ka!—Mer-de-ka!'

On the wharf the band struggled against the growing chant. Dutch officials and soldiers stared at the Scotsmen with unconcealed fury.

Cox turned questioningly to King. 'Sir?'

King shook his head, smiling, then coughed. *'Mer-de-ka*, RSM!'

Cox grinned. 'Absolutely, Sir!'

With a short blast of her whistle, *Bulolo* eased away from the wharf. As one the Seaforths cheered. Finally they were going home.

The last British service personnel left Java in November 1946. The Netherlands refused to recognise Indonesia's independence and continued to oppose the Republican Government until December 1949 when, after political and economic pressure from the United States, Dutch military intervention ceased and a peace agreement was signed. The Republic of Indonesia became a member of the United Nations on 1st January 1950.

Epilogue

A weary Ota re-checked the name and address of their hotel, put his reading glasses away and got into the front seat of the taxi. Nagumo was already snoring in the back seat between Sano and Harada. Ota leant back and closed his eyes. He felt a slight twinge of arthritis in his left knee but it passed.

It had been a tiring but certainly entertaining ten days in Paris, Rome, Florence and two nights in Amsterdam before the short flight to Glasgow. Time had flown by and they were almost at the end of their reunion trip. Ota wondered if it would be the last...he was approaching seventy after all. Kudo and Kondo had died the year before. Another heart-attack would finish Sano, and Nagumo's liver was failing....

Ota forced himself to think of something more pleasant. In Amsterdam they had toured the canals and seen the Old Master paintings in the Rijksmuseum. After dinner on their second night Nagumo had, inevitably, insisted on leading them to the famous red-light district to see the girls on display in their brightly lit windows.

'Look at this!' Nagumo had exclaimed with delight. 'Almost like the old days in Tokyo! It takes me back!'

They had dawdled, in a boisterous humour, managing to lose the years for a few precious minutes. Nagumo "window shopped" for them, pointing out the undeniable charms of the waiting women. A dark-skinned temptress had caught his eye. 'What I'd give to be twenty years younger!'

'Forget it, Nagumo-san,' Harada had quipped. 'We're just pedestrians now!'

Beside Ota the taxi driver gave two quick pips on the horn to an errant cyclist. Ota's eyes half-opened, no more. He, smiled, still thinking of the scene at Amsterdam's Schiphol airport. Their late afternoon flight had been rescheduled for the early evening, giving Nagumo ample time for yet more 'Dutch courage' before he took to the air.

Ota had gone in search of a Japanese newspaper. When he arrived at the gate his jaw had dropped. Nagumo, rather the worse for drink, was stripping to his underwear while explaining in Japanese to the bemused security team that if he had lost his right arm instead of his left, he would at least have been able to play a bit of golf at Gleneagles.

Sano, who had been doubled over with laughter, told Ota that the metal detector was sounding every time Nagumo walked through it, to the immense frustration of the guards who could find nothing on him. Eventually they had accepted that forty-five-year-old shrapnel deep in Nagumo's back was triggering their sensors. Nagumo had been summarily dressed and escorted patiently onto the aircraft....

The taxi radio crackled and Ota woke again. He was nursing a small flight bag on his knees. In it was the gift he would present at the dinner the next evening. It was beautifully wrapped in delicate, handmade paper and tied with red, blue and white ribbon. They were not quite the colours of the British flag but were the nearest match available in the gift-wrapping section of the Mitsukoshi department store in Tokyo.

The present, a gold Seiko carriage clock, was the reason they had come to Scotland. It was a gift from the 16th

Imperial Japanese Army Veterans' Association to their last commanding officer, General Sir Philip Chrishaw.

Ota still had his doubts that a clock was the most suitable gift for a man aged ninety-six.

Melrose

Chrishaw sat in front of a roaring fire in the farmhouse's sitting room, nursing a shot of ten-year-old Talisker single-malt on his stomach. Birthday cards filled the mantelpiece. He was smartly dressed in jacket and collar and trademark cravat. What little was left of his now white hair was brushed back.

There was soft knock on the door from his part-time secretary, the long-retired but sprightly Major Robert McCrae, formerly of the Seaforth Highlanders. 'Sir Philip, everyone is here now.'

'Right,' said Chrishaw, his gaze on the graceful curve of the Japanese sword propped against the mantelpiece where it had stood for over four decades. 'I'll be with you in a moment.'

Many of the older guests in the crowded lounge were members of the Burma Star Association. Others were some of his regular correspondents—military researchers and scholars—for whom Philip Chrishaw was a living piece of military history.

The evening went well. Though Chrishaw was a little frail and preferred to sit in a wheelchair, he was, as usual, the perfect host. He took the presentation of the clock in his stride, shaking Ota's hand and posing for some group photographs. Afterwards, drink flowed and people mingled.

A woman in a smart but practical trouser-suit button-holed Ota. She held a note pad. 'Hello, my name's Judith

Stott. 'I'm a journalist with the Daily Telegraph's Scottish bureau.' They shook hands. 'Tell me, Mr Ota,' she asked with interest, 'it must cause some surprise in Japan that your last commander was a British general?'

Ota shook his head. 'I must tell you that outside our *senyukai*—our war-comrade clubs—we rarely speak of the war, not even to our families. It was a long time ago. No one is interested in old men's tales.'

Stott looked at him quizzically. 'You think so? Look over there.' She indicated the small group hovering around Chrishaw. Some of them had already produced maps of the Burma campaign or copies of once-secret signals and were asking the General questions. 'They and others like them all over the world would visit everyday if they could,' said Stott. 'You should see his mailbag!'

'I can imagine,' said Ota, 'but General Chrishaw was a very important man... It's different in Japan. Since the war, most people are anti-military.'

She nodded. 'I see. When I heard you were making the presentation I decided to read some of the old news reports,' I couldn't find any mention of Japanese soldiers helping the British. Perhaps the government did not want to admit what was happening? It must have been very strange for both sides...I mean for the British and Japanese?'

'Oh, yes', replied Ota. 'It was chaos. Though I think the Indonesians got the biggest surprise. I'm sure they never expected us to fight them.'

Stott smiled as Chrishaw escaped a group of historians and directed McCrae to wheel him to join her.

'Very smart, Sir Philip, as always,' Stott said beaming. 'You, too, Major.'

The two old soldiers were clearly pleased.

'Thanks, Judith,' Chrishaw replied warmly. He grinned slyly at McCrae. 'It's good to have a young woman in the house who's not a granddaughter or a great-granddaughter!'

They all laughed.

'I only said I liked your tie, Sir Philip!', she replied smiling.

Chrishaw beamed. 'Old soldiers don't die, you know, Judith, their medal ribbons just fade away.'

She went on, notebook poised. 'I was just telling Mr Ota that I've been reading some of the press reporting on Java. I found one by Meg Graham in one of her books. I hadn't realised she had been in Java, too. Did you ever meet her? She's something of a role model.'

'Oh, yes indeed,' Chrishaw said nodding. 'Sharp as a pin! Good dancer if I recall. Sense of humour, too! Her writing was perceptive. I always thought she'd leave her mark.'

'Miss Stott,' Ota asked politely, 'Did you say she wrote a book?'

'Several actually, the one I mentioned is called Masks of Conflict.

Ota wrote down the title and saw a contented-looking Nagumo approaching, glass of whiskey in hand.

The evening drew to a close with the taking of some more group photographs. Just before the farewells, Chrishaw slipped out of the lounge and went into his sitting room. He returned with the sword across his knees.

Ota and the others stared, jolted by the sight of the weapon.

Gradually the room fell silent as people realised something unplanned was about to happen. Chrishaw unwound the red-and-gold tassel and partially unsheathed the blade. 'Ladies and Gentlemen, forty-five years ago, General Yamagami surrendered this sword to me on Java.' He paused, looking down at the still-bright steel. 'I think it's time it was returned.'

A rush of applause and appreciative murmurs followed his words.

As Ota interpreted, his former comrades appeared stunned. Chrishaw slid the blade back in its scabbard and offered the sword horizontally with both hands just as the Japanese had done decades before. 'Here, Mr Ota, please take it and return it to the General's family. Tell them that though I cannot forget what I lost in that terrible war, I can perhaps, forgive.'

Ota took the sword and bowed. 'General, I am honoured. General Yamagami's family will be very grateful.'

There was another round of applause and yet more photographs were taken, this time of Chrishaw and the Japanese with the sword.

Judith Stott was beaming. 'That was a marvellous gesture, Sir Philip. You've given me the title for my piece.'

'Oh, let me guess,' Chrishaw said with an amused nod. 'Something about an old soldier....'

Schiphol Airport, Amsterdam, The Netherlands

The young Dutch woman in the flower kiosk greeted her elderly customer with a friendly. *'Goeiemiddag'*—Good Day. 'May I help you?'

Good morning,' replied Ota. 'I'd like a box of the red tulips.'

'Certainly,' said the woman smiling. 'They're lovely bright blooms aren't they. Shall I wrap them as a present?'

Ota nodded. 'Yes, please. They always bring back memories.'

'Nice memories of Holland, I hope?'

He shook his head, his eyes suddenly a little distant. 'No, memories of a promise kept in Java.'

Slightly perplexed, the assistant smiled anyway, convinced her elderly customer had misunderstood her. She wished him a good journey. *'Goede reis!'*

Ota thanked her and headed back to the departure gate where Nagumo and the others were waiting. KLM-Royal Dutch Airlines flight 861 to Tokyo was ready to board.

'By the way,' Nagumo said pointing across the terminal. 'Look at the sign over there.'

Ota turned. At the gate opposite the information board listed flight 837 to Jakarta's Sukarno-Hatta Airport. Bored-looking Asian and western passengers sat together, waiting quietly. He looked back at Nagumo. 'Are you thinking what I'm thinking?'

Nagumo nodded. 'We left behind many friends...we should go and pray for them where they fell.'

Ota looked at the board again and smiled. 'You're right, we'll return to Java. But let's go home first.'

終

The End

The origins of *Black Sun, Red Moon: A Novel of Java* and *Merdeka Rising*.

Some years ago my father sent me a copy of an article published in the London *Daily Telegraph* newspaper entitled 'Old soldier returns surrender sword'. I was intrigued by a reference to 'an extraordinary incident after the surrender, when Japanese troops were re-armed by the British to help them liberate the Java internment camps'. That single sentence fired my curiosity, which led me to research and, eventually, to write my story. The newspaper article is reproduced in full on my website (see below). *Black Sun, Red Moon* and *Merdeka Rising* are fiction. The violence, death and valour on Java in 1945-46 is fact.

RM

For background information, some research-related photographs, maps and other memorabilia, please visit:

http://www.rorymarron.com

If you have spotted a spelling or grammatical mistake, please email: editorial@seventhcitadel.com.

Seventh Citadel
www.seventhcitadel.com

Lightning Source UK Ltd.
Milton Keynes UK
UKOW06f1216280216

269243UK00005B/24/P